Ripley knew what was going on. Knew what was coming.

She could sense it even if they couldn't see it, like a wave rushing a black sand beach at night.

She found her voice and the mike simultaneously.

"Pull your team out, Gorman. Get them out of there *now*."

The lieutenant spared her an irritated glare. "Don't give me orders, lady. I know what I'm doing."

"Maybe, but you don't know what's being *done*."

Down on C-level the walls and ceiling of the alien chamber were coming to life. Biomechanical fingers extended talons that could tear metal. Slime lubricated jaws began to flex, pistoning silently as their owners awoke. Uncertain movements dimly glimpsed through smoke and steam by the nervous human intruders.

Master Sergeant Apone found himself starting to back up. "Go to infrared. Look sharp, people!"

"Multiple signals," Comtech Corporal Hudson declared, "all around. Closing from all directions."

The medtech's nerves snapped and she whirled to retreat. As she turned something tall and immensely powerful loomed above the smoke to wrap long arms around her . . .

BOOKS BY
ALAN DEAN FOSTER

Alien
Aliens
Clash of the Titans
The I Inside
Krull
Outland
Pale Rider
Shadowkeep
Starman

THE SPELLSINGER SERIES:

Spellsinger
The Hour of the Gate
The Day of the Dissonance
The Moment of the Magician
The Paths of the Perambulator

Published by
WARNER BOOKS

A L I E N S

a novelization by
ALAN DEAN FOSTER
based on the screenplay by
JAMES CAMERON

story by
JAMES CAMERON and **DAVID GILER** & **WALTER HILL**
based on characters created by
DAN O'BANNON and **RONALD SHUSETT**

WARNER BOOKS

A Warner Communications Company

WARNER BOOKS EDITION

Warner Books, Inc.
666 Fifth Avenue
New York, N.Y. 10103

A Warner Communications Company

Printed in the United States of America

First Printing: June, 1986

10   9   8   7   6   5   4   3   2   1

For H. R. Giger,
Master of the sinister airbrush.
Who reveals more about us than we wish to know.
From ADF and points west.

Two dreamers.

Not so very much difference between them despite the more obvious distinctions. One was of modest size, the other larger. One was female, the other male. The mouth of the first contained a mixture of sharp and flat teeth, a clear indication that it was omnivorous, while the maxillary cutlery of the other was intended solely for slicing and penetrating. Both were the scions of a race of killers. This was a genetic tendency the first dreamer's kind had learned to moderate. The other dreamer remained wholly feral.

More differences were apparent in their dreams than in their appearance. The first dreamer slept uneasily, memories of unmentionable terrors recently experienced oozing up from the depths of her subconscious to disrupt the normally placid stasis of hypersleep. She would have tossed and turned dangerously if not for the capsule that contained and restrained her movements—that and the fact that in deep sleep, muscular activity is reduced to a minimum. So she tossed and turned mentally. She was not aware of this. During hypersleep one is aware of nothing.

Every so often, though, a dark and vile memory would rise to the fore, like sewage seeping up beneath a city street. Temporarily it would overwhelm her rest. Then she would moan within the capsule. Her heartbeat would increase. The computer that watched over her like an electronic angel would note the accelerated activity and respond by lowering her body temperature another degree while increasing the flow of stabilizing drugs to her system. The moaning would stop. The dreamer would quiet and sink back into her cushions. It would take time for the nightmare to return.

Next to her the small killer would react to these isolated episodes by twitching as if in response to the larger sleeper's distress. Then it, too, would relax again, dreaming of small, warm bodies and the flow of hot blood, of the comfort to be found in the company of its own kind, and the assurance that this would come again. Somehow it knew that both dreamers would awaken together or not at all.

The last possibility did not unsettle its rest. It was possessed of more patience than its companion in hypersleep, and a more realistic perception of its position in the cosmos. It was content to sleep and wait, knowing that if and when consciousness returned, it would be ready to stalk and kill again. Meanwhile it rested.

Time passes. Horror does not.

In the infinity that is space, suns are but grains of sand. A white dwarf is barely worthy of notice. A small spacecraft like the lifeboat of the vanished vessel *Nostromo* is almost too tiny to exist in such emptiness. It drifted through the great nothing like a freed electron broken loose from its atomic orbit.

Yet even a freed electron can attract attention, if others equipped with appropriate detection instruments happen to chance across it. So it was that the lifeboat's course took it close by a familiar star. Even so, it was a stroke of luck that it was not permanently overlooked. It passed very near another ship; in space, "very near" being anything less than a light-year. It appeared on the fringe of a range spanner's screen.

Some who saw the blip argued for ignoring it. It was too small to be a ship, they insisted. It didn't belong where it was. And ships talked back. This one was as quiet as the dead. More likely it was only an errant asteroid, a renegade chunk of nickel-iron off to see the universe. If it was a ship, at the very least it would have been blaring to anything within hearing range with an emergency beacon.

But the captain of the ranging vessel was a curious fellow. A minor deviation in their course would give them a chance to check out the silent wanderer, and a little clever bookkeeping would be sufficient to justify the detour's cost to the owners. Orders were given, and computers worked to adjust trajectory. The captain's judgment was confirmed when they drew alongside the stranger: it was a ship's lifeboat.

Still no sign of life, no response to polite inquiries. Even the running lights were out. But the ship was not completely dead. Like a body in frigid weather, the craft had withdrawn power from its extremities to protect something vital deep within.

The captain selected three men to board the drifter. Gently as an eagle mating with a lost feather, the larger craft sidled close to the *Narcissus*. Metal kissed metal. Grapples were applied. The sounds of the locking procedure echoed through both vessels.

Wearing full pressure suits, the three boarders entered their airlock. They carried portable lights and other equipment. Air being too precious to abandon to vacuum, they waited patiently while the oxygen was inhaled by their ship. Then the outer-lock door slid aside.

Their first sight of the lifeboat was disappointing: no internal lights visible through the port in the door, no sign of life within. The door refused to respond when the external controls were pressed. It had been jammed shut from inside. After the men made sure there was no air in the lifeboat's cabin, a robot welder was put to work on the door. Twin torches flared brightly in the darkness, slicing into the door from two sides. The flames met at the bottom of the barrier.

Two men braced the third, who kicked the metal aside. The way was open.

The lifeboat's interior was as dark and still as a tomb. A section of portable grappling cable snaked along the floor. Its torn and frayed tip ended near the exterior door. Up close to the cockpit a faint light was visible. The men moved toward it.

The familiar dome of a hypersleep capsule glowed from within. The intruders exchanged a glance before approaching. Two of them leaned over the thick glass cover of the transparent sarcophagus. Behind them, their companion was studying his instrumentation and muttered aloud.

"Internal pressure positive. Assuming nominal hull and systems integrity. Nothing appears busted; just shut down to conserve energy. Capsule pressure steady. There's power feeding through, though I bet the batteries have about had it. Look how dim the internal readouts are. Ever see a hypersleep capsule like this one?"

"Late twenties." The speaker leaned over the glass and murmured into his suit pickup. "Good-lookin' dame."

"Good-lookin', my eye." His companion sounded disappointed. "Life function diodes are all green. That means she's alive. There goes our salvage profit, guys."

The other inspector gestured in surprise. "Hey, there's something in there with her. Nonhuman. Looks like it's alive too. Can't see too clearly. Part of it's under her hair. It's orangish."

"Orange?" The leader of the trio pushed past both of them and rested the faceplate of his helmet against the transparent barrier. "Got claws, whatever it is."

"Hey." One of the men nudged his companion. "Maybe it's an alien life-form, huh? That'd be worth some bucks."

Ripley chose that moment to move ever so slightly. A few strands of hair drifted down the pillow beneath her head, more fully revealing the creature that slept tight against her.

The leader of the boarders straightened and shook his head disgustedly.

"No such luck. It's just a cat."

Listening was a struggle. Sight was out of the question. Her throat was a seam of anthracite inside the lighter pumice of her skull; black, dry, and with a faintly resinous taste. Her tongue moved loosely over territory long forgotten. She tried to remember what speech was like. Her lips parted. Air came rushing up from her lungs, and those long-dormant bellows ached with the exertion. The result of this strenuous interplay between lips, tongue, palate, and lungs was a small triumph of one word. It drifted through the room.

"Thirsty."

Something smooth and cool slid between her lips. The shock of dampness almost overwhelmed her. Memory nearly caused her to reject the water tube. In another time and place that kind of insertion was a prelude to a particularly unique and loathsome demise. Only water flowed from this tube, however. It was accompanied by a calm voice intoning advice.

"Don't swallow. Sip slowly."

She obeyed, though a part of her mind screamed at her to suck the restoring liquid as fast as possible. Oddly enough, she did not feel dehydrated, only terribly thirsty.

"Good," she whispered huskily. "Got anything more substantial?"

"It's too soon," said the voice.

"The heck it is. How about some fruit juice?"

"Citric acid will tear you up." The voice hesitated, considering, then said, "Try this."

Once again the gleaming metal tube slipped smoothly into her mouth. She sucked at it pleasurably. Sugared iced tea cascaded down her throat, soothing both thirst and her first cravings for food. When she'd had enough, she said so, and the tube was withdrawn. A new sound assailed her ears: the trill of some exotic bird.

She could hear and taste; now it was time to see. Her eyes opened to a view of pristine rain forest. Trees lifted bushy green crowns heavenward. Bright iridescent winged creatures buzzed as they flitted from branch to branch. Birds trailed long tail feathers like jet contrails behind them as they dipped and soared in pursuit of the insects. A quetzal peered out at her from its home in the trunk of a climbing fig.

Orchids bloomed mightily, and beetles scurried among leaves and fallen branches like ambulatory jewels. An agouti appeared, saw her, and bolted back into the undergrowth. From the stately hardwood off to the left, a howler monkey dangled, crooning softly to its infant.

The sensory overload was too much. She closed her eyes against the chattering profusion of life.

Later (another hour? another day?) a crack appeared in the middle of the big tree's buttressing roots. The split widened to obliterate the torso of a gamboling marmoset. A woman emerged from the gap and closed it behind her, sealing the temporary bloodless wound in tree and animal. She touched a hidden wall switch, and the rain forest went away.

It was very good for a solido, but now that it had been shut off, Ripley could see the complex medical equipment the rain forest imagery had camouflaged. To her immediate left was the medved that had responded so considerately to her request for first water and then cold tea. The machine hung motionless and ready from the wall, aware of everything that was happening inside her body, ready to adjust medication, provide food and drink, or summon human help should the need arise.

The newcomer smiled at the patient and used a remote control attached to her breast pocket to raise the backrest of Ripley's bed. The patch on her shirt, which identified her as a senior medical technician, was bright with color against the background of white uniform. Ripley eyed her warily, unable to tell if the woman's smile was genuine or routine. Her voice was pleasant and maternal without being cloying.

"Sedation's wearing off. I don't think you need any more. Can you understand me?" Ripley nodded. The medtech considered her patient's appearance and reached a decision. "Let's try something new. Why don't I open the window?"

"I give up. Why don't you?"

The smile weakened at the corners, was promptly recharged. Professional and practiced, then; not heartfelt. And why should it be? The medtech didn't know Ripley, and Ripley didn't know her. So what. The woman pointed her remote toward the wall across from the foot of the bed.

"Watch your eyes."

Now there's a choice non sequitur for you, Ripley thought. Nevertheless, she squinted against the implied glare.

A motor hummed softly, and the motorized wall plate slid into the ceiling. Harsh light filled the room. Though filtered and softened, it was still a shock to Ripley's tired system.

Outside the port lay a vast sweep of nothingness. Beyond the nothingness was everything. A few of Gateway Station's modular habitats formed a loop off to the left, the plastic cells strung together like children's blocks. A couple of communications antennae peeped into the view from below. Dominating the scene was the bright curve of the Earth. Africa was a brown, white-streaked smear swimming in an ocean blue, the Mediterranean a sapphire tiara crowning the Sahara.

Ripley had seen it all before, in school and then in person. She was not particularly thrilled by the view so much as she was just glad it was still there. Events of recent memory suggested it might not be, that nightmare was reality and this soft, inviting globe only mocking illusion. It was comforting, familiar, reassuring, like a worn-down teddy bear. The scene was completed by the bleak orb of the moon drifting in the background like a vagrant exclamation point: planetary system as security blanket.

"And how are we today?" She grew aware that the med-tech was talking to her instead of at her.

"Terrible." Someone or two had told her once upon a time that she had a lovely and unique voice. Eventually she should get it back. For the moment no part of her body was functioning at optimum efficiency. She wondered if it ever would again, because she was very different from the person she'd been before. That Ripley had set out on a routine cargo run in a now vanished spacecraft. A different Ripley had returned, and lay in the hospital bed regarding her nurse.

"Just terrible?" You had to admire the medtech, she mused. A woman not easily discouraged. "That's better than yesterday, at least. I'd call 'terrible' a quantum jump up from atrocious."

Ripley squeezed her eyelids shut, opened them slowly. The Earth was still there. Time, which heretofore she hadn't given a hoot about, suddenly acquired new importance.

"How long have I been on Gateway Station?"

"Just a couple of days." Still smiling.

"Feels longer."

The medtech turned her face away, and Ripley wondered whether she found the terse observation boring or disturbing. "Do you feel up to a visitor?"

"Do I have a choice?"

"Of course you have a choice. You're the patient. After the doctors you know best. You want to be left alone, you get left alone."

Ripley shrugged, mildly surprised to discover that her shoulder muscles were up to the gesture. "I've been alone long enough. Whattheheck. Who is it?"

The medtech walked to the door. "There are two of them, actually." Ripley could see that she was smiling again.

A man entered, carrying something. Ripley didn't know him, but she knew his fat, orange, bored-looking burden.

"Jones!" She sat up straight, not needing the bed support now. The man gratefully relinquished possession of the big tomcat. Ripley cuddled it to her. "Come here, Jonesey, you ugly old moose, you sweet ball of fluff, you!"

The cat patiently endured this embarrassing display, so typical of humans, with all the dignity his kind was heir too. In so doing, Jones displayed the usual tolerance felines have for human beings. Any extraterrestrial observer privy to the byplay would not have doubted for an instant which of the two creatures on the bed was the superior intelligence.

The man who'd brought the good orange news with him pulled a chair close to the bed and patiently waited for Ripley to take notice of him. He was in his thirties, good-looking without being flashy, and dressed in a nondescript business suit. His smile was no more or less real than the medtech's, even though it had been practiced longer. Ripley eventually acknowledged his presence with a nod but continued to reserve her conversation for the cat. It occurred to her visitor that if he was going to be taken for anything more than a delivery man, it was up to him to make the first move.

"Nice room," he said without really meaning it. He looked like a country boy, but he didn't talk like one, Ripley thought as he edged the chair a little closer to her. "I'm Burke. Carter Burke. I work for the Company, but other than that, I'm an okay guy. Glad to see you're feeling better." The last at least sounded as though he meant it.

"Who says I'm feeling better?" She stroked Jones, who purred contentedly and continued to shed cat hair all over the sterile bed.

"Your doctors and machines. I'm told the weakness and disorientation should pass soon, though you don't look particularly disoriented to me. Side effects of the unusually long hypersleep, or something like that. Biology wsn't my favorite subject. I was better at figures. For example, yours seems to have come through in pretty good shape." He nodded toward the bed covers.

"I hope I look better than I feel, because I feel like the inside of an Egyptian mummy. You said 'unusually long hypersleep.' How long was I out there?" She gestured toward the watching medtech. "They won't tell me anything."

Burke's tone was soothing, paternal. "Well, maybe you shouldn't worry about that just yet."

Ripley's hand shot from beneath the covers to grab his arm. The speed of her reaction and the strength of her grip clearly surprised him. "No. I'm conscious, and I don't need any more coddling. How *long*?"

He glanced over at the medtech. She shrugged and turned away to attend to the needs of some incomprehensible tangle of lights and tubes. When he looked back at the woman lying in the bed, he found he was unable to shift his eyes away from hers.

"All right. It's not my job to tell you, but my instincts say you're strong enough to handle it. Fifty-seven years."

The number hit her like a hammer. Fifty-seven too many hammers. Hit her harder than waking up, harder than her first sight of the home world. She seemed to deflate, to lose strength and color simultaneously as she sank back into the mattress. Suddenly the artificial gravity of the station seemed thrice Earth-normal, pressing her down and back. The air-filled pad on which she rested was ballooning around her, threatening to stifle and smother. The medtech glanced at her warning lights, but all of them stayed silent.

Fifty-seven years. In the more than half century she'd been dreaming in deepsleep, friends left behind had grown old and died, family had matured and faded, the world she'd left behind had metamorphosed into who knew what. Governments had risen and fallen; inventions had hit the market and been outmoded and discarded. No one had ever survived more than sixty-five years in hypersleep. Longer than that and the body begins to fail beyond the ability of the capsules to sustain life. She'd barely survived; she'd pushed the limits of the physiologically possible, only to find that she'd outlived life.

"Fifty-seven!"

"You drifted right through the core systems," Burke was telling her. "Your beacon failed. It was blind luck that that deep salvage team caught you when they..." he hesitated. She'd suddenly turned pale, her eyes widening. "Are you all right?"

She coughed once, a second time harder. There was a pressure—her expression changed from one of concern to dawning horror. Burke tried to hand her a glass of water from the nightstand, only to have her slap it away. It struck the floor and shattered. Jones's fur was standing on end as the cat leapt to the floor, yowling and spitting. His claws made rapid scratching sounds on the smooth plastic as he scrambled away from the bed. Ripley grabbed at her chest, her back arching as the convulsions began. She looked as if she were strangling.

The medtech was shouting at the omnidirectional pickup. "Code Blue to Four Fifteen! Code Blue, Four One Five!"

She and Burke clutched Ripley's shoulders as the patient began bouncing against the mattress. They held on as a doctor and two more techs came pounding into the room.

It couldn't be happening. It couldn't!

"No—nooooooo!"

The techs were trying to slap restraints on her arms and legs as she thrashed wildly. Covers went flying. One foot sent a medtech sprawling while the other smashed a hole in the soulless glass eye on a monitoring unit. From beneath a cabinet Jones glared out at his mistress and hissed.

"Hold her," the doctor was yelling. "Get me an airway, stat! And fifteen cc's of—!"

An explosion of blood suddenly stained the top sheet crimson, and the linens began to pyramid as something unseen rose beneath them. Stunned, the doctor and the techs backed off. The sheet continued to rise.

Ripley saw clearly as the sheet slid away. The medtech fainted. The doctor made gagging sounds as the eyeless, toothed worm emerged from the patient's shattered rib cage.

It turned slowly until its fanged mouth was only a foot from its host's face, and screeched. The sound drowned out everything human in the room, filling Ripley's ears, overloading her numbed cortex, echoing, reverberating through her entire being as she...

... sat up screaming, her body snapping into an upright position in the bed. She was alone in the darkened hospital room. Colored light shone from the insectlike dots of glowing LEDs. Clutching pathetically at her chest she fought to regain the breath the nightmare had stolen.

Her body was intact: sternum, muscles, tendons, and ligaments all in place and functional. There was no demented horror ripping itself out of her torso, no obscene birth in progress. Her eyes moved jerkily in their sockets as she scanned the room. Nothing lying in ambush on the floor, nothing hiding behind the cabinets waiting for her to let down her guard. Only silent machines monitoring her life and the comfortable bed maintaining it. The sweat was pouring off her even though the room was pleasantly cool. She held one fist protectively against her sternum, as if to reassure herself constantly of its continued inviolability.

She jumped slightly as the video monitor suspended over the bed came to life. An older woman gazed anxiously down at her. Night-duty medtech. Her face was full of honest, not merely professional, concern.

"Bad dreams again? Do you want something to help you sleep?" A robot arm whirred to life left of Ripley's arm. She regarded it with distaste.

"No. I've slept enough."

"Okay. You know best. If you change your mind, just use your bed buzzer." She switched off. The screen darkened.

Ripley slowly leaned back against the raised upper section of mattress and touched one of the numerous buttons set in the side of her nightstand. Once more the window screen that covered the far wall slid into the ceiling. She could see out again. There was the portion of Gateway, now brilliantly lit by nighttime lights and, beyond it, the night-shrouded globe of the Earth. Wisps of cloud masked distant pinpoints of light. Cities—alive with happy people blissfully ignorant of the stark reality that was an indifferent cosmos.

Something landed on the bed next to her, but this time she didn't jump. It was a familiar, demanding shape, and she hugged it tightly to her, ignoring the casual _meowrr_ of protest.

"It's okay, Jones. We made it, we're safe. I'm sorry I scared you. It'll be all right now. It's going to be all right."

All right, yes, save that she was going to have to learn how to sleep all over again.

Sunlight streamed through the stand of poplars. A meadow was visible beyond the trees, green stalks splattered with the brightness of bluebells, daisies, and phlox. A robin pranced near the base of one tree, searching for insects. It did not see the sinewy predator stalking it, eyes intent, muscles taut. The bird turned its back, and the stalker sprang.

Jones slammed into the solido of the robin, neither acquiring prey nor disturbing the image, which continued its blithe quest for imaged insects. Shaking his head violently, the tomcat staggered away from the wall.

Ripley sat on a nearby bench regarding this cat-play. "Dumb cat. Don't you know a solido by now when you see one?" Although maybe she shouldn't be too hard on the cat. Solido design had improved during the last fifty-seven years. Everything had been improved during the last fifty-seven years. Except for her and Jones.

Glass doors sealed the atrium off from the rest of Gateway Station. The expensive solido of a North American temperate forest was set off by potted plants and sickly grass underfoot. The solido looked more real than the real plants, but at least the latter had an honest smell. She leaned slightly toward one pot. Dirt and moisture and growing things. Of cabbages and kings, she mused dourly. Horsepucky. She wanted off Gateway. Earth was temptingly near, and she longed to put blue sky between herself and the malign emptiness of space.

Two of the glass doors that sealed off the atrium parted to admit Carter Burke. For a moment she found herself regarding him as a man and not just a company cipher. Maybe that was a sign that she was returning to normal. Her appraisal of him was mitigated by the knowledge that when the *Nostromo* had departed on its ill-fated voyage, he was two decades short of being born. It shouldn't have made any difference. They were approximately the same physical age.

"Sorry." Always the cheery smile. "I've been running behind all morning. Finally managed to get away."

Ripley never had been one for small talk. Now more than ever, life seemed too precious to waste on inconsequential banter. Why couldn't people just say what they had to say instead of dancing for five minutes around the subject?

"Have they located my daughter yet?"

Burke looked uncomfortable. "Well, I was going to wait until after the inquest."

"I've waited fifty-seven years. I'm impatient. So humor me."

He nodded, set down his carrying case, and popped the lid. He fumbled a minute with the contents before producing several sheets of thin plastic.

"Is she . . . ?"

Burke spoke as he read from one of the sheets. "Amanda Ripley-McClaren. Married name, I guess. Age sixty-six at . . . time of death. That was two years ago. There's a whole history here. Nothing spectacular or notable. Details of a pleasant, ordinary life. Like the kind most of us lead, I expect. I'm sorry." He passed over the sheets, studied Ripley's face as she scanned the printouts. "Guess this is my morning for being sorry."

Ripley studied the holographic image imprinted on one of the sheets. It showed a rotund, slightly pale woman in her mid-sixties. Could have been anyone's aunt. There was nothing distinctive about the face, nothing that leapt out and shouted with familiarity. It was impossible to reconcile the picture of this older woman with the memory of the little girl she'd left behind.

"Amy," she whispered.

Burke still held a couple of sheets, read quietly as she continued to stare at the hologram. "Cancer. Hmmm. They still haven't licked all varieties of that one. Body was cremated. Interred Westlake Repository, Little Chute, Wisconsin. No children."

Ripley looked past him, toward the forest solido but not at it. She was staring at the invisible landscape of the past.

"I promised her I'd be home for her birthday. Her eleventh birthday. I sure missed that one." She glanced again at the picture. "Well, she'd already learned to take my promises with a grain of salt. When it came to flight schedules, anyway."

Burke nodded, trying to be sympathetic. That was difficult for him under ordinary circumstances, much more so this morning. At least he had the sense to keep his mouth shut instead of muttering the usual polite inanities.

"You always think you can make it up to somebody— later, you know." She took a deep breath. "But now I never can. I never can." The tears came then, long overdue. Fifty-seven years overdue. She sat there on the bench and sobbed softly to herself, alone now in a different kind of space.

Finally Burke patted her reassuringly on her shoulder, uncomfortable at the display and trying hard not to show it. "The hearing convenes at oh-nine-thirty. You don't want to be late. It wouldn't make a good first impression."

She nodded, rose. "Jones. Jonesey, c'mere." Meowing, the cat sauntered over and allowed her to pick him up. She wiped self-consciously at her eyes. "I've got to change. Won't take long." She rubbed her nose against the cat's back, a small outrage it suffered in silence.

"Want me to walk you back to your room?"

"Sure, why not?"

He turned and started for the proper corridor. The doors parted to permit them egress from the atrium. "You know, that cat's something of a special privilege. They don't allow pets on Gateway."

"Jones isn't a pet." She scratched the tom behind the ears. "He's a survivor."

As Ripley promised, she was ready in plenty of time. Burke elected to wait outside her private room, studying his own reports, until she emerged. The transformation was impressive. Gone was the pale, waxy skin; gone the bitterness of expression and the uncertain stride. Determination? he wondered as they headed for the central corridor. Or just clever makeup?

Neither of them said anything until they neared the sublevel where the hearing room was located. "What are you going to tell them?" he finally asked her.

"What's to tell that hasn't already been told? You read my deposition. It's complete and accurate. No embellishments. It didn't need any embellishments."

"Look, *I* believe you, but there are going to be some heavyweights in there, and every one of them is going to try to pick holes in your story. You got feds, you got Interstellar Commerce Commission, you got Colonial Administration, insurance company guys—"

"I get the picture."

"Just tell them what happened. The important thing is to stay cool and unemotional."

Sure, she thought. All of her friends and shipmates and relatives were dead, and she'd lost fifty-seven years of reality to an unrestoring sleep. Cool and unemotional. Sure.

Despite her determination, by midday she was anything but cool and collected. Repetition of the same questions, the same idiotic disputations of the facts as she'd reported them, the same exhaustive examination of minor points that left the major ones untouched—all combined to render her frustrated and angry.

As she spoke to the somber inquisitors the large videoscreen behind her was printing out mug shots and dossiers. She was glad it was behind her, because the faces were those of the _Nostromo_'s crew. There was Parker, grinning like a goon. And Brett, placid and bored as the camera did its duty. Kane was there, too, and Lambert. Ash the traitor, his soulless face enriched with programmed false piety. Dallas...

Dallas. Better the picture behind her, like the memories.

"Do you have earwax or what?" she finally snapped. "We've been here three hours. How many different ways do you want me to tell the same story? You think it'll sound better in Swahili, get me a translator and we'll do it in Swahili. I'd try Japanese, but I'm out of practice. Also out of patience. How long does it take you to make up your collective mind?"

Van Leuwen steepled his fingers and frowned. His expression was as gray as his suit. It was approximated by the looks on the faces of his fellow board members. There were eight of them on the official board of inquiry, and not a friendly one in the lot. Executives. Administrators. Adjusters. How could she convince them? They weren't human beings. They were expressions of bureaucratic disapproval. Phantoms. She was used to dealing with reality. The intricacies of politicorporate maneuvering were beyond her.

"This isn't as simple as you seem to believe," he told her quietly. "Look at it from our perspective. You freely admit to detonating the engines of, and thereby destroying, an M-Class interstellar freighter. A rather expensive piece of hardware."

The insurance investigator was possibly the unhappiest member of the board. "Forty-two million in adjusted dollars. That's minus payload, of course. Engine detonation wouldn't leave anything salvageable, even if we could locate the remains after fifty-seven years."

Van Leuwen nodded absently before continuing. "It's

not as if we think you're lying. The lifeboat shuttle's flight recorder corroborates some elements of your account. The least controversial ones. That the *Nostromo* set down on LV-426, an unsurveyed and previously unvisited planet, at the time and date specified. That repairs were made. That it resumed its course after a brief layover and was subsequently set for self-destruct and that this, in fact, occurred. That the order for engine overload was provided by you. For reasons unknown."

"Look, I told you—"

Van Leuwen interrupted, having heard it before. "It did not, however, contain any entries concerning the hostile alien life-form you *allegedly* picked up during your short stay on the planet's surface."

"We didn't 'pick it up,'" she shot back. "Like I told you, it—"

She broke off, staring at the hollow faces gazing stonily back at her. She was wasting her breath. This wasn't a real board of inquiry. This was a formal wake, a post-interment party. The object here wasn't to ascertain the truth in hopes of vindication, it was to smooth out the rough spots and make the landscape all nice and neat again. And there wasn't a thing she could do about it, she saw now. Her fate had been decided before she'd set foot in the room. The inquiry was a show, the questions a sham. To satisfy the record.

"Then somebody's gotten to it and doctored the recorder. A competent tech could do that in an hour. Who had access to it?"

The representative of the Extrasolar Colonization Administration was a woman on the ungenerous side of fifty. Previously she'd looked bored. Now she just sat in her chair and shook her head slowly.

"Would you just listen to yourself for one minute? Do you really expect us to believe some of the things you've been telling us? Too much hypersleep can do all kinds of funny things to the mind."

Ripley glared at her, furious at being so helpless. "You want to hear some funny things?"

Van Leuwen stepped in verbally. "The analytical team that went over your shuttle centimeter by centimeter found no physical evidence of the creature you describe or anything like it. No damage to the interior of the craft. No etching of metal surfaces that might have been caused by an unknown corrosive substance."

Ripley had kept control all morning, answering the most inane queries with patience and understanding. The time for being reasonable was at an end, and so was her store of patience.

"That's because I blew it out the airlock!" She subsided a little as this declaration was greeted by the silence of the tomb. "Like I said."

The insurance man leaned forward and peered along the desk at the ECA representative. "Are there any species like this 'hostile organism' native to LV-426?"

"No." The woman exuded confidence. "It's a rock. No indigenous life bigger than a simple virus. Certainly nothing complex. Not even a flatworm. Never was, never will be."

Ripley ground her teeth as she struggled to stay calm. "I told you, it wasn't indigenous." She tried to meet their eyes, but they were having none of it, so she concentrated on Van Leuwen and the ECA rep. "There was a signal coming from the surface. The _Nostromo_'s scanner picked it up and woke us from hypersleep, as per standard regulations. When we traced it, we found an alien spacecraft like nothing you or anyone else has ever seen. _That_ was on the recorder too.

"The ship was a derelict. Crashed, abandoned ... we never did find out. We homed in on its beacon. We found the ship's pilot, also like nothing previously encountered. He was dead in his chair with a hole in his chest the size of a welder's tank."

Maybe the story bothered the ECA rep. Or maybe she

was just tired of hearing it for the umpteenth time. Whatever, she felt it was her place to respond.

"To be perfectly frank, we've surveyed over three hundred worlds, and no one's ever reported the existence of a creature, which, using your words"—and she bent to read from her copy of Ripley's formal statement—"'gestates in a living human host' and has 'concentrated molecular acid for blood.'"

Ripley glanced toward Burke, who sat silent and tight-lipped at the far end of the table. He was not a member of the board of inquiry, so he had kept silent throughout the questioning. Not that he could do anything to help her. Everything depended on how her official version of the *Nostromo*'s demise was received. Without the corroborating evidence from the shuttle's flight recorder the board had nothing to go on but her word, and it had been made clear from the start how little weight they'd decided to allot to that. She wondered anew who had doctored the recorder and why. Or maybe it simply had malfunctioned on its own. At this point it didn't much matter. She was tired of playing the game.

"Look, I can see where this is going." She half smiled, an expression devoid of amusement. This was hardball time, and she was going to finish it out even though she had no chance of winning. "The whole business with the android—why we followed the beacon in the first place—it all adds up, though I can't prove it." She looked down the length of the table, and now she did grin. "Somebody's covering their Ash, and it's been decided that I'm going to take the muck for it. Okay, fine. But there's one thing you can't change, one fact you can't doctor away.

"Those things *exist*. You can wipe me out, but you can't wipe that out. Back on that planet is an alien ship, and on that ship are thousands of eggs. *Thousands*. Do you understand? Do you have any idea what that implies? I suggest you go back there with an expedition and find it, using the flight recorder's data, and find it fast. Find it and deal with it, preferably with an orbital nuke. before one of your survey teams comes back with a little surprise."

"Thank you, Officer Ripley," Van Leuwen began, "that will be—"

"Because just one of those things," she went on, stepping on him, "managed to kill my entire crew within twelve hours of hatching."

The administrator rose. Ripley wasn't the only one in the room who was out of patience. "*Thank* you. That will be all."

"That's not all!" She stood and glared at him. "If those things get back here, that *will* be all. Then you can just kiss it goodbye, Jack. Just *kiss it goodbye*!"

The ECA representative turned calmly to the administrator. "I believe we have enough information on which to base a determination. I think it's time to close this inquest and retire for deliberation."

Van Leuwen glanced at his fellow board members. He might as well have been looking at mirror images of himself, for all the superficial differences of face and build. They were of one mind.

That was something that could not be openly expressed, however. It would not look good in the record. Above all, everything had to look good in the record.

"Gentlemen, ladies?" Acquiescent nods. He looked back down at the subject under discussion. Dissection was more like it, she thought sourly. "Officer Ripley, if you'd excuse us, please?"

"Not likely." Trembling with frustration, she turned to leave the room. As she did so, her eyes fastened on the picture of Dallas that was staring blankly back down from the videoscreen. Captain Dallas. Friend Dallas. Companion Dallas.

Dead Dallas. She strode out angrily.

There was nothing more to do or say. She'd been found guilty, and now they were going to go through the motions of giving her an honest trial. Formalities. The Company and its friends loved their formalities. Nothing wrong with death and tragedy, as long as you could safely suck all the emotion out of it. Then it would be safe to put in the annual report. So the inquest had to be held, emotion translated into sanitized figures in neat columns. A verdict had to be rendered. But not too loudly, lest the neighbors overhear.

None of which really bothered Ripley. The imminent demise of her career didn't bother her. What she couldn't forgive was the blind stupidity being flaunted by the all-powerful in the room she'd left. So they didn't believe her. Given their type of mind-set and the absence of solid evidence, she could understand that. But to ignore her story totally, to refuse to check it out, that she could never forgive. Because there was a lot more at stake than one lousy life, one unspectacular career as a flight transport officer. And they didn't care. It didn't show as a profit or a loss, so they didn't care.

She booted the wall next to Burke as he bought coffee and doughnuts from the vending machine in the hall. The machine thanked him politely as it accepted his credcard. Like practically everything else on Gateway Station, the machine had no odor. Neither did the black liquid it poured. As for the alleged doughnuts, they might once have flown over a wheat field.

"You had them eating out of your hand, kiddo." Burke was trying to cheer her up. She was grateful for the attempt, even as it failed. But there was no reason to take her anger out on him. Multiple sugars and artificial creamer gave the ersatz coffee some taste.

"They had their minds made up before I even went in there. I've wasted an entire morning. They should've had scripts printed up for everyone to read from, including me. Would've been easier just to recite what they wanted to hear instead of trying to remember the truth." She glanced at him. "You know what they think?"

"I can imagine." He bit into a doughnut.

"They think I'm a headcase."

"You are a headcase," he told her cheerfully. "Have a doughnut. Chocolate or buttermilk?"

She eyed the precooked torus he proffered distastefully. "You can taste the difference?"

"Not really, but the colors are nice."

She didn't grin, but she didn't sneer at him, either.

The "deliberations" didn't take long. No reason why they should, she thought as she reentered the room and resumed her seat. Burke took his place on the far side of the chamber. He started to wink at her, thought better of it, and aborted the gesture. She recognized the eye twitch for what it almost became and was glad he hadn't followed through.

Van Leuwen cleared his throat. He didn't find it necessary to look to his fellow board members for support.

"It is the finding of this board of inquiry that Warrant Officer Ellen Ripley, NOC-14672, has acted with questionable judgment and is therefore declared unfit to hold an ICC license as a commercial flight officer."

If any of them expected some sort of reaction from the condemned, they were disappointed. She sat there and stared silently back at them, tight-lipped and defiant. More likely they were relieved. Emotional outbursts would have to be recorded. Van Leuwen continued, unaware that Ripley had reattired him in black cape and hood.

"Said license is hereby suspended indefinitely, pending review at a future date to be specified later." He cleared his throat, then his conscience. "In view of the unusual length of time spent by the defendant in hypersleep and the concomitant indeterminable effects on the human nervous system, no criminal charges will be filed at this time."

At this time, Ripley thought humorlessly. That was corporatese for "Keep your mouth shut and stay away from the media and you'll still get to collect your pension."

"You are released on your own recognizance for a six-month period of psychometric probation, to include monthly review by an approved ICC psychiatric tech and treatment and or medication as may be prescribed."

It was short, neat, and not at all sweet, and she took it all without a word, until Van Leuwen had finished and departed. Burke saw the look in her eye and tried to restrain her.

"Lay off," he whispered to her. She threw off his hand and continued up the corridor. "It's over."

"Right," she called back to him as she lengthened her stride. "So what else can they do to me?"

She caught up with Van Leuwen as he stood waiting for the elevator. "Why won't you check out LV-426?"

He glanced back at her. "Ms. Ripley, it wouldn't matter. The decision of the board is final."

"The heck with the board's decision. We're not talking about me now. We're talking about the next poor souls to find that ship. Just tell me why you won't check it out."

"Because I don't have to," he told her brusquely. "The people who live there checked it out years ago, and they've never reported any 'hostile organism' or alien ship. Do you think I'm a complete fool? Did you think the board wouldn't seek some sort of verification, if only to protect ourselves from future inquiries? And by the way, they call it Acheron now."

Fifty-seven years. Long time. People could accomplish a lot in fifty-seven years. Build, move around, establish new colonies. Ripley struggled with the import of the administrator's words.

"What are you talking about? What people?"

Van Leuwen joined the other passengers in the elevator car. Ripley put an arm between the doors to keep them from closing. The doors' sensors obediently waited for her to remove it.

"Terraformers," Van Leuwen explained. "Planetary engineers. Much has happened in that field while you slept,

Ripley. We've made significant advances, great strides. The cosmos is not a hospitable place, but we're changing that. It's what we call a shake-'n'-bake colony. They set up atmosphere processors to make the air breathable. We can do that now, efficiently and economically, as long as we have some kind of resident atmosphere to work with. Hydrogen, argon—methane is best. Acheron is swimming in methane, with a portion of oxygen and sufficient nitrogen for beginning bonding. It's nothing now. The air's barely breathable. But given time, patience, and hard work, there'll be another habitable world out there ready to comfort and succor humanity. At a price, of course. Ours is not a philanthropic institution, though we like to think of what we do as furthering mankind's progress.

"It's a big job. Decades worth. They've already been there more than twenty years. *Peacefully.*"

"Why didn't you tell me?"

"Because it was felt that the information might have biased your testimony. Personally I don't think it would have made a bit of difference. You obviously believe what you believe. But some of my colleagues were of a differing opinion. I doubt it would have changed our decision."

The doors tried to close, and she slammed them apart. The other passengers began to exhibit signs of annoyance.

"How many colonists?"

Van Leuwen's brow furrowed. "At last count I'd guess sixty, maybe seventy, families. We've found that people work better when they're not separated from their loved ones. It's more expensive, but it pays for itself in the long run, and it gives the community the feeling of a real colony instead of merely an engineering outpost. It's tough on some of the women and the kids, but when their tour of duty ends, they can retire comfortably. Everyone benefits from the arrangement."

"Sweet Jesus," Ripley whispered.

One of the passengers leaned forward, spoke irritably. "Do you mind?"

Absently she dropped her arm to her side. Freed of their responsibility, the doors closed quietly. Van Leuwen had already forgotten her, and she him. She was looking instead into her imagination.

Not liking what she saw there.

It was not the best of times, and it certainly was the worst of places. Driven by unearthly meteorological forces, the winds of Acheron hammered unceasingly at the planet's barren surface. They were as old as the rocky globe itself. Without any oceans to compete with they would have scoured the landscape flat eons ago, had not the uneasy forces deep within the basaltic shell continually thrust up new mountains and plateaus. The winds of Acheron were at war with the planet that gave them life.

Heretofore there'd been nothing to interfere with their relentless flow. Nothing to interrupt their sand-filled storms, nothing to push against the gales instead of simply conceding mastery of the air to them—until humans had come to Acheron and claimed it for their own. Not as it was now, a landscape of tortured rock and dust dimly glimpsed through yellowish air, but as it would be once the atmosphere processors had done their work. First the atmosphere itself would be transformed, methane relinquishing its dominance to oxygen and nitrogen. Then the winds would be tamed, and the surface. The final result would be a benign climate whose offspring would take the form of snow and rain and growing things.

That would be the present's legacy to future generations. For now the inhabitants of Acheron ran the processors and struggled to make a dream come true, surviving on a ration of determination, humor, and oversize paychecks. They would not live long enough to see Acheron become a land of milk and honey. Only the Company would live long enough for that. The Company was immortal as none of them could ever be.

The sense of humor common to all pioneers living under difficult conditions was evident throughout the colony, most notably in a steel sign set in concrete pylons outside the last integrated structure:

HADLEY'S HOPE - Pop. 159
Welcome to Acheron

Beneath which some local wag had, without official authorization, added in indelible spray paint "Have a Nice Day." The winds ignored the request. Airborne particles of sand and grit had corroded much of the steel plate. A new visitor to Acheron, courtesy of the atmosphere processors, had added its own comment with a brown flourish: the first rains had produced the first rust.

Beyond the sign lay the colony itself, a cluster of bunk-erlike metal and plasticrete structures joined together by conduits seemingly too fragile to withstand Acheron's winds. They were not as impressive to look upon as was the surrounding terrain with its wind-blasted rock formations and crumbling mountains, but they were almost as solid and a lot more homey. They kept the gales at bay, and the still-thin atmosphere, and protected those who worked within.

High-wheeled tractors and other vehicles crawled down
the open roadways between the buildings, emerging from or
disappearing into underground garages like so many com-
munal pillbugs. Neon lights flickered fitfully on commercial
buildings, advertising the few pitiful, but earnest, entertain-
ments to be had at outrageous prices that were paid without
comment. Where large paychecks are found, there are always
small businesses operated by men and women with outsize
dreams. The company had no interest in running such penny-
ante operations itself, but it gladly sold concessions to those
who desired to do so.

Beyond the colony complex rose the first of the atmosphere processors. Fusion-powered, it belched a steady storm
of cleansed air back into the gaseous envelope that surrounded
the planet. Particulate matter and dangerous gases were removed either by burning or by chemical breakdown; oxygen
and nitrogen were thrown back into the dim sky. In with the
bad air, out with the good. It was not a complicated process,
but it was time-consuming and very expensive.

But how much is a world worth? And Acheron was not
as bad as some that the Company had invested in. At least
it possessed an existing atmosphere capable of modification.
Much easier to fine-tune the composition of a world's air than
to provide it from scratch. Acheron had weather and near
normal gravity. A veritable paradise.

The fiery glow that emanated from the crown of the
volcanolike atmosphere processor suggested another realm
entirely. None of the symbolism was lost on the colonists. It
inspired only additional humor. They hadn't agreed to come
to Acheron because of the weather.

There were no soft bodies or pallid, weak faces visible
within the colony corridors. Even the children looked tough.
Not tough as in mean or bullying, but strong within as well
as without. There was no room here for bullies. Cooperation
was a lesson learned early. Children grew up faster than their
Earthbound counterparts and those who lived on fatter, gentler

worlds. They and their parents were a breed unto themselves, self-reliant yet interdependent. They were not unique. Their predecessors had ridden in wagons instead of starships.

It helped to think of oneself as a pioneer. It sounded much better than a numerical job description.

At the center of this ganglion of men and machines was the tall building known as the control block. It towered above every other artificial structure on Acheron with the exception of the atmosphere processing stations themselves. From the outside it looked spacious. Within, there wasn't a spare square meter to be found. Instrumentation was crowded into corners and sequestered in the crawl spaces beneath the floors and the serviceways above the suspended ceilings. And still there was never enough room. People squeezed a little closer to one another so that the computers and their attendant machines could have more room. Paper piled up in corners despite unceasing efforts to reduce every scrap of necessary information to electronic bytes. Equipment shipped out new from the factory quickly acquired a plethora of homey scratches, dents, and coffee-cup rings.

Two men ran the control block and therefore the colony. One was the operations manager, the other his assistant. They called one another by their first names. Formality was not in vogue on frontier worlds. Insistence on titles and last names and too much supercilious pulling of rank could find a man lost outside without a survival suit or communicator.

Their names were Simpson and Lydecker, and it was a toss-up as to which looked more harried than the other. Both wore the expression of men for whom sleep is a teasing mistress rarely visited. Lydecker looked like an accountant haunted by a major tax deduction misplaced ten years earlier. Simpson was a big, burly type who would have been more comfortable running a truck than a colony. Unfortunately he'd been stuck with brains as well as brawn and hadn't managed to hide it from his employers. The front of his shirt was perpetually sweat-stained. Lydecker confronted him before he could retreat.

"See the weather report for next week?" Simpson was chewing on something fragrant, which stained the inside of his mouth. Probably illegal, Lydecker knew. He said nothing about it. It was Simpson's business, and Simpson was his boss. Besides, he'd been considering borrowing a chew. Small vices were not encouraged on Acheron, but as long as they didn't interfere with a person's work, neither were they held up to ridicule. It was tough enough to keep one's sanity, hard enough to get by.

"What about it?" the operations manager said.

"We're going to have a real Indian summer. Winds should be all the way down to forty knots."

"Oh, good. I'll break out the inner tubes and the suntan lotion. Heck, I'd settle for just one honest glimpse of the local sun."

Lydecker shook his head, affecting an air of mock disapproval. "Never satisfied, are you? Isn't it enough to know it's still up there?"

"I can't help it; I'm greedy. I should shut up and count my blessings, right? You got something else on your mind, Lydecker, or are you just on one of your hour-long coffee breaks?"

"That's me. Goof off every chance I get. I figure my next chance will be in about two years." He checked a printed readout. "You remember you sent some wildcatters out to that high plateau out past the Ilium Range a couple days ago?"

"Yeah. Some of our dreamers back home thought there might be some radioactives out that way. So I asked for volunteers, and some guy named Jorden stuck up his mitt. I told 'em to go look if they wanted to. Some others might've taken off in that direction also. What about it?"

"There's a guy on the horn right now. Mom-and-pop

survey team. Says he's homing something and wants to know if his claim will be honored."

"Everybody's a lawyer these days. Sometimes I think I should've gone in for it myself."

"What, and ruin your sophisticated image? Besides, there's not much call for lawyers out here. And you make better money."

"Keep telling me that. It helps." Simpson shook his head and turned to gaze at a green screen. "Some honch in a cushy office on Earth says go look at a grid reference in the middle of nowhere, we look. They don't say why, and I don't ask. I don't ask because it takes two weeks to get an answer from back there, and the answer's always 'Don't ask.' Sometimes I wonder why we bother."

"I just told you why. For the money." The assistant operations officer leaned back against a console. "So what do I tell this guy?"

Simpson turned to stare at a videoscreen that covered most of one wall. It displayed a computer-generated topographical map of the explored portion of Acheron. The map was not very extensive, and the features it illustrated made the worst section of the Kalahari Desert look like Polynesia. Simpson rarely got to see any of Acheron's surface in person. His duties required him to remain close to Operations at all times, and he liked that just fine.

"Tell him," he informed Lydecker, "that as far as I'm concerned, if he finds something, it's his. Anybody with the guts to go crawling around out there deserves to keep what he finds."

The tractor had six wheels, armored sides, oversize tires, and a corrosion-proof underbody. It was not completely Acheron-proof, but then, very little of the colony's equipment was. Repeated patching and welding had transformed the once-sleek exterior of the tractor into a collage composed of off-color metal blotches held together with solder and epoxy sealant. But it kept the wind and sand at bay and climbed steadily forward. That was enough for the people it sheltered.

At the moment it was chugging its way up a gentle slope, the fat tires kicking up sprays of volcanic dust that the wind was quick to carry away. Eroded sandstone and shale crumbled beneath its weight. A steady westerly gale howled outside its armored flanks, blasting the pitted windows and light ports in its emotionless, unceasing attempt to blind the vehicle and those within. The determination of those who drove combined with the reliable engine to keep it moving uphill. The engine hummed reassuringly, while the air filters cycled ceaselessly as they fought to keep dust and grit out of the sacrosanct interior. The machine needed clean air to breathe just as much as did its occupants.

He was not quite as weather-beaten as his vehicle, but Russ Jorden still wore the unmistakable look of someone who'd spent more than his share of time on Acheron. Weathered and wind-blasted. To a lesser degree the same description applied to his wife, Anne, though not to the two children who bounced about in the rear of the big central cabin. Somehow they managed to dart in and around portable sampling equipment and packing cases without getting themselves smashed against the walls. Their ancestors had learned at an early age how to ride something called a horse. The action of the tractor was not very different from the motion one has to cope with atop the spine of that empathetic quadruped, and the children had mastered it almost as soon as they learned how to walk.

Their clothing and faces were smeared with dust despite the nominally inviolable interior of the vehicle. That was a fact of life on Acheron. No matter how tight you tried to seal yourself in, the dust always managed to penetrate vehicles, offices, homes. One of the first colonists had coined a name for this phenomenon that was more descriptive than scientific. "Particulate osmosis," he'd called it. Acheronian science. The more imaginative colonists insisted that the dust was sentient, that it hid and waited for doors and windows to open a crack before deliberately rushing inside. Homemakers argued face-tiously whether it was faster to wash clothes or scrape them clean.

Russ Jorden wrestled the massive tractor around boulders too big to climb and negotiated a path through narrow crevices in the plateau they were ascending. He was sustained in his efforts by the music of the Locater's steady pinging. It grew louder the nearer they came to the source of the electromagnetic disturbance, but he refused to turn down the volume. Each ping was a melody unto itself, like the chatter of old-time cash registers. His wife monitored the tractor's condition and the life-support systems while her husband drove.

"Look at this fat, juicy, magnetic profile." Jorden tapped the small readout on his right. "And it's mine, mine, mine. Lydecker says that Simpson said so, and we've got it recorded. They can't take that away from us now. Not even the Company can take it away from us. Mine, all mine."

"Half mine, dear." His wife glanced over at him and smiled.

"And half mine!" This cheerful desecration of basic mathematics came from Newt, the Jorden's daughter. She was six years old going on ten, and she had more energy than both her parents and the tractor combined. Her father grinned affectionately without taking his eyes from the driver's console.

"I got too many partners."

The girl had been playing with her older brother until she'd finally worn him out. "Tim's bored, Daddy, and so am I. When are we going back to town?"

"When we get rich, Newt."

"You always say that." She scrambled onto her feet, as agile as an otter. "I wanna go back. I wanna play Monster Maze."

Her brother stuck his face into hers. "You can play by yourself this time. You cheat too much."

"Do not!" She put small fists on unformed hips. "I'm just the best, and you're jealous."

"Am not! You go in places we can't fit."

"So? That's why I'm the best."

Their mother spared a moment to glance over from her bank of monitors and readouts. "Knock it off. I catch either of you two playing in the air ducts again, I'll tan your hides. Not only is it against colony regulations, it's dangerous. What if one of you missed a step and fell down a vertical shaft?"

"Aw, Mom. Nobody's dumb enough to do that. Besides, all the kids play it, and nobody's been hurt yet. We're careful." Her smile returned. "An' I'm the best 'cause I can fit places nobody else can."

"Like a little worm." Her brother stuck his tongue out at her.

She duplicated the gesture. "Nyah, nyah! Jealous, jealous." He made a grab for her protruding tongue. She let out a childish shriek and ducked behind a mobile ore analyzer.

"Look, you two." There was more affection than anger in Anne Jorden's tone. "Let's try to calm down for two minutes, okay? We're almost finished up here. We'll head back toward town soon and—"

Russ Jorden had half risen from his seat to stare through the windshield. Childish confrontations temporarily put aside, his wife joined him.

"What is it, Russ?" She put a hand on his shoulder to steady herself as the tractor lurched leftward.

"There's something out there. Clouds parted for just a second, and I *saw* it. I don't know what it is, but it's big. And it's ours. Yours and mine—and the kids'."

The alien spacecraft dwarfed the tractor as the big six-wheeler trundled to a halt nearby. Twin arches of metallic glass swept skyward in graceful, but somehow disturbing, curves from the stern of the derelict. From a distance they resembled the reaching arms of a prone dead man, locked in advanced rigor mortis. One was shorter than the other, and yet this failed to ruin the symmetry of the ship.

The design was as alien as the composition. It might have been grown instead of built. The slick bulge of the hull still exhibited a peculiar vitreous luster that the wind-borne grit of Acheron had not completely obliterated.

Jorden locked the tractor's brakes. "Folks, we have scored big this time. Anne, break out the suits. I wonder if the Hadley Café can synthesize champagne?"

His wife stood where she was, staring out through the tough glass. "Let's check it out and get back safely before we start celebrating, Russ. Maybe we're not the first to find it."

"Are you kidding? There's no beacon on this whole plateau. There's no marker outside. Nobody's been here before us. Nobody! She's all ours." He was heading toward the rear of the cabin as he talked.

Anne still sounded doubtful. "Hard to believe that anything that big, putting out that kind of resonance, could have sat here for this long without being noticed."

"Bulll." Jorden was already climbing into his environment suit, flipping catches without hunting for them, closing seal-tights with the ease of long practice. "You worry too much. I can think of plenty of reasons why it's escaped notice until now."

"For instance?" Reluctantly she turned from the window and moved to join him in donning her own suit.

"For instance, it's blocked off from the colony's detectors by these mountains, and you know that surveillance satellites are useless in this kind of atmosphere."

"What about infrared?" She zipped up the front of her suit.

"What infrared? Look at it: dead as a doornail. Probably been sitting here just like that for thousands of years. Even if it got here yesterday, you couldn't pick up any infrared on this part of the planet; new air coming out of the atmosphere processor is too hot."

"So then how did Operations hit on it?" She was slipping on her equipment, filling up the instrument belt.

He shrugged. "How the heck should I know? If it's bugging you, you can winkle it out of Lydecker when we get back. The important thing is that we're the ones they picked to check it out. We lucked out." He turned toward the airlock door. "C'mon, babe. Let's crack the treasure chest. I'll bet that baby's insides are just crammed with valuable stuff."

Equally enthusiastic but considerably more self-possessed, Anne Jorden tightened the seals on her own suit. Husband and wife checked each other out: oxygen, tools, lights, energy cells, all in place. When they were ready to leave the tractor, she popped her wind visor and favored her offspring with a stern gaze.

"You kids stay inside. I mean it."

"Aw, Mom." Tim's expression was full of childish disappointment. "Can't I come too?"

"No, you cannot come too. We'll tell you all about it when we get back." She closed the airlock door behind her.

Tim immediately ran to the nearest port and pressed his nose against the glass. Outside the tractor, the twilight landscape was illuminated by the helmet beams of his parents.

"I dunno why I can't go too."

"Because Mommy said so." Newt was considering what to play next as she pressed her own face against another window. The lights from her parents' helmets grew dim as they advanced toward the strange ship.

Something grabbed her from behind. She squealed and turned to confront her brother.

"Cheater!" he jeered. Then he turned and ran for a place to hide. She followed, yelling back at him.

The bulk of the alien vessel loomed over the two bipeds as they climbed the broken rubble that surrounded it. Wind howled around them. Dust obscured the sun.

"Shouldn't we call in?" Anne stared at the smooth-sided mass.

"Let's wait till we know what to call it in as." Her husband kicked a chunk of volcanic rock out of his path.

"How about 'big weird thing'?"

Russ Jorden turned to face her, surprise showing on his face behind the visor. "Hey, what's the matter, honey? Nervous?"

"We're preparing to enter a derelict alien vessel of unknown type. You bet I'm nervous."

He clapped her on the back. "Just think of all that beautiful money. The ship alone's worth a fortune, even if it's empty. It's a priceless relic. Wonder who built it, where they came from, and why it ended up crashed on this godforsaken lump of gravel?" His voice and expression were full of enthusiasm as he pointed to a dark gash in the ship's side. "There's a place that's been torn open. Let's check her out."

They turned toward the opening. As they drew near, Anne Jorden regarded it uneasily. "I don't think this is the result of damage, Russ. It looks integral with the hull to me. Whoever designed this thing didn't like right angles."

"I don't care what they liked. We're going *in*."

A single tear wound its way down Newt Jorden's cheek. She'd been staring out the fore windshield for a long time now. Finally she stepped down and moved to the driver's chair to shake her sleeping brother. She sniffed and wiped away the tear, not wanting Tim to see her cry.

"Timmy—wake up, Timmy. They've been gone a long time."

Her brother blinked, removed his feet from the console, and sat up. He glanced unconcernedly at the chronometer set in the control dash, then peered out at the dim, blasted landscape. Despite the tractor's heavy-duty insulation, one could still hear the wind blowing outside when the engine was shut down. Tim sucked on his lower lip.

"It'll be okay, Newt. Dad knows what he's doing."

At that instant the outside door slammed open, admitting wind, dust, and a tall dark shape. Newt screamed, and Tim scrambled out of the seat as their mother ripped off her visor and threw it aside, heedless of the damage it might do to the delicate instrumentation. Her eyes were wild, and the tendons stood out in her neck as she shoved past her children. She snatched up the dash mike and yelled into the condenser.

"Mayday! Mayday! This is Alpha Kilo Two Four Niner calling Hadley Control. Repeat. This is Alpha Kil . . ."

Newt barely heard her mother. She had both hands pressed over her mouth as she sucked on stale atmosphere. Behind her, the tractor's filters whined as they fought to strain the particulate-laden air. She was staring out the open door at the ground. Her father lay there, sprawled on his back on the rocks. Somehow her mother had dragged him all the way back from the alien ship.

There was something on his face.

It was flat, heavily ribbed, and had lots of spiderlike chitinous legs. The long, muscular tail was tightly wrapped around the neck of her father's environment suit. More than anything else, the creature resembled a mutated horseshoe crab with a soft exterior. It was pulsing in and out, in and out, like a pump. Like a machine. Except that it was not a machine. It was clearly, obviously, obscenely alive.

Newt began screaming again, and this time she didn't stop.

It was quiet in the apartment except for the blare of the wallscreen. Ripley ignored the simpcom and concentrated instead on the smoke rising from her denicotined cigarette. It formed lazy, hazy patterns in the stagnant air.

Even though it was late in the day, she'd managed to avoid confronting a mirror. Just as well, since her haggard, unkempt appearance could only depress her further. The apartment was in better shape than she was. There were just enough decorative touches to keep it from appearing spartan. None of the touches were what another might call personal. That was understandable. She'd outlived everything that once might have been considered personal. The sink was full of dirty dishes even though the dishwasher sat empty beneath it.

She wore a bathrobe that was aging as rapidly as its owner. In the adjoining bedroom, sheets and blankets lay in a heap at the base of the mattress. Jones prowled the kitchen, hunting overlooked morsels. He would find none. The kitchen kept itself reasonably antiseptic despite a deliberate lack of cooperation from its owner.

"Hey, Bob!" the wallscreen bleated vapidly, "I heard that you and the family are heading off for the colonies!"

"Best decision I ever made, Phil," replied a fatuously grinning nonentity from the opposite side of the wall. "We'll

39

be starting a new life from scratch in a clean world. No crime, no unemployment . . ."

And the two chiseled performers who were acting out this administration-approved spiel probably lived in an expensive Green Ring on the East Coast, Ripley thought sardonically as she listened to it with half an ear. In Cape Cod condos overlooking Martha's Vineyard or Hilton Head or some other unpolluted, high-priced snob refuge for the fortunate few who knew how to bill and coo and dance, yassuh, dance when imperious corporate chieftains snapped their fingers. None of that for her. No smell of salt, no cool mountain breezes. Inner-city Company dole, and lucky she was to have that much.

She'd find something soon. They just wanted to keep her quiet for a while, until she calmed down. They'd be glad to help her relocate and retrain. After which they'd conveniently forget about her. Which was just dandy keeno fine as far as she was concerned. She wanted no more to do with the Company than the Company wanted to do with her.

If only they hadn't suspended her license, she'd long since have been out of here and away.

The door buzzed sharply for attention and she jumped. Jones merely glanced up and meowed before trundling off toward the bathroom. He didn't like strangers. Always had been a smart cat.

She put the cigarette (guaranteed to contain no carcinogens, no nicotine, and no tobacco—harmless to your health, or so the warning label on the side of the packet insisted) aside and moved to open the door. She didn't bother to check through the peephole. Hers was a full-security building. Not that after her recent experiences there was anything in an Earthside city that could frighten her.

Carter Burke stood there, wearing his usual apologetic smile. Standing next to him and looking formal was a younger man clad in the severe dress-black uniform of an officer in the Colonial Marines.

"Hi, Ripley." Burke indicated his companion. "This is Lieutenant Gorman of the Co—"

The closing door cut his sentence in half. Ripley turned her back on it, but she'd neglected to cut power to the hall speaker. Burke's voice reached her via the concealed membrane.

"Ripley, we have to talk."

"No, we don't. Get lost, Carter. And take your friend with you."

"No can do. This is important."

"Not to me it isn't. Nothing's important to me."

Burke went silent, but she sensed he hadn't left. She knew him well enough to know that he wouldn't give up easily. The Company rep wasn't demanding, but he was an accomplished wheedler.

As it developed, he didn't have to argue with her. All he had to do was say one sentence.

"We've lost contact with the colony of Acheron."

A sinking feeling inside as she mulled over the ramifications of that unexpected statement. Well, perhaps not entirely unexpected. She hesitated a moment longer before opening the door. It wasn't a ploy. That much was evident in Burke's expression. Gorman's gaze shifted from one to the other. He was clearly uncomfortable at being ignored, even as he tried not to show it.

She stepped aside. "Come in."

Burke surveyed the apartment and gratefully said nothing, shying away from inanities like "Nice place you have here" when it obviously wasn't. He also forbore from saying, "You're looking well," since that also would have constituted an obvious untruth. She could respect him for his restraint. She gestured toward the table.

"Want something? Coffee, tea, spritz?"

"Coffee would be fine," he replied. Gorman added a nod.

She went into the compact kitchen and dialed up a few

cups. Bubbling sounds began to emanate from the processor as she turned back to the den.

"You didn't need to bring the Marines." She smiled thinly at him. "I'm past the violent stage. The psych techs said so, and it's right there on my chart." She waved toward a desk piled high with discs and papers. "So what's with the escort?"

"I'm here as an official representative of the corps." Gorman was clearly uneasy and more than willing to let Burke handle the bulk of the conversation. How much did he know, and what had they told him about her? she wondered. Was he disappointed in not encountering some stoned harridan? Not that his opinion of her mattered.

"So you've lost contact." She feigned indifference. "So?"

Burke looked down at his slim-line, secured briefcase. "It has to be checked out. Fast. All communications are down. They've been down too long for the interruption to be due to equipment failure. Acheron's been in business for years. They're experienced people, and they have appropriate backup systems. Maybe they're working on fixing the problem right now. But it's been no-go dead silence for too long. People are getting nervous. Somebody has to go and check it out in person. It's the only way to quiet the nervous Nellies.

"Probably they'll correct the trouble while the ship's on its way out and the whole trip will be a waste of time and money, but it's time to set out."

He didn't have to elaborate. Ripley had already gotten where he was going and returned. She went into the kitchen and brought out the coffees. While Gorman sipped his cup of brew she began pacing. The den was too small for proper pacing, but she tried, anyway. Burke just waited.

"No," she said finally. "There's no way."

"Hear me out. It's not what you think."

She stopped in the middle of the floor and stared at him in disbelief. "Not what I think? Not what I *think*? I don't have to think, Burke. I was reamed, steamed, and dry-cleaned by you guys, and now you want me to go back out *there*? Forget it!"

She was trembling as she spoke. Gorman misinterpreted the reaction as anger, but it was pure fear. She was scared. Gut-scared and trying to mask it with indignation. Burke knew what she was feeling but pressed on, anyway. He had no choice.

"Look," he began in what he hoped was his best conciliatory manner, "we don't know what's going on out there. If their relay satellite's gone out instead of the ground transmitter, the only way to fix it is with a relief team. There are no spacecraft in the colony. If that's the case, then they're all sitting around out there cursing the Company for not getting off its collective butt and sending out a repair crew pronto. If it is the satellite relay, then the relief team won't even have to set foot on the planet itself. But we don't know what the trouble is, and if it's *not* the orbital relay, then I'd like to have you there. As an adviser. That's all."

Gorman lowered his coffee. "You wouldn't be going in with the troops. Assuming we even have to go in. I can guarantee your safety."

She rolled her eyes and glanced at the ceiling.

"These aren't your average city cops or army accompanying us, Ripley," Burke said forcefully. "These Colonial Marines are some tough hombres, and they'll be packing state-of-the-art firepower. Man plus machine. There's nothing they can't handle. Right, Lieutenant?"

Gorman allowed himself a slight smile. "We're trained to deal with the unexpected. We've handled problems on worse worlds than Acheron. Our casualty rate for this kind of operation hovers right around zero. I expect the percentage to improve a little more after this visit."

If this declaration was intended to impress Ripley, it failed miserably. She looked back to Burke.

"What about you? What's your interest in this?"

"Well, the Company cofinanced the colony in tandem

with the Colonial Administration. Sort of an advance against mineral rights and a portion of the long-term developmental profits. We're diversifying, getting into a lot of terraforming. Real estate on a galactic scale. Building better worlds and all that."

"Yeah, yeah," she muttered. "I've seen the commercials."

"The corporation won't see any substantial profits out of Acheron until terraforming's complete, but a big outfit like that has to consider the long term." Seeing that this was having no effect on his host, Burke switched to another tack. "I hear you're working in the cargo docks over Portside?"

Her reply was defensive, as was to be expected. "That's right. What about it?"

He ignored the challenge. "Running loaders, forklifts, suspension grates; that sort of thing?"

"It's all I could get. I'm crazy if I'm going to live on charity all my life. Anyway, it keeps my mind off . . . everything. Days off are worse. Too much time to think. I'd rather keep busy."

"You like that kind of work?"

"Are you trying to be funny?"

He fiddled with the catch on his case. "Maybe it's not all you can get. What if I said I could get you reinstated as a flight officer? Get you your license back? And that the Company has agreed to pick up your contract? No more hassles with the commission, no more arguments. The official reprimand comes out of your record. Without a trace. As far as anyone will be concerned, you've been on a leave of absence. Perfectly normal following a long tour of duty. It'll be like nothing happened. Won't even affect your pension rating."

"What about the ECA and the insurance people?"

"Insurance is settled, over, done with. They're out of it. Since nothing will appear on your record, you won't be considered any more of a risk than you were before your last trip. As far as the ECA is concerned, they'd like to see you go out with the relief team too. It's all taken care of."

"*If* I go."

"*If* you go." He nodded, leaning slightly toward her. He wasn't exactly pleading. It was more like a practiced sales pitch. "It's a second chance, kiddo. Most people who get taken down by a board of inquiry never have the opportunity to come back. If the problem's nothing more than a busted relay satellite, all you have to do is sit in your cubbyhole and read while the techs take care of it. That, and collect your trip pay while you're in hypersleep. By going, you can wipe out all the unpleasantness and put yourself right back up there where you used to be. Full rating, full pension accumulation, the works. I've seen your record. One more long out-trip and you qualify for a captain's certificate.

"And it'll be the best thing in the world for you to face this fear and beat it. You gotta get back on the horse."

"Spare me, Burke," she said frostily. "I've had my psych evaluation for the month."

His smile slipped a little, but his tone grew more determined. "Fine. Let's cut the crap, then. I've read your evaluations. You wake up every night, sheets soaking, the same nightmare over and over—"

"No! The answer is no." She retrieved both coffee cups even though neither was empty. It was another form of dismissal. "Now please go. I'm sorry. Just go, would you?"

The two men exchanged a look. Gorman's expression was unreadable, but she had the feeling that his attitude had shifted from curious to contemptuous. The heck with him: what did he know? Burke mined a pocket, removed a translucent card, and placed it on the table before heading for the door. He paused in the portal to smile back at her.

"Think about it."

Then they were gone, leaving her alone with her thoughts. Unpleasant company. Wind. Wind and sand and a moaning sky. The pale disc of an alien sun fluttering like a paper cutout beyond the riven atmosphere. A howling, rising in pitch and intensity, coming closer, closer, until it was right on top of you, smothering you, cutting off your breath.

With a guttural moan Ripley sat straight up in her bed, clutching her chest. She was breathing hard, painfully. Sucking in a particularly deep breath, she glanced around the tiny bedroom. The dim light set in the nightstand illuminated bare walls, a dresser, and a highboy, sheets kicked to the foot of the bed. Jones lay sprawled atop the highboy, the highest point in the room, staring impassively back at her. It was a habit the cat had acquired soon after their return. When they went to bed, he would curl up next to her, only to abandon her soon after she fell asleep in favor of the safety and security of the highboy. He knew the nightmare was on its way and gave it plenty of space.

She used a corner of the sheet to mop the sweat from her forehead and cheeks. Fingers fumbled in the nightstand drawer until they found a cigarette. She flicked the tip and waited for the cylinder to ignite. Something—her head snapped around. Nothing there. Only the soft hum of the clock. There was nothing else in the room. Just Jones and her. Certainly no wind.

Leaning to her left, she pawed through the other nightstand drawer until she'd located the card Burke had left behind. She turned it over in her fingers, then inserted it into a slot in the bedside console. The videoscreen that dominated the far wall immediately flashed the words STAND BY at her. She waited impatiently until Burke's face appeared. He was bleary-eyed and unshaven, having been roused from a sound sleep, but he managed a grin when he saw who was calling.

"Yello? Oh, Ripley. Hi."

"Burke, just tell me one thing." She hoped there was enough light in the room for the monitor to pick up her expression as well as her voice. "That you're going out there to kill them. Not to study. Not to bring back. Just burn them out, clean, forever."

He woke up rapidly, she noted. "That's the plan. If there's anything dangerous walking around out there, we get rid of it. Got a colony to protect. No monkeying around with potentially dangerous organisms. That's Company policy. We find anything lethal, anything at all, we fry it. The scientists can go suck eggs. My word on it." A long pause and he leaned toward his own pickup, his face looming large on the screen. "Ripley. Ripley? You still there?"

No more time to think. Maybe it was time to stop thinking and to _do_. "All right. I'm in." There, she'd gone and said it. Somehow she'd said it.

He looked like he wanted to reply, to congratulate or thank her. Something. She broke the connection before he could say a word. A thump sounded on the sheets next to her, and she turned to gaze fondly down at Jones. She trailed short nails down his spine, and he primped delightedly, rubbing against her hip and purring.

"And _you_, my dear, are staying right here."

The cat blinked up at her as he continued to caress her fingers with his back. It was doubtful that he understood either her words or the gist of the previous phone call, but he did not volunteer to accompany her.

At least one of us still has some sense left, she thought as she slid back beneath the covers.

IV

It was an ugly ship. Battered, overused, parts repaired that should have been replaced, too tough and valuable to scrap. Easier for its masters to upgrade it and modify it than build a new one. Its lines were awkward and its engines oversize. A mountain of metal and composites and ceramic, a floating scrap heap, weightless monument to war, it shouldered its way brutally through the mysterious region called hyperspace. Like its human cargo, it was purely functional. Its name was *Sulaco*.

Fourteen dreamers this trip. Eleven engaged in related morphean fantasies, simple and straightforward as the vessel that carried them through the void. Two others more individualistic. A last sleeping under sedation necessary to mute the effects of recurring nightmares. Fourteen dreamers—and one for whom sleep was a superfluous abstraction.

Executive Officer Bishop checked readouts and adjusted controls. The long wait was ended. An alarm sounded throughout the length of the massive military transport. Long dormant machinery, powered down to conserve energy, came back to life. So did long dormant humans as their hypersleep capsules were charged and popped open. Satisfied that his charges had survived their long hibernation, Bishop set about the business of placing *Sulaco* in a low geo-stationary orbit around the colony world of Acheron.

Ripley was the first of the sleepers to awake. Not because

she was any more adaptive than her fellow travelers or more
used to the effects of hypersleep, but simply because her
capsule was first in line for recharge. Sitting up in the enclosed
bed, she rubbed briskly at her arms, then started to work on
her legs. Burke sat up in the capsule across from her, and
the lieutenant—what was his name?—oh, yeah, Gorman,
beyond him.

The other capsules contained the *Sulaco*'s military com-
plement: eight men and three women. They were a select
group in that they chose to put their lives at risk for the
majority of the time they were awake: individuals used to
long periods of hypersleep followed by brief, but intense,
periods of wakefulness. The kind of people others made room
for on a sidewalk or in a bar.

PFC Spunkmeyer was the dropship crew chief, the man
responsible along with Pilot-Corporal Ferro for safely con-
veying his colleagues to the surface of whichever world they
happened to be visiting, and then taking them off again in
one piece. In a hurry if necessary. He rubbed at his eyes and
groaned as he blinked at the hypersleep chamber.

"I'm getting too old for this." No one paid any attention
to this comment, since it was well known (or at least widely
rumored) that Spunkmeyer had enlisted when underage. However, nobody joked about his maturity or lack of it when they
were plummeting toward the surface of a new world in the
PFC-directed dropship.

Private Drake was rolling out of the capsule next to
Spunkmeyer's. He was a little older than Spunkmeyer and a
lot uglier. In addition to sharing similarities in appearance
with the *Sulaco*, likewise he was built a lot like the old
transport. Drake was heavy-duty bad company, with arms
like a legendary one-eyed sailor, a nose busted beyond repair
by the cosmetic surgeons, and a nasty scar that curled one
side of his mouth into a permanent sneer. The scar surgery
could have fixed, but Drake hung on to it. It was one medal

he was allowed to wear all the time. He wore a tight-fitting floppy cap, which no living soul dared refer to as "cute."

Drake was a smartgun operator. He was also skilled in the use of rifles, handguns, grenades, assorted blades, and his teeth.

"They ain't payin' us enough for this," he mumbled.

"Not enough to have to wake up to your face, Drake." This from Corporal Dietrich, who was arguably the prettiest of the group except when she opened her mouth.

"Suck vacuum," Drake told her. He eyed the occupant of another recently opened capsule. "Hey, Hicks, you look like I feel."

Hicks was the squad's senior corporal and second in command among the troops after Master Sergeant Apone. He didn't talk much and always seemed to be in the right place at the potentially lethal time, a fact much appreciated by his fellow Marines. He kept his counsel to himself while the others spouted off. When he did speak, what he had to say was usually worth hearing.

Ripley was back on her feet, rubbing the circulation back into her legs and doing standing knee-bends to loosen up stiffened joints. She examined the troopers as they shuffled past her on their way to a bank of lockers. There were no supermen among them, no overly muscled archetypes, but every one of them was lean and hardened. She suspected that the least among them could run all day over the surface of a two-gee world carrying a full equipment pack, fight a running battle while doing so, and then spend the night breaking down and repairing complex computer instrumentation. Brawn and brains aplenty, even if they preferred to talk like common street toughs. The best the contemporary military had to offer. She felt a little safer—but only a little.

Master Sergeant Apone was making his way up the center aisle, chatting briefly with each of his newly revived soldiers in turn. The sergeant looked as though he could take apart a medium-size truck with his bare hands. As he passed

Comtech Corporal Hudson's pallet, the latter voiced a complaint.

"This floor's *freezing*."

"So were you, ten minutes ago. I never saw such a bunch of old women. Want me to fetch your slippers, Hudson?"

The corporal batted his eyelashes at the sergeant. "Would you, sir? I'd be ever so grateful?" A few rough chuckles acknowledged Hudson's riposte. Apone smiled to himself as he resumed his walk, chiding his people and urging them to speed it up.

Ripley stayed out of their way as they trudged past. They were a tightly knit bunch, a single fighting organism with eleven heads, and she wasn't a part of their group. She stood outside, isolated. A couple of them nodded to her as they strode past, and there were one or two cursory hellos. That was all she had any right to expect, but it didn't make her feel any more relaxed in their company.

PFC Vasquez just stared as she walked past. Ripley had received warmer inspections from robots. The other smartgun operator didn't blink, didn't smile. Black hair, blacker eyes, thin lips. Attractive if she'd make half an effort.

It required a special talent; a unique combination of strength, mental ability, and reflexes, to operate a smartgun. Ripley waited for the woman to say something. She didn't open her mouth as she passed by. Every one of the troopers looked tough. Drake and Vasquez looked tough *and* mean.

Her counterpart called out to her as she came abreast of his locker. "Hey, Vasquez, you ever been mistaken for a man?"

"No. Have you?"

Drake proffered an open palm. She slapped it, and his fingers immediately clenched right around her smaller fingers. The pressure increased on both sides—a silent, painful greeting. Both were glad to be out from under hypersleep and alive again.

Finally she whacked him across the face and their hands

parted. They laughed, young Dobermans at play. Drake was the stronger but Vasquez was faster, Ripley decided as she watched them. If they had to go down, she resolved to try to keep them on either side of her. It would be the safest place.

Bishop was moving quietly among the group, helping with massages and a bottle of special postsleep fluid, acting more like a valet than a ship's officer. He appeared older than any of the troopers, including Lieutenant Gorman. As he passed close to Ripley she noticed the alphanumeric code tattooed across the back of his left hand. She stiffened in recognition but said nothing.

"Hey," Private Frost said to someone out of Ripley's view, "you take my towel?" Frost was as young as Hudson but better-looking, or so he would insist to anyone who would waste time listening. When it came time for bragging, the two younger troopers usually came out about even. Hudson tended to rely on volume while Frost hunted for the right words.

Spunkmeyer was up near the head of the line and still complaining. "I need some slack, man. How come they send us straight back out like this? It ain't fair. We got some slack comin', man."

Hicks murmured softly. "You just got three weeks. You want to spend your whole life on slack time?"

"I mean breathing, not this frozen stuff. Three weeks in the freezer ain't real off-time."

"Yeah, Top, what about it?" Dietrich wanted to know.

"You know it ain't up to me." Apone raised his voice above the griping. "Awright, let's knock off the jawing. First assembly's in fifteen. I want everybody looking like human beings by then—most of you will have to fake it. Let's shag it."

Hypersleep wear was stripped off and tossed into the disposal unit. Easier to cremate the remains and provide fresh new attire for the return journey than to try to recycle shorts

and tops that had clung to a body for several weeks. The line
of lean, naked bodies moved into the shower. High-pressure
water jets blasted away accumulated sweat and grime, set
nerve endings tingling beneath scoured skin. Through the
swirling steam Hudson, Vasquez, and Ferro watched Ripley
dry off.

"Who's the freshmeat again?" Vasquez asked the question as she washed cleanser out of her hair.

"She's supposed to be some kinda consultant. Don't
know much about her." The diminutive Ferro wiped at her
belly, which was as flat and muscular as a steel plate, and
exaggerated her expression and tone. "She saw an *alien* once.
Or so the skipchat says."

"Whooah!" Hudson made a face. "I'm impressed."

Apone yelled back at them. He was already out in the
drying room, toweling off his shoulders. They were as devoid
of fat as those of troopers twenty years younger.

"Let's go, let's go. Buncha lazybutts'll run the recyclers
dry. C'mon, cycle through. You got to get dirty before you
can get clean."

Informal segregation was the order of the day in the
mess room. It was automatic. There was no need for whispered words or little nameplates next to the glasses. Apone
and his troopers requisitioned the large table while Ripley,
Gorman, Burke, and Bishop sat at the other. Everyone nursed
coffee, tea, spritz, or water while they waited for the ship's
autochef to deal out eggs and ersatz bacon, toast and hash,
condiments, and vitamin supplements.

You could identify each trooper by his or her uniform.
No two were exactly alike. This was the result not of specialized identification insignia, but of individual taste. The
Sulaco was no barracks and Acheron no parade ground. Occasionally Apone would have to chew someone out for a
particularly egregious addition, like the time Crowe had
showed up with a portrait of his latest girlfriend computer-

stenciled across the back of his armor. But for the most part
he let the troopers decorate their outfits as they liked.

"Hey, Top," Hudson chivvied, "what's the op?"

"Yeah." Frost blew bubbles in his tea. "All I know is I
get shipping orders and not time to say hello-goodbye to
Myrna."

"Myrna?" Private Wierzbowski raised a bushy eyebrow.
"I thought it was Leina?"

Frost looked momentarily uncertain. "I think Leina was
three months ago. Or six."

"It's a rescue mission." Apone sipped his coffee. "There's
some juicy colonists' daughters we gotta rescue."

Ferro made a show of looking disappointed. "Hell, that
lets me out."

"Says who?" Hudson leered at her. She threw sugar at
him.

Apone just listened and watched. No reason for him to
intervene. He could have quieted them down, could have
played it by the book. Instead he left it loose and fair, but
only because he knew that his people were the best. He'd
walk into a fight with any one of them watching his back
and not worry about what he couldn't see, knowing that
anything trying to sneak up on him would be taken care of
as efficiently as if he had eyes in the back of his head. Let
'em play, let 'em curse ECA and the corps and the Company
and him too. When the time came, the playing would stop,
and every one of them would be all business.

"Dumb colonists." Spunkmeyer looked to his plate as
food began to put in an appearance. After three weeks asleep
he was starving, but not so starving that he couldn't offer the
obligatory soldier's culinary comment. "What's this stuff supposed to be?"

"Eggs, dimwit," said Ferro.

"I know what an egg is, bubblebrain. I mean this soggy
flat yellow stuff on the side."

"Corn bread, I think." Wierzbowski fingered his portion

and added absently, "Hey, I wouldn't mind getting me some more a that Arcturan poontang. Remember that time?"

Hicks was sitting on his right side. The corporal glanced up briefly, then looked back to his plate. "Looks like that new lieutenant's too good to eat with us lowly grunts. Kissing up to the Company rep."

Wierzbowski stared past the corporal, not caring if anyone should happen to notice the direction of his gaze. "Yeah."

"Doesn't matter if he knows his job," said Crowe.

"The magic word." Frost hacked at his eggs. "We'll find out."

Perhaps it was Gorman's youth that bothered them, even though he was older than half the troopers. More likely it was his appearance: hair neat even after weeks in hypersleep, slack creases sharp and straight, boots gleaming like black metal. He looked too good.

As they ate and muttered and stared, Bishop took the empty seat next to Ripley. She rose pointedly and moved to the far side of the table. The ExO looked wounded.

"I'm sorry you feel that way about synthetics, Ripley."

She ignored him as she glared down at Burke, her tone accusing. "You never said anything about there being an android on board! Why not? Don't lie to me, either, Carter. I saw his tattoo outside the showers."

Burke appeared nonplussed. "Well, it didn't occur to me. I don't know why you're so upset. It's been Company policy for years to have a synthetic on board every transport. They don't need hypersleep, and it's a lot cheaper than hiring a human pilot to oversee the interstellar jumps. They won't go crazy working a longhaul solo. Nothing special about it."

"I prefer the term 'artificial person' myself," Bishop interjected softly. "Is there a problem? Perhaps it's something I can help with."

"I don't think so." Burke wiped egg from his lips. "A synthetic malfunctioned on her last trip out. Some deaths were involved."

"I'm shocked. Was it long ago?"

"Quite a while, in fact." Burke made the statement without going into specifics, for which Ripley was grateful.

"Must have been an older model, then."

"Hyperdine Systems 120-A/2."

Bending over backward to be conciliatory, Bishop turned to Ripley. "Well, that explains it. The old A/2s were always a bit twitchy. That could never happen now, not with the new implanted behavioral inhibitors. Impossible for me to harm or, by omission of action, allow to be harmed a human being. The inhibitors are factory-installed, along with the rest of my cerebral functions. No one can tamper with them. So you see, I'm quite harmless." He offered her a plate piled high with yellow rectangles. "More corn bread?"

The plate did not shatter when it struck the far wall as Ripley smacked it out of his hand. Corn bread crumbled as the plate settled to the floor.

"Just stay away from me, Bishop! You got that straight? You keep away from me."

Wierzbowski observed this byplay in silence, then shrugged and turned back to his food. "She don't like the corn bread, either."

Ripley's outburst sparked no more conversation than that as the troopers finished breakfast and retired to the ready room. Ranks of exotic weaponry lined the walls behind them. Some clustered their chairs and started an improvised game of dice. Tough to pick up a floating crap game after you've been unconscious for three weeks, but they tried nonetheless. They straightened lazily as Gorman and Burke entered, but snapped to when Apone barked at them.

"Tench-hut!" The men and women responded as one, arms vertical at their sides, eyes straight ahead, and focused only on what the sergeant might say to them next.

Gorman's eyes flicked over the line. If possible, the troopers were more motionless standing at attention than they

had been when frozen in hypersleep. He held them a moment
longer before speaking.

"At ease." The line flexed as muscles were relaxed. "I'm
sorry we didn't have time to brief you before we left Gateway,
but—"

"Sir?" said Hudson.

Annoyed, Gorman glanced toward the speaker. Couldn't
let him finish his first sentence before starting with the questions. Not that he'd expected anything else. He'd been warned
that this bunch might be like that.

"Yes, what is it, Hicks?"

The speaker nodded at the man standing next to him.
"Hudson, sir. He's Hicks."

"What's the question, soldier?"

"Is this going to be a stand-up fight, sir, or another bug-
hunt?"

"If you'd wait a moment, you might find some of your
questions anticipated, Hudson. I can understand your impa-
tience and curiosity. There's not a great deal to explain. All
we know is that there's still been no contact with the colony.
Executive Officer Bishop tried to rise Hadley the instant the
Sulaco hove within hailing distance of Acheron. He did not
obtain a response. The planetary deepspace satellite relay
checks out okay, so *that's* not the reason for the lack of
contact. We don't know what it is yet."

"Any ideas?" Crowe asked.

"There is a possibility, just a possibility at this point,
mind, that a xenomorph may be involved."

"A whaaat?" said Wierzbowski.

Hicks leaned toward him, whispered softly. "It's a bug-
hunt." Then louder, to the lieutenant, "So what are these
things, if they're there?"

Gorman nodded to Ripley, who stepped forward. Eleven
pairs of eyes locked on her like gun sights: alert, intent,
curious, and speculative. They were sizing her up, still unsure
whether to class her with Burke and Gorman or somewhere

else. They neither cared for her nor disliked her, because they didn't know her yet.

Fine. Leave it at that. She placed a handful of tiny recorder disks on the table before her.

"I've dictated what I know on these. There are some duplicates. You can read them in your rooms or in your suits."

"I'm a slow reader." Apone lightened up enough to smile slightly. "Tease us a bit."

"Yeah, let's have some previews." Spunkmeyer leaned back against enough explosive to blow a small hotel apart, snuggling back among the firing tubes and detonators.

"Okay. First off, it's important to understand the organism's life cycle. It's actually two creatures. The first form hatches from a spore, a sort of large egg, and attaches itself to its victim. Then it injects an embryo, detaches, and dies. It's essentially a walking reproductive organ. Then the—"

"Sounds like you, Hicks." Hudson grinned over at the older man, who responded with his usual tolerant smile.

Ripley didn't find it funny. She didn't find anything about the alien funny, but then, she'd seen it. The troopers still weren't convinced she was describing something that existed outside her imagination. She'd have to try to be patient with them. That wasn't going to be easy.

"The embryo, the second form, hosts in the victim's body for several hours. Gestating. Then it"—she had to swallow, fighting a sudden dryness in her throat—"emerges. Molts. Grows rapidly. The adult form advances quickly through a number of intermediate stages until it matures in the form of—"

This time it was Vasquez who interrupted. "That's all fine, but I only need to know one thing."

"Yes?"

"Where they are." She pointed her finger at an empty space between Ripley and the door, cocked her thumb, and blew away an imaginary intruder. Hoots and guffaws of approval came from her colleagues.

"Yo Vasquez!" As always, Drake delighted in his counterpart's demure bloodthirstiness. Her nickname was the Gamin Assassin. It was not misplaced.

She nodded brusquely. "Anytime. Anywhere."

"Somebody say 'alien'?" Hudson leaned back in his seat, idly fingering a weapon with an especially long and narrow barrel. "She thought they said 'illegal alien' and signed up."

"Fuck you." Vasquez threw the comtech a casual finger. He responded by mimicking her tone and attitude as closely as possible.

"Anytime. Anywhere."

Ripley's tone was as cold as the skin of the *Sulaco*. "Am I disturbing your conversation, Mr. Hudson? I know most of you are looking at this as just another typical police action. I can assure you it's more than that. I've seen this creature. I've seen what it can do. If you run into it, I can guarantee that you won't do so laughingly."

Hudson subsided, smirking. Ripley shifted her attention to Vasquez. "I hope it'll be as easy as you make it out to be, Private. I really do." Their eyes locked. Neither woman looked away.

Burke broke it up by stepping between them to address the assembled troops. "That's enough for a preview. I suggest all of you take the time to study the disks Ripley has been kind enough to prepare for you. They contain additional basic information, as well as some highly detailed speculative graphics put together by an advanced imaging computer. I believe you'll find them interesting. I promise they'll hold your attention." He relinquished the floor to Gorman. The lieutenant was brisk, sounding like a commander even if he didn't quite look like one.

"Thank you Mr. Burke, Ms. Ripley." His gaze roved over the indifferent faces of his squad. "Any questions?" A hand waved casually from the back of the group and he sighed resignedly. "Yes, Hudson?"

The comtech was examining his fingernails. "How do I get out of this outfit?"

Gorman scowled and forbore from offering the first thought that came to mind. He thanked Ripley again, and gratefully she took a seat.

"All right. I want this operation to go smoothly and by the numbers. I want full DCS and tactical data-base assimilation by oh-eight-thirty." A few groans rose from the group but nothing in the way of a strong protest. It was no less than what they expected.

"Ordnance loading, weapons strip and checkout, and dropship prep will have seven hours. I want everything and everybody ready to go on time. Let's hit it. You've had three weeks rest."

The *Sulaco* was a giant metallic seashell drifting in a black sea. Bluish lights flared soundlessly along the flanks of the unlovely hull as she settled into final orbit. On the bridge, Bishop regarded his instruments and readouts unblinkingly. Occasionally he would touch a switch or tap a flurry of commands into the system. For the most part all he had to do was observe while the ship's computers parked the vessel in the desired orbit. The automation that made interstellar navigation possible had reduced man to the status of a last-recourse backup system. Now synthetics like Bishop had replaced man. Exploration of the cosmos had become a chauffeured profession.

When the dials and gauges had lined up to his satisfaction, he leaned toward the nearest voice pickup. "Attention to the bridge. Bishop speaking. This concludes final intraorbital maneuvering operations. Geosynchronous insertion has been completed. I have adjusted artificial gravity to Acheron norm. Thank you for your cooperation. You may resume work."

In contrast to the peace and quiet that reigned throughout most of the ship, the cargo loading bay was swarming with activity. Spunkmeyer sat in the roll cage of a big powerloader, a machine that resembled a skeletal mechanical elephant and was much stronger. The waldo gloves in which his hands and feet were inserted picked up the PFC's movements and transferred them to the metal arms and legs of the machine, multiplying his carrying capacity by a factor of several thousand.

He slid the long, reinforced arms into a bulging ordnance rack and lifted out a rack of small tactical missiles. Working with the smooth, effortless movements of his external prosthesis, he swung the load up into the dropship's belly. Clicks and clangs sounded from within as the vessel accepted the offering and automatically secured the missiles in place. Spunkmeyer retreated in search of another load. The powerloader was battered and dirty with grease. Across its back the word *Caterpillar* was faintly visible.

Other troopers drove tow motors or ran loading arms. Occasionally they called to one another, but for the most part the loading and prep operation proceeded without conversation. Also without accident, the members of the squad meshed like the individual gears and wheels of some halfmetal, half-organic machine. Despite the close quarters in which they found themselves, and the amount of dangerous machinery in constant motion, no one so much as scraped his neighbor. Hicks watched over it all, checking off one item after another on an electronic manifest, occasionally nodding to himself as one more necessary predrop procedure was satisfactorily completed.

In the armory Wierzbowski, Drake, and Vasquez were fieldstripping light weapons, their fingers moving with as much precision as the loading machines in the cargo bay. Tiny circuit boards were removed, checked, and blown clean of dust and lint before being reinserted into sleek metal and plastic sculptures of death.

Vasquez removed her heavy smartgun from its rack and locked it into a work stand and lovingly began to run it through the computer-assisted final checkout. The weapon was designed to be worn, not carried. It was equipped with an integral computer lock-and-fire, its own search-and-detection equipment, and was balanced on a precision gimbal that stabilized itself according to its operator's movements. It could do just about everything except pull its own trigger.

Vasquez smiled affectionately as she worked on it. It was a difficult child, a complex child, but it would protect her and her comrades and keep them safe from harm. She lavished more understanding and care on it than she did on any of her colleagues.

Drake understood completely. He also talked to his weapon, albeit silently. None of their fellow troopers found such behavior abnormal. Everyone knew that all Colonial Marines were slightly unbalanced and that smartgun operators were the strangest of the lot. They tended to treat their weapons as extensions of their own bodies. Unlike their colleagues, gun operation was their principal function. Drake and Vasquez didn't have to worry about mastering communications equipment, piloting a dropship, driving the armored personnel carrier, or even helping to load the ship for landing. All they were required to do was shoot at things. Death-dealing was their designated specialty.

Both of them loved their work.

Not everyone was as busy as the troopers. Burke had completed his few personal preparations for landing while

Gorman was able to leave the actual supervision of final prep to Apone. As they stood off to the side and watched, the Company representative spoke casually to the lieutenant.

"Still nothing from the colony?"

Gorman shook his head and noted something about the loading procedure that induced him to make a notation on his electronic pad. "Not even a background carrier wave. Dead on all channels."

"And we're sure about the relay satellite?"

"Bishop insists that he checked it out thoroughly and that it responded perfectly to every command. Says it gave him something to do while we were on final system approach. He ran a standard signal check along the relay back to Earth, and we should get a response in a few days. That'll be the final confirmation, but he felt sure enough of his own check to guarantee the system's performance."

"Then the problem's down on the surface somewhere."

Gorman nodded. "Like we've suspected all along."

Burke looked thoughtful. "What about local communications? Community video, operations to tractors, relays between the atmosphere processing stations, and the like?"

The lieutenant shook his head regretfully. "If anybody's talking to anybody else down there, they're doing it with smoke signals or mirrors. Except for the standard low-end hiss from the local sun, the electromagnetic spectrum's dead as lead."

The Company rep shrugged. "Well, we didn't expect to find anything else. Still, there was always hope."

"There still is. Maybe the colony's taken a mass vow of silence. Maybe all we'll run into is a collective pout."

"Why would they do something like that?"

"How should I know? Mass religious conversion or something else that demands radio silence."

"Yeah. Maybe." Burke wanted to believe Gorman. Gorman wanted to believe Burke. Neither man believed the other for a moment. Whatever had silenced the colony of

Acheron hadn't been a matter of choice. People liked to talk, colonists more than most. They wouldn't shut down all communications willingly.

Ripley had been watching the two men. Now she shifted her attention back to the ongoing process of loading and predrop prep. She'd seen military dropships on the newscasts, but this was the first time she'd stood close to one. It made her feel a little safer. Heavily armed and armored, it looked like a giant black wasp. As she looked on, a six-wheeled armored personnel carrier was being hoisted into the ship's belly. It was built like an iron ingot, low and squatty, unlovely in profile and purely functional.

Movement on her left made her stumble aside as Frost wheeled a rack of incomprehensible equipment toward her.

"Clear, please," the trooper said politely.

As she apologized and stepped away she was forced to retreat in another direction in order to get out of Hudson's way.

"Excuse me." He didn't look at her, concentrating on his lift load of supplies.

Cursing silently to herself, she hunted through the organized confusion until she found Apone. The NCO was chatting with Hicks, both of them studying the corporal's checklist as she approached. She kept quiet until the sergeant acknowledged her presence.

"Something?" he asked curiously.

"Yeah, there's something. I feel like a fifth wheel down here, and I'm sick of doing nothing."

Apone grinned. "We're all sick of doing nothing. What about it?"

"Is there anything I can do?"

He scratched the back of his head, eyeing her. "I don't know. *Is* there anything you can do?"

She turned and pointed. "I can drive that loader. I've got a class-two dock rating. My latest career move."

Apone glanced in the direction in which she was pointing. The *Sulaco*'s backup powerloader squatted dormant in its maintenance bay. His people were versatile, but they were soldiers first. Marines, not construction workers. An extra couple of hands would be welcome loading the heavy stuff, especially if they were fashioned of titanium alloy, as were the powerloader's.

"That's no toy." The skepticism in Apone's voice was matched by that on Hicks's face.

"That's all right," she replied crisply. "This isn't Christmas."

The sergeant pursed his lips. "Class-two, huh?"

By way of response, she spun on her heel and strode over to the loader, climbed the ladder, and settled into the seat beneath the safety cage. A quick inspection revealed that, as she'd suspected, the loader was little different from the ones she'd operated Portside on Earth. A slightly newer model, maybe. She jabbed at a succession of switches. Motors turned over. A basso whine emanated from the guts of the machine, rising to a steady hum.

Hands and feet slipped into waldo gloves. Like some paralyzed dinosaur suddenly shocked back to life, the loader rose on titanium pads. It boomed as she walked it over to the stack of cargo modules. Huge claws extended and dipped, slipping into lifting receptacles beneath the nearest container. She raised it from the top of the pile and swung it back toward the watching men. Her voice rose above the hum of the motors.

"Where you want it?"

Hicks glanced at his sergeant and cocked an eyebrow appreciatively.

Personal preparation proceeded at the same pace as dropship loading but with additional care. Something could go wrong with the APC, or the supplies crammed into it, or with communications or backup, but no soldier would allow anything to go wrong with his or her personal weaponry. Each of them was capable of fighting and winning a small war on his or her own.

First the armor was snapped together and checked for cracks or warps. Then the special combat boots, capable of resisting any combination of weather, corrosion, and teeth. Backpacks that would enable a fragile human being to survive for over a month in a hostile environment without any supplemental aid whatsoever. Harnesses to keep you from bouncing around during a rough drop or while the APC was grinding a path over difficult terrain. Helmets to protect your skull and visors to shield your eyes. Comsets for communicating with the dropship, with the APC, with whichever buddy happened to be guarding your rear.

Fingers flowed smoothly over fastenings and snaps. When everything was done and ready, when all had been checked out and operational, the whole procedure was run again from scratch. And when *that* was over, if you had a minute, you spent it checking out your neighbor's work.

Apone strode back and forth among his people, doing his own unobtrusive checking even though he knew it was unnecessary. He was, however, a firm believer in the for-want-of-a-nail school. Now was the time to spot the overlooked snap, the forgotten catch. Once things turned hairy, regrets were usually fatal.

"Let's move it, girls! On the ready-line. Let's go, let's go. You've slept long enough."

They formed up and headed for the dropship, chatting excitedly and shuffling along in twos and threes. Apone could have made it pretty if he'd wanted to, formed them up and called cadence, but his people weren't pretty, and he wasn't about to tell them how to walk. The sergeant was pleased to see that their new lieutenant had learned enough by now to keep his mouth shut. They filed into the ship muttering among themselves, no flags flying, no prerecorded bands tootling. Their anthem was a string of well-worn and familiar obscenities passed down from one to the next: defiant words from men and women ready to challenge death. Apone shared them. As all foot soldiers have known for thousands of years, there's nothing noble about dying. Only an irritating finality.

Once inside the dropship, they filed directly into the APC. The carrier would deploy the instant the shuttle craft touched down. It made for a rougher ride, but Colonial Marines do not expect coddling.

As soon as everyone was aboard and the dropship doors secured, a klaxon sounded, signaling depressurization of the *Sulaco*'s cargo bay. Service robots scurried for cover. Warning lights flashed.

The troopers sat in two rows opposite each other, a single aisle running between. Next to the soldiers in their hulking armor, Ripley felt small and vulnerable. In addition to her duty suit she wore only a flight jacket and a communications headset. No one offered her a gun.

Hudson was too juiced up to sit still. The adrenaline was flowing and his eyes were wide. He prowled the aisle, his movements predatory and exaggerated, a cat ready to pounce. As he paced, he kept up a steady stream of psychobabble, unavoidable in the confined space.

"I am *ready*, man. Ready to get it *on*. Check it out. I am the ultimate. State-of-the-art. You *do not* want to mess with me. Hey, Ripley." She glanced up at him, expressionless. "Don't worry, little lady. Me and my squad of ultimate killing machines will protect you. Check it out." He slapped the controls of the servocannon mounted in the overhead gun bay, careful not to hit any of the ready studs.

"Independently targeting particle-beam phalanx gun. Ain't she a cutey? *Vwap!* Fry half a city with this puppy. We got tactical smart missiles, phased-plasma pulse-rifles, RPGs. We got sonic ee-lectronic cannons, we got nukes no flukes, we got knives, sharp sticks—"

Hicks reached up, grabbed Hudson by his battle harness, and yanked him down into an empty seat. His voice was low but it carried.

"Save it."

"Sure, Hicks." Hudson sat back, suddenly docile.

Ripley nodded her thanks to the corporal. Young face, old eyes, she thought as she studied him. Seen more than he should have in his time. Probably more than he's wanted to. She didn't mind the quiet that followed Hudson's soliloquy. There was hysteria enough below. She didn't need to listen to any extra. The corporal leaned toward her.

"Don't mind Hudson. Don't mind any of 'em. They're all like that, but in a tight spot there're none better."

"If he can shoot his gun as well as he does his mouth, maybe it'll take my blood pressure down a notch."

Hicks grinned. "Don't worry on that score. Hudson's a comtech, but he's a close-combat specialist, just like everyone else."

"You too?"

He settled back in his seat: content, self-contained, ready. "I'm not here because I wanted to be a pastry chef."

Motors began to throb. The dropship lurched as it was lowered out of the cargo bay on its grapples.

"Hey," Frost muttered, "anybody check the locks on this coffin? If they're not tight, we're liable to bounce right out the bottom of the shuttle."

"Keep cool, sweets," said Dietrich. "Checked 'em out myself. We're secure. This six-wheeler goes nowhere until we kiss dirt." Frost looked relieved.

The dropship's engines rumbled to life. Stomachs lurched as they left the artificial gravity field of the *Sulaco* behind. They were free now, floating slowly away from the big transport. Soon they would be clear and the engines would fire fully. Legs and hands began to float in zero-gee, but their harnesses held them tight to their seats. The floor and walls of the APC quivered as the engines thundered. Gravity returned with a vengeance.

Burke looked like he was on a fishing cruiser off

Jamaica. He was grinning eagerly, anxious for the real adventure to begin. "Here we go!"

Ripley closed her eyes, then opened them almost immediately. Anything was better than staring at the black backsides of her lids. They were like tiny videoscreens alive with wild sparks and floating green blobs. Malign shapes appeared in the blobs. The taut, confident faces of Frost, Crowe, Apone, and Hicks made for more reassuring viewing.

Up in the cockpit, Spunkmeyer and Ferro studied readouts and worked controls. Gees built up within the APC as the dropship's speed increased. A few lips trembled. No one said a word as they plunged toward atmosphere.

Gray limbo below. The dark mantle of clouds that shrouded the surface of Acheron suddenly became something more than a pearlescent sheen to be admired from above. The atmosphere was dense and disturbed, boiling over dry deserts and lifeless rocks, rendering the landscape invisible to everything but sophisticated sensors and imaging equipment.

The dropship bounced through alien jet streams, shuddering and rocking. Ferro's voice sounded icy calm over the open intercom as she shouldered the streamlined craft through the dust-filled gale.

"Switching to DCS ranging. Visibility zero. A real picnic ground. What a bowl of crap."

"Two-four-oh." Spunkmeyer was too busy to respond in kind to her complaints. "Nominal to profile. Picking up some hull ionization."

Ferro glanced at a readout. "Bad?"

"Nothing the filters can't handle. Winds two hundred plus." A screen between them winked to life, displaying a topographic model of the terrain they were overflying. "Surface ranging on. What'd you expect, Ferro? Tropical beaches?" He nudged a trio of switches. "Starting to hit thermals. Vertical shift unpredictable. Lotta swirling."

"Got it." Ferro thumbed a button. "Nothing that ain't in

our programming. At least the weather hasn't changed down there." She eyed a readout. "Rough air ahead."

The pilot's voice sounded briskly over the APC's intercom system. "Ferro, here. You all read the profile on this dirtball. Summertime fun it ain't. Stand by for some chop."

Ripley's eyes flicked rapidly over her companions, crammed tightly together in the confines of the armored personnel carrier. Hicks lay slumped to one side, asleep in his seat harness. The bouncing seemed not to bother him in the slightest. Most of the other troopers sat quietly, staring straight ahead, their minds mulling over private thoughts. Hudson was talking steadily and silently to himself. His lips moved ceaselessly. Ripley didn't try to read them.

Burke was studying the interior layout of the APC with professional interest. Across from him Gorman sat with his eyes shut tight. His skin was pale, and the sweat stood out on his forehead and neck. His hands were in nonstop motion, rubbing the backs of his knees. Massaging away tenseness— or attempting to dry clamminess, she thought. Maybe it would help him to have someone to talk to.

"How many drops is this for you, Lieutenant?"

His eyes snapped open and he blinked at her. "Thirty-eight—simulated."

"How many *combat* drops?" Vasquez asked pointedly.

Gorman tried to reply as though it made no difference. A minor point, and what did it have to do with anything, anyway? "Well—two. Three, including this one."

Vasquez and Drake exchanged a glance, said nothing. They didn't have to. Their respective expressions were sufficiently eloquent. Ripley gave Burke an accusing look, and he responded with one of indifferent helplessness, as if to say, "Hey, I'm a civilian. Got no control over military assignments."

Which was pure bull, of course, but there was nothing to be gained by arguing about it now. Acheron lay beneath them, Earthside bureaucracy very far away indeed. She chewed her lower lip and tried not to let it bother her. Gorman seemed competent enough. Besides, in any actual confrontation or combat, Apone would run the show. Apone and Hicks.

Cockpit voices continued to reverberate over the intercom. Ferro managed to outgripe Spunkmeyer three to one. In between gripes and complaints they managed to fly the dropship.

"Turning on final approach," she was saying. "Coming around to a seven-zero-niner. Terminal guidance locked in."

"Always knew you were terminal," said Spunkmeyer. It was an old pilot's joke, and Ferro ignored it.

"Watch your screen. I can't fly this sucker and watch the terrain readouts too. Keep us off the mountains." A pause, then, "Where's the beacon?"

"Nothing on relay." Spunkmeyer's voice was calm. "Must've gone out along with communications."

"That's crazy and you know it. Beacons are automatic and individually powered."

"Okay. *You* find the beacon."

"I'll settle for somebody waving a lousy flag." Silence followed. None of the troopers appeared concerned. Ferro and Spunkmeyer had set them down softer than a baby's kiss in worse weather than Acheron's.

"Winds easing. Good kite-flying weather. We'll hold her steady up here for a while so you kids in back can play with your toys."

A flurry of motion as the troopers commenced final touchdown preparations. Gorman slipped out of his flight harness and headed up the aisle toward the APC's tactical operations center. Burke and Ripley followed, leaving the Marines to their work.

The three of them crowded into the bay. Gorman slid behind the control console while Burke took up a stance behind him so he could look over the lieutenant's shoulder. Ripley was pleased to see that there was nothing wrong with Gorman's mechanical skills. He looked relieved to have something to do. His fingers brought readouts and monitor screens to life like an organist extracting notes from stops and keys. Ferro's voice reached them from the cockpit, mildly triumphant.

"Finally got the beacons. Signal is hazy but distinct. And the clouds have cleared enough for us to get some visual. We can see Hadley."

Gorman spoke toward a pickup. "How's it look?"

"Just like the brochures," she said sardonically. "Vacation spot of the galaxy. Massive construction, dirty. A few lights on, so they've got power somewheres. Can't tell at this distance if they're regular or emergency. Not a lot of 'em. Maybe it's nap time. Give me two weeks in the Antarctic anytime."

"Spunkmeyer, your impressions?"

"Windy as all get out. They haven't been bombed. Structural integrity looks good, but that's from up here, looking through bad light. Sorry we're too busy to do a ground scan."

"We'll take care of that in person." Gorman turned his attention back to the multiple screens. The closer they came to setdown, the more confident he seemed to become. Maybe a fear of heights was his only weakness, Ripley mused. If that proved to be the case, she'd be able to relax.

In addition to the tactical screens there were two small ones for each soldier. All were name-labeled. The upper set relayed the view from the video cams built into the crown of each battle helmet. The lower provided individual bio readouts: EEG, EKG, respiratory rate, circulatory functioning, visual acuity, and so on. Enough information for whoever was monitoring the screens to build up a complete physiological profile of every trooper from the inside out.

Above and to the side of the double set of smaller screens were larger monitors that offered those riding inside the APC a complete wraparound view of the terrain outside. Gorman thumbed controls. Hidden telltales beeped and responded on cue.

"Looking good," he murmured to himself, as much as to his civilian observers. "Everybody on line." Ripley noted that the blood-pressure readouts held remarkably steady. And not one of the soldiers' heart rates rose above seventy-five.

One of the small video monitors displayed static instead of a clear view of the APC's interior. "Drake, check your camera," Gorman ordered. "I'm not getting a picture. Frost, show me Drake. Might be an external break."

The view on the screen next to Drake's shifted to reveal the helmeted face of the smartgun operator as he whacked himself on the side of the head with a battery pack. His screen snapped into focus instantly.

"That's better. Pan it around a bit."

Drake complied. "Learned that one in tech class," he informed the occupants of the operations bay. "Got to make sure you hit the left side only or it doesn't work."

"What happens if you hit the right side?" Ripley asked curiously.

"You overload the internal pressure control, the one that keeps your helmet on your head." She could see Drake smiling wolfishly into Frost's camera. "Your eyeballs implode and your brains explode."

"What brains?" Vasquez let out a snort. Drake promptly leaned forward and tried to smack the right side of her helmet with a battery pack.

Apone quieted them. He knew it didn't matter what was wrong with Drake's helmet, because the smartgun operator would abandon it the first chance he got. Likewise Vasquez. Drake would appear in his floppy cap and Vasquez in her red bandanna. Nonregulation battle headgear. Both claimed the helmets obstructed the movement of their gun sights, and if that was the way they felt about it, Apone wasn't about to argue with them. They could shave their skulls and fight bald-headed if they wished as long as they shot straight.

"Awright. Fire team A, gear up. Check your backup systems and your power packs. Anybody goes dead when we

spread out is liable to end up that way. If some boogeyman
doesn't kill you, I will. Let's move. Two minutes." He glanced
to his right. "Somebody wake up Hicks."

A few guffaws sounded from the assembled troopers.
Ripley had to smile as she let her gaze drop to the biomonitor
with the corporal's name above it. The readings indicated a
man overwhelmed with boredom. Apone's second in command was deep in REM sleep. Dreaming of balmier climes,
no doubt. She wished she could relax like that. Once upon
a time she'd been able to. Once this trip was over, maybe
she'd be able to again.

The passenger compartment saw a new rush of activity
as backpacks were donned and weapons presented. Vasquez
and Drake assisted each other in buckling on their complex
smartgun harnesses.

The forward-facing viewscreen gave those in the operations bay the same view as Ferro and Spunkmeyer. Directly
ahead a metal volcano thrust its perfect cone into the clouds,
belching hot gas into the sky. Audio pickups muted the atmosphere processor's thunder.

"How many of those are on Acheron?" Ripley asked
Burke.

"That's one of thirty or so. I couldn't give you all the
grid references. They're scattered all over the planet. Well,
not scattered. Placed, for optimum injection into the atmosphere. Each is fully automated, and their output is controlled
from Hadley Operations Central. Their production will be
adjusted as the air here becomes more Earth-normal. Eventually they'll shut themselves down. Until that happens, they'll
work around the clock for another twenty to thirty years.
They're expensive and reliable. We manufacture them, by
the way."

The ship was a drifting mote alongside the massive,
rumbling tower. Ripley was impressed. Like everyone else
whose work took them out into space, she'd heard about the

big terraforming devices, but she'd never expected to see one in person.

Gorman nudged controls, swinging the main external imager around and down to reveal the silent roofs of the colony. "Hold at forty," he commanded Ferro via the console pickup. "Make a slow circle of the complex. I don't think we'll spot anything from up here, but that's the way the regs say to go, so that's how we'll do it."

"Can do," the pilot responded. "Hang on back there. Might bounce a little while we spiral in. This isn't an atmosphere flyer, remember. It's just a lousy dropship. Tight suborbital maneuvering ain't a highlight of its repertoire."

"Just do as you're told, Corporal."

"Yes, *sir*." Ferro added something else too low for her mike to unscramble. Ripley doubted that it was flattering.

They circled in over the town. Nothing moved among the buildings beneath them. The few lights they'd spotted from afar continued to burn. The atmosphere processor roared in the background.

"Everything looks intact," Burke commented. "Maybe some kind of plague has everyone on their backs."

"Maybe." To Gorman the colony structures looked like the wrecks of ancient freighters littering the ocean floor. "Okay," he said sharply to Apone, "let's do it."

Back in the passenger bay, the master sergeant rose from his seat and glared at his troops, hanging on to an overhead handgrip as the dropship rocked in Acheron's unceasing gale.

"Awright! You heard the lieutenant. I want a nice clean dispersal this time. Watch the suit in front of you. Anybody trips over anybody else's boots going out gets booted right back up to the ship."

"Is that a promise?" Crowe looked innocent.

"Hey, Crowe, you want your mommy?" Wierzbowski grinned at his colleague.

"Wish she were here," the private responded. "She'd wipe the floor with half you lot."

They filed toward the front lock, squeezing past operations. Vasquez gave Ripley a nudge as she strolled by. "You staying in here?"

"You bet."

"Figures." The smartgun operator turned away, shifting her attention to the back of Drake's head.

"Set down sixty meters this side of the main telemetry mast." Gorman swiveled the imager's trakball control. Still no sign of life below. "Immediate dust-off on my 'clear,' then find a soft cloud and stay on station."

"Understood," said Ferro perfunctorily.

Apone was watching the chronometer built into his suit sleeve. "Ten seconds, people. Look sharp!"

As the dropship descended to within a hundred and fifty meters of the colony landing pad, its exterior lights flashed on automatically, the powerful beams penetrating a surprising distance into the gloom. The tarmac was damp and freckled with wind-blown garbage, none of which was large enough to upset Ferro's carefully timed touchdown. Hydraulic legs absorbed the shock of contact as tons of metal settled to ground. Seconds later the APC roared out of the cargo bay and away from the compact vessel. Having barely made contact with the surface of Acheron, the dropship's engines thundered, and it crawled back up into the dark sky.

Nothing materialized out of the muck to challenge or confront the personnel carrier as it rumbled up to the first of the silent colony buildings. Spray and mud flew from beneath its solid, armored wheels. It swerved sharply left so that the crew door would face the town's main entrance. Before the door was half open, Hudson had piled out and hit the ground running. His companions were right behind him. They spread out fast, to cover as much ground as possible without losing sight of one another.

Apone's attention was riveted to the screen of his visor's image intensifier as he scanned the buildings surrounding them. The scanner's internal computer magnified the available light and cleaned up the view as much as it could, resulting in a bright picture that was still luridly tinted and full of contrast. It was enough.

Colony architecture tended to the functional. Beautification of surroundings would come later, when the wind wouldn't ruin all such efforts no matter how modest. Wind whipped trash between the buildings—that detritus that was too heavy to blow away. A chunk of metal rocked on an uneven base, banging mindlessly against a nearby wall, any echo subsumed by the wind. A few neonic lights flickered unsteadily. Gorman's voice sounded crisply over everyone's suit communicator.

"First squad up, on line. Hicks, get your people in a cordon between the entrance and the APC. Watch your rear. Vasquez, take point. Let's move."

A line of troopers advanced on the main entrylock. No one expected a greeting committee to meet them, any more than they expected to cycle the lock and stroll in without difficulty, but it was still something of a shock to encounter the pair of heavy-duty tractors that were parked nose-to-nose in front of the big door, barring any entry. It implied a conscious effort on the part of those inside to keep something outside.

Vasquez reached the silent machines first and paused to peer inside the operator's cab of the nearest. The controls had been ripped out and strewn around the interior. Impassive, she squeezed between the earthmovers, her tone phlegmatic as she reported back.

"Looks like somebody took a crowbar to the instrumentation." She reached the main doorway and nodded to her right, where Drake flanked her. Apone arrived, scanned the barrier, and moved to the external door controls. His fingers tried every combination. None of the telltale lights came alive.

"Busted?" Drake inquired.

"Sealed. There's a difference. Hudson, get up here. We need a bypass."

No funny cracks now as the comtech, all business, put his gun aside and bent to examine the door panel. "Standard stuff," he said in less than a minute. Using a tool taken from his work belt, he pried away the protective weather facing and studied the wiring. "Take two puffs, Sarge." His fingers deft and deliberate in their movements, despite the wind and cold, he began patching around the ruined circuitry. Apone and the others waited and watched.

"First squad," the sergeant snapped into his suit pickup, "assemble on me at the main lock."

A sign creaked and groaned overhead where it had broken loose from its moorings. The wind howled around them, buffeting nerves more than bodies. Hudson made a connection. Two indicator lights flickered fitfully. Moaning against the dust that had accumulated in its guide rail, the big door slid back on its tracks, traveling in fits and starts, in sync with the blinking lights. Halfway open it jammed. It was more than enough.

Apone motioned Vasquez forward. The muzzle of her smartgun preceding her, she stepped inside. Her companions followed as Gorman's voice crackled in their headsets.

"Second team, move up. Flanking positions, close quarters. How's it look, Sergeant?"

Apone's eyes scanned the interior of the silent structure. "Clean so far, sir. Nobody home yet."

"Right. Second team, keep watching behind you as you advance." The lieutenant spared a moment to glance up and behind him. "You okay, Ripley?"

She was abruptly aware that she was breathing too fast, as though she'd just finished running a marathon instead of having been standing in one place. She nodded curtly, angry at herself, angry at Gorman for his concern. He returned his attention to the console.

Vasquez and Apone strode down the wide, deserted corridor. A few lights burned blue overhead. Emergency illumination, already beginning to weaken. No telling how long the batteries had been burning. The wind accompanied them partway in, whistling down the metal concourse. Pools of water stained the floor. Farther along, rain dripped through blast holes in the ceiling. Apone tilted his head back so that his helmet camera would simultaneously record the evidence of the firefight and transmit it back to the APC.

"Pulse-rifles," he murmured, explaining the cause of the ragged holes. "Somebody's a wild shot."

In the operations bay, Ripley glanced sharply at Burke. "People confined to bed don't run around firing pulse-rifles inside their habitat. People with inoperative communications equipment don't go around firing off pulse-rifles. Something else makes them do things like that." Burke simply shrugged and turned to watch the screens.

Apone made a face at the blast holes. "Messy." It was a professional opinion, not an aesthetic one. The master sergeant couldn't abide sloppy work. Of course, these were only colonists, he reminded himself. Engineers, structural technicians, service classifications. No soldiers. Maybe one or two cops. No need for soldiers—until now. And why now? The wind taunted him. He searched the corridor ahead, seeking answers and finding only darkness.

"Move out."

Vasquez resumed her advance, more machinelike in her movements than any robot. Her smartgun cannon shifted slowly from left to right and back again, covering every inch ahead every few seconds. Her eyes were downcast, intent on the gun's tracking monitor instead of the floor underfoot. Footsteps echoed around and behind her, but ahead it was silent.

Gorman tapped a finger alongside a large red button. "Quarter and search by twos. Second team, move inside. Hicks, take the upper level. Use your motion trackers. Anybody sees *anything* moving, sing out."

Someone ventured a couple of lines a capella from Thor's storm-calling song at the end of *Das Rheingold*. It sounded like Hudson, but Ripley couldn't be sure, and no one owned up to the chorus. She tried to watch all the individual camera monitors simultaneously. Every dark corner inside the building was a gateway to Hell, every shadow a lethal threat. She had to fight to keep her breathing steady.

Hicks led his squad up a deserted stairwell to the town's second level. The corridor was a mirror image of the one directly beneath, maybe a little narrower but just as empty. It did offer one benefit: They were pretty well out of the wind.

Standing in the middle of a knot of troops, he unlimbered a small metal box with a glass face. It had delicate insides and, like most marine equipment, a heavily armored exterior. He aimed it down the hallway and adjusted the controls. A couple of LEDs lit up brightly. The gauges stayed motionless. He panned it slowly from right to left.

"Nothing," he reported. "No movement, no signs of life."

"Move out" was Gorman's disappointed response.

Hicks held the scanner out in front of him while his squad covered him, front, back, and sideways. They passed rooms and offices. Some of the doors stood ajar, others shut tight. The interiors were similar and devoid of surprises.

The farther they went, the more blatant became the evidence of struggle. Furniture was overturned and papers scattered about. Irreplaceable computer storage disks had been trampled underfoot. Personal possessions, shipped at great cost over interstellar distances, had been thrown thoughtlessly aside, smashed and broken. Priceless books of real paper floated soddenly in puddles of water that had leaked from frozen pipes and holes in the ceiling.

"Looks like my room in college." Burke was trying to be funny. He failed.

Several of the rooms Hicks's squad passed had not just

been turned upside down; they'd been burned. Black streaks
seared walls of metal and composite. In several offices the
triple-paned safety-glass windows had been blown out. Rain
and wind gusted through the gaps. Hicks stepped inside one
office to lift a half-eaten doughnut from a listing table. A
nearby coffee cup overflowed with rainwater. The dark grounds
lay scattered across the floor, floating like water mites in the
puddles.

Apone's people systematically searched the lower level,
moving in pairs that functioned as single organisms. They
went through the colonists' modest, compact living quarters
one apartment at a time. There wasn't much to see. Hudson
kept his eyes on his scanner as he prowled alongside Vasquez,
looking up only long enough to take note of a particular stain
on one wall. He didn't need sophisticated electronic analyzers
to tell him what it was: dried blood. Everyone in the APC
saw it too. No one said anything.

Hudson's tracker let out a beep, the sound explosively
loud in the empty corridor. Vasquez whirled, her gun ready.
Tracker and smartgun operator exchanged a glance. Hudson
nodded, then walked slowly toward a half-open door that was
splintered partway off its frame. Holes produced by pulse-
rifle rounds peppered the remnants of the door and the walls
framing it.

As the comtech eased out of the way, Vasquez sidled up
close to the ruined barrier and kicked it in. She came as close
as possible to firing without actually unleashing a stream of
destruction on the room's interior.

Dangling from a length of flex conduit, a junction box
swung back and forth like a pendulum, driven by the wind
that poured in through a broken window. The heavy metal
box clacked against the rails of a child's bunk bed as it swung.

Vasquez uttered a guttural sound. "Motion detectors. I
hate 'em." They both turned back to the hallway.

Ripley was watching the view provided by Hicks's monitor. Suddenly she leaned forward. "Wait! Tell him to—"

Abruptly aware that only Burke and Gorman could hear her, she hurried to plug in her headset jack, patching herself into the intersuit communications net. "Hicks, this is Ripley. I saw something on your screen. Back up." He complied, and the picture on his monitor retreated. "That's it. Now swing left. There!"

The two men who shared the operations bay with her watched as the image provided by the corporal's camera panned until it stabilized on a section of wall full of holes and oddly shaped gouges and depressions. Ripley went cold. She knew what had caused the irregular pattern of destruction.

Hicks ran a glove over the battered metal. "You seeing this okay? Looks melted."

"Not melted," Ripley corrected him. "Corroded."

Burke looked over at her, raised an eyebrow. "Hmm. Acid for blood."

"Looks like somebody bagged them one of Ripley's bad guys here." Hicks sounded less impressed than the Company rep.

Hudson had been making his own inspection of a room on the lower level. Now he beckoned to his companions to join him. "Hey, if you like that, you're gonna love this." Ripley and her companions shifted their attention to the view being relayed back to the APC by the voluble private's camera.

He was looking down. His feet framed a gaping hole. As he leaned forward over the edge they could see another hole directly below the first and beyond, dimly illuminated by his helmet light, a section of the maintenance level. Pipes, conduits, wiring—all had been eaten away by the action of some ferocious liquid.

Apone examined the view, turned away. "Second squad, talk to me. What's your status?"

Hicks's voice replied. "Just finished our sweep. There's nobody home."

The master sergeant nodded to himself, spoke to the

occupants of the distant APC. "The place is dead, sir. Dead and deserted. All's quiet on the Hadley front. Whatever happened here, we missed it."

"Late for the party again." Drake kicked a lump of corroded metal aside.

Gorman leaned back and looked thoughtful. "All right. The area's secured. Let's go in and see what their computer can tell us. First team, head for Operations. You know where that is, Sergeant?"

Apone nudged a sleeve switch. A small map of the Hadley colony appeared on the inside of his helmet visor. "That tall structure we saw coming in. It's not far, sir. We're on our way."

"Good. Hudson, when you get there, see if you can bring their CPU on-line. Nothing fancy. We don't want to use it; we just want to talk to it. Hicks, we're coming in. Meet me at the south lock by the uplink tower. Gorman out."

"Out is right." Hudson would have spat save for the fact that no suitable target presented itself. "He's coming in. I feel safer already."

Vasquez made sure her suit mike was off before agreeing.

The powerful arc lights mounted on the front of the APC illuminated the stained, wind-scoured walls of the colony buildings as the armored vehicle trundled down the main service street. They passed a couple of smaller vehicles parked in a shielded area. The APC's gleaming metal wheels threw up sheets of dirty water as it rumbled through oversize potholes. Internal shocks absorbed the impact. Wind-blown rain lashed the headlights.

In the driver's compartment, Bishop and Wierzbowski worked smoothly side by side, man and synthetic functioning in perfect harmony. Each respected the other's abilities. Both knew, for example, that Wierzbowski could ignore any advice Bishop gave. Both also knew that the human would probably take it. Wierzbowski squinted through the narrow driver's port and pointed.

"Over there, I think."

Bishop checked the flashing, brightly colored map on the screen between them. "That has to be it. There's no other lock in this area." He leaned on the wheel, and the heavy machine swung toward a cavernous opening in the wall nearby.

"Yeah, there's Hicks."

Apone's second in command emerged from the open lock as the armored personnel carrier ground to a halt. He watched while the crew door cycled and slid aside. A suited Gorman was first down the ramp, followed closely by Burke, Bishop, and Wierzbowski. Burke looked back, searching for the tank's remaining occupant, only to see her hesitate in the portal. She wasn't looking at him. Her attention was focused on the dark entrance leading deep into the colony.

"Ripley?"

Her eyes lowered to meet his. By way of reply, she shook her head sharply from side to side.

"The area's secured." Burke tried to sound understanding. "You heard Apone."

Another negative gesture. Hudson's voice sounded in their headsets.

"Sir, the colony CPU is on-line."

"Good work, Hudson," said the lieutenant. "Those of you in Operations, stand by. We'll be there soon." He nodded to his companions. "Let's go."

VI

In person the devastation looked much worse than it had on the APC's monitors.

"Looks like your company can write off its share of *this* colony," he murmured to Burke.

"The buildings are mostly intact." The company rep didn't sound concerned. "The rest's insured."

"Yeah? What about the colonists?" Ripley asked him.

"We don't know what's happened to them yet." He sounded slightly irritated by the question.

It was chilly inside the complex. Internal control had failed along with the power, and in any case, the blown-out windows and gaping holes in the walls would have overloaded the equipment quickly, anyway. Ripley found that she was sweating despite her environment suit's best efforts to keep her comfortable. Her eyes were as active as any trooper's as she checked out every hole in the walls and floor, every shadowed corner.

This was where it had all begun. This was the place where *it* had come from. The alien. There was no doubt in her mind what had happened here. An alien like the one that had caused the destruction of the *Nostromo* and the deaths of all her shipmates had gotten loose in Hadley Colony.

Hicks noticed her nervousness as she scanned the ravaged hallway and the fire-gutted offices and storage rooms. Wordlessly he motioned to Wierzbowski. The trooper nodded imperceptibly, adjusted his stride so that he fell into position on Ripley's right. Hicks slowed down until he was flanking her on the left. Together they formed a protective cordon around her. She noticed the shift and glanced at the corporal. He winked, or at least she thought he might have. It was too fast for her to be certain. Might just have been blinking at something in his eye. Even in the corridor there was enough of a breeze to blow sand and soot around.

Frost emerged from the side corridor just ahead. He beckoned to the new arrivals, speaking to Gorman but looking at Hicks.

"Sir, you should check this out."

"What is it, Frost?" Gorman was in a hurry to rendezvous with Apone. But the soldier was insistent.

"Easier to show you, sir."

"Right. It's up this way?" The lieutenant gestured down the corridor. Frost nodded and turned up into darkness, the others following.

He led them into a wing that was completely without power. Their suit lights revealed scenes of destruction worse than anything yet encountered. Ripley found that she was trembling. The APC, safe, solid, heavily armed, and not far off, loomed large in her thoughts. If she ran hard, she'd be back there in a few minutes. And alone once again. No matter how secure the personnel carrier was, she knew she was safer here, surrounded by the soldiers. She kept telling herself that as they advanced.

Frost was gesturing. "Right ahead here, sir."

The corridor was blocked. Someone had erected a make-shift barricade of welded pipes and steel plate, extra door panels, ceiling sheathing, and composite flooring. Acid holes and gashes scarred the hastily raised barrier. The metal had been torn and twisted by hideously powerful forces. Just to the right of where Frost was standing the barricade had been ripped open like an old soup can. They squeezed through the narrow opening one at a time.

Lights played over the devastation beyond. "Anybody know where we are?" Gorman asked.

Burke studied an illuminated company map. "Medical wing. We're in the right section, and it has the right look."

They fanned out, the lights from their suits illuminating overturned tables and cabinets, broken chairs and expensive surgical equipment. Smaller medical instruments littered the floor like steel confetti. Additional tables and furniture had been piled, bolted, and welded to the inside of the barricade that once had sealed the wing off from the rest of the complex. Black streaks showed where untended fire had flamed, and the walls were pockmarked with holes from pulse-rifle fire and acid.

Despite the absence of lights, the wing wasn't completely energy-dead. A few isolated instruments and control boards glowed softly with emergency power. Wierzbowski ran a gloved hand over a hole in the wall the size of a basketball.

"Last stand. They threw up that barricade and holed up in here."

"Makes sense." Gorman kicked an empty plastic bottle aside. It went clattering across the floor. "Medical would have the longest-lasting emergency power supply plus its own stock of supplies. This is where I'd come also. No bodies?"

Frost was sweeping the far end of the wing with his light. "I didn't see any when I came in here, sir, and I don't see any now. Looks like it was a fight."

"Don't see any of your bad guys, either, Ripley." Wierzbowski looked up and around. "Hey, Ripley?" His finger tensed on the pulse-rifle's trigger. "Where's Ripley?"

"Over here."

The sound of her voice led them into a second room. Burke examined their new surroundings briefly before pronouncing identification. "Medical lab. Looks pretty clean. I don't think the fight got this far. I think they lost it in the outer room."

Wierzbowski's eyes roved the emergency-lit chamber until they found what had attracted Ripley's attention. He muttered something under his breath and walked toward her. So did the others.

At the far side of the lab seven transparent cylinders glowed with violet light. Combined with the fluid, they contained the light served to preserve the organic material within. All seven cylinders were in use.

"It's a still. Somebody makes booze here," Gorman said. Nobody laughed.

"Stasis tubes. Standard equipment for a colony med lab this size." Burke approached the glass cylinders.

Seven tubes for seven specimens. Each cylinder held something that looked like a severed hand equipped with too many fingers. The bodies to which the long fingers were attached were flattened and encased in a material like beige leather, thin and translucent. Pseudo-gills drifted lazily in the stasis suspension fluid. There were no visible organs of sight or hearing. A long tail hung from the back of each abomination, trailing freely in the liquid. A couple of the creatures held their tails coiled tightly against their undersides.

Burke spoke to Ripley without taking his eyes off the specimens. "Are these the same as the one you described in your report?" She nodded without speaking.

Fascinated, the Company rep moved toward one cylinder, leaning forward until his face was almost touching the special glass.

"Watch it, Burke," Ripley warned him.

As she concluded the warning the creature imprisoned in the tube lunged sharply, slamming against the inner lining of the cylinder. Burke jumped back, startled. From the ventral portion of the flattened handlike body a thin, fleshy projection had emerged. It looked like a tapered section of intestine as it slithered tonguelike over the tube's interior. Eventually it retracted, curling up inside a protective sheath between the gill-like structures. Legs and tail contracted into a resting position.

Hicks glanced emotionlessly at Burke. "It likes you."

The Company rep didn't reply as he moved down the line, inspecting each of the cylinders in turn. As he passed a tube he would press his hand against the smooth exterior. Only one of the remaining six specimens reacted to his presence. The others drifted aimlessly in the suspension fluid, their fingers and tails floating freely.

"These are dead," he said when he'd finished with the last tube. "There's just two alive. Unless there's a different state they go into, but I doubt it. See, the dead ones have a completely different color. Faded, like."

A file folder rested atop each cylinder. By exerting every ounce of self-control she possessed, Ripley was able to remove the file from the top of a tube containing a live facehugger. Retreating quickly, she opened the folder and began reading with the aid of her suit light. In addition to the printed material the file was overflowing with charts and sonographs. There were a couple of nuclear magnetic resonance image plates, which attempted to show something of the creatures' internal structure. They were badly blurred. All of the lengthy computer printouts had copious notes scribbled freehand in the margins. A physician's handwriting, she decided. They were mostly illegible.

"Anything interesting?" Burke was leaning around the stasis cylinder whose file she was perusing, studying the creature it contained from every possible angle.

"Probably a great deal, but most of it's too technical for me." She tapped the file. "Report of the examining physician. Doctor named Ling."

"Chester O. Ling." Burke tapped the tube with a fingernail. This time the creature inside failed to respond. "There were three doctors stationed at Hadley. Ling was a surgeon, I believe. What's he have to say about this little prize here?"

"Removed surgically before embryo implantation could be completed. Standard surgical procedures useless."

"Wonder why?" Gorman was as interested in the specimen as the rest of them but not to the point of taking his eyes off the rest of the room.

"Body fluids dissolved the instruments as they were applied. They had to use surgical lasers to both remove and cauterize the specimen. It was attached to somebody named Marachuk, John L." She glanced up at Burke, who shook his head.

"Doesn't ring a bell. Not an administrator or one of the higher-ups. Must've been a tractor driver or roustabout."

She looked back down at the report. "He died during the procedure. They killed him getting it off."

Hicks walked over to have a look at the report, peering over Ripley's shoulder. He didn't have the chance to read it. His motion tracker emitted an unexpected and startlingly loud beep.

The four soldiers spun, checking first the entrance to the lab, moving on to squint at dark corners. Hicks aimed the tracker back toward the barricade.

"Behind us." He gestured toward the corridor they'd just left.

"One of us?" Without thinking, Ripley moved closer to the corporal.

"No way of telling. This baby isn't a precision instrument. She's made to take a lot of abuse from dumb grunts like me and still keep on working, but she doesn't render judgments."

Gorman addressed his headset pickup. "Apone, we're up in medical and we've got something. Where are your people?" He gave his visor map a quick scan. "Anybody in D-Block?"

"Negative." All of them could hear the sergeant's filtered reply. "We're all over in Operations, as ordered. You want some company?"

"Not yet. We'll keep you posted." He nudged the aural pickup away from his mouth. "Let's go, Vasquez."

She nodded tersely and swung the smartgun into the ready position on its support arm. It locked in place with an authoritative click. She and Hicks started off in the direction of the signal source while Frost and Wierzbowski brought up the rear.

The corporal led them back out into the main corridor and turned right, into a stainless-steel labyrinth. "Getting stronger. Definitely not mechanical." He held the tracker firmly in one hand, cradled his rifle with the other. "Irregular movement. Where the heck are we, anyway?"

Burke surveyed their surroundings. "Kitchen. We'll be in among the food-processing equipment if we keep going this way."

Ripley had slowed until she fell behind Wierzbowski and Frost. Realizing suddenly that there was nothing behind her but darkness, she hurried to catch up to her companions.

Burke's appraisal was confirmed as they advanced and their lights began to bounce off the shiny surfaces of bulky machinery: freezers, cookers, defrosters, and sterilizers. Hicks ignored it all, intent on his tracker.

"It's moving again."

Vasquez's gaze was cold as she scanned her environment. Plenty of cover in here. Her fingers caressed the smartgun's controls. A long preparation table loomed in their path.

"Which way?"

Hicks hesitated briefly, then nodded toward a complicated array of machinery designed to process freeze-dried meats and vegetables. The soldiers advanced on it, their tread a deliberate, solemn march. Wierzbowski stumbled over a metal canister and angrily booted it aside, sending it clanging off into the shadows. He kept his balance and his aplomb, but Ripley half climbed the nearest wall.

The corporal's tracker was beeping steadily now, almost humming. The hum rose to a sharp whine. A pile of stockpots suddenly came crashing down off to their right, and a dim shape was faintly glimpsed moving through the shadows behind the preparation counters.

Vasquez pivoted smoothly, her finger already contracting on the trigger. At the same instant Hick's rifle slammed the heavier barrel upward. Tracer fire ripped into the ceiling, sending droplets of molten metal flying. She whirled and screamed at him.

Ignoring her, he hurried forward into her line of fire and aimed his bright-light under a row of metal cabinets. He stayed like that for what seemed a short eternity before beckoning for Ripley to join him. Her legs wouldn't work, and her feet seemed frozen to the floor. Hicks gestured again, more urgently this time, and she found herself moving forward in a daze.

He was bending over, trying to work his light beneath a high storage locker. She crouched down next to him.

Pinned against the wall by his light like a butterfly on a mounting pin was a tiny, terrified figure. Filthy and staring, the little girl cowered away from the intruders. In one hand she held a plastic food packet that had been half gnawed. The other clutched tight the head of a large doll, holding it by its hair. Of the remainder of the plastic body there was no sign. The child was as emaciated as she was dirty, the skin taut around her small face. She looked far more fragile than the doll's head she carried. Her blond hair was tangled and matted, a garland of steel wool framing her face.

Ripley tried but couldn't hear her breathing.

The girl blinked against the light, the brief gesture sufficient to jump-start Ripley's mind. She extended a hand toward the waif slowly, fingers closed, and smiled at her.

"Come on out," she said soothingly. "It's all right. There's nothing to be afraid of here." She tried to reach farther behind the cabinet.

The girl retreated from the extending fingers, backing away and trembling visibly. She had the look of a rabbit paralyzed by oncoming headlights. Ripley's fingers almost reached her. She opened her hand, intending to gently caress the torn blouse.

Like a shot, the girl bolted to her right, scuttling along beneath the cabinetry with incredible agility. Ripley dove forward, scrambling on elbows and knees as she fought to keep the child in view. Outside the cabinets Hicks crabbed frantically sideways until a small gap appeared between two storage lockers. He snapped out a hand, and his fingers locked around a tiny ankle. An instant later he drew it back.

"Ow! Watch it, she bites."

Ripley reached for the other retreating foot and missed. A second later the girl reached a ventilation duct whose grille had been kicked out. Before Hicks or anyone else could make another grab for her, she'd scrambled inside, wriggling like a fish. Hicks didn't even try to follow. He wouldn't have fit through the narrow opening stark naked, much less clad in his bulky armor.

Ripley dove without thinking, squirming into the duct with her arms held out in front of her, moving with thighs and arms. Her hips barely cleared the opening. The girl was just ahead of her, still moving. As Ripley followed, her breathing loud in the confined tunnel, the child slammed a metal hatch in place ahead of her. With a lunge Ripley reached the barrier and shoved it open before it could be latched from the other side. She cursed as she banged her forehead against the metal overhead.

Shining her light ahead, she forgot the pain. The girl was backed against the far end of a small spherical chamber, one of the colony's ventilation system's pressure-relief bubbles. She was not alone.

Surrounding her were wadded-up blankets and pillows mixed with a haphazard collection of toys, stuffed animals, dolls, cheap jewelry, illustrated books, and empty food packets. There was even a battery-operated disk player muffled by cut-up pillows. The entire array was the result of the girl's foraging through the complex. She'd hauled it back to this place by herself, furnishing her private hideaway according to her own childish plan.

It was more like a nest than a room, Ripley decided.

Somehow this child had survived. Somehow she had coped with and adapted to her devastated environment when all the adults had succumbed. As Ripley struggled with the import of what she was seeing, the girl continued to edge around the back wall. She was heading for another hatch. If the conduit it barred was no bigger in diameter than the cover protecting it, the girl would be out of their grasp. Ripley saw that she could never enter it.

The child turned and dove, and Ripley timed her own lunge to coincide. She managed to get both arms around the girl, locking her in a bear hug. Finding herself trapped, the girl went into a frenzy, kicking and hitting and trying to use her teeth. It was not only frightening, it was horrifying: because, as she fought, the child stayed dead silent. The only noise in the confined space as she struggled in Ripley's grasp was her frantic breathing, and even that was eerily subdued. Only once in her life had Ripley had to try to control someone small who'd fought with similar ferocity, and that was Jones, when she'd had to take him to the vet.

She talked to the child as she kept clear of slashing feet and elbows and small sharp teeth. "It's okay, it's okay. It's over, you're going to be all right now. It's okay, you're safe."

Finally the girl ran out of strength, slowing down like a failing motor. She went completely limp in Ripley's arms, almost catatonic, and allowed herself to be rocked back and forth. It was hard to look at the child's face, to meet her traumatized, vacant stare. Lips white and trembling, eyes darting wildly and seeing nothing, she tried to bury herself in the adult's chest, shrinking back from a dark nightmare world only she could see.

Ripley kept rocking the girl back and forth, back and forth, cooing to her in a steady, reassuring voice. As she whispered, she let her gaze roam the chamber until it fell on something lying on the top of the pile of scavenged goods. It was a framed solido of the girl, unmistakable and yet so different. The child in the picture was dressed up and smiling, her hair neat and recently shampooed, a bright ribbon shining in the blond tresses. Her clothing was immaculate and her skin scrubbed pink. The words beneath the picture were embossed in gold:

FIRST-GRADE CITIZENSHIP AWARD
REBECCA JORDEN

"Ripley. Ripley?" Hicks voice, echoing down the air shaft. "You okay in there?"

"Yes." Aware they might not have heard her, she raised her voice. "I'm okay. We're both okay. We're coming out now."

The girl did not resist as Ripley retraced her crawl feet first, dragging the child by the ankles.

VII

The girl sat huddled against the back of the chair, hugging her knees to her chest. She looked neither right nor left, nor at any of the adults regarding her curiously. Her attention was focused on a distant point in space. A biomonitor cuff had been strapped to her left arm. Dietrich had been forced to modify it so that it would fit properly around the child's shrunken arm.

Gorman sat nearby while the medtech studied the information the cuff was providing. "What's her name again?"

Dietrich made a notation on an electronic caduceus pad. "What?"

"Her name. We got a name, didn't we?"

The medtech nodded absently, absorbed by the readouts. "Rebecca, I think."

"Right." The lieutenant put on his best smile and leaned forward, resting his hands on his knees. "Now think, Rebecca. Concentrate. You have to try to help us so that we can help you. That's what we're here for, to help you. I want you to take your time and tell us what you remember. Anything at all. Try to start from the beginning."

The girl didn't move, nor did her expression change. She was unresponsive but not comatose, silent but not mute. A disappointed Gorman sat back and glanced briefly to his left as Ripley entered carrying a steaming coffee mug.

"Where are your parents? You have to try to—"

"Gorman! Give it a rest, would you?"

The lieutenant started to respond sharply. His reply faded to a resigned nod. He rose, shaking his head. "Total brainlock. Tried everything I could think of except yelling at her, and I'm not about to do that. It could send her over the edge. If she isn't already."

"She isn't." Dietrich turned off her portable diagnostic equipment and gently removed the sensor cuff from the girl's unresisting arm. "Physically she's okay. Borderline malnutrition, but I don't think there's any permanent damage. The wonder of it is that she's alive at all, scrounging unprocessed food packets and freeze-dried powder." She looked at Ripley. "You see any vitamin packs in there?"

"I didn't have time for sight-seeing, and she didn't offer to show me around." She nodded toward the girl.

"Right. Well, she must know about supplements because

she's not showing any signs of critical deficiencies. Smart little thing."

"How is she mentally?" Ripley sipped at her coffee, staring at the waif in the chair. The child's skin was like parchment over the backs of her hands.

"I can't tell for sure, but her motor responses are good. I think it's too early to call it brainlock. I'd say she's on hold."

"Call it anything you want." Gorman rose and headed for the exit. "Whatever it is, we're wasting our time trying to talk to her." He strode out of the side room and back into Operations to join Burke and Bishop in staring at the colony's central computer terminal. Dietrich headed off in another direction.

For a while Ripley watched the three men, who were intent on the terminals Hudson had resurrected, then knelt alongside the girl. Gently she brushed the child's unkempt hair back out of her eyes. She might have been combing a statue for all the response she elicited. Still smiling, she proffered the steaming cup she was holding.

"Here, try this. If you're not hungry, you must be thirsty. I'll bet it gets cold in that vent bubble, what with the heat off and everything." She moved the cup around, letting the air carry the warm, aromatic smell of the contents to the girl's nostrils. "It's just a little instant hot chocolate. Don't you like chocolate?" When the girl didn't react, Ripley wrapped the small hands around the cup, bending the fingers toward each other. Then she tilted hands and cup upward.

Dietrich was correct about the child's motor responses. She drank mechanically and without watching what she was doing. Cocoa spilled down her chin, but most of it went down the small throat and stayed down. Ripley felt vindicated.

Not wanting to overwhelm an obviously shrunken stomach, she pulled the cup away when it was still half full. "There, wasn't that nice? You can have some more in a minute. I don't know what you've been eating and drinking, and we don't want to make you sick by giving you too much rich stuff too quickly." She pushed at the blond tresses again.

"Poor thing. You don't talk much, do you? That's okay by me. You feel like keeping quiet, you keep quiet. I'm kind of the same way. I've found that most people do a lot of talking and they wind up not saying very much. Especially adults when they're talking to children. It's kind of like they enjoy talking at you but not to you. They want you to listen to them all the time, but they don't want to listen to you. I think that's pretty stupid. Just because you're small doesn't mean you don't have some important things to say." She set the cup aside and dabbed at the brown-stained chin with a cloth. It was easy to feel the ridge of unfinished bone beneath the tightly drawn skin.

"Uh-oh." She grinned broadly. "I made a clean spot here. Now I've gone and done it. Guess I'll just have to do the whole thing. Otherwise nothing will match."

From an open supply packet she withdrew a squeeze bottle full of sterilized water and used it to soak the cloth she was holding. Then she applied the makeshift scrubber firmly to the girl's face, wiping away dirt and accumulated grime in addition to the remaining cocoa spots. Throughout the operation the child sat quietly. But the bright blue eyes shifted and seemed to focus on Ripley for the first time.

She felt a surge of excitement and fought to suppress it. "Hard to believe there's a little girl under all this." She made a show of examining the cloth's surface. "Enough dirt there to file a mining claim on." Bending over, she stared appraisingly at the newly revealed face. "Definitely a little girl. And a pretty one, at that."

She looked away just long enough to assure herself that no one from Operations was about to barge in. Any interruption at this critical moment might undo everything that she'd worked so hard to accomplish with the aid of a little hot chocolate and clean water.

No need to worry. Everyone in Operations was still clustered around the main terminal. Hudson was seated at the console fingering controls while the others looked on.

A three-dimensional abstract of the colony drifted across the main screen, lazy geometric outlines tumbling from left to right, then bottom to top, as Hudson manipulated the program. The comtech was neither playing nor showing off; he was hunting something. No rude comments spilled from his lips now, no casual profanity filled the air. It was work time. If he cursed at all, it was to himself. The computer knew all the answers. Finding the right questions was an agonizingly slow process.

Burke had been inspecting other equipment. Now he shifted his position for a better view as he whispered to Gorman.

"What's he scanning for?"

"PDTs. Personal data transmitters. Every colonist has one surgically implanted as soon as they arrive."

"I know what a PDT is," Burke replied mildly. "The Company manufactures them. I just don't see any point in running a PDT scan. Surely if there was anyone else left alive in the complex, we'd have found them by now. Or they'd have found us."

"Not necessarily." Gorman's reply was polite without being deferential. Technically Burke was along on the expedition as an observer for the Company, to look after its financial interests. His employer was paying for this little holiday excursion in tandem with the colonial administration, but what authority he had was largely unwritten. He could give advice but not orders. This was a military expedition, and Gorman was in charge. On paper Burke was his equal. The reality was very different.

"Someone could be alive but unable to move. Injured, or maybe trapped inside a damaged building. Sure the scan's a long shot, but procedure demands it. We have to run the check." He turned to the comtech. "Everything functioning properly, Hudson?"

"If there's anyone alive within a couple of kilometers of base central, we'll read it out here." He tapped the screen. "So far I've got zip except for the kid."

Wierzbowski offered a comment from the far side of the room. "Don't PDTs keep broadcasting if the owner dies?"

"Not these new ones." Dietrich was sorting through her instruments. "They're partly powered by the body's own electrical field. If the owner fades out, so does the signal. A stiff's electrical capacitance is nil. That's the only drawback to using the body as a battery."

"No kidding?" Hudson spared the comely medtech a glance. "How can you tell if somebody's AC or DC?"

"No problem in your case, Hudson." She snapped her medical satchel shut. "Clear case of insufficient current."

It was easier to find another clean cloth than to try to scrub out the first one. Ripley was working on the girl's small hands now, excavating dirt from between the fingers and beneath the nails. Pink skin emerged from behind a mask of dark grime. As she cleaned, she kept up a steady stream of reassuring chatter.

"I don't know how you managed to stay alive with everybody else gone away, but you're one brave kid, Rebecca."

A sound new to Ripley's ears, barely audible. "N-newt."

Ripley tensed and looked away so her excitement wouldn't show. She kept moving the washcloth as she leaned closer. "I'm sorry, kid, I didn't hear you. Sometimes my hearing's not so good. What did you say?"

"Newt. My n-name's Newt. That's what everybody calls me. Nobody calls me Rebecca except my brother."

Ripley was finishing off the second hand. If she didn't respond, the girl might lapse back into silence. At the same time she had to be careful not to say anything that might upset her. Keep it casual and don't ask any questions.

"Well, Newt it is, then. My name's Ripley—and people call me Ripley. You can call me anything you like, though." When no reply was forthcoming from the girl, Ripley lifted the small hand she'd just finished cleaning and gave it a formal shake.

"Pleased to meet you, Newt." She pointed at the disembodied doll head that the girl still clutched fiercely in one hand. "And who is that? Does she have a name? I bet she does. Every doll has a name. When I was your age, I had lots of dolls, and every one of them had a name. Otherwise, how can you tell them apart?"

Newt glanced down at the plastic sphere with its vacant, glassy eyes. "Casey. She's my only friend."

"What about me?"

The girl looked at her so sharply that Ripley was taken aback. The assurance in Newt's eyes bespoke a hardness that was anything but childish. Her tone was flat, neutral.

"I don't want you for a friend."

Ripley tried to conceal her surprise. "Why not?"

"Because you'll be gone soon, like the others. Like everybody." She gazed down at the doll head. "Casey's okay. She'll stay with me. But you'll go away. You'll be dead and you'll leave me alone."

There was no anger in that childish declamation, no sense of accusation or betrayal. It was delivered coolly and with complete assurance, as though the event had already occurred. It was not a prediction, but rather a statement of fact soon to take place. It chilled Ripley's blood and frightened her more than anything that had happened since the dropship had departed the safety of the orbiting *Sulaco*.

"Oh, Newt. Your mom and dad went away like that, didn't they? You just don't want to talk about it." The girl nodded, eyes downcast, staring at her knees. Her fingers were white around the doll head. "They'd be here if they could, honey," Ripley told her solemnly. "I know they would."

"They're dead. That's why they can't come see me any-

more. They're dead like everybody else." This delivered with
a cold certainty that was terrifying to see in so small a child.

"Maybe not. How can you be sure?"

Newt raised her eyes and stared straight at Ripley. Small
children do not look adults in the eye like that, but Newt was
a child in stature only. "I'm sure. They're dead. They're dead,
and soon you'll be dead, and then Casey and I'll be alone
again."

Ripley didn't look away and she didn't smile. She knew
this girl could see straight through anything remotely phony.
"Newt. Look at me, Newt. I'm not going away. I'm not going
to leave you and I'm *not* going to be dead. I promise. I'm
going to stay around. I'll be with you as long as you want
me to."

The girl's eyes remained downcast. Ripley could see her
struggling with herself, wanting to believe what she'd just
heard, trying to believe. After a while she looked up again.

"You promise?"

"Cross my heart." Ripley performed the childish gesture.

"And hope to die?"

Now Ripley did smile, grimly. "And hope to die."

Girl and woman regarded one another. Newt's eyes began to brim, and her lower lip to tremble. Slowly the tension
fled from her small body, and the indifferent mask she'd
pulled across her face was replaced by something much more
natural: the look of a frightened child. She threw both arms
around Ripley's neck and began to sob. Ripley could feel the
tears streaming down the newly washed cheeks, soaking her
own neck. She ignored them, rocking the girl back and forth
in her arms, whispering soothing nothings to her.

She closed her own eyes against the tears and the fear
and lingering sensation of death that permeated Hadley Operations Central and hoped that the promise she'd just made
could be kept.

The breakthrough with the girl was matched by another
in Operations as Hudson let out a triumphant whoop. "Hah!

Stop your grinnin' and drop your linen! Found 'em. Give old Hudson a decent machine and he'll turn up your money, your secrets, and your long-lost cousin Jed." He rewarded the control console with an affectionate whack. "This baby's been battered, but she can still play ball."

Gorman leaned over the comtech's shoulder. "What kind of shape are they in?"

"Unknown. These colonial PDTs are long on signal and short on details. But it looks like all of them."

"Where?"

"Over at the atmosphere processing station." Hudson studied the schematic. "Sublevel C under the south part of the complex." He tapped the screen. "This charmer's a sweetheart when it comes to location."

Everyone in Operations had clustered around the comtech for a look at the monitor. Hudson froze the colony scan and enlarged one portion. In the center of the processing station's schematic a cluster of glowing blue dots pulsed like deep-sea crustaceans.

Hicks grunted as he stared at the screen. "Looks like a town meeting."

"Wonder why they all went over there?" Dietrich mused aloud. "I thought we'd decided that this was where they made their last stand?"

"Maybe they were able to make a break for it and secure themselves in a better place." Gorman turned away, brisk and professional. "Remember, the processing station still has full power. That'd be worth a lot. Let's saddle up and find out."

"Awright, let's go, girls." Apone was slipping his pack over his shoulders. Operations became a hive of activity. "They ain't payin' us by the hour." He glanced at Hudson. "How do we get over there?"

The comtech adjusted the screen, reducing the magnification. An overview of the colony appeared on the monitor. "There's one small service corridor. It's a pretty good hike, Sarge."

Apone looked to Gorman, waiting for orders. "I don't know about you, Sergeant," the lieutenant told him, "but I'm not fond of long, narrow corridors. And I'd like for everyone to be fresh when we arrive. I'd also like to have the APC's armament backing us up when we go in there."

"My thoughts exactly, sir." The sergeant looked relieved. He'd been ready to suggest and argue and was glad that neither was going to be necessary. A couple of the troops nodded and looked satisfied. Gorman might be inexperienced in the field, but at least he wasn't a fool.

Hicks yelled back toward the small ready room. "Hey, Ripley, we're going for a ride in the country. You coming?"

"We're both coming." A few looks of surprise greeted her as she led the girl out of the back room. "This is Newt. Newt, these are my friends. They're your friends too."

The girl simply nodded, unwilling to extend that privilege beyond Ripley as yet. A couple of the soldiers nodded to the child as they shouldered their equipment. Burke smiled encouragingly at her. Gorman looked surprised.

Newt looked up at her live friend, still clutching the disembodied doll head tightly in her right hand. "Where are we going?"

"To a safe place. Soon."

Newt almost smiled.

The atmosphere in the APC during the ride from colony Operations to the processing station was more subdued than it had been when they'd first roared out of the dropship. The universal devastation; the hollow, wounded buildings; and the unmistakable evidence of hard fighting had put a damper on the Marines' initial high spirits.

It was clear that the cause of the colony's interrupted communications with Earth had nothing to do with its relay satellite or base instrumentation. It had to do with Ripley's critter. The colonists had ceased communicating because something had compelled them to do so. If Ripley was to be believed, that something was still hanging around. Undoubtedly the little girl was a storehouse of information on the subject, but no one tried to press questions on her. Dietrich's orders. The child's recovery was still too fragile to jeopardize with traumatizing inquiries. So as they rode along in the APC they had to fill in the gaps in Ripley's library disks with their imaginations. Soldiers have active imaginations.

Wierzbowski drove the personnel carrier across the twilight landscape, traversing a causeway that connected the rest of the colony complex to the atmosphere-processing station a kilometer away. Wind tore at the massive vehicle but could not sway it. The APC was designed for comfortable travel in winds up to three hundred kph. A typical Acheronian gale didn't bother it. Behind it, the dropship had settled to ground at the landing field, awaiting the soldiers' return. Ahead, the conical tower of the massive processing unit glowed with a spectral light as it continued with its business of terraforming Acheron's inhospitable atmosphere.

Ripley and Newt sat side by side just aft of the driver's cab. Wierzbowski kept his attention on his driving. Within the comparative safety of the heavily armored vehicle the girl gradually grew more voluble. Though there were at least a dozen questions Ripley badly wanted to ask her, she just sat patiently and listened, letting her charge ramble on. Occasionally Newt would offer the answer to an unasked question, anyway. Like now.

"I was best at the game." She hugged the doll head and stared at the opposite wall. "I knew the whole maze."

"The 'maze'?" Ripley thought back to where they'd found her. "You mean the air-duct system?"

"Yeah, you know," she replied proudly. "And not just the air ducts. I could even get into tunnels that were full of wires and stuff. In the walls, under the floor. I could get into anywhere. I was the *ace*. I could hide better than anybody. They all said I was cheating because I was smaller than everybody else, but it wasn't 'cause I was smaller. I was just smarter, that's all. And I've got a real good memory. I could remember anyplace I'd been before."

"You're really something, ace." The girl looked pleased. Ripley's gaze shifted forward. Through the windshield the processing station loomed directly ahead.

It was an unbeautiful structure, strictly utilitarian in design. Its multitude of pipes and chambers and conduits had been scoured and pitted by decades of wind-blown rock and sand. It was as efficient as it was ugly. Working around the clock for years on end, it and its sister stations scattered around the planet would break down the components of Acheron's atmosphere, scrub them clean, add to them, and eventually produce a pleasant biosphere equipped with a balmy, homelike climate. A great deal of beauty to spring forth from so much ugliness.

The monolithic metal mass towered over the armored personnel carrier as Wierzbowski braked to a stop across from the main entryway. Led by Hicks and Apone, the waiting troopers deployed in front of the oversize door. Up close to the complex, the *thrum* of heavy machinery filled their ears, rising above the steady whistle of the wind. The well-built machinery continued to do its job even in the absence of its human masters.

Hudson was first to the entrance and ran his fingers over the door controls like a locksmith casing his next crack.

"Surprise, chiluns. Everything works." He thumbed a single button, and the heavy barrier slid aside to reveal an interior walkway. Off to the right a concrete ramp led downward.

"Which way, sir?" Apone inquired.

"Take the ramp," Gorman instructed them from inside the APC. "There'll be another at the bottom. Take it down to C-level."

"Check." The sergeant gestured at his troops. "Drake, take point. The rest of you follow by twos. Let's go."

Hudson hesitated at the control panel. "What about the door?"

"There's nobody here. Leave it open."

They started down the broad ramp into the guts of the station. Light filtered down from above, slanting through floors and catwalks fashioned of steel mesh, bending around conduits ranked side by side like organ pipes. They had their suit lights switched on, anyway. Machinery pounded steadily around them as they descended.

The multiple views provided by their suit cameras bounced and swayed as they walked, making viewing difficult for those watching the monitors inside the APC. Eventually the floor leveled out and the images steadied. Multiple lenses revealed a floor overflowing with heavy cylinders and conduits, stacks of plastic crates, and tall metal bottles.

"B-level." Gorman addressed the operations bay pickup. "They're on the next one down. Try to take it a little slower. It's hard to make anything out when you're moving fast on a downslope."

Dietrich turned to Frost. "Maybe he wants us to fly? That way the picture wouldn't bounce."

"How about if I carry you instead?" Hudson called back to her.

"How about if I throw you over the railing?" she responded. "Picture would be steady that way, too, until you hit bottom."

"Shut up back there," Apone growled as they swung around a turn in the descending rampway. Hudson and the rest obliged.

In the Operations bay Ripley peered over Gorman's right shoulder, and Burke around the other, while Newt tried to squeeze in from behind. Despite all the video wizardry the lieutenant could command, none of the individual suit cameras provided a clear picture of what the troops were seeing.

"Try the low end gain," Burke suggested.

"I did that first thing, Mr. Burke. There's an awful lot of interference down there. The deeper they go, the more junk their signals have to get through, and those suit units don't put out much power. What's an atmosphere-processing station's interior built out of, anyway?"

"Carbon-fiber composites and silica blends up top wherever possible, for strength and lightness. A lot of metallic glass in the partitions. Foundations and sublevels don't have to be so fancy. Concrete and steel floors with a lot of titanium alloy thrown in."

Gorman was unable to contain his frustration as he fiddled futilely with his instruments. "If the emergency power was out and the station shut down, I'd be getting clearer reception, but then they'd be advancing with nothing but suit lights to guide them. It's a trade-off." He shook his head as he studied the blurred images and leaned toward the pickup.

"We're not making that out too well ahead of you. What is it?"

Static garbled Hudson's voice as well as the view provided by his camera. "You tell me. I only work here."

The lieutenant looked back at Burke. "Your people build that?"

The Company rep leaned toward the row of monitors, squinting at the dim images being relayed back from the bowels of the atmosphere-processing station.

"Hell, no."

"Then you don't know what it is?"

"I've never seen anything like it in my life."

"Could the colonists have added it?"

Burke continued to stare, finally shook his head. "If they did, they improvised it. That didn't come out of any station construction manual."

Something had been added to the latticework of pipes and conduits that crisscrossed the lowest level of the processing station. There was no question that it was the result of design and purpose, not some unknown industrial accident.

Visibly damp and lustrous in spots, the peculiar material that had been used to construct the addition resembled a solidified liquid resin or glue. In places light penetrated the material to a depth of several centimeters, revealing a complex internal structure. At other locations the substance was opaque. What little color it displayed was muted: greens and grays, and here and there a touch of some darker green.

Intricate chambers ranged in size from half a meter in diameter to a dozen meters across, all interconnected by strips of fragile-looking webwork that on closer inspection turned out to be about as fragile as steel cable. Tunnels led off deeper into the maze while peculiar conical pits dead-ended in the floor. So precisely did the added material blend with the existing machinery that it was difficult to tell where human handiwork ended and something of an entirely different nature began. In places the addition almost mimicked existing station equipment, though whether it was imitation with a purpose or merely blind duplication, no one could tell.

The whole gleaming complex extended as far back into C-level as the trooper's cameras could penetrate. Although it filled every available empty space, the epoxylike incrustation did not appear to have in any way impaired the functioning of the station. It continued to rumble on, having its way with Acheron's air, unaffected by the heteromorphic chambering that filled much of its lower level.

Of them all, only Ripley had some idea of what the troopers had stumbled across, and she was momentarily too numb with horrid fascination to explain. She could only stare and remember.

Gorman happened to glance back long enough to catch the expression on her face. "What is it?"

"I don't know."

"You know something, which is more than any of the rest of us. Come on, Ripley. Give. Right now I'd pay a hundred credits for an informed guess."

"I really don't know. I think I've seen something like it

once before, but I'm not sure. It's different, somehow. More elaborate and—"

"Let me know when your brain starts working again." Disappointed, the lieutenant turned back to the mike. "Proceed with your advance, Sergeant."

The troopers resumed their march, their suit lights shining on the vitreous walls surrounding them. The deeper they went into the maze, the more it took on the appearance of having been grown or secreted rather than built. The labyrinth looked like the interior of a gigantic organ or bone. Not a human organ, not a human bone.

Whatever else its purpose, the addition served to concentrate waste heat from the processor's fusion plant. Steam from dripping water formed puddles on the floor and hissed around them. Factory respiration.

"It's opening up a little just ahead." Hicks panned his camera around. The troop was entering a large, domed chamber. The walls abruptly changed in character and appearance. It was a testimony to their training that not one of the troopers broke down on the spot.

Ripley muttered, "Oh, God." Burke mumbled a shocked curse.

Cameras and suit lights illuminated the chamber. Instead of the smooth, curving walls they'd passed earlier, these were rough and uneven. They formed a rugged bas-relief composed of detritus gathered from the town: furniture, wiring, solid- and fluid-state components, bits of broken machinery, personal effects, torn clothing, human bones and skulls, all fused together with that omnipresent, translucent, epoxylike resin.

Hudson reached out to run a gloved hand along one wall, casually caressing a cluster of human ribs. He picked at the resinous ooze, barely scratching it.

"Ever see anything like this stuff before?"

"Not me." Hicks would have spat if he'd had room. "I'm not a chemist."

Dietrich was expected to render an opinion and did so.

"Looks like some kind of secreted glue. Your bad guys spit this stuff out or what, Ripley?"

"I—I don't know how its manufactured, but I've seen it before, on a much smaller scale."

Gorman pursed his lips, analysis taking over from the initial shock. "Looks like they ripped apart the colony for building materials." He indicated the view offered by Hicks's screen. "There's a whole stack of blank storage disks imbedded there."

"And portable power cells." Burke gestured toward another of the individual monitors. "Expensive stuff. Tore it all apart."

"And the colonists," Ripley pointed out, "when they were done with them." She turned to look down at the somber-visaged little girl standing next to her.

"Newt, you'd better go sit up front. Go on." She nodded and obediently headed for the driver's cab.

The steam on C-level intensified as the troops moved still deeper into the chamber. It was accompanied by a corresponding increase in temperature.

"Hotter'n a furnace in here," Frost grumbled.

"Yeah," Hudson agreed sarcastically, "but it's a *dry* heat."

Ripley looked to her left. Burke and Gorman stayed intent on the videoscreens. To the lieutenant's left was a small monitor that showed a graphic readout of the station's ground plan.

"They're right under the primary heat exchangers."

"Yeah." A fascinated Burke was unable to take his eyes off the view being relayed by Apone's camera. "Maybe the organisms like the heat. That's why they built—"

"That's not what I mean. Gorman, if your people have to use their weapons in there, they'll rupture the cooling system."

Burke abruptly realized what Ripley was driving at. "She's right."

"So?" asked the lieutenant.

"So," she continued, "that releases the freon and/or the water that's been condensed out of the air for cooling purposes."

"Fine." He tapped the screens. "It'll cool everybody off."

"It'll do more than cool them off."

"For instance?"

"Fusion containment shuts down."

"So? *So?*" Why didn't she get to the point? Didn't the woman realize that he was trying to direct a search-and-clear expedition here?

"We're talking thermonuclear explosion."

That made Gorman sit back and think. He weighed his options. His decision was made easier by the fact that he didn't have any. "Apone, collect rifle magazines from everybody. We can't have any firing in there."

Apone wasn't the only one who overheard the order. The troopers eyed one another with a combination of disbelief and dismay.

"Is he crazy?" Wierzbowski clutched his rifle protectively to his ribs, as if daring Gorman to come down and disarm it personally.

Hudson all but growled. "What're we supposed to use, man? Harsh language?" He spoke into his headset. "Hey, Lieutenant, you want maybe we should try judo? What if they ain't got any arms?"

"They've got arms," Ripley assured him tightly.

"You're not going in naked, Hudson," Gorman told him. "You've got other weapons you can use."

"Maybe that wouldn't be such a bad idea," Dietrich muttered.

"What, using alternates?" Wierzbowski muttered.

"No. Hudson going in naked. No living thing could stand the shock."

"Screw you, Dietrich," the comtech shot back.

"Not a chance." With a sigh the medtech yanked the fully charged magazine from her rifle.

"Flame units only." Gorman's tone was no-nonsense. "I want all rifles slung."

"You heard the lieutenant." Apone began circulating among them, collecting magazines. "Pull 'em out."

One by one the rifles were rendered harmless. Vasquez turned over the power packs for her smartgun with great reluctance. Three of the troopers carried portable incinerator units in addition to their penetration weapons. These were unlimbered, warmed up, and checked. Unnoticed by Apone or any of her colleagues, Vasquez slipped a spare power cell from the back of her pants and slipped it into her smartgun. As soon as the sergeant's eyes and all suit cameras were off them, Drake did likewise. The two smartgun operators exchanged a grim wink.

Hicks had no one to wink at and no smartgun to jimmy with. What he did have was a cylindrical sheath attached to the inner lining of his battle harness. Unzipping his torso armor, he opened the sheath to reveal the gunmetal-gray twin barrels of an antique pump twelve-gauge shotgun with a sawed-off butt stock. As Hudson looked on with professional interest the corporal resealed his armor, clicked back the stock of the well-maintained relic, and chambered a round.

"Where'd you get that, Hicks? When I saw that bulge, I thought you were smuggling liquor, except that'd be out of character for you. Steal it from a museum?"

"Been in my family for a long time. Cute, isn't it?"

"Some family. Can it do anything?"

Hicks showed him a single shell. "Not your standard military-issue high-velocity armor-piercing round, but you don't want it going off in your face, either." He kept his voice down. "I always keep this handy. For close encounters. I don't think it'll penetrate anything far enough to set off any mushrooms."

"Yeah, real cute." Hudson favored the sawed-off with a last admiring look. "You're a traditionalist, Hicks."

The corporal smiled thinly. "It's my tender nature."

Apone's voice carried back to them from just ahead. "Let's move. Hicks, since you seem to like it back there, you take rear guard."

"My pleasure, Sarge." The corporal rested the old shotgun against his right shoulder, balancing it easily with one hand, his finger light on the heavy trigger. Hudson grinned appreciatively, gave Hicks the high sign, and jogged forward to take up his assigned position near the point.

The air was thick, and their lights were diffused by the roiling steam. Hudson felt as though they were advancing through a steel-and-plastic jungle.

Gorman's voice echoed in his headset. "Any movement?" The lieutenant sounded faint and far away, even though the comtech knew he was only a couple of levels above and just outside the entrance to the processing station. He kept his eyes on his tracker as he advanced.

"Hudson here, sir. Nothing so far. Zip. The only thing moving around down here is the air."

He turned a corner and glanced up from the miniature readouts. What he saw made him forget the tracker, forget his rifle, forget everything.

Another encrusted wall lay directly in front of them. It was marred by bulges and ripples and had been sculpted by some unknown, inhuman hand, a teratogenic version of Rodin's *Gates of Hell*. Here were the missing colonists, entombed alive in the same epoxylike resin that had been used to construct the latticework and tunnels, chambers and pits, and had transformed the lowest level of the processing station into something out of a xenopsychotic nightmare.

Each had been cocooned in the wall without regard for human comfort. Arms and legs had been grotesquely twisted, broken when necessary in order to make the unfortunate victim fit properly into the alien scheme and design. Heads lolled at unnatural angles. Many of the bodies had been reduced to desiccated lumps of bone from which the flesh and skin had decayed. Others had been cleaned to the naked bone. They were the fortunate ones who had been granted the gift of death. Every corpse had one thing in common, no matter where it was situated or how it had been placed in the wall: the rib cages had been bent outward, as though the sternum had exploded from behind.

The troopers moved slowly into the embryo chamber. Their expressions were grim. No one said anything. There wasn't one among them who hadn't laughed at death, but this was worse than death. This was obscene.

Dietrich approached the still-intact figure of a woman. The body was ghostly white, drained. The eyelids fluttered and opened as the woman sensed movement, a presence, something. Madness dwelt within. The figure spoke in a hollow, sepulchral voice, a whisper conjured up out of desperation. Trying to hear, Dietrich leaned closer.

"Please—kill me."

Wide-eyed, the medtech stumbled back. Within the safety of the APC Ripley could only stare helplessly, biting down hard on the knuckles of her left hand. She knew what was coming, knew what prompted the woman's ultimate request, just as she knew that neither she nor anyone else could do anything except comply. The sound of somebody retching came over the Operations bay speakers. Nobody made jokes about that, either.

The woman imprisoned in the wall began to convulse. Somewhere she summoned up the energy to scream, a steady, sawing shriek of mindless agony. Ripley took a step toward the nearest mike, wanting to warn the troopers of what was coming but unable to make her throat work.

It wasn't necessary. They'd studied the research disks she'd prepared for them.

"Flamethrower!" Apone snapped. "Move!"

Frost handed his incinerator to the sergeant, stepped

aside. As Apone took possession, the woman's chest erupted in a spray of blood. From the cavity thus formed, a small fanged skull emerged, hissing viciously.

Apone's finger jerked the trigger of the flamethrower. The two other soldiers who carried similar devices imitated his action. Heat and light filled the chamber, searing the wall and obliterating the screaming horror it contained. Cocoons and their contents melted and ran like translucent taffy. A deafening screeching echoed in their ears as they worked the fire over the entire end of the room. What wasn't carbonized by the intense heat melted. The wall puddled and ran, pooling around their boots like molten plastic. But it didn't smell like plastic. It gave off a thick, organic stench.

Everyone in the chamber was intent on the wall and the flamethrowers. No one saw a section of another wall twitch.

VIII

The alien had been lying dormant, prone in a pocket that blended in perfectly with the rest of the room. Slowly it emerged from its resting niche. Smoke from burning cocoons and other organic matter billowed roofward, reducing visibility in the chamber to near zero.

Something made Hudson glance briefly at his tracker. His pupils expanded, and he whirled to shout a warning. "Movement! I've got movement."

"Position?" inquired Apone sharply.

"Can't lock up. It's too tight in here, and there's too many other bodies."

An edge crept into the master sergeant's voice. "Don't tell me that. Talk to me, Hudson. Where is it?"

The comtech struggled to refine the tracker's information. That was the trouble with these field units: They were tough but imprecise.

"Uh, seems to be in front *and* behind."

In the Operations bay of the APC, Gorman frantically adjusted gain and sharpness controls on individual monitors. "We can't see anything back here, Apone. What's going on?"

Ripley knew what was going on. Knew what was coming. She could sense it, even if they couldn't see it, like a wave rushing a black sand beach at night. She found her voice and the mike simultaneously.

"Pull your team out, Gorman. Get them out of there *now*."

The lieutenant spared her an irritated glare. "Don't give me orders, lady. I know what I'm doing."

"Maybe, but you don't know what's being *done*."

Down on C-level the walls and ceiling of the alien chamber were coming to life. Biomechanical fingers extended talons that could tear metal. Slime-lubricated jaws began to flex, pistoning silently as their owners awoke. Uncertain movements were glimpsed dimly through smoke and steam by the nervous human intruders.

Apone found himself starting to back up. "Go to infrared. Look sharp, people!" Visors were snapped into place. On their smooth, transparent insides images began to materialize, nightmare silhouettes moving in ghostly silence through the drifting mist.

"Multiple signals," Hudson declared, "all around. Closing from all directions."

Dietrich's nerves snapped, and she whirled to retreat. As she turned, something tall and immensely powerful loomed above the smoke to wrap long arms around her. Limbs like metal bars locked across her chest and contracted. The med-tech screamed, and her finger tensed reflexively on the trigger of her flamethrower. A jet of flame engulfed Frost, turning him into a blindly stumbling bipedal torch. His shriek echoed through everyone's headset.

Apone pivoted, unable to see anything in the dense atmosphere and poor light but able to hear entirely too much. The heat from the cooling exchangers on the level above distorted the imaging ability of the troopers' infrared visors.

In the APC, Gorman could only stare as Frost's monitor went to black. At the same time his bioreadouts flattened, hills and valleys signifying life being replaced by grim, straight lines. On the remaining monitor screens, images and outlines bobbed and panned confusedly. Blasts of glowing napalm from the remaining operative flamethrowers combined to overload the light-sensing ability of suit cameras, flaring what images they did provide.

In the midst of chaos and confusion Vasquez and Drake found each other. High-tech harpy nodded knowingly to new-wave neanderthal as she slammed her sequestered magazine back in place.

"Let's rock," she said curtly.

Standing back to back, they opened up simultaneously with their smartguns, laying down two arcs of fire like welders sealing the skin of a spaceship. In the confined chamber the din from the two heavy weapons was overpowering. To the operators of the smartguns the thunder was a Bach fugue and Grimoire stanthisizer all rolled into one.

Gorman's voice echoed in their ears, barely audible over the roar of battle. "Who's firing? I ordered a hold on heavy fire!"

Vasquez reached up just long enough to rip away her headset, her eyes and attention riveted on the smartgun's targeting screen. Feet, hands, eyes, and body became exten-sions of the weapon, all dancing and spinning in unison. Thunder, lightning, smoke, and screams filled the chamber, a little slice of Armageddon on C-level. A great calmness flowed through her.

Surely Heaven couldn't be any better than this.

Ripley flinched as another scream reverberated through the Operations bay speakers. Wierzbowski's suit camera crumbled, followed by the immediate flattening of his bio-monitors. Her fingers clenched, the nails digging into the palms. She'd liked Wierzbowski.

What was she doing here, anyway? Why wasn't she back home, poor and unlicensed, but safe in her little apartment, surrounded by Jones and ordinary people and common sense? Why had she voluntarily sought the company of nightmares? Out of altruism? Because she'd suspected all along what had been responsible for the break in communications between Acheron and Earth? Or because she wanted a lousy flight certificate back?

Down in the depths of the processing station, frantic, panicky voices ran into one another on the single personal communications frequency. Headset components sorted sense from the babble. She recognized Hudson's above everyone else's. The comtech's unsophisticated pragmatism shone through the breakdown in tactics.

"Let's get out of here!"

She heard Hicks yelling at someone else. The corporal sounded more frustrated than anything else. "Not that tunnel, the other one!"

"You sure?" Crowe's picture swung crazily as he ducked something unseen, the view provided by his suit camera a wild blur full of smoke, haze, and biomechanical silhouettes. "Watch it—behind you. Move, will you!"

Gorman's hands slowed. Something besides button-pushing was required now, and Ripley could see from the ashen expression that had come over the lieutenant's face that he didn't have it.

"Get them out of there!" she screamed at him. "Do it _now_!"

"Shut up." He was gulping air like a grouper, studying his readouts. Everything was unraveling, his careful plan of advance coming apart on the remaining monitors too fast for him to think it through. Too fast. "Just shut up!"

The groan of metal being ripped apart sounded over Crowe's headset pickup as his telemetry went black. Gorman stuttered something incomprehensible, trying to keep control of himself even as he was losing control of the situation.

"Uh, Apone, I want you to lay down a suppressing fire with the incinerators and fall back by squads to the APC. Over."

The sergeant's distant reply was distorted by static, the roar of the flamethrowers, and the rapid fire stutter of the smartguns.

"Say again? All after incinerators?"

"I said . . ." Gorman repeated his instructions. It didn't matter if anyone heard them. The men and women trapped in the cocoon chamber had time only to react, not to listen.

Only Apone fiddled with his headset, trying to make sense of the garbled orders. Gorman's voice was distorted beyond recognition. The headsets were designed to operate and deliver a clear signal under any conditions, including under water, but there was something happening here that hadn't been anticipated by the communications equipment designers, something that couldn't have been foreseen by anyone because it hadn't been encountered before.

Someone screamed behind the sergeant. Forget Gorman. He switched the headset over to straight intersuit frequency. "Dietrich? Crowe? Sound off! Wierzbowski, where are you?"

Movement to his left. He whirled and came within a millimeter of blowing Hudson's head off. The comtech's eyes were wild. He was teetering on the edge of sanity and barely recognized the sergeant. No bold assertions now; all false bravado fled. He was terrified out of his skin and made no effort to conceal the fact.

"We're getting juked! We're gonna die in here!"

Apone passed him a rifle magazine. The comtech slapped it home, trying to look every which way at once. "Feel better?" Apone asked him.

"Yeah, right. Right!" Gratefully the comtech chambered a pulse-rifle round. "Forget the heat exchanger." He sensed movement, turned, and fired. The slight recoil imparted by the weapon traveled up his arm to restore a little of his lost confidence.

Off to their right, Vasquez was laying down an uninterrupted field of fire, destroying everything not human that came within a meter of her—be it dead, alive, or part of the processing plant's machinery. She looked out of control. Apone knew better. If she was out of control, they'd all be dead by now.

Hicks ran toward her. Pivoting smoothly, she let loose a long burst from the heavy weapon. The corporal ducked as the smartgun's barrel swung toward his face, stumbling clear as the nightmarish figure stalking him was catapulted backward by Vasquez's blast. Biomechanical fingers had been centimeters from his neck.

Within the APC, Apone's monitor suddenly spun crazily and went dark. Gorman stared at it, as though by doing so, he could will it back to life, along with the man it represented.

"I told them to fall back." His tone was distant, disbelieving. "They must not have heard the order."

Ripley shoved her face into his, saw the dazed, baffled expression. "They're cut off in there! *Do* something!"

He looked up at her slowly. His lips worked, but the mumble they produced was unintelligible. He was shaking his head slightly.

No help from that quarter. The lieutenant was out of it. Burke had backed up against the opposite wall, as though by putting distance between himself and the images on the remaining active monitors he could somehow remove himself from the battle that was raging in the bowels of the processing station.

There was only one thing that would do the surviving soldiers any good now, and that was some kind of immediate help. Gorman wasn't going to do anything about it, and Burke couldn't. So that left Jones's favorite human.

If the cat had been present and capable of taking action on Ripley's behalf, she knew what he would have done: turned the armored personnel carrier around and driven that sucker at top speed for the landing field. Piled into the dropship, lifted back to the *Sulaco*, slipped into hypersleep, and *gone home*. Not likely anyone in colonial administration would dispute her report this time. Not with a shell-shocked Gorman and half-comatose Burke to back her up. Not with the recordings automatically stored by the APC's computer taken directly from the soldier's suit cameras to flash in the faces of those smug, content Company representatives.

Get out, go home, get *away*, the voice inside her skull screamed at her. You've got the proof you came for. The colony's kaput, one survivor, the others dead or worse than dead. Go back to Earth and come back with an army next time, not a platoon. Atmosphere fliers for air cover. Heavy weapons. Level the place if they have to, but let 'em do it without you.

There was only one problem with that comforting line of reasoning. Leaving now would mean abandoning Vasquez and Hudson and Hicks and everyone else still alive down in C-level to the tender ministrations of the aliens. If they were lucky, they would die. If they were not, they'd end up cemented into a cocoon wall as replacement for the still-living host colonists they'd mercifully carbonized.

She couldn't do that and live with it. She'd see their faces and hear their screams every time she rested her head on a pillow. If she fled, she'd be swapping the immediate nightmare for hundreds later on. A bad trade. One more time the numbers were against her.

She was terrified of what she had to do, but the anger that had been building inside her at Gorman's ineffectiveness and at the Company for sending her out here with an inexperienced field officer and less than a dozen troops (to save money, no doubt) helped drive her past the paralyzed lieutenant toward the APC's cockpit.

The sole survivor of Hadley Colony awaited her with a solemn stare.

"Newt, get in the back and put your seat belt on."

"You're going after the others, aren't you?"

She paused as she was strapping herself into the driver's chair. "I have to. There are still people alive down there, and they need help. You understand that, don't you?"

The girl nodded. She understood completely. As Ripley clicked home the latches on the driver's harness, the girl raced back down the aisle.

The warm glow of instruments set in the hold mode greeted Ripley as she turned to the controls. Gorman and Burke might be incapable of reaction, but no such psychological restraints inhibited the APC's movements. She started slapping switches and buttons, grateful now for the time spent during the past year operating all sorts of heavy loading and transport equipment out in Portside. The oversize turbocharged engine raced reassuringly, and the personnel carrier shook, eager to move out.

The vibration from the engine was enough to shock Gorman back to the real world. He leaned back in his chair and shouted forward. "Ripley, what are you doing?"

Easy to ignore him, more important to concentrate on the controls. She slammed the massive vehicle into gear. Drive wheels spun on damp ground as the APC lurched toward the gaping entrance to the station.

Smoke was pouring out of the complex. The big armored wheels skidded slightly on the damp pavement as she wrenched the machine sideways and sent it hurtling down the wide, descending rampway. The ramp accommodated the APC with room to spare. It had been designed to admit big earthmovers and service vehicles. Colonial construction was typically overbuilt. Even so, the roadway was depressed by the weight of the APC's armor, but no cracks appeared in its wake as Ripley sent it racing downward. Her hands hammered the controls of the independently powered wheels as she took out some of her anger on the uncomplaining plastic.

Mist and haze obscured the view provided by the external monitors. She switched to automatic navigation, and the APC kept itself from crashing into the enclosing walls, ranging lasers reading the distance between wheels and obstacles twenty times a second and reporting back to the vehicle's central computer. She maintained speed, knowing that the machine wouldn't let her crash.

Gorman stopped staring at the dimly seen walls rushing by on the Operations bay screens, released his suit harness, and stumbled forward, bouncing off the walls as Ripley sent the APC careening wildly around tight corners.

"What are you doing?"

"What's it look like I'm doing?" She didn't turn to face him, absorbed in controlling the carrier.

He put a hand on her shoulder. "Turn around! That's an order!"

"You can't give me orders, Gorman. I'm a civilian, remember?"

"This is a military expedition under military control. As commanding officer, I am ordering you to turn this vehicle around!"

She gritted her teeth, attention focused on the forward viewscreens. "Go sit on a grenade, Gorman. I'm busy."

He reached down and tried to pull her out of the chair. Burke got both arms around him and pulled him off. She would have thanked the Company rep, but she didn't have the time.

They reached C-level and the big wheels screamed as she sent the APC into a mad turn, simultaneously switching off the automatic navigation system and the ranging lasers. The engine revved as they rumbled forward, tearing away pipes and conduits, equipment modules, and chunks of alien encrustation. She glanced at the control console until she located the external instrumentation she wanted: strobe beacon, siren, running lights. She wiped the entire panel with the palm of her right hand.

The exterior of the APC came alive with sodium-arc lights, infrared homing beacons, spinning locater flashers, and the piercing whine of the battle siren. The individual suit monitors were all back in the Operations bay, but she didn't need to see them, zeroing in on the flash of weapons fire just ahead. The lights and roar came from beyond a thick wall of translucent alien resin, the material eerily distributing the light from the guns throughout its substance, giving the cocoon chamber the appearance of a dome pulsing from within.

She nudged the accelerator. The APC smashed through the curving wall like an iron ingot shot from a cannon. Fragments of resin and biomechanical mortar went flying. Huge chunks were crushed beneath the armored wheels. She wrenched on the wheel, and the personnel carrier pivoted neatly. The rear of the powerful machine swung around and brought down another section of alien wall.

Hicks appeared out of the smoke. He was firing back the way he'd come, holding the big pulse-rifle in one hand while supporting a limping Hudson with the other. Adrenaline, muscle, and determination were all that kept the two men going. Ripley looked away from the windshield and back down the APC's central aisle.

"Burke, they're coming!"

A faint reply as he hollered back toward the cockpit: "I'm on my way! Hang on."

The Company rep stumbled to the crew access door, fumbled with unfamiliar controls until the armored hatch cycled wide. Following in Hicks's and Hudson's footsteps, the two smartgun operators materialized out of the dense mist. They were retreating with precision, side by side, firing and covering the retreat as they fell back on the personnel carrier.

As Ripley looked on, Drake's gun went empty. Automatically he snapped the release buckles on the smartgun harness. It sloughed away like an old skin. Before it hit the ground, he'd pulled a flamethrower from his back and had brought it into play. The hollow *whoosh* of napalm mixed with the deep-throated chatter of Vasquez's still operative smartgun.

Hicks reached the APC, put his weapon aside, and all but threw the injured Hudson through the opening. Then he tossed his pulse-rifle after the comtech and cleared the hatch in two strides. Vasquez was still firing as the corporal got both hands under her arms and heaved, pulling her in after him. At the same time she saw a dark, towering silhouette lunge toward Drake from behind, and she changed her field of fire as Hicks was dumping her onto the APC's deck.

A flash of contact lit up an inhuman, frozen grin as the smartgun shells tore apart the alien's thorax. Bright yellow body fluid sprayed in all directions. It splashed across Drake's face and chest. Smoke rose from the staggering body of the smartgun operator as the acid chewed rapidly through flesh and bone. His muscles spasmed, and his flamethrower fired as he toppled backward.

Vasquez and Hicks rolled as a gout of flame slashed through the open crew door, setting portions of the APC's flammable interior ablaze. As Drake fell, Hicks charged the hatch and started to cycle the door. Moving on hands and knees, Vasquez lunged wildly at the opening. The corporal had to leave the controls to grab her. It was a struggle to keep her from plunging outside.

"Drake!" She was screaming, not calm and controlled anymore. "He's down!"

It took all of Hicks's superior size and strength to wrench her around to face him. "He's gone! Forget it, Vasquez. He's gone."

She stared up at him, irrational, her face streaked with soot and grime. "No. No, he's not! He's . . ."

Hicks looked back at the APC's other occupants. "Get

her away from here. We've got to get this door closed."
Hudson nodded. Together he and Burke dragged the dazed
smartgun operator away from the entry hatch. The corporal
looked toward the cockpit and raised what was left of his
voice. "Let's go! We're clear back here."

"Going!" Ripley jammed on the controls and nailed the
accelerator. The armored personnel carrier roared and shuddered as she sent it racing backward up the ramp.

A storage rack broke free, burying Hudson beneath a
pile of equipment. Cursing and flailing, he threw the stuff
aside, indifferent to whether it was marked EMERGENCY RA-
TIONS or EXPLOSIVES.

Hicks turned his attention back to the door, fumbled with
the controls. It was nearly shut when two sets of long claws
suddenly appeared to slam into the metal flange like a pair
of power hammers. From her seat Newt let out a primordial
child's scream. The saber-tooth, the giant bear, the boogeyman was at the entrance to the cave, and this time she had
no place to hide.

Vasquez stumbled to her feet and joined Hicks and Burke
in leaning on the door. Despite their combined efforts, the
metal barrier was slowly being wrenched open from the outside. Locks and seals groaned in protest.

Hicks managed to find enough wind to yell at the still
numbed Gorman. "Get on the door!"

The lieutenant heard him and reacted. Reacted by backing away and shaking his head, his eyes wide. Hicks muttered
a curse and jammed his shoulder against the latching lever.
This freed one hand to pull out the sawed-off twelve-gauge
just as a nightmare alien head wedged its way through the
opening. Outer jaws parted to reveal the pistonlike inner
throat and penetrating teeth. As slime-covered fangs swung
toward him, Hicks jammed the muzzle of the shotgun between
the gaping demon jaws and pulled the trigger. The explosion
of the ancient projectile weapon echoed through the personnel
carrier as the shattered skull fell backward, fountaining acid

blood. The spray immediately began to eat into the door and deck.

Hicks and Vasquez fell aside, but some of the droplets struck Hudson on the arm. Smoke rose from skin as hissing flesh dissolved. The comtech operator let out a howl and stumbled into the empty seats.

Hicks and Burke slammed the hatch shut and locked it.

Like a runaway comet, the APC rumbled backward up the ramp and slammed into a mass of conduit. Ripley worked on the wheels, spinning the oversize metal rims and ripping free. Sparks showered over the vehicle. In the crew quarters behind her, everyone seemed to be yelling simultaneously. Extinguishers were unbolted and brought into play on the internal fire. Newt stayed out of the way, sitting silently in her seat as panicky adults ran to and fro around her. She was breathing hard but steadily, eyes alert, watching. None of what was happening was new to her. She'd been through it all before.

Something made a soft metallic thump as it landed on the roof.

Gorman had retreated into a corner to the left of the aisle. He was staring blankly at his frantic companions. Consequently he did not see the small gun hatch, against which he was leaning, begin to vibrate. But he felt it when the hatch cover was ripped from its seals. He started to turn, not nearly fast enough, and was snatched through the opening.

There was something at the tip of the alien's tail, something silver-sharp and superfast. It whipped around one leg to bury itself in the lieutenant's shoulder. He screamed. Hicks threw himself into the crew bay fire-control chair and clutched the controls, jabbing contact points and switches with his other hand as the seat motor hummed and swung him around. Brightly colored telltales came to life on the board, adding no cheer to the beleaguered APC's interior but bringing a smile to the corporal's face.

In response to his actions servomotors whirred and a

small turret came to life on the personnel carrier's roof. It spun in a half circle. The alien holding Gorman two-thirds of the way out of the vehicle turned sharply in the direction of the new sound just as twin guns fired in its direction. The heavy shells blew it right off the top of the machine, the impact knocking it clear before the acid in its body began to spill.

Burke dragged the unconscious Gorman back inside while Vasquez hunted for something to plug the opening with.

Trailing fire and smoke, the APC tore up the ramp. Ripley wrestled with the controls as the big vehicle slewed sideways, broadsiding a control room outbuilding. Office furniture and splintered sections of wall exploded in all directions, forming a wake of plastic and composite fiber behind the retreating machine.

Almost clear now, almost out. Another minute or two, and if nothing broke down, they'd be free of the station's confines. Free to...

An alien arm arced down right in front of her face to smash the shatterproof windshield. Glistening, slime-coated jaws lunged inside. Ripley threw up both arms to shield her face and leaned away. Once before, she'd been this close to perdition. In the shuttle *Narcissus*, secure in its pilot's seat, luring another alien close so that she could blow it out the airlock. But there was no airlock here, no comforting atmosphere suit enclosing her, no tricks left to pull, and no time to think of any.

She tried to crush the brakes underfoot. The big wheels locked up at high speed, screeching over the sound of the chaos outside. She felt herself being thrown forward, her head flying toward those gaping jaws. But her seat harness checked her motion and kept her in the chair.

No such restraints secured the alien. Leaning over the windshield, it was clinging awkwardly to the edge of the roof, and not even its inhuman strength could prevent it from being thrown forward. As soon as it landed on the ground she threw the personnel carrier back in gear. It didn't even bump as it trundled over the skeletal body, crushing it beneath its massive weight. Acid squirted over armored wheels, but the APC's forward movement carried it clear before more than a few inconsequential pits had been eaten in the spinning disks. Their movement was not affected.

Darkness ahead. Clean, welcoming darkness. Not a blank falling over her mind but the darkness of a dimly lit world: the surface of Acheron, framed by the walls of the station. A moment later they were through, rumbling over the connecting causeway toward the landing field.

A noise like bolts dropped in a food processor was coming from the rear of the APC. Occasionally a louder clunk could be heard. It was a sound beyond the soothing effects of lubrication, beyond repair. She fiddled with controls and tried to adjust the noise out of existence, but like her recurring nightmares, it refused early dismissal.

Hicks came forward and, gently but firmly, eased her fingers off the accelerator control. Her face was as white as her knuckles. She blinked, glanced back up at him.

"It's okay," he assured her, "we're clear. They're all behind us. I don't think fighting out in the open suits them. Ease up. We're not going much further in this hunk of junk, anyway."

The grinding noise was overpowering as they slowed. She listened intently as she brought the big vehicle to a halt.

"Don't ask me for an analysis. I'm an operator, not a mechanic."

Hicks cocked an ear in the direction of the metallic gargling. "Sounds like a blown transaxle. Maybe two. You're just grinding metal. Actually I'm surprised that the underside of this baby isn't lying back on B-level somewhere. They build these things tough."

"Not tough enough." That was Burke's voice, filtering up to them from somewhere in the passenger compartment.

"Nobody expected to have to face anything like these

creatures. Ever." Hicks leaned toward the console and rotated an exterior viewer. The APC looked terrible on the outside, a smoking, acid-scarred hulk. It was supposed to be invulnerable. Now it was scrap.

Ripley spun her seat, glanced at the empty one next to her, and then turned to stare down the aisle that led back through the personnel carrier.

"Newt. Where's Newt?"

A tug on her pants leg. Not hard, so she didn't jump. Newt was squeezed into the tiny space between the driver's seat and the APC's armored bulkhead. She was trembling and terrified but alert. No catatonia this time, no withdrawal from reality. No reason for an extreme reaction, Ripley knew. Doubtless the girl had been witness to much worse when the aliens had overwhelmed the colony.

Had she been watching the Operations bay monitors when the soldiers had initially penetrated the alien cocoon chamber? Had she seen the face of the woman who had whispered in agony to Dietrich? What if the woman had been . . . ?

But she couldn't have been. If that had been Newt's mother, the girl would be beyond catatonia by now. Gone, withdrawn, and unreachable, perhaps forever.

"You okay?" Sometimes inanities had to be asked. Besides, she wanted, needed, to hear the child respond.

Newt did so with a thumbs-up gesture, still employing selective silence as a defense mechanism. Ripley didn't push her to talk. Keeping quiet while everyone around her was being killed had kept her alive.

"I have to check on the others," she told the upturned face. "Will you be all right?"

A nod this time, accompanied by a shy little smile that made Ripley swallow hard. She tried to conceal what she was feeling inside, because this wasn't the time or place to break down. They could do that when they were safely back aboard the *Sulaco*.

"Good. I'll be right back. If you get tired of staying under there, you can come back and join the rest of us, okay?" The smile widened slightly and was followed by a more vigorous nod, but the girl stayed put. She still trusted her own instincts more than she trusted any adult. Ripley wasn't offended. She unbuckled herself and headed back down the aisle.

Hudson was standing off to one side inspecting his arm. The fact that he still had an arm showed that he'd only been lightly misted by the alien acid. He was reliving the last twenty minutes of his life, replaying every second over and over in his mind and not believing what he saw there. She could hear him muttering to himself.

"—I don't believe it. It didn't happen. It didn't happen, man."

Burke tried to have a look at the injured comtech's arm, more curious than sympathetic. Hudson jerked away from the Company rep.

"I'm all right. Leave it!"

Burke pursed his lips, wanting to see but not willing to push. "Better let somebody take a look at it. Can't tell what the side effects are. Might be toxic."

"Yeah? And if it is, I suppose you're going to check stores and break out an antidote in a couple of minutes, right? Dietrich's the medtech." He swallowed and his anger faded. "Was our medtech. Stinking bugs."

Hicks was bending over the motionless Gorman, checking for a pulse. Ripley joined him.

"Anything?" she asked tightly.

"Heartbeat's slow but steady. He's breathing the same way. It's the same with the rest of his vital signs: slowed down but regular. He's alive. If I didn't know better, I'd say he was sleeping, but it ain't sleep. I think he's paralyzed."

Vasquez pushed both of them aside and grabbed the unconscious lieutenant by his collar. She was too furious to cry. "He's dead is what he is!" She hauled the upper half of

Gorman's body upright with one hand and drew back the other in a fist, screaming in his face.

"Wake up, *pendejo*! Wake up. I'm gonna kill you, you useless waste!"

Hicks inserted his bulk between her and the frozen lieutenant. Same soft voice employed, but with a slight edge to it now. Same hard eyes staring into the smartgun operator's face.

"Hold it. Hold it. Back off—right now."

Their eyes locked. Vasquez continued to hold Gorman half off the deck. Something basic cut its way through her fury. Marine—she was a Marine, and Marines live by basics. The basics in this case were simple. Apone was gone and therefore Hicks was in charge.

"It ain't worth bruising my knuckles," she finally muttered. She released the lieutenant's collar, and his head bounced off the deck as she turned away, still cursing to herself. Ripley didn't doubt for an instant that if Hicks hadn't intervened, the smartgun operator would have beaten the unconscious Gorman to a pulp.

With Vasquez out of the way Ripley bent over the paralyzed officer and opened his tunic. The bloodless purple puncture wound that marred his shoulder had already sealed itself.

"Looks like it stung him or something. Interesting. I didn't know they could do that."

"Hey!"

The excited shout made Hicks and her turn toward the Operations bay. Hudson was in there. He'd been staring morosely at the biomonitors and videoscreens, and something had caught his eye. Now he beckoned to his remaining companions.

"Look. Crowe and Dietrich aren't dead, man." He gestured at the bio readouts, swallowed uneasily. "They must be like Gorman. Their signs are real low, but they ain't dead. . . ."

His voice trailed off, along with his initial excitement.

If they weren't dead and they were like Hudson, that meant— The comtech started to shake with a mixture of anger and sorrow. He was standing on the thin edge of hysteria. They all were. It clung to them like a psychic leech, hanging on the fringes of their sanity, threatening to invade and take over the instant anyone let down his mental guard.

Ripley knew what those soporific bioreadouts meant. She tried to explain, but she couldn't meet Hudson's eyes as she did so.

"You can't help them."

"Hey, but if they're still alive—"

"Forget it. Right now they're being cocooned, just like those others. Like the colonists you found in the wall when you went in there. You can't do a damn thing for them. Nobody can. That's the way it is. Just be glad you're here talking about them instead of down there with them. If Dietrich was here, she'd know she couldn't do anything to help you."

The comtech seemed to sag in on himself. "This ain't happening."

Ripley turned away from him. As she did so, her gaze met Vasquez's. It would have been easy for her to say "I told you so" to the smartgunner. It also would have been superfluous. That one look communicated everything the two women needed to say.

This time it was Vasquez who turned away.

IX

In the colony medical lab Bishop stood hunched over an ocular probe. Beneath the lens was a stretched slice of one of the dead facehugger parasites, extracted from the specimen in the nearest stasis cylinder. Even in death the biopsied creature looked threatening, lying on its back on the dissection table. The clutching legs looked poised to grab any face that bent too close, the powerful tail ready to propel the creature clear across the room in a single pistoning leap.

The internal structure was as fascinating as the functional exterior, and Bishop was glued to the probe's eyepiece. By combining the probe's resolving power with the versatility of his own artificial eye, he was able to see a great deal that the colonists might have missed.

One of the questions that particularly intrigued him, and which he was anxious to answer, involved the definite possibility of an alien parasite attempting to attach itself to a synthetic like himself. His insides were radically different from those of a purely biological human being. Would a parasite be able to detect the differences before it sprang? If not and it attempted to utilize a synthetic as a host, what might be the probable results of such an enforced union? Would it simply drop off and go searching for another body, or would it mindlessly insert the embryonic seed it carried into an artificial host? If so, would the embryo be able to

135

grow or would it be the more surprised of the couple as it struggled to mature within a body devoid of flesh and blood?

Could a robot be parasitized?

Something made a noise near the doorway. Bishop looked up long enough to see the dropship crew chief roll a pallet full of equipment and supplies into the lab.

"Where you want this stuff?"

"Over there." Bishop gestured. "By the end of the bench will do nicely."

Spunkmeyer began unloading the shipping pallet. "Need anything else?"

Bishop waved vaguely without taking his gaze from the probe.

"Right. I'll be back in the ship. Buzz me if you need anything."

Another wave. Spunkmeyer shrugged and turned to leave.

Bishop was a funny sort of bird, the crew chief mused as he wheeled his hand truck down the empty corridors and back out onto the landing tarmac. Funny sort of hybird, he thought, correcting himself and smiling at the pun. He whistled cheerfully as he snugged his collar higher up around his neck. The wind wasn't blowing too badly, but it was still chilly outside without a full environment suit. Concentrating on a tune also helped to keep his mind off the disaster that had befallen the expedition.

Crowe, Dietrich, old Apone—all gone. Hard to believe, as Hudson kept mumbling over and over to himself. Hard to believe and a shame. He'd known them all; they'd flown together on a number of missions. Though he couldn't say he knew any of them intimately.

He shrugged, even though there was no one around to see the gesture. Death was something they were all used to, an acquaintance each of them fully expected to encounter prior to retirement. Crowe and Dietrich had early appointments, that was all. Nothing to be done about it. But Hicks and the rest had made it out okay. They'd finish their studies and cleanup here and be out by tomorrow. That was the plan. A little more study, make a few last recordings, and get out of there. He knew he wasn't the only one looking forward to the moment when the dropship would heave mass and head back to the good ol' *Sulaco*.

His thoughts went back to Bishop again. Maybe there'd been some sort of subtle improvement in the new model synthetics, or maybe it was just Bishop himself, but he found that he rather liked the android. Everybody said that the artificial-intelligence boys had been working hard to improve personality programming for years, even adding a bit of randomness to each new model as it walked off the assembly line. Sure, that was it—Bishop was an individual. You could tell him from another synthetic just by talking to him. And it didn't hurt to have one quiet, courteous companion among all the boastful loudmouths.

As he rolled the hand truck to the top of the dropship's loading ramp, he slipped. Catching his balance, he bent to examine the damp spot. Since there was no depression in which rainwater could pool up, he thought he must have busted a container of Bishop's precious preserving fluid, but there was no tickling, lingering odor of formaldehyde. The shiny stuff clinging to the metal ramp looked more like a thick slime or gel.

He shrugged and straightened. He couldn't remember busting a bottle containing anything like that, and as long as nobody asked him about it, there was no point in worrying. No time for worrying, either. Too much to do so they could get ready to leave.

The wind beat at him. Lousy atmosphere, and yet it was a lot milder than what it had been before the atmosphere processors had started work here. "Unbreathable," the pre-sleep briefing had said. Pulling the hand truck in behind him, he hit the switch to retract the ramp and close the door.

Vasquez was pacing the length of the APC. Inactivity in what was still a combat situation was a foreign sensation to her. She wanted a gun in her hands and something to shoot at. She knew the situation called for careful analysis, and it frustrated her because she wasn't the analytical type. Her methods were direct, final, and didn't involve any talk. But she was smart enough to realize that this wasn't your standard operation anymore. Standard operating procedure had been chewed up and spit out by the enemy. Knowing this failed to calm her, however. She wanted to kill something.

Occasionally her fingers would flex as though they were still gripping the controls of her smartgun. Watching her would have made Ripley nervous if she wasn't already as tense as it was possible to be without snapping like the overwound mainspring of an ancient timepiece.

It got to the point where Vasquez knew she could say something or start tearing her hair out. "All right, we can't blow them up. We can't go down there as a squad; we can't even go back down in the APC because they'll take us apart like a can full of peas. Why not roll some canisters of CN-20 down there? Nerve gas the whole nest? We've got enough on the dropship to make the whole colony uninhabitable."

Hudson was pleading with his eyes, glancing at each of them in turn. "Look man, let's just bug out and call it even, okay?" He glanced at the woman standing next to him. "I'm with Ripley. Let 'em make the whole colony into a playpen if they want to, but we get out now and come back with a warship."

Vasquez stared at him out of slitted eyes. "Getting queasy, Hudson?"

"Queasy!" He straightened a little in reaction to the implicit challenge. "We're in over our heads here. Nobody said we'd run into anything like this. I'll be the first one to volunteer to come back, but when I do, I want the right kind of equipment to deal with the problem. This ain't like mob control, Vasquez. You try kicking some butts here and they'll eat your leg right off."

Ripley looked at the smartgun operator. "The nerve gas won't work, anyway. How do we know if it'll affect their biochemistry? Maybe they'll just snort the stuff. The way these things are built, nerve gas might just give them a pleasant high. I blew one of them out an airlock with an emergency grapple stuck in its gut, and all it did was slow it down. I had to fry it with my ship's engines." She leaned back against the wall.

"I say we take off and nuke the entire site from orbit and the whole high plateau where we originally found the ship that brought them here. It's the only way to be sure."

"Now hold on a second." Having been silent during the ongoing discussion, Burke abruptly came to life. "I'm not authorizing that kind of action. That's about as extreme as you can get."

"You don't think the situation's extreme?" growled Hudson. He toyed with the bandage on his acid-scarred arm and glared hard at the Company representative.

"Of course it's extreme."

"Then why won't you authorize the use of nukes?" Ripley pressed him. "You lose the colony and one processing station, but you've still got ninety-five percent of your terraforming capability unimpaired and operational on the rest of the planet. So why the hesitation?"

Sensing the challenge in her tone, the Company rep backpedaled flawlessly into a conciliatory mode.

"Well, I mean, I know this is an emotional moment. I'm as upset as anybody else. But that doesn't mean we have to resort to snap judgments. We have to move cautiously here. Let's think before we throw out the baby with the bathwater."

"The baby's dead, Burke, in case you haven't noticed." Ripley refused to be swayed.

"All I'm saying," he argued, "is that it's time to look at the whole situation, if you know what I mean."

She crossed her arms over her chest. "No, Burke, what do you mean?"

He thought fast. "First of all, this installation has a substantial monetary value attached to it. We're talking about an entire colony setup here. Never mind the replacement cost. The investment in transportation alone is enormous, and the process of terraforming Acheron is just starting to show some real progress. It's true that the other atmosphere-processing stations function automatically, but they still require regular maintenance and supervision. Without the means to house and service an appropriate staff locally, that would mean keeping several transports in orbit as floating hotels for the necessary personnel. That involves an ongoing cost you can't begin to imagine."

"They can bill me," she told him unsmilingly. "I got a tab running. What else?"

"For another thing, this is clearly an important species we're dealing with here. We can't just arbitrarily exterminate those who've found their way to this world. The loss to science would be incalculable. We might never encounter them again."

"Yeah, and that'd be just too bad." She uncrossed her arms. "Aren't you forgetting something, Burke? You told me that if we encountered a hostile life-form here, we'd take care of it and forget the scientific concerns. That's why I never liked dealing with administrators: you guys all have selective memories."

"It just isn't the way to handle things," he protested.

"Forget it!"

"Yeah, forget it." Vasquez echoed Ripley's sentiments as well as her words. "Watch us."

"Maybe you haven't been keeping up on current events," Hudson put in, "but we just got fragged, pal."

"Look, Burke." Clearly Ripley was not pleased. "We had an agreement. I think I've proved my case, made my point, whatever you want to call it. We came here for confirmation of my story and to find out what caused the break in communications between Acheron and Earth. You got your confirmation, the Company's got its explanation, and I've got my vindication. Now it's time to get away from here."

"I know, I know." He put an arm over her shoulders, careful not to make it look as if he were being familiar, and turned her away from the others as he lowered his voice. "But we're dealing with changing scenarios here. You have to be ready to put aside the first reaction that comes to mind, put aside your natural emotions, and know how to take advantage. We've survived here; now we've got to be ready to survive back on Earth."

"What are you getting at, Burke?"

Either he didn't notice the chill in her eyes or else he chose not to react to it. "What I'm trying to say is that this thing is *major*, Ripley. I mean, really major. We've never encountered anything like these creatures before, and we might never have the chance to do so again. Their strength and their resourcefulness is unbelievable. You don't just annihilate something like that, not with the kind of potential they imply. You back off until you learn how to handle them, sure, but you don't just blow them away."

"Wanna bet?"

"You're not thinking rationally. Now, I understand what you're going through. Don't think that I don't. But you've got to put all that aside and look at the larger picture. What's done is done. We can't help the colonists, and we can't do anything for Crowe and Apone and the others, but we can help ourselves. We can learn about these things and make use of them, turn them to our advantage, master them."

"You don't master something like these aliens. You get out of their way; and if the opportunity presents itself, you blow them to atoms. Don't talk to me about 'surviving' back on Earth."

He took a deep breath. "Come on, Ripley. These aliens are special in ways we haven't begun to understand. Uniqueness is one thing the cosmos is stingy with. They need to be studied, carefully and under the right conditions, so that we can learn from them. All that went wrong here was that the colonists started studying them without the proper equipment. They didn't know what to expect. We do."

"Do we? Look what happened to Apone and the rest."

"They didn't know what they were up against, and they went in a little overconfident. They got caught in a tight spot. That's a mistake we won't make again."

"You can bet on that."

"What happened here is tragic, sure, but it won't be repeated. When we come back, we'll be properly equipped. That acid can't eat through everything. We'll take a sample back somehow, have it analyzed in company labs. They'll develop a defense, a shield. And we'll figure out a way to immobilize the mature form so it can be manipulated and used. Sure, the aliens are strong, but they're not omnipotent. They're tough but they're not invulnerable. They can be killed by hand weapons as small as pulse-rifles and flamethrowers. That's one thing this expedition *has* proved. You proved it yourself," he added in a tone of admiration she didn't believe for an instant.

"I'm telling you, Ripley, this is an opportunity few people are given. We can't blow it on an emotional spur-of-the-moment decision. I didn't think you were the type to throw away the chance of a lifetime for something as abstract as a little revenge."

"It doesn't have anything to do with revenge," she told him evenly. "It has to do with survival. Ours."

"You're still not hearing me." He dropped his voice to a whisper. "See, since you're the representative of the company that discovered this species, your percentage of the eventual profits to be derived from the study and concomitant exploitation of them will naturally be some serious money. The fact that the Company once prosecuted you and then had the decision of the prosecuting board overturned doesn't enter into it. Everybody knows that you're the sole survivor of the crew that first encountered these creatures. The law requires that you receive an appropriate royalty. You're going to be richer than you dreamed possible, Ripley."

She stared silently at him for a long time, as though she were observing an entirely new species of alien just encountered. A particularly loathsome variety at that.

"You son of a. . . ."

He backed off, his expression hardening. The false sense of camaraderie he'd tried to promote was sloughed off like a mask. "I'm sorry you feel that way. Don't make me pull rank, Ripley."

"What rank? We've been through all this before." She nodded down the aisle. "I believe Corporal Hicks has authority here."

Burke started to laugh at her. Then he saw that she was serious. "You're kidding. What is this, a joke? *Corporal* Hicks? Since when was a corporal in charge of anything except his own boots?"

"This operation is under military jurisdiction," she reminded him quietly. "That's the way the *Sulaco*'s dispatch orders read. Maybe you didn't bother to read them. I did. That's the way Colonial Administration worded it. You and I, Burke, we're just observers. We're just along for the ride. Apone's dead and Gorman might as well be. Hicks is next in the chain of command." She peered past the stunned Company rep. "Right?"

Hicks's reply was matter-of-fact. "Looks that way."

Burke's careful corporate self-control was beginning to slip. "Look, this is a multimillion credit operation. He can't make that kind of decision. Corporals don't authorize nukes. He's just a grunt." Second thoughts and a hasty glance in the soldier's direction prompted Burke to add a polite, "No offense."

"None taken." Hicks's response was cool and correct.

He spoke to his headset pickup. "Ferro, you been copying all of this?"

"Standing by" came the dropship pilot's reply over their speakers.

"Prepare for dust-off. We're gonna need an immediate evac."

"Figured as much from what we heard over here. Tough."

"You don't know the half of it." Hicks's expression was unchanged as he regarded the tight-lipped Burke. "You're right about one thing. You can't make a decision like this on the spur of the moment."

Burke relaxed slightly. "That's more like it. So what are we going to do?"

"Think it over, like you said we should." The corporal closed his eyes for about five seconds. "Okay, I've thought it over. What I think is that we'll take off and nuke the site from orbit. It's the only way to be *sure*."

He winked. The color drained from the Company rep's face. He took an angry step in Hicks's direction before realizing that what he was thinking of doing bore no relation to reality. Instead he had to settle for expressing his outrage verbally.

"This is absurd! You seriously can't be thinking of dropping a nuclear device on the colony site."

"Just a little one," Hicks assured him calmly, "but big enough." He put his hands together, smiled and pushed them apart. "*Whoosh*."

"I'm telling you for the last time that you don't have the authority to do something like—"

His tirade was interrupted by a loud *clack*: the sound of a pulse-rifle being activated. Vasquez cradled the powerful weapon beneath her right arm. It wasn't pointed in Burke's direction, but then it wasn't exactly aimed away from him, either. Her expression was blank. He knew it wouldn't change if she decided to put a pulse-shell through his chest, either.

End of discussion. He sat down heavily in one of the empty seats that lined the wall.

"You're all crazy," he muttered. "You know that."

"Man," Vasquez told him softly, "why else would anyone join the Colonial Marines?" She glanced over at the corporal. "Tell me something, Hicks: Does that mean I can plead insanity for shooting this *mierda*? If I can, I might as well shoot that sorry excuse for a lieutenant while I'm at it. Don't want to waste a good defense."

"Nobody's shooting anybody," the corporal informed her firmly. "We're getting out of here."

Ripley met his eyes, nodded once, then turned and sat down. She put a reassuring arm around the only conscious nonparticipant in the discussion. Newt leaned against her shoulder.

"We're going home, honey," she told the girl.

Now that their course of action had been determined, Hicks took a moment to check out the interior of the APC. Between the fire damage and the holes eaten by alien acid, it was clearly a write-off.

"Let's get together what we can carry. Hudson, give me a hand with the lieutenant."

The comtech eyed the paralyzed form of his commanding officer with undisguised distaste. "How about we just sit him up in Operations and strap him to the chair? He'll feel right at home."

"No sell. He's still alive, and we've got to get him out of here."

"Yeah, I know, I know. Just don't keep reminding me."

"Ripley, you keep an eye on the child. She's sort of taken to you, anyway."

"The feeling's mutual." She clasped Newt tightly to her.

"Vasquez, can you cover us until the dropship touches down?"

She smiled at him, showing perfect teeth. "Can pigs fly?" She tapped the stock of the pulse-rifle.

The corporal turned to face the landing team's last human member. "You coming?"

"Don't be funny," Burke grumbled.

"I won't. Not here. This isn't a funny place." He switched on his headset pickup. "Bishop, you found anything out?"

The synthetic's voice filled the passenger bay. "Not much. The equipment here is colonial-style basic. I've gone about as far as I can go with the tools available."

"It doesn't matter. We're getting out. Pack it up and meet us on the tarmac. Can you make it okay? I don't want to abandon the APC until the dropship's on final approach."

"No problem. It's been quiet back here."

"Okay. Don't take anything you can't carry easily. Move it."

The dropship rose from its place on the concrete pad, fighting the wind as it lifted. Under Ferro's steady hand it hovered, pivoted in midair, and began to move over the colony toward the stalled APC.

"Got you on visual. Wind's let up a little. I'll set her down as close as I can," Ferro informed them.

"Roger." Hicks turned to his companions. "Ready?" Everyone nodded except Burke, who looked sour but said nothing. "Then let's get out of here." He cycled the door.

Wind and rain poured in as the ramp extended. They filed rapidly out of the vehicle. The dropship was already in plain sight, edging toward them. Searchlights blazed from its flanks and belly. One illuminated a single human shape striding through the mist toward them.

"Bishop!" Vasquez waved. "Long time no see."

He called across to her. "Didn't work out so good, huh?"

"It stank." She spat downwind. "Tell you all about it sometime."

"Later. After hypersleep. After we've put this place far behind us."

She nodded, the only one of the waiting group whose attention was not monopolized by the approaching dropship.

Her dark eyes continuously scanned the landscape around the personnel carrier. Nearby, Ripley waited, gripping Newt's small hand tightly. Hudson and Hicks carried the still-unconscious Gorman between them.

"Hold it there," Ferro instructed them. "Give me a little room. I don't want to come down on top of you." She thumped her headset pickup. "It'd be nice if I had a little help up here, Spunkmeyer. Get off the pot."

The compartment door slid aside behind her. She glanced back over her shoulder, angry and not bothering to hide the fact. "It's about time. Where the . . . ?"

Her eyes widened, and the rest of the accusation trailed away.

It wasn't Spunkmeyer.

The alien barely fit through the opening. Outer jaws flared to reveal the inner set of teeth. There was a blur of movement and an explosive, organic *whoosh*. Ferro barely had time to scream as she was slammed backward into the control console.

From below, the would-be refugees watched in dismay as the dropship veered wildly to port. Its main engines roared to life, and it accelerated even as it lost altitude. Ripley grabbed Newt and sprinted toward the nearest building.

"Run!"

The dropship clipped a rock formation at the edge of the causeway, slewed left, and struck a basalt ridge. It tumbled, turning completely on its back like a dying dragonfly, struck the tarmac, and exploded. Sections and compartments began to break away from the mainframe, some of them already afire. The body of the ship arced into the air once more, bouncing off the unyielding stone, fire blazing from it engines and superstructure.

Part of an engine module slammed into the APC, setting off its armament. The personnel carrier blew itself to bits as shells and fuel exploded inside it. A flaming Catherine wheel, the remains of the dropship skipped past and rolled into the outskirts of the atmosphere processing station. A tremendous fireball lit the dark sky of Acheron. It faded rapidly.

Emerging from concealment, the stunned survivors stared at the debris in disbelief as their superior firepower and hopes of getting off the planet were simultaneously reduced to charred metal and ash.

"Well that's *great*!" said a near hysterical Hudson. "That's just great, man. *Now* what are we supposed to do? We're in some real fine shape now."

"Are you finished?" Hicks stared hard at the comtech until Hudson looked abashed. Then he glanced at Ripley. "You okay?"

She nodded and tried to hide her real feelings as she looked down at Newt. She could have spared herself the effort. It was impossible to hide anything from the child. Newt looked calm enough. She was breathing hard, true, but it was from the effort of racing for cover, not from fear. The girl shrugged, sounding remarkably grown-up.

"I guess we're not leaving, right?"

Ripley bit her lip. "I'm sorry, Newt."

"You don't have to be sorry. It wasn't your fault." She stared silently at the flaming wreckage of the dropship.

Hudson was kicking aside rocks, bits of metal, anything smaller than his boot. "Just tell me what we're supposed to do now. What're we gonna do *now*?"

Burke looked annoyed. "Maybe we could build a fire and sing songs."

Hudson took a step toward the Company rep, and Hicks had to intervene.

"We should get back." Everyone turned to look down at Newt, who was still staring at the burning dropship. "We should get back 'cause it'll be dark soon. *They* come mostly at night. Mostly."

"All right." Hicks nodded in the direction of the ruined APC. It was mostly metal and composites and shouldn't burn much longer. "The fire's about had it. Let's see what we can find."

"Scrap metal," suggested Burke.

"And maybe something more. You coming?"

The Company rep rose from where he'd been sitting. "I'm sure not staying here."

"Up to you." The corporal turned to their synthetic. "Bishop, see if you can make Operations livable. What I mean is, make sure it's . . . clear."

The android responded with a gentle smile. "Take point? I know what that means. I'm expendable, of course."

"Nobody's expendable." Hicks started across the tarmac toward the smoking APC. "Let's move it."

Day on Acheron was dim twilight; night was darker than the farthest reaches of interstellar space, because not even the stars shone through its dense atmosphere to soften the barren surface with twinkling light. The wind howled around the battered metal buildings of Hadley town, whistling down corridors and rattling broken doors. Sand pattered against cracked windows, a perpetual snare-drum roll. Not a comforting sound to be heard. Inside, everyone waited for the nightmare to come.

Emergency power was sufficient to light Operations and its immediate environs but not much else. There the weary and demoralized survivors gathered to consider their options. Vasquez and Hudson had made one final run to the hulk that was the armored personnel carrier. Now they set down their prize, a large, scorched, dented packing case. Several similar cases were stacked nearby.

Hicks glanced at the case and tried not to sound too disappointed. He knew what the answer to his question would be but asked it, anyhow. Maybe he was wrong.

"Any ammo?" Vasquez shook her head and slumped into an office chair.

"Everything was stored in the airspace between the APC's walls. It all went up when it caught fire." She pulled off her sweat-soaked bandanna and wiped a forearm across her hairline. "Man, what I wouldn't give for some soap and a hot shower."

Hicks turned toward the table on which reposed their entire weapons inventory.

"This is it, then. Everything we could salvage." His gaze examined the stock, wishing he could triple it by looking at it. "We've got four pulse-rifles with about fifty rounds each. Not so good. About fifteen M-40 grenades and two flame-throwers less than half full—one damaged. And we've got four of these robot-sentry units with their scanners and display relays intact." He approached the stack of packing cases and broke the seal on the nearest. Ripley joined him in inspecting the contents.

Stabilized in packing foam was a squat automatic weapon. Secured in a separate set of boxes next to it was matching video and movement-sensor instrumentation.

"Looks pretty efficient," she commented.

"They are." Hicks shut the case. "Without them I'd say we might as well cut our wrists right now. With them, well, our chances are better than none, anyway. Trouble is we need about a hundred like this one and ten times the ammunition. But I'm grateful for small favors." He rapped his knuckles on the hard plastic case. "If these hadn't been packed like this, they would've gone blooey with the rest of the APC."

"What makes you think we stand a chance, anyway?" Hudson said.

Ripley ignored him. "How long after we're declared overdue can we expect a rescue?"

Hicks looked thoughtful. He'd been too absorbed with the problems of their immediate survival to think about the possibility of help from outside.

"We should have filed a mission update yesterday. Call it about seventeen days from tonight."

The comtech whirled and stomped off, waving his arms disconsolately. "Man, we're not going to make it seventeen *hours.* Those things are going to come in here just like they did before, man. They're going to come in here and get us long before anyone from Earth comes poking around to see what's left of us. And they're gonna find us, too, all sucked out and blown dry like those poor colonists we cremated down on C-level. Like Dietrich and Crowe, man." He started to sob.

Ripley indicated the silently watching Newt. "*She* survived longer than that with no weapons and no training. The colonists didn't know what hit them. We know what to expect, and we've got more than wrenches and hammers to fight back with. We don't have to clean them out. All we have to do is survive for a couple of weeks. Just keep them away from us and stay alive."

Hudson laughed bitterly. "Yeah, no sweat. Just stay alive. Dietrich and Crowe are alive too."

"We're here, we've got some armaments, and we know what's coming. So you'd better just start dealing with it. Just deal with it, Hudson. Because we need you and I'm tired of your comments." He gaped at her, but she wasn't through.

"Now get on that central terminal and call up some kind of floor-plan file. Construction blueprints, maintenance schematics, anything that shows the layout of this place. I want to see air ducts, electrical access tunnels, subbasements, water pipes: every possible way into this wing of the colony. I want to see the guts of this building, Hudson. If they can't reach us, they can't hurt us. They haven't ripped through these walls yet, so maybe that means they can't. This is colony Operations. We're in the most solid structure on the planet, excepting maybe the big atmosphere-processing stations. We're up off the ground, and they haven't shown any signs of being able to climb a sheer wall."

Hudson hesitated, then straightened slightly, relieved to have something to concentrate on. Hicks nodded his approval to Ripley.

"Aye-firmative," the comtech told her, a little of his

cockiness restored. With it came a dram of confidence. "I'm on it. You want to know where every plug is in this dump, I'll find it." He headed for the vacant computer console. Hicks turned to the synthetic.

"You want a job or have you already got something in mind?"

Bishop looked uncertain. This was part of his social programming. An android could never be actually uncertain. "If you require me for something specific . . ." Hicks shook his head. "In that case I'll be in Medical. I'd like to continue my research. Perhaps I may stumble across something that will prove useful to us."

"Fine," Ripley told him. "You do that." She was watching him closely. If Bishop was conscious of this excessive scrutiny, he gave no sign of it as he turned and headed for the lab.

Once Hudson had something to work on, he moved fast. Before long, Ripley, Hicks, and Burke were clustered around the comtech, peering past him at the large flat video display. It illuminated a complex series of charts and mechanical drawings. Newt hopped from one foot to the other, trying to see around the adults' bulk.

Ripley tapped the screen. "This service tunnel has to be what they're using to move back and forth."

Hudson studied the readout. "Yeah, right. It runs from

the processing station right into the colony maintenance sub-level, here." He traced the route with a fingertip. "That's how they slipped in and surprised the colonists. That's the way I'd come too."

"All right. There's a fire door at this end. This first thing we do is put one of the remote sentries in the tunnel and seal that door."

"That won't stop them." Hicks's gaze roved over the plans. "Once they've been stopped in the service tunnel, they'll find another way in. We gotta figure on them getting into the complex eventually."

"That's right. So we put up welded barricades at these intersections"—she pointed to the schematic as she spoke—"and seal these ducts here, and here. Then they can only come at us from these two corridors, and we create a free field of fire for the other two sentry units, here." She tapped the location, her nail clicking on the hard surface of the illuminated screen. "Of course, they can always tear the roof off, but I think that'd take them a while. By then our relief should arrive, and we'll be out of here."

"We'd better be," Hicks muttered. He studied the layout of Operations intently. "Otherwise this looks outstanding. Seal the fire door in the tunnel, weld the corridors shut, then all we need is a deck of cards to pass the time." He straightened and eyed his companions. "All right, let's move like we got a purpose."

Hudson half snapped to attention. "Aye-firmative."

Next to him Newt copied the gesture and the inflection. "Aye-firmative." The comtech looked down at her and smiled before he caught himself. Hopefully no one noticed the transient grin. It would ruin his reputation as an incorrigible hard-case.

Hudson grunted as he set the second heavy sentry gun onto its recoil-absorbing tripod. The weapon was squat, ugly, unencumbered by sights or triggers. Vasquez locked the weapon in place, then snapped on the connectors that led from the firing mechanism to the attached motion sensor. When she was certain the comtech was out of the way, she nudged a single switch marked ACTIVATE. A small green light came to life atop the gun. On the small diagnostic readout set flush in the side, READY flashed yellow, then red.

Both troopers stepped clear. Vasquez picked up a battered wastebasket that had rolled into the corridor and shouted toward the weapon's aural pickup. "Testing!" Then she threw the empty metal container out into the middle of the corridor.

Both guns swiveled and let loose before the basket hit the floor, reducing the container to dime-size shrapnel. Hudson whooped with delight.

"Take that, suckers!" He lowered his voice as he turned to Vasquez, his eyes rolling. "Oh, give me a home, where the firepower roams, and the deer and the antelope get shot to hamburger."

"You always were the sensitive type," Vasquez told him.

"I know. It shows in my face." Turning, he put a shoulder against the fire door. "Give me a hand with this."

Vasquez helped him roll the heavy steel barrier into place. Then she unpacked the high-intensity portable welding torch she'd brought with her and snapped it alight. Blue flame roared from the muzzle. She turned a dial on the handle, refining the acetylene finger.

"Give me some room, man, or I'm liable to seal your foot to your boot." Hudson complied, stepping back to watch her. He began to pace, staring down the empty serviceway and listening. He fingered the controls of his headset nervously.

"Hudson here."

Hicks responded instantly. "How're you two doing? We're working on the big air duct you located in the plans."

"A and B sentries are in place and activated. Looks good. Nothing comes up this tunnel they can't pick out." Vasquez's torch hissed nearby. "We're sealing the fire door right now."

"Roger. When you're through, get yourselves back up here."

"Hey, you think I want a ticket for loitering?"

Hicks smiled to himself. That sounded more like the old Hudson. He nudged the tiny mike away from his lips and adjusted the thick metal plate he was carrying so that it covered the duct opening. Ripley nodded at him and shoved her plate in place. He unlimbered a duplicate of Vasquez's welder and began sealing the plate to the floor.

Behind him, Burke and Newt worked busily, stacking containers of medicine and food in a corner. The aliens hadn't touched the colony's food supplies. More importantly the water-distillation system was still functioning. Since it was self-pressurized, no power was needed to draw it from the taps. They wouldn't starve or go thirsty.

When he'd sealed down two-thirds of the plate, Hicks set the welder aside and extracted a small bracelet from a belt pouch. He flicked a tiny switch set flush with the metal, and a minuscule LED came to life as he handed the circlet to Ripley.

"What is it?"

"Emergency beeper. Military version of the PDTs the colonists had surgically implanted. Doesn't have the range they do, and you wear it outside instead of inside your body, but the idea's the same. With that on I can locate you anywhere near the complex on this." He tapped the miniature tracker that was built into his battle harness.

She studied it curiously. "I don't need this."

"Hey, it's just a precaution. You know."

She regarded him quizzically for a moment, then shrugged and slipped the bracelet over her wrist. "Thanks. You wearing one?"

He smiled and looked away. "Only got one tracker." He tapped his harness. "I know where I am. What's next?"

She forgot all about the bracelet as she consulted the hard-copy printout of Hudson's schematic.

Something very strange happened while they worked. They were too busy to notice, and it was left to Newt to point it out.

The wind had died. Stopped utterly. In the unAcheronic stillness outside the colony, a diffuse mist swirled and roiled uncertainly. In two visits to Acheron this was the first time Ripley hadn't heard the wind. It was disquieting.

The absence of wind reduced outside visibility from poor to nonexistent. Fog swirled around Operations, giving the world beyond the triple-paned windows the look of being under water. Nothing moved.

In the service tunnel that connected the buildings of the colony to the processing station and each other, a pair of robot guns sat silently, their motion scanners alert and humming. C gun surveyed the empty corridor, its ARMED light flashing green. Through a hole in the ceiling at the far end of the passageway, fog swirled in. Water condensed on bare metal walls and dripped to the floor. The gun did not fire on the falling drops. It was smarter, more selective than that, able to distinguish between harmless natural phenomena and inimical movement. The water made no attempt to advance, and so the weapon held its fire, waiting patiently for something to kill.

Newt had carried boxes until she'd worn herself out. Ripley carried her from Operations into the medical wing, the small head resting wearily on the woman's shoulder. Occasionally she would try to say something, and Ripley would reply as though she understood. She was hunting for a place where the child could rest quietly and in comparative safety.

The operating theater was located at the far end of the medical section. Much of its complex equipment sat in recesses in the walls while the rest hung from the ceiling at the tips of extensible arms. A large globe containing lights and additional surgical instrumentation dominated the ceiling. Cabinets and equipment not fastened down had been shoved into a corner to provide room for several folding metal cots.

This was where they would sleep. This was where they would retreat to if the aliens breached the outer defenses. The inner redoubt. The keep. The operating room was sealed tighter and had thicker walls than any other part of the colony complex, or so the schematics Hudson had called forth insisted. It looked a lot like an oversize, high-tech vault. If they had to shoot themselves in order to keep from falling alive into the aliens' hands, this was where any future rescuers would find the bodies.

But for now it was a safe haven, snug and quiet. Gently Ripley lowered the girl to the nearest cot, smiling down at the upturned face.

"Now you just lie there and have a nap. I have to go help the others, but I'll come in every chance I get to check on you. You deserve a rest. You're exhausted."

Newt stared up at her. "I don't want to sleep."

"You have to, Newt. Everybody has to sometime. You'll feel better after you've had a rest."

"But I have scary dreams."

It struck a familiar chord in Ripley, but she managed to feign cheerfulness. "Everybody has bad dreams, Newt."

The girl snuggled deeper into the padded cot. "Not like mine."

Don't bet on it, child, she thought. Aloud she said, "I'll bet Casey doesn't have bad dreams." She disengaged the doll head from the girl's small fingers and made a show of peering inside. "Just as I thought: Nothing bad in there. Maybe you could try to be like Casey. Pretend there's nothing in here." She tapped the girl's forehead, and Newt smiled back.

"You mean, try to make it all empty-like?"

"Yes, empty-like. Like Casey." She caressed the delicate face, brushing hair back from Newt's forehead. "If you do that, I'll bet you'll be able to sleep without having any bad dreams."

She closed the doll head's unblinking eyes and handed it back to its owner. Newt took it, rolling her own eyes as if to say, "Don't pull that five-year-old stuff on me, lady. I'm six."

"Ripley, she doesn't have bad dreams, because she's just a piece of plastic."

"Oh. Sorry, Newt. Well, then, maybe you could pretend you're like her that way. Just made of plastic."

The girl almost smiled. Almost. "I'll try."

"Good girl. Maybe I'll try it myself."

Newt pulled Casey close up to her neck, looking thoughtful. "My mommy always said there were no such things as monsters. No real ones. But there *are*."

Ripley continued to brush isolated strands of blond hair back from the pale forehead. "Yes, there are, aren't there?"

"They're as real as you and me. They're not make-believe, and they didn't come out of a book. They're really real, not fake-real like the ones I used to watch on the video. Why do they tell little kids things like that, things that aren't true?" There was a faint tinge of betrayal in her voice.

No lying to this child, Ripley knew. Not that she had the slightest intention of doing so. Newt had experienced too much reality to be fooled by a simple fib. Ripley instinctively sensed that to lie to this girl would be to lose her trust forever.

"Well, some kids can't handle it like you can. The truth, I mean. They're too scared, or their grown-ups think they'll be too scared. Grown-ups have a way of always underestimating little kids' ability to handle the truth. So they try to make things easier for them by making things up."

"About the monsters. Did one of those things grow inside mommy?"

Ripley found some blankets and began pulling them up around the small body, tucking them tightly around narrow ribs. "I don't know, Newt. Neither does anybody else. That's the truth. I don't think anybody will ever know."

The girl considered. "Isn't that how babies come? I mean, people babies. They grow inside you?"

A chill went down Ripley's spine. "No, not like that,

not like that at all. It's different with people, honey. The way
it gets started is different, and the way the baby comes is
different. With people the baby and the mother work together.
With these aliens the—"

"I understand," Newt said, interrupting. "Did you ever
have a baby?"

"Yes." She pushed the blanket up under the child's chin.
"Just once. A little girl."

"Where is she? Back on Earth?"

"No. She's gone."

"You mean, dead."

It wasn't a question. Ripley nodded slowly, trying to
remember a small female thing not unlike Newt running and
playing, a miracle with dark curls bouncing around her face.
Trying to reconcile that memory with the picture of an older
woman briefly glimpsed, child and mature lady linked together through time overspent in the stasis of hypersleep. The
child's father was a more distant memory still. So much of
a life lost and forgotten. Youthful love marred by a lack of
common sense, a brief flare of happiness smothered by reality.
Divorce. Hypersleep. Time.

She turned away from the bed and reached for a portable
space heater. While it wasn't uncomfortable in the operating
theater, it would be more comfortable with the heater on. It
looked like a slab of plastic, but when she thumbed the "on"
switch, it emitted a whirr and a faint glow as its integral
warming elements came to life. As the heat spread, the operating room became a little less sterile, a shade cozier. Newt
blinked sleepily.

"Ripley, I was thinking. Maybe I could do you a favor
and fill in for her. Your little girl, I mean. Nothing permanent.
Just for a while. You can try it, and if you don't like it, it's
okay. I'll understand. No big deal. Whattaya think?"

It took what little remained of Ripley's determination
and self-control not to break down in front of the child. She
settled for hugging her tightly. She also knew that neither of

them might see the light of another dawn. That she might have to turn Newt's face away during a very possible apocalyptic last moment and put the muzzle of a pulse-rifle to those blond tresses.

"I think it's not the worst idea I've heard all day. Let's talk about it later, okay?"

"Okay." A shy, hopeful smile.

Ripley switched off the room light and started to rise. A small hand grabbed her arm with desperate force.

"Don't go! Please."

With great reluctance Ripley disengaged her arm from Newt's grip. "It'll be all right. I'll be in the other room, right next door. I'm not going to go anywhere else. And don't forget that that's there." She indicated the miniature video pickup that was imbedded over the doorway. "You know what that is, don't you?" A small nod in the darkness.

"Uh-huh. It's a securcam."

"That's right. See, the green light's on. Mr. Hicks and Mr. Hudson checked out all the securcams in this area to make sure all of them were operating properly. It's watching you, and I'll be watching its monitor over in the other room. I'll be able to see you just as clearly in there as I can when I'm right here."

When Newt still seemed to hesitate, Ripley unsnapped the tracer bracelet Hicks had given her. She slipped it around the girl's smaller wrist, cinching it tight.

"Here. This is for luck. It'll help me keep an eye on you too. Now go to sleep—and don't dream. Okay?"

"I'll try." The sound of a small body sliding down between clean sheets.

Ripley watched in the dim light from the instruments on standby as the girl turned onto her side, hugging the doll head and gazing through half-lidded eyes at the steadily glowing function light imbedded in the bracelet. The space heater hummed comfortingly as she backed out of the room.

Other half-opened eyes were twitching erratically back

and forth. They were the only visible evidence that Lieutenant Gorman was still alive. It was an improvement of sorts. One step further from complete paralysis.

Ripley leaned over the table on which the lieutenant was lying, studying the eye movements and wondering if he could recognize her. "How is he? I see he's got his eyes open."

"That might be enough to wear him out." Bishop looked up from a nearby workbench. He was surrounded by instruments and shining medical equipment. The light of the single high-intensity lamp he was working with threw his features into sharp relief, giving his face a macabre cast.

"Is he in pain?"

"Not according to his bioreadouts. They're hardly conclusive, of course. I'm sure he'll let us know as soon as he regains the use of his larynx. By the way, I've isolated the poison. Interesting stuff. It's a muscle-specific neurotoxin. Affects only the nonvital parts of the system; leaves respiratory and circulatory functions unimpaired. I wonder if the creatures instinctively adjust the dosage for different kinds of potential hosts?"

"I'll ask one of them first chance I get." As she stared, one eyelid rose all the way before fluttering back down again. "Either that was an involuntary twitch or else he winked at me. Is he getting better?"

Bishop nodded. "The toxin seems to be metabolizing. It's powerful, but the body appears capable of breaking it down. It's starting to show up in his urine. Amazing mechanism, the human body. Adaptable. If he continues to flush the poison at a constant rate, he should wake up soon."

"Let me get this straight. The aliens paralyzed the colonists they didn't kill, carried them over to the processing station, and cocooned them to serve as hosts for more of those." She pointed into the back room where the stasis cylinders held the remaining facehugger specimens.

"Which would mean lots of those parasites, right? One

for each colonist. Over a hundred, at least, assuming a mortality rate during the final fight of about a third."

"Yes, that follows," Bishop readily agreed.

"But these things, the parasitic facehugger form, come from eggs. So where are all the eggs coming from? When the guy who first found the alien ship reported back to us, he said there were a lot of eggs inside, but he never said how many, and nobody else ever went in after him to look. And not all those eggs may have been viable.

"The thing is, judging from the way the colony here was overwhelmed, I don't think the first aliens had time to haul eggs from that ship back here. That means they had to come from somewhere else."

"That is the question of the hour." Bishop swiveled his chair to face her. "I have been pondering it ceaselessly since the true nature of the disaster here first became apparent to us."

"Any ideas, bright or otherwise?"

"Without additional solid evidence it is nothing more than a supposition."

"Go ahead and suppose, then."

"We could assume a parallel to certain insect forms who have a hivelike organization. An ant or termite colony, for example, is ruled by a single female, a queen, who is the source of new eggs."

Ripley frowned. Interstellar navigation to entomology was a mental jump she wasn't prepared to make. "Don't insect queens come from eggs also?"

The synthetic nodded. "Absolutely."

"What if there was no queen egg aboard the ship that brought these things here?"

"There's no such thing in a social insect society as a 'queen egg,' until the workers decide to create one. Ants, bees, termites, all employ essentially the same method. They select an ordinary egg and feed the pupa developing inside a special food high in certain nutrients. Among bees, for example, it is called royal jelly. The chemicals in the jelly act to change the composition of the maturing pupa so that what eventually emerges is an adult queen and not another worker. Theoretically any egg can be used to hatch a queen. Why the insects choose the particular eggs they do is something we still do not know."

"You're saying that one of those things lays *all* the eggs?"

"Well, not exactly like one we're familiar with. Only if the insect analogy holds up. Assuming it does, there could be other similarities. An alien queen analogous to an ant or termite queen could be much larger physically than the aliens we have so far encountered. A termite queen's abdomen is so bloated with eggs that she can't move by herself at all. She is fed and tended by workers, mated to drones, and defended by highly specialized warriors. She is also quite harmless. On the other hand, a queen bee is far more dangerous than any worker bee because she can sting many times. She is the center of their lives, quite literally the mother of their society.

"In one respect, at least, we are fortunate that the analogy does not hold up. Ants and bees develop from eggs directly to larvae, pupae, and adults. Each alien embryo requires a live host in which to mature. Otherwise Acheron would be covered with them by now."

"Funny, but that doesn't reassure me a whole lot. These things are a lot bigger than any ant or termite. Could they be intelligent? Could this hypothetical queen? That's something we never could decide on back on the *Nostromo*. We were too busy trying to keep from getting killed. Not much time for speculation."

"It's hard to say." Bishop looked thoughtful. "There is one thing worth considering, though."

"What's that?"

"It may have been nothing more than blind instinct, attraction to the heat or whatever, but she did choose, assuming she exists, to incubate her eggs in the one spot in the colony where we couldn't destroy her without destroying ourselves. Beneath the heat exchangers at the processing plant. If that site was chosen from instinct, it means that they may be no brighter than your average termite. If, on the other hand, it was selected on the basis of intelligence, well, then I think we're in very deep trouble indeed.

"That's *if* there's any reality to these suppositions at all. Despite the distance involved, the eggs these aliens hatched from might have been brought down here by the first ones to emerge. There might be no queen involved at all, no complex alien society. Whether by intelligence or instinct, though, we have seen that they cooperate. That's something we don't have to speculate on. We've seen them in action."

Ripley stood there and considered the ramifications of Bishop's analysis. None of them were encouraging, nor had she expected any to be. She nodded toward the stasis cylinders.

"I want those specimens destroyed as soon as you're done with them. You understand?"

The android glanced toward the two live facehuggers pulsing malevolently in their tubular prisons. He looked unhappy. "Mr. Burke gave instructions that they were to be kept alive in stasis for return to the Company laboratories. He was very specific."

The wonder of it was that she went for the intercom instead of the nearest weapon. "Burke!"

A faint whisper of static failed to mar his reply. "Yes? That's you, isn't it, Ripley?"

"You bet it's me! Where are you?"

"Scavenging while there's still time. I thought I might learn something on my own, since I just seem to be in everybody's way up there."

"Meet me in the lab."

"Now? But I'm still—"

"Now!" She closed the connection and glared at the inoffensive Bishop. "You come with me." Obediently he put his work aside and rose to follow her. That was all she was after; to make sure that he'd obey an order if she gave it. It meant he wasn't completely under Burke's sway, Company machine or no Company machine. "Never mind, forget it."

"I shall be happy to accompany you if that is what you wish."

"That's all right. I've decided to handle it on my own. You continue with your research. That's more important than anything else."

He nodded, looking puzzled, and resumed his seat.

Burke was waiting for her outside the entrance to the lab. His expression was bland. "This better be important. I think I was onto something, and we may not have much time left."

"You may not have _any_ time left." He started to protest, and she cut him off with a gesture. "No, in there." She gestured at the operating theater. It was soundproofed inside, and she could scream at him to her heart's content without drawing everyone else's attention. Burke ought to be grateful for her thoughtfulness. If Vasquez overheard what the Company representative had been planning, she wouldn't waste time arguing with him. She'd put a bullet through him on the spot.

"Bishop tells me you have intentions of taking the live parasites home in your pocket. That true?"

He didn't try to deny it. "They're harmless in stasis."

"Those suckers aren't harmless unless they're dead. Don't you understand that yet? I want them killed as soon as Bishop's gotten everything out of them he can."

"Be reasonable, Ripley." A ghost of the old, self-assured corporate smile stole over Burke's face. "Those specimens are worth millions to the Bioweapons Division of the Company. Okay, so we nuke the colony. I'm outvoted on that one. But not on this. Two lousy specimens, Ripley. How much trouble could they cause while secured in stasis? And if you're worried about something happening when we get them back to Earthside labs, don't. We have people who know how to handle things like these."

"Nobody knows how to handle 'things like these.' Nobody's ever encountered anything like them. You think it'd be dangerous for some germs to get loose from a weapons lab? Try to imagine what would happen if just one of those parasites got loose in a major city, with its thousands of kilometers of sewers and pipes and glass-fiber channels to hide in."

"They're not going to get loose. Nothing can break a stasis field."

"No sale, Burke. There's too much we don't know about these monsters. It's too risky."

"Come on, I know you're smarter than this." He was trying to mollify and persuade her at the same time. "If we play it right, we can both come out of this heroes. Set up for life."

"Is that the way you really see it?" She eyed him askance. "Carter Burke, alien smasher? Didn't what happened in C-level of the processing station make any impression on you at all?"

"They went in unprepared and overconfident." Burke's tone was flat, unemotional. "They got caught in tight quarters where they couldn't use the proper tactics and weapons. If they'd all used their pulse-rifles and kept their heads and managed to get out without shooting up the heat exchangers, they'd all be here now and we'd be on our way back to the *Sulaco* instead of holed up in Operations like a bunch of frightened rabbits. Sending them in like that was Gorman's decision, not mine. And besides, those were adult aliens they were fighting, not parasites."

"I didn't hear you object loudly when strategy was being discussed."

"Who would've listened to me? Don't you remember what Hicks said? What you said? Gorman wouldn't have been any different." His tone turned sarcastic. "This is a *military* expedition."

"Forget the whole idea, Burke. You couldn't pull it off even if I let you. Just try getting a dangerous organism past ICC quarantine. Section 22350 of the Commerce Code."

"You've been doing your homework. That's what the code says, all right. But you're forgetting one thing. The code's nothing but words on paper. Paper never stopped a determined man. If I have five minutes alone with the customs inspector on duty when we turn through Gateway Station, we'll get them through. Leave that end of it to me. The ICC can't impound something they don't know anything about."

"But they *will* know about it, Burke."

"How? First they'll want to talk to us, then they'll make us walk through a detection tunnel. Big deal. By the time the relief team gets around to inspecting our luggage, I'll have made the necessary arrangements with ship's personnel to set up the stasis tubes somewhere down near the engine or waste-products recycling. We'll pick them up and slip them off the relief ship the same way. Everyone'll be so busy shooting questions at us, they'll have no time for checking cargo.

"Besides, everyone will know we found a devastated colony and that we got out as fast as we could. No one will be looking for us to smuggle anything back in. The Company will back me up on this, Ripley, especially when they see what we've brought them. They'll take good care of you, too, if that's what you're worrying about."

"I'm sure they'll back you up," she said. "I don't doubt that for an instant. Any outfit that would send less than a dozen soldiers out here with an inexperienced goofball like Gorman in charge after hearing my story is capable of anything."

"You worry too much."

"Sorry. I like living. I don't like the idea of waking up some morning with an alien monstrosity exploding out of my chest."

"That's not going to happen."

"You bet it isn't. Because if you try taking those ugly little teratoids out of here, I'll tell everyone on the rescue ship what you're up to. This time I think people will listen to me. Not that it would ever get that far. All I have to do is tell Vasquez, or Hicks, or Hudson what you have in mind. They won't wait around for a directive, and they'll use more than angry words. So you might as well give it up, Burke." She nodded in the direction of the cylinders. "You're not getting them out of this lab, much less off the surface of this planet."

"Suppose I can convince the others?"

"You can't, but supposing for a minute that you could, how would you go about convincing them that you're not responsible for the deaths of the one hundred and fifty-seven colonists here?"

Burke's combativeness drained away and he turned pale. "Now wait a second. What are you talking about?"

"You heard me. The colonists. All those poor, unsuspecting good Company people. Like Newt's family. You said I'd been doing my homework, remember? *You* sent them to that ship, to check out the alien derelict. I just checked it out in the colony log. It's as intact as the plans Hudson called up. Would make interesting reading in court. 'Company Directive Six Twelve Nine, dated five thirteen seventy-nine. Proceed to inspect possible electromagnetic emission at coordinates—but I'm not telling you anything you don't already know, am I? Signed Burke, Carter J.'" She was trembling with anger. It was all spilling out of her at once, the frustration and fury at the incompetence and greed that had brought her back to this world of horror.

"You sent them out there, and you didn't even warn them, Burke. You sat through the inquest. You heard my story. Even if you didn't believe everything, you must have believed enough of it to want the coordinates checked out. You must have thought there was something to it or you wouldn't have gone to the trouble of having anyone go out there to look around. Out to the alien ship. You might not have believed, but you suspected. You wondered. Fine. Have it checked out. But checked out carefully by a fully equipped team, not some independent prospector. And warn them of what you suspected. Why didn't you warn them, Burke?"

"Warn them about what?" he protested. He'd heard only her words, hadn't sensed the moral outrage in her voice. That in itself explained a great deal. She was coming to understand Carter J. Burke quite well.

"Look, maybe the thing didn't even exist, right? Maybe there wasn't much to it. All we had to go on was your story, which was a bit much to take at face value."

"Was it? The _Narcissus_'s recorder was tampered with, Burke. Remember me telling the board of inquiry about that? You wouldn't happen to know what happened to the recorder, would you?"

He ignored the question. "What do you think would've happened if I'd stuck my neck out and made it into a major security situation?"

"I don't know," she said tightly. "Enlighten me."

"Colonial Administration would've stepped in. That means government officials looking over your shoulder at every turn, paperwork coming out your ears, no freedom of movement at all. Inspectors crawling all over the place looking for an excuse to shut you down and take over in the name of the almighty public interest. No exclusive development rights, nothing. The fact that your story turned out to be right is as much a surprise to me as everyone else." He shrugged, his manner as blasé as ever. "It was a bad call, that's all."

Something finally snapped inside Ripley. Surprising both of them, she grabbed him by the collar and slammed him against the wall.

"_Bad call_? These people are _dead_, Burke! One hundred and fifty-seven of them less one kid, all dead because of your 'bad call.' That's not counting Apone and the others torn apart or paralyzed over there." She jerked her head in the direction of the processing station.

"Well, they're going to nail your hide to the shed, and I'll be standing there helping to pass out the nails when they do. That's assuming your 'bad call' lets any of us get off this chunk of gravel alive. Think about that for a while." She stepped away from him, shaking with anger.

At least the aliens' motivations were comprehensible.

Burke straightened his back and his shirt, pity in his voice. "You just can't see the big picture, can you? Your worldview is restricted exclusively to the here and now. You've no interest in what your life could be like tomorrow."

"Not if it includes you, I don't."

"I expected more of you, Ripley. I thought you would be smarter than this. I thought I'd be able to count on you when the time came to make the critical decisions."

"Another bad call on your part, Burke. Sorry to disappoint you." She spun on her heel and abandoned the observation room, the door closing behind her. Burke followed her with his eyes, his mind a whirl of options.

Breathing hard, she strode toward Operations as the alarm began to sound. It helped to take her mind off the confrontation with Burke. She broke into a run.

XI

Hudson had the portable tactical console set up next to the colony's main computer terminal. Wires trailed from the console to the computer, a rat's nest of connections that enabled whoever sat behind the tactical board to interface with the colony's remaining functional instrumentation. Hicks looked up as Ripley entered Operations and slapped a switch to kill the alarm. Vasquez and Hudson joined her in clustering around the console.

"They're coming," he informed them quietly. "Just thought you'd like to know. They're in the tunnel already."

Ripley licked her lips as she stared at the console readouts. "Are we ready for them?"

The corporal shrugged, adjusted a gain control. "Ready as we can be. Assuming everything we've set up works. Manufacturers' warranties aren't going to be a lot of use to us if something shorts out when it's supposed to be firing, like those sentry guns. They're about all we've got."

"Don't worry, man, they'll work." Hudson looked better than at any time since the initial assault on the processing station's lower levels. "I've set up hundreds of those suckers. Once the ready lights come on, you can leave 'em and forget 'em. I just don't know if they'll be enough."

"No use worrying about it. We're throwing everything we've got left at them. Either the RSS guns'll stop them or they won't. Depends on how many of them there are." Hicks thumbed a couple of contact switches. Everything read out on-line and operational. He glanced at the readouts for the motion sensors mounted on A and B guns. They were blinking rapidly, the strobe speeding up until both lights shone steadily. At the same time a crash of heavy gunfire made the floor quiver slightly.

"Guns A and B. Tracking and firing on multiple targets." He looked up at Hudson. "You give good firepower."

The comtech ignored Hicks, watching the multiple readouts. "Another dozen guns," he muttered under his breath. "That's all it would take. If we had another dozen guns . . ."

A steady rumble echoed through the complex as the automatic weapons pounded away beneath them. Twin ammo counters on the console shrank inexorably toward single digits.

"Fifty rounds per gun. How are we going to stop them with only fifty rounds per gun?" Hicks murmured.

"They must all be wall-to-wall down there." Hudson gestured at the readouts. "Look at those ammo counters go. It's a shooting gallery down there."

"What about the acid?" Ripley wondered. "I know those guns are armored, but you've seen that stuff at work. It'll eat through anything."

"As long as the guns keep firing, they ought to be okay," Hicks told her. "Those RSS shells have a lot of impact. If it keeps blowing them backward, that'll keep the acid away. It'll spray all over the walls and floor, but the guns should stay clear."

That certainly seemed to be what was happening in the service tunnel because the robot sentries kept up their steady barrage. Two minutes went by; three. The counter on B gun reached zero, and the thunder below was reduced by half. Its motion sensor continued to flicker on the tactical readout as the empty weapon tracked targets it could no longer fire upon.

"B gun's dry. Twenty left on A." Hicks watched the counter, his throat dry. "Ten. Five. That's it."

A grim silence descended over Operations. It was shattered by a reverberating boom from below. It was repeated at regular intervals like the thunder of a massive gong. Each of them knew what the sound meant.

"They're at the fire door," Ripley muttered. The booming increased in strength and ferocity. Audible along with the deeper rumble was another new sound: the nerve-racking scrape of claws on steel.

"Think they can break through there?" Ripley thought Hicks looked remarkably calm. Assurance—or resignation?

"One of them ripped a hatch right off the APC when it tried to pull Gorman out, remember?" she reminded him.

Vasquez nodded toward the floor. "That ain't no hatch down there. It's a Class double-A fire door, three layers of steel alloy with carbon-fiber composite laid between. The door will hold. It's the welds I'm worried about. We didn't have much time. I'd feel better if I'd had a couple bars of chromite solder and a laser instead of a gas torch to work with."

"And another hour," Hudson added. "Why don't you wish for a couple of Katusha Six antipersonnel rockets while you're at it. One of those babies would clean out the whole tunnel."

The intercom buzzed for attention, startling them. Hicks clicked it on.

"Bishop here. I heard the guns. How are we doing?"

"As well as can be expected. A and B sentries are out of ammo, but they must've done some damage."

"That's good, because I'm afraid I have some bad news."

Hudson made a face and leaned back against a cabinet. "Well, now, that's a switch."

"What kind of bad news?" Hicks inquired.

"It will be easier to explain and show you at the same time. I'll be right over."

"We'll be here." Hicks flipped the intercom off. "Charming."

"Hey, no sweat," said the jaunty comtech. "We're already in the toilet, so why worry?"

The android arrived quickly and moved to the single high window that overlooked much of the colony complex. The wind had picked back up and blown off the clinging fog. Visibility was still far from perfect, but it was sufficient to permit them a glimpse of the distant atmosphere-processing station. As they stared, a column of flame unexpectedly jetted skyward from the base of the station. For an instant it was brighter than the steady glow that emanated from the top of the cone itself.

"What was that?" Hudson pressed his face closer to the glass.

"Emergency venting," Bishop informed him.

Ripley was standing close to the comtech. "Can the construction contain the overload?"

"Not a chance. Not if the figures I've been monitoring are half accurate, and I have no reason to suppose that they are anything other than completely accurate."

"What happened?" Hicks spoke as he walked back to the tactical console. "Did the aliens cause that, monkeying around inside?"

"There's no way to tell. Perhaps. More likely someone hit something vital with a smartgun shell or a blast from a pulse-rifle during the fight on C-level. Or the damage might have been done when the dropship smashed into the base of the complex. The cause is of no import. All that matters is the result, which is not good."

Ripley started to tap her fingers on the window, thought better of it, and brought her hand back to her side. There might be something out there listening. As she stared, another gush of superheated gas flared from the base of the processing station.

"How long before it blows?"

"There's no way to be sure. One can extrapolate from the available figures but without any degree of certainty. There are too many variables involved that can only be roughly compensated for, and the requisite calculations are complex."

"How long?" Hicks asked patiently.

The android turned to him. "Based on the information I've been able to gather, I'm projecting total systems failure in a little under four hours. The blast radius will be about thirty kilometers. It will be nice and clean. No fallout, of course. About ten megatons."

"That's very reassuring," said Hudson dryly.

Hicks sucked air. "We got problems."

The comtech unfolded his arms and turned away from his companions. "I don't believe this," he said disconsolately. "Do you believe this? The RSS guns blow a pack of them to bits, the fire door's still holding, and it's all a waste!"

"It's too late to shut the station down? Assuming the instrumentation necessary to do it is still operational?" Ripley stared at the android. "Not that I'm looking forward to jogging across the tarmac, but if that's the only chance we've got, I'll take a shot at it."

He smiled regretfully. "Save your legs. I'm afraid it's too late. The dropship impact, or the guns, or whatever, did too much damage. At this point overload is inevitable."

"Terrific. So what's the recommended procedure now?"

Vasquez grinned at her. "Bend over, put your head between your legs, and kiss your ass goodbye."

Hudson was pacing the floor like a caged cat. "Oh, man. And I was getting short too! Four more weeks and out. Three of that in hypersleep. Early retirement. Ten years in the Marines and you're out and sitting pretty, they said. Recruiters. Now I'm gonna buy it on this rock. It ain't fair, man!"

Vasquez looked bored. "Give us a break, Hudson."

He spun on her. "That's easy for you to say, Vasquez. You're a lifer. You love mucking around on these alien dirtballs so you can blow away anything that sticks up bug eyes.

Me, I joined for the pension. Ten years and out, take the credit, and buy into a little bar somewhere, hire somebody else to run the joint so I can kick back and jabchat with the customers while the money rolls in."

The smartgun operator looked back toward the window as another gas jet lit up the mist-shrouded landscape. Her expression was hard. "You're breaking my heart. Go cross a wire or something."

"It's simple." Ripley looked over at Hicks. "We can't stay here, so we've got to get away. There's only one way to do that: We need the other dropship. The one that's still on the *Sulaco*. Somehow we have to bring it down on remote. There's got to be a way to do that."

"There *was*. You think I haven't been thinking about that ever since Ferro rolled ours into the station?" Hudson stopped pacing. "You use a narrow-beam transmitter tuned just for the dropship's controls."

"I know," she said impatiently. "I thought about that, too, but we can't do it that way."

"Right. The transmitter was on the APC. It's wasted."

"There's got to be another way to bring that shuttle down. I don't care how. Think of a way. You're the comtech. Think of something."

"Think of what? We're dead."

"You can do better than that, Hudson. What about the colony's transmitter? That uplink tower down at the other end of the complex? We could program it to send that dropship a control frequency. Why can't we use that? It looked like it was intact."

"The thought had occurred to me earlier." All eyes turned toward Bishop. "I've already checked it out. The hardwiring between here and the tower was severed in the fighting between the colonists and the aliens—one more reason why they were unable to communicate with the relay satellite overhead, even if only to leave a warning for anyone who might come to check on them."

Ripley's mind was spinning like a dynamo, exploring options, considering and disregarding possible solutions until only one was left. "So what you're saying is that the transmitter itself is still functional but that it can't be utilized from here?"

The android looked thoughtful, finally nodded. "If it is receiving its share of emergency power, then yes, I don't see why it wouldn't be capable of sending the requisite signals. A lot of power would not be necessary, since all the other channels it would normally be broadcasting are dead."

"That's it, then." She scanned her companions' faces. "Somebody's just going to have to go out there. Take a portable terminal and go out there and plug in manually."

"Oh, right, right!" said Hudson with mock enthusiasm. "With those things running around. No way."

Bishop took a step forward. "I'll go." Quiet, matter of fact. As though there was no alternative.

Ripley gaped at him. "What?"

He smiled apologetically. "I'm really the only one present who is qualified to remote-pilot a dropship, anyway. And the outside weather won't bother me the way it would the rest of you. Nor will I be subject to quite the same degree of . . . mental distractions. I'll be able to concentrate on the job."

"If you aren't accosted by any passing pedestrians," Ripley pointed out.

"Yes, I will be fine if I am not interrupted." His smile widened. "Believe me, I'd prefer not to have to attempt this. I may be synthetic, but I'm not stupid. As nuclear incineration is the sole alternative, however, I am willing to give it a try."

"All right. Let's get on it. What'll you need?"

"The portable transmitter, of course. And we'll need to check to make sure the antenna is still drawing power. Since we're making an extra-atmospheric broadcast on a narrow beam, the transmitter will have to be realigned as precisely as possible. I will also need some—"

Vasquez interrupted sharply. "Listen!"

"To what?" Hudson turned a slow circle. "I don't hear anything."

"Exactly. It's stopped."

The smartgun operator was right. The booming and scratching at the fire door had ceased. As they listened, the silence was broken by the high-pitched trill of a motion-sensor alarm. Hicks looked at the tactical console.

"They're into the complex."

It didn't take long to get together the equipment Bishop needed. Finding a safe way out for him was another matter entirely. They debated possible exit routes, mixing information from the colony computer with suggestions from the tactical console, and spicing the results with their own heated personal opinions. The result was a consensual route that was the best of an unpromising bunch.

It was presented to Bishop. Android or not, he had the final say. Along with a multitude of other human emotions the new synthetics were also fully programmed for self-preservation. Or as Bishop ventured when the discussion of possible escape paths grew too heated, on the whole he would rather have been in Philadelphia.

There was little to argue about. Everyone agreed that the route selected was the only one that offered half a chance for him to slip out of Operations without drawing unwelcome attention. An uncomfortable silence ensued once this course was agreed upon, until Bishop was ready to depart.

One of the acid holes that was part of the colonists' losing battle with the aliens had formed a sizable gap in the floor of the medical lab. The hole offered access to the maze of subfloor conduits and serviceways. Some of these had been added subsequent to the colony's original construction and tacked on as required by Hadley's industrious inhabitants. It was one of these additions that Bishop was preparing to enter.

The android lowered himself through the opening, sliding and twisting until he was lying on his back, looking up at the others.

"How is it?" Hicks asked him.

Bishop looked back between his feet, then arched his neck to stare straight ahead. The chosen path. "Dark. Empty. Tight, but I guess I can make it."

You'd better, Ripley mused silently. "Ready for the terminal?"

A pair of hands lifted, as if in supplication. "Pass it down." She handed him the heavy, compact device.

Turning with an effort, he shoved it into the constricted shaft ahead of him. Fortunately the instrument was sheathed in protective plastic. It would make some noise as it was pushed along the conduit but not as much as metal scraping on metal. He turned on his back and raised his hands a second time.

"Let's have the rest."

Ripley passed him a small satchel. It contained tools, patch cables and replacement circuit boards, energy bypasses, a service pistol, and a small cutting torch, together with fuel for same. More weight and bulk, but it couldn't be helped. Better to take a little more time reaching the uplink tower than to arrive short of some necessary item.

"You're sure about which way you're going?" Ripley asked him.

"If the updated colony schematic is correct, yes. This duct runs almost out to the uplink assembly. One hundred eighty meters. Say, forty minutes to crawl down there. It would be easier on treads or wheels, but my designers had to go and get sentimental. They gave me legs." No one laughed.

"After I get there, one hour to patch in and align the antenna. If I get an immediate response, thirty minutes to prep the ship, then about fifty minutes' flight time."

"Why so long?" Hicks asked him.

"With a pilot on board the dropship it would take half

that, but remote-piloting from a portable terminal's going to be damn tricky. The last thing I want to do is rush the descent and maybe lose contact or control. I need the extra time to bring her in slow. Otherwise she's liable to end up like her sister ship."

Ripley checked her chronometer. "It's going to be close. You'd better get going."

"Right. See you soon." His farewell was full of forced cheerfulness. Entirely for their benefit, Ripley knew. No reason to let it get to her. He was only a synthetic, a near-machine.

She turned away from the hole as Vasquez slid a metal plate over the opening and began spot-welding it in place. There wasn't any maybe about what Bishop had to do. If he failed, they wouldn't have to worry about holding off the aliens. The bonfire that was slowly being ignited inside the processing station would finish them all.

Bishop lay on his back, watching the glow from Vasquez's welder transcribe a circle over his head. It was pretty, and he was sophisticated enough to appreciate beauty, but he was wasting time enjoying it. He rolled onto his belly and began squirming forward, pushing the terminal and the sack of equipment ahead of him. Push, squirm, push, squirm: slow going. The conduit was barely wide enough for his shoulders. Fortunately he was not subject to claustrophobia, any more than he suffered from vertigo or any of the other mental ills mankind was heir to. There was much to be said for artificial intelligence.

In front of him the conduit dwindled toward infinity. This is how a bullet must feel, he mused, lodged in the barrel of a gun. Except that a bullet wasn't burdened with feelings and he was. But only because they'd been programmed into him.

The darkness and loneliness gave him plenty of time for thinking. Moving forward didn't require much mental effort, so he was able to spend the rest considering his condition.

Feelings and programming. Organic tantrums or byte snits? Was there in the last analysis that much difference between himself and Ripley or, for that matter, any of the other humans? Beyond the fact that he was a pacifist and most of them were warlike, of course. How did a human being acquire its feelings?

Slow programming. A human infant came into the world already preprogrammed by instinct but could be radically reprogrammed by environment, companions, education, and a host of other factors. Bishop knew that his own programming was not affected by environment. What had happened to his earlier relative, then, the one that had gone berserk and caused Ripley to hate him so? A breakdown in programming—or a deliberate bit of malicious reprogramming by some still unidentified human? Why would a human do such a thing?

No matter how sophisticated his own programming or how much he learned during his allotted term of existence, Bishop knew that the species that had created him would remain forever shrouded in mystery. To a synthetic mankind would always be an enigma, albeit an entertaining and resourceful one.

In contrast to his companions there was nothing mysterious about the aliens. No incomprehensible mysteries to ponder, no double meanings to unravel. You could readily predict how they would act in a given situation. Moreover, a dozen aliens would likely react in the same fashion, whereas a dozen humans might do a dozen completely different and unrelated things, at least half of them illogical. But then, humans were not members of a hive society. At least they chose not to think of themselves as such. Bishop still wasn't sure he agreed.

Not all that much difference between human, alien, and android. All hive cultures. The difference was that the human hive was ruled by chaos brought about by this peculiar thing called individuality. They'd programmed him with it. As a

result he was part human. An honorary organic. In some
respects he was better than a human being, in others, less.
He felt best of all when they acted as though he were one of
them.

He checked his chronometer. He'd have to crawl faster
or he'd never make it in time.

The robot guns guarding the entrance to Operations
opened up, their metallic clatter ringing along the corridors.
Ripley picked up her flamethrower and headed for computer
central. Vasquez finished welding the floor plate that blocked
Bishop's rabbit hole into place with a flourish, put the torch
aside, and followed the other woman.

Hicks was staring at the tactical console, mesmerized
by the images the video pickups atop the guns were displaying. He barely glanced up long enough to beckon to the two
arrivals.

"Have a look at this," he said quietly.

Ripley forced herself to look. Somehow the fact that
they were distant two-dimensional images instead of an immediate reality made it easier. Each time a gun fired, the
brief flare from the weapon's muzzle whited out the video,
but they could still see clearly enough and often enough to
watch the alien horde as it pushed and stumbled up the corridor. Each time one was struck by an RSS shell, the chitinous
body would explode, spraying acid blood in all directions.
The gaping holes and gouges in the floor and walls stood out
sharply. The only thing the acid didn't chew through was
other aliens.

Tracer fire lit the swirling mist that poured into the corridor from jagged gashes in the walls as the automatic weapons continued to hammer away at the invaders.

"Twenty meters and closing." Hicks's attention was drawn
to the numerical readouts. "Fifteen. C and D guns down about
fifty percent." Ripley checked the safety on her flamethrower

to make sure it was off. Vasquez didn't need to check her pulse-rifle. It was a part of her.

The readouts flickered steadily. Between the bursts of fire a shrill, inhuman screeching was clearly audible.

"How many?" Ripley asked.

"Can't tell. Lots. Hard to tell how many of them are alive and which are down. They lose arms and legs and keep coming until the guns hit them square." Hudson's gaze flicked to another readout. "D gun's down to twenty rounds. Ten." He swallowed. "It's out."

Abruptly all firing ceased as the remaining gun ran out of shells. Smoke and mist obscured the double pickup view from below. Small fires burned where tracers had set flammable material ablaze in the corridor. The floor was littered with twisted and blackened corpses, a biomechanical boneyard. As they stared at the monitors several bodies collapsed and disappeared as the acid leaking from their limbs chewed a monstrous hole in the floor.

Nothing lunged from the clinging pall of smoke to rip the silent weapons from their mounts. The motion-sensor alarm was silent.

"What's going on?" Hudson fiddled uncertainly with his instruments. "What's going on, where are they?"

"I'll be..." Ripley exhaled sharply. "They gave up. They retreated. The guns stopped them. That means they can reason enough to connect cause and effect. They didn't just keep coming mindlessly."

"Yeah, but check this out." Hicks tapped the plastic between a pair of readouts. The counter that monitored D gun rested on zero. C gun was down to ten—a few seconds worth of firepower at the previous rate. "Next time they can walk right up to the door and knock. If only the APC hadn't blown."

"If the APC hadn't blown, we wouldn't be standing here talking about it. We'd be driving somewhere talking with the turret gun," Vasquez pointed out sharply.

Only Ripley wasn't discouraged. "But *they* don't know how far the guns are down. We hurt them. We actually hurt them. Right now they're probably off caucusing somewhere, or whatever it is they do to make group decisions. They'll start looking for another way to get in. That'll take them awhile, and when they decide on another approach, they'll be more cautious. They're going to start seeing those sentry guns everywhere."

"Maybe we got 'em demoralized." Hudson picked up on her confidence. He had some color back in his face. "You were right, Ripley. The ugly monsters aren't invulnerable."

Hicks looked up from the console and spoke to Vasquez and the comtech. "I want you two walking the perimeter. Operations to Medical. That's about all we can cover. I know we're all strung-out, but try to stay frosty and alert. If Ripley's right, they'll start testing the walls and conduits. We've got to stop any entries before they get out of hand. Pick them off one at a time as they try to get through."

The two troopers nodded. Hudson abandoned the console, picked up his rifle, and joined Vasquez in heading for the main corridor. Ripley located a half cup of coffee, picked it up, and drained the tepid contents in a single swallow. It tasted lousy but soothed her throat. The corporal watched her, waited until she'd finished.

"How long since you slept? Twenty-four hours?"

Ripley shrugged indifferently. She wasn't surprised by the question. The constant tension had drained her. If she looked half as tired as she felt, it was no wonder that Hicks had expressed concern. Exhaustion threatened to overwhelm her before the aliens did. When she replied, her voice was distant and detached.

"What difference does it make? We're just marking time."

"That's not what you've been saying."

She nodded toward the corridor that had swallowed Hudson and Vasquez. "That was for their benefit. Maybe a little for myself too. We can sleep but *they* won't. They won't slow down and they won't back off until they have what they want, and what they want is us. They'll get us too."

"Maybe. Maybe not." He smiled slightly.

She tried to smile back but wasn't sure if she accomplished it or not. Right then she'd have traded a year's flight salary for a hot cup of fresh coffee, but there was no one to trade with, and she was too tired to work on the dispenser. She slung the flamethrower over her shoulder.

"Hicks, I'm not going to wind up like those others. Like the colonists and Dietrich and Crowe. You'll take care of it, won't you, if it comes to that?"

"_If_ it comes to that," he told her softly, "I'll do us both. Although if we're still here when the processing station blows, it won't be necessary. That'll take care of everything, us and them. Let's see that it doesn't."

This time she was sure she managed a grin. "I can't figure you, Hicks. Soldiers aren't supposed to be optimists."

"Yeah, I know. You're not the first to point it out. I'm a freakin' anomaly." Turning, he picked something up from behind the tactical console. "Here, I'd like to introduce you to a close personal friend of mine."

With the smoothness and ease of long practice he disengaged the pulse-rifle's magazine and set it aside. Then he handed her the weapon.

"M-41A 10-mm pulse-rifle, over and under with a 30-mm pump-action grenade launcher. A real cutie-pie. The Marine's best friend, spouses notwithstanding. Almost jamproof, self-lubricating, works under water or in a vacuum and can blow a hole through steel plate. All she asks is that you keep her clean and don't slam her around too much and she'll keep you alive."

Ripley hefted the weapon. It was bulky and awkward, stuffed with recoil-absorbent fiber to counter the push from the high-powered shells it fired. It was much more impressive than her flamethrower. She raised the muzzle and pointed it experimentally at the far wall.

"What do you think?" Hicks asked her. "Can you handle one?"

She looked back at him, her voice level. "What do I do?"

He nodded approvingly and handed her the magazine.

No matter how quiet he tried to be, Bishop still made noise as the portable flight terminal and his sack of equipment scraped along the bottom of the conduit. No human being could have maintained the pace he'd kept up since leaving Operations, but that didn't mean he could keep going indefinitely. There were limits even to a synthetic's abilities.

Enhanced vision enabled him to perceive the walls of the pitch-dark tunnel as it continued receding ahead of him. A human would have been totally blinded in the cylindrical duct. At least he didn't have to worry about losing his way. The conduit provided almost a straight shot to the transmitter tower.

An irregular hole appeared in the right-hand wall, admitting a feeble shaft of light. Among the emotions that had been programmed into him was curiosity. He paused to peer through the acid-etched crack. It would be nice to be able to take a bearing in person instead of having to rely exclusively on the computer printout of the service-shaft plans.

Drooling jaws flashed toward his face to slam against the enclosing steel with a vicious scraping sound.

Bishop flattened himself against the far side of the conduit as the echo of the attack rang along the metal. The curve of the wall where the jaws had struck bent slightly inward. Hurriedly he resumed his forward crawl. To his considerable surprise the attack was not repeated, nor could he sense any apparent pursuit.

Maybe the creature had simply sensed motion and had struck blindly. When no reaction had been forthcoming from inside the duct, there was no reason for it to strike again. How did it detect potential hosts? Bishop went through the motions of breathing without actually performing respiration. Nor did he smell of warmth or blood. To a marauding alien an android might seem like just another piece of machinery. So long as one didn't attack or offer resistance, you might be able to walk freely among them. Not that such an excursion appealed to Bishop, since the reactions and motives of the aliens remained unpredictable, but it was a useful bit of information to have acquired. If the hypothesis could be verified, it might offer a means of studying the aliens.

Let someone else study the monsters, he thought. Let someone else seek verification. A bolder model than himself was required. He wanted off Acheron as much for his own sake as for that of the humans he was working with.

He glanced at his chronometer, faintly aglow in the darkness. Still behind schedule. Pale and strained, he tried to move faster.

Ripley had the stock of the big gun snugged up against her cheek. She was doing her best to keep pace with Hicks's instructions, knowing that they didn't have much time, knowing that if she had to use the weapon, she wouldn't be able to ask a second time how something worked. Hicks was as patient with her as possible, considering that he was trying to compress a complete weapons instruction course into a couple of minutes.

The corporal stood close behind her, positioning her arms as he explained how to use the built-in sight. It required a mutual effort to ignore the intimacy of their stance. There was little enough warmth in the devastated colony, little enough humanity to cling to, and this was the first physical, rather than verbal, contact between them.

"Just pull it in real tight," he was telling her. "Despite the built-in absorbers, it'll still kick some. That's the price you have to pay for using shells that'll penetrate just about anything." He indicated a readout built into the side of the stock. "When this counter reads zero, hit this." He ran a thumb over a button, and the magazine dropped out, clattering on the floor.

"Usually we're required to recover the used ones: they're expensive. I wouldn't worry about following regs just now."

"Don't worry," she told him.

"Just leave it where it falls. Get the other one in quick." He handed her another magazine, and she struggled to balance the heavy weapon with one hand while loading with the other. "Just slap it in hard, it likes abuse." She did so and was rewarded with a sharp click as the magazine snapped home. "Now charge it." She tapped another switch. A red telltale sprang to life on the side of the arming mechanism.

Hicks stepped back, eyed her firing stance approvingly. "That's all there is to it. You're ready for playtime again. Give it another run-through."

Ripley repeated the procedure: release magazine, check, reload, arm. The gun was awkward physically, comforting mentally. Her hands were trembling from supporting the weight. She lowered the barrel and indicated the metal tube that ran underneath.

"What's this for?"

"That's the grenade launcher. You probably don't want to mess with that. You've got enough to remember already. If you have to use the gun, you want to be able to do it without thinking."

She stared back at him. "Look, you started this. Now show me everything. I can handle myself."

"So I've noticed."

They ran through sighting procedures again, then grenade loading and firing, a complete course in fifteen minutes. Hicks showed her how to do everything short of breaking down and cleaning the weapon. Satisfied that she'd missed nothing, she left him to ponder the tactical console's readouts as she headed for Medical to check on Newt. Slung from its field straps, her newfound friend bounced comfortingly against her shoulder.

She slowed when she heard footsteps ahead, then relaxed. Despite its greater bulk, an alien would make a lot less noise than the lieutenant. Gorman emerged from the doorway, looking weak but sound. Burke was right behind him. He barely glanced at her. That was fine with Ripley. Every time the Company representative opened his mouth, she had an urge to strangle him, but they needed him. They needed every hand they could get, including those stained with blood. Burke was still one of them, a human being.

Though just barely, she thought.

"How do you feel?" she asked Gorman.

The lieutenant leaned against the wall for support and put one hand to his forehead. "All right, I guess. A little dizzy. One beauty of a hangover. Look, Ripley, I—"

"Forget it." No time to waste on useless apologies. Besides, what had happened wasn't entirely Gorman's fault. Blame for the fiasco beneath the atmosphere-proessing station needed to be apportioned among whoever had been foolish or incompetent enough to have put him in command of the relief team. Gorman's lack of experience aside, no amount of training could have prepared anyone for the actuality of the aliens. How do you organize combat along accepted lines of battle with an enemy that's as dangerous when it's bleeding to death as it is when it's alive? She pushed past him and into the Med lab.

Gorman followed her with his eyes, then turned to head up the corridor. As he did so he encountered Vasquez approaching from the other direction. She regarded him out of cold, slitted eyes. Sweat stained her colorful bandanna and plastered it to her dark hair and skin.

"You still want to kill me?" he said quietly.

Her reply mixed contempt with acceptance. "It won't be necessary." She continued past him, striding toward the next checkpoint.

With Gorman and Burke gone, Medical was deserted. She crossed through to the operating theater where she'd left

Newt. The light was dim, but not so weak that she couldn't make out the empty bed. Fear racing through her like a drug, she spun, her eyes frantically scanning the room, until a thought made her bend to look beneath the cot.

She relaxed, the tension draining back out of her. Sure enough, the girl was curled up against the wall, jammed as far back in as she could get. She was fast asleep, Casey clutched tightly in one small hand.

The angelic expression further reassured Ripley, innocent and undisturbed despite the demons that had plagued the child through waking as well as through sleeping hours. Bless the children, she thought, who can sleep anyplace through anything.

Carefully she laid the rifle on the cot. Getting down on hands and knees, she crawled beneath the springs. Without waking the girl she slipped both arms around her. Newt twitched in her sleep, instinctively snuggling her body closer to the adult's comforting warmth. A primal gesture. Ripley turned slightly on her side and sighed.

Newt's face contorted with the externalization of some private, tormented dreamscape. She cried out inarticulately, a vague dream-distorted plea. Ripley rocked her gently.

"There, there. Hush. It's all right. It's all right."

Several of the high-pressure cooling conduits that encircled the massive atmosphere-processing tower had begun to glow red with excess heat. High-voltage discharges arced around the conical crown and upper latticework, strobing the blighted landscape of Acheron and the silent structures of Hadley town with irregular, intense flashes of light. It would have been obvious to anyone that something was drastically wrong with the station. Damping units fought to contain a reaction that was already out of control. They continued, anyway. They were not programmed for futility.

Across from the landing platform a tall metal spire poked

toward the clouds. Several parabolic antennae clustered around the top, like birds flocking to a tree in wintertime.

At the base of the tower a solitary figure stood hunched over an open panel, his back facing into the wind.

Bishop had the test-bay cover locked in the open position and had managed to patch the portable terminal console into the tower's instrumentation. Thus far everything had gone as well as anyone dared hope. It hadn't started out that way. He'd arrived late at the tower, having underestimated the length of time it would take him to crawl through the conduit. As if by way of compensation, the preliminary checkout and testing had come off without a hitch, enabling him to make up some of that lost time. Whether he'd made up enough remained to be seen.

His jacket lay draped over the keyboard and monitor of the terminal to shield them from blowing sand and dust. The electronics were far more sensitive to the inclement weather than he was. The last several minutes had seen him typing frenetically, his fingers a blur on the input keys. He accomplished in a minute what would have taken a trained human ten.

Had he been human he might have uttered a small prayer. Perhaps he did anyway. Synthetics have their own secrets. He surveyed the keyboard a last time and muttered to himself.

"Now, if I did it right, and nothing's busted inside . . ." He punched a peripheral function key inscribed with the signal word ENABLE.

Far overhead, the *Sulaco* drifted patiently and silently in the emptiness of space. No busy figures moved through its empty corridors. No machines hummed efficiently as they worked the huge loading bay. Instruments winked on and off silently, maintaining the ship in its geo-stationary orbit above the colony.

A klaxon sounded, though there were none to hear it. Rotating warning lights came to life within the vast cargo hold, though there was no one to witness the interplay of red, blue, and green. Hydraulics whined. Immensely powerful lifters rumbled along their tracks as the second dropship was trundled out on its overhead rack. Wheels locked in place, and pulleys and levers took over. The shuttle was lowered into the gaping drop bay.

As soon as it was locked in drop position, service booms and automatic decouplers extended from walls and floor to plug into the waiting vessel. Predrop fueling and final check-out commenced. These were mundane, routine tasks for which human attention was unnecessary. Actually the ship could do the job better without any people around. They would only get in the way and slow down the operation.

Engines were brought on-line, shut down, and restarted. Locks were cycled open and sealed shut. Internal commu-nications flared to life and exchanged numerical sequences with the *Sulaco*'s main computer. A recorded announcement boomed across the vast, open chamber. Procedure required it, even though there was no one present to listen.

"Attention. Attention. Final fueling operations have be-gun. Please extinguish all smoking materials."

Bishop witnessed none of the activity, saw no lights rotating rapidly, heard no warning. He was satisfied none-theless. The tiny readouts that came alive on the portable guidance console were as eloquent as a Shakespearean sonnet. He knew that the dropship had been prepared and that fueling was taking place because the console told him so. He'd done more than make contact with the *Sulaco*: he was communi-cating. He didn't have to be there in person. The portable was his electronic surrogate. It told him everything he needed to know, and what it told him was good.

XII

She hadn't intended to go to sleep. All she'd wanted was to share a little space, some warmth, and a few moments of quiet with the girl. But her body knew what she needed better than she did. When she relinquished control and allowed it the chance to minister to its own requirements, it took over immediately.

Ripley awoke with a start and just missed banging her head against the underside of the cot. She was wide-awake instantly.

Dim light from the Med lab filtered into the operating room. Checking her watch, she was startled to see that more than an hour had passed. Death could have visited and departed in that much time, but nothing seemed to have changed. No one had come in to wake her, which wasn't surprising. Their minds were occupied with more important matters. The fact that she'd been left alone was in itself a good sign. If the final assault had begun, Hicks or someone else surely would have rousted her out of the warm corner beneath the bed by now.

Gently she disengaged herself from Newt, who slept on, oblivious to adult obsessions with time. Ripley made sure the small jacket was pulled up snugly around the girl's chin before turning to crawl out from beneath the cot. As she turned to roll, she caught another glimpse of the rest of the Med lab— and froze.

The row of stasis cylinders stood just inside the doorway that led toward the rest of Hadley central. Two of them were dark, their tops hinged open, the stasis fields quiescent. Both were empty.

Hardly daring to breathe, she tried to see into every dark corner, under every counter and piece of freestanding equipment. Unable to move, she frantically tried to assess the situation as she nudged the girl sleeping behind her with her left hand.

"Newt," she whispered. Could the things sense sound waves? They had no visible ears, no obvious organs of hearing, but who could tell how primitive alien senses interpreted their environment? "Newt, wake up."

"What?" The girl rolled over and rubbed sleepily at her eyes. "Ripley? Where are—"

"Shssh!" She put a finger to her lips. "Don't move. We're in trouble."

The girl's eyes widened. She responded with a single nod, now as wide-awake and alert as her adult protector. Ripley didn't have to tell her a second time to be quiet. During her solitary nightmare sojourn deep within the conduits and service ducts that honeycombed the colony, the first thing Newt had learned was the survival value of silence. Ripley pointed to the sprung stasis tubes. Newt saw and nodded again. She didn't so much as whimper.

They lay close to each other and listened in the darkness. Listened for sounds of movement, watching for lethal low-slung shapes skittering across the polished floor. The compact space heater hummed efficiently nearby.

Ripley took a deep breath, swallowed, and started to move. Reaching up, she grabbed the springs that lined the underside of the cot and began trying to push it away from the wall. The squeal of metal as the legs scraped across the floor was jarringly loud in the stillness.

When the gap between bed rail and wall was wide enough, she cautiously slid herself up, keeping her back pressed against the wall. With her right hand she reached across the mattress for the pulse-rifle. Her fingers groped among the sheets and blanket.

The pulse-rifle was gone.

Her eyes cleared the rim of the bed. Surely she'd left it lying there in the middle of the mattress! A faint hint of movement caught her attention, and her head snapped around to the left. As it did so, something that was all legs and vileness jumped at her from its perch on the foot of the bed. She uttered a startled, mewling cry of pure terror and ducked back down. Horny talons clutched at her hair as the loathsome shape struck the wall where her head had been a moment earlier. It slid, fighting for a grip while simultaneously searching for the vulnerable face that had shown itself a second ago.

Rolling like mad and digging her bare fingers into the springs, Ripley slammed the cot backward, pinning the teratoid against the wall only centimeters above her face. Its legs twitched and writhed with maniacal ferocity while the muscular tail banged against springs and wall like a demented python. It emitted a shrill, piercing noise, a cross between a squeal and a hiss.

Ripley heaved Newt across the floor and, in a frenzied scramble, rolled out after her. Once clear, she put both hands against the side of the cot and shoved harder against the imprisoned facehugger. Timing her move carefully, she flipped the cot and managed to trap it underneath one of the metal rails.

Clutching Newt close to her, she backed away from the overturned bed. Her eyes were in constant motion, darting from shadow to cupboard, searching out every corner. The whole lab area was fraught with fatal promise. As they retreated, the facehugger, displaying terrifying strength for something so small, shoved the bulk of the bed off its body and scuttled away beneath a bank of cabinets. Its multiple legs were a blur of motion.

Trying to keep to the center of the room as much as possible, Ripley continued backing toward the doorway. As soon as her back struck the door, she reached up to run a hand over the wall switch. The barrier at her back should have rolled aside. It didn't move. She hit the switch again then started pounding on it, regardless of the noise she was making. Nothing. Deactivated, broken, it didn't matter. She tried the light switch. Same thing. They were trapped in the darkness.

Trying to keep her eyes on the floor in front of them, she used one fist to pound on the door. Dull thunks resounded from the acoustically dampened material. Naturally the entrance to the operating theater would be soundproofed. Wouldn't want unexpected screams to unsettle a queasy colonist who happened to be walking past.

Keeping Newt with her, she edged away from the door and around the wall until they were standing behind the big observation window that fronted on the main corridor. Hardly daring to spare a glance away from the threatening floor, she turned and shouted.

"Hey—hey!"

She hammered desperately on the window. No one appeared on the other side of the triple-glazed transparency. A scrabbling noise from the floor made her whirl. Now Newt began to whimper, feeding off the adult's fear. Desperately Ripley stepped out in line with the wall-mounted video surveillance pickup and began waving her arms.

"Hicks! Hicks!"

There was no response, not from the pickup, nor from the empty room on the other side of the glass. The camera didn't pan to focus on her and no curious voice came from its speaker. In frustration Ripley picked up a steel chair and slammed it against the observation window. It bounced off without even scarring the tough material. She kept trying.

Wasting her strength. The window wasn't going to break, and there was no one in the outer lab to witness her frantic efforts. She put the chair aside and struggled to control her breathing as she surveyed the room.

A nearby counter yielded a small, high-beam examination light. Switching it on, she played the narrow beam over the walls. The circle of light whipped over the stasis tubes, past tall assemblies of surgical and anaesthesiological equipment, over flush-mounted storage bins and cabinets and research instrumentation. She could feel Newt shaking next to her as she clung to the tall woman's leg.

"Mommy—Mommmyyyy..."

Perversely it helped to steady Ripley. The child was completely dependent on her, and her own obvious fear was only making the girl panic. She swept the beam across the ceiling, brought it back to something. An idea took hold.

Removing her lighter from a jacket pocket, she hastily crumpled together a handful of paper gleaned from the same cabinet that had provided the beam. Moving as slowly as she dared, she boosted Newt up onto the surgical table that occupied the center of the room, then clambered up after her.

"Mommy—I mean, Ripley—I'm scared."

"I know, honey," she replied absently. "Me too."

Twisting the paper tightly, she touched the lighter's flame to the top of her improvised torch. It caught instantly, blazing toward the ceiling. She raised her hand and held the fire toward the temperature sensor at the bottom of one of the Med lab's fire-control sprinkler heads. Like much of the self-contained safety equipment that was standard issue for frontier worlds, the sprinkler had its own battery-powered backup power supply. It wasn't affected by whatever had killed the door and the lights.

The flames rapidly consumed her handful of paper, threatening to burn her ungloved skin. She gritted her teeth and held tight to the torch as it illuminated the room, bouncing off the mirror-bright surface of the globular surgical instrument cluster that hung suspended above the operating table.

"Come on, come *on*," she muttered tightly.

A red light winked to life on the side of the sprinkler head as the flames from her makeshift torch finally got hot enough to trigger internal sensors. As it was activated, the sensor automatically relayed its information to the other sprinklers set into the ceiling. Water gushed from several dozen outlets, flooding cabinets and floor with an artificial downpour. Simultaneously the Operations complex fire alarm came to life like a waking giant.

In Operations central, Hicks jumped at the sound of the alarm. His gaze darted from the tactical console to the main computer screen. One small section of the floor plan was flashing brightly. He rose and bolted for the exit, shouting into his headset pickup as he ran.

"Vasquez, Hudson, meet me in Medical! We got a fire!" Both troopers abandoned their guard positions and moved to rendezvous with the corporal.

Ripley's clothes clung to her as the sprinklers continued to drench the room and everything in it. The siren continued to hoot wildly. Between its steady howl and the splatter of water on metal and floor, it was impossible to hear anything else.

She tried to see through the heavy spray, wiping water and hair away from her eyes. One elbow banged against the surgical multiglobe and its assortment of cables, high-intensity lights, and tools, setting it swaying. She glanced at it and turned away to resume her inspection of the room. Something made her look a second time.

The something leapt at her face.

Falling water and the shrieking siren drowned out the sound of her scream as she stumbled backward, falling off the table and splashing to the floor, arms flailing, legs kicking wildly. Newt screamed and scrambled clear as Ripley hurled the chittering facehugger away. It slammed into a wall, clung there like an obscene parody of a climbing tarantula, then leapt back at her as though propelled by a steel spring.

Ripley scrambled desperately, pulling equipment down

on herself, trying to put something solid between her and the abomination as she retreated. It went over, under, or around everything she heaved in its path, its multijointed legs a frenzy of relentless motion. Claws caught at her boots and it scuttled up her body. She pushed at it again, the feel of the slick, leathery hide making her nauseous. The one thing she dared not do was throw up.

It was unbelievably strong. When it had jumped at her from atop the multiglobe, she'd managed to fling it away before it could get a good grip. This time it refused to be dislodged, hung on tight as it ascended her torso. She tried to rip at it, to pull it away, but it avoided her hands as it climbed toward her head with single-minded purpose. Newt screamed abjectly, backing away until she was pressed up against a desk in one corner.

With a last, desperate gesture Ripley slid both hands up her chest until they blocked her face, just as the facehugger arrived. She pushed with all her remaining strength, trying to force it away from her. As she fought, she stumbled blindly, knocking over equipment, sending instruments flying. On the wet floor her feet threatened to slip out from under her. Water continued to pour from the ceiling, flooding the room and blinding her. It also hindered the facehugger's movements somewhat, but it made it impossible for her to get a strong grip on its body or legs.

Newt continued to scream and stare. In consequence she failed to see the crablike legs that appeared above the rim of the desk she was leaning against. But her ability to sense motion had become almost as acute as that of the sentry-gun sensors. Whirling, she jammed the desk against the wall, fear lending strength to her small form. Pinned against the wall, the creature writhed wildly, fighting to free itself with its legs and tail as she leaned against the desk and wailed.

"Ripleyyy!"

The desk bounced and shuddered with the teratoid's

struggles. It slipped one leg free, then another. A third, as it began to squeeze itself out of the trap.

"*Ripleeyyy!*"

The facehugger's legs clawed at Ripley's head, trying to reach behind it to interlock even as she whipped her face from side to side. As it fought for an unbreakable grip it extruded the ovipositorlike tubule from its ventral opening. The organ pushed wetly at Ripley's arms, trying to force its way between.

A shape appeared outside the observation window, dim behind mist-shrouded glass. A hand wiped a clear place. Hicks's face pressed against the glass. His eyes grew wide as he saw that was happening inside. There was no thought of trying to repair the inoperative door mechanism. He stepped back and raised the muzzle of his pulse-rifle.

The heavy shells shattered the triple-paned barrier in several places. The corporal then dove at the resulting spiderweb patterns and exploded into the room in a shower of glittering fragments, a human comet with a glass tail. He hit the floor rolling, his armor grinding through the shards and protecting him from their sharp edges, sliding across to where the facehugger finally got its powerful tail secured around Ripley's throat. It began to choke her and pull itself closer to her face.

Hicks slipped his fingers around the thrashing arachnoidal limbs and pulled with superhuman force. Between the two of them they forced the monstrosity away from her face.

Hudson followed Hicks into the room, stared a moment at Ripley and the corporal as they struggled with the facehugger. Then he spotted Newt leaning against the desk. He shoved her aside, sending her spinning across the damp floor, and, in the same motion, raised his rifle to blast the second parasite to bits before it could crawl free of the desk's imprisoning bulk. Acid splattered, chewing into desk, wall, and floor as the crablike body was blown apart.

Gorman leaned close to Ripley and got both hands around

the end of the facehugger's tail. Like a herpetologist removing a boa constrictor from its favorite branch, he unwound it from her throat. She gasped, swallowing air and water and choking spasmodically. But she kept her grip on it as the three of them held it between them.

Hicks blinked against the spray, nodded to his right. "The corner! Together. Don't let it keep a grip on you." He glanced over his shoulder toward the watching Hudson. "Ready?"

"Do it!" The comtech raised his weapon.

The three of them threw the thing into the empty corner. It scrabbled upright in an instant and jumped back at them with demented energy. Hudson's shot caught it in midair, blowing it apart. The heavy downpour from the sprinklers helped to localize the resultant gush of acid. Smoke began to mix with water vapor as the yellow liquid ate into the floor.

Gagging, Ripley fell to her knees. Red streaks like rope burns scarred her throat. As she knelt next to Hicks and Hudson the sprinklers finally shut down. Water dripped from cabinets and equipment, racing away through the holes the acid had eaten in the floor. The fire siren died.

Hicks was staring at the stasis cylinders. "How did they get out of there? You can't break a stasis field from the inside." His gaze rose to the security pickup mounted on the far wall. "I was watching the monitors. Why didn't I see what was going on here?"

"Burke." It came out as a long wheeze. "It was Burke."

It was very quiet in Operations. Everyone's thoughts were racing at breakneck speed, but no one spoke. None of the thoughts were pleasant. Finally Hudson gestured at the subject of all this solemn contemplation and spoke with his usual eloquence.

"I say we grease him right now."

Burke tried hard not to stare at the menacing muzzle of the comtech's pulse-rifle. One twitch of Hudson's finger and the Company rep knew his head would explode like an over-

ripe melon. He managed to maintain an icy calm betrayed
only by the isolated beads of sweat that dotted his forehead.
The last five minutes had seen him compose and discard half
a dozen speeches as he decided it was best to say nothing.
Hicks might listen to his arguments, but the wrong word,
even the wrong movement, could set any of the others off.
In this he was quite correct.

The corporal was pacing back and forth in front of the
Company rep's chair. Occasionally he would look down at
him and shake his head in disbelief.

"I don't get it. It doesn't make any sense."

Ripley crossed her arms as she regarded the man-shape
in the chair. In her eyes it had ceased to be human. "It makes
plenty of sense. He wanted an alien, only he couldn't figure
out a way to sneak it back through Gateway quarantine. I
guaranteed him I'd inform the appropriate authorities if he
tried it. That was *my* mistake."

"Why would he want to try something like that?" Hicks
bemusement was plain on his face.

"For weapons research. Bioweapons. People—and I use
the word advisedly—like him do things like that. If it's new
and unique, they see a profit in it to the exclusion of everything else." She shrugged. "At first I thought he might be
different. When I figured otherwise, I made the mistake of
not thinking far enough ahead. I'm probably being too hard
on myself. I couldn't think beyond what a sane human being
might do."

"I don't get it," said Vasquez. "Where's his angle if
those things killed you? What's that get him?"

"He had no intention of letting them kill us—right away.
Not until we got his toys back to Earth for him. He had it
timed just right. Bishop'll have the dropship down pretty
soon. By then the facehuggers would've done their job, and
Newt and I would be flat-out with nobody knowing the cause.
The rest of you would have hauled us unconscious onto the
dropship. See, if we were impregnated, parasitized, whatever

you want to call it, and then frozen in hypersleep before we woke up, the effects of hypersleep would slow down the embyronic alien's growth just like it does ours. It wouldn't mature during the flight home. Nobody would know what we were carrying, and as long as our vital signs stayed stable, no one would think anything was radically wrong. We'd unload at Gateway, and the first thing the authorities would do is ship us Earthside to a hospital.

"That's where Burke and his Company cronies would step in. They'd claim responsibility, or bribe somebody, and check us into one of their own facilities where they could study us in private. Me and Newt."

She looked over at the frail figure of the girl sitting nearby. Newt hugged her knees to her chest and watched the proceedings with somber eyes. She was all but lost in the adult jacket someone had scrounged for her, scrunched down inside the copious padding and high collar. Her still-damp hair was plastered to her forehead and cheeks.

Hicks stopped pacing to stare at Ripley. "Wait a minute. *We*'d know about it. Maybe we wouldn't be sure, but we'd sure have it checked out the instant we arrived at the Station. No way would we let anybody ship you Earthside without a complete medical scan."

Ripley considered this, then nodded. "The only way it would work is if he sabotaged the sleep capsules for the trip back. With Dietrich gone, each of us would have to put ourselves into hypersleep. He could set his timer to wake him a few days down the road, climb out of his capsule, shut down everybody else's bio-support systems, and jettison the bodies. Then he could make up any story he liked. With most of your squad already killed by the aliens, and the details of the fight over on C-level recorded by your suit scanners and stored in the *Sulaco*'s records, it would be an easy matter to attribute your deaths to the aliens as well."

"He's *dead*." Hudson switched his attention from Ripley

back to the Company rep. "You hear that? You're dog meat, pal."

"This is a totally paranoid delusion." Burke saw no harm in finally speaking out, convinced that he couldn't hurt himself any more than he already had. "You saw how strong those things are. I had nothing to do with their escaping."

"Bullcrap. Nothing's strong enough to force its way out of a stasis tube," Hicks said evenly.

"I suppose after they climbed out they locked the operating room from the outside, shut down the emergency power to the overhead lights, hid my rifle, and killed the videoscan too." Ripley looked tired. "You know, Burke, I don't know which species is worse. You don't see *them* killing each other for a percentage."

"Let's waste him." Hicks's expression was unreadable as he gazed down at the Company rep. "No offense."

Ripley shook her head. Inside, the initial rage was giving way to a sickened emptiness. "Just find someplace to lock him up until it's time to leave."

"Why?" Hudson was shaking with suppressed anger, his finger taut on the trigger of his rifle.

Ripley glanced at the comtech. "Because I'd like to take him back. I want people to know what he's done. They need to know what happened to the colony here, and why. I want—"

The lights went out. Hicks turned immediately to the tactical console. The screen still glowed on battery power, but no images flashed across it because the power to the colony's computer had been cut. A quick check of Operations revealed that everything was out: power doors, videoscreens, sensor cameras, the works.

"They cut the power." Ripley stood motionless in the near blackness.

"What do you mean, *they* cut the power?" Hudson turned a slow circle and started backing toward a wall. "How could they cut the power, man? They're dumb animals."

"Who knows what they really are? We don't know enough about them to say that for sure yet." She picked up the pulse-rifle that Burke had taken and thumbed off the safety. "Maybe they act like that individually, but they could also have some kind of collective intelligence. Like ants or termites. Bishop talked about that, before he left. Termites build mounds three meters high. Leaf-cutter ants have agriculture. Is that just instinct? What is intelligence, anyway?" She glanced left.

"Stay close, Newt. The rest of you, let's get some trackers going. Come on, get moving. Gorman, keep an eye on Burke."

Hudson and Vasquez switched on their scanners. The glow of the motion-tracker sensors was comforting in the darkness. Modern technology hadn't failed them completely yet. With the two troopers leading the way, they headed for the corridor. With all power out to Operations, Vasquez had to slide the barrier aside manually.

Ripley's voice sounded behind the smartgun operator. "Anything?"

"Nothing here." Vasquez was a shadow against one wall.

She didn't have to put the same question to Hudson because everyone heard the comtech's tracker beep loudly. All eyes turned in his direction.

"There's something. I've got something." He panned the tracker around. It beeped again, louder this time. "It's moving. It's _inside_ the complex."

"I don't see anything." Vasquez's tracker remained silent. "You're just reading me."

Hudson's voice cracked slightly. "No. No! It ain't you. They're inside. Inside the perimeter. They're in _here_."

"Stay cool, Hudson." Ripley tried to see to the far end of the corridor. "Vasquez, you ought to be able to confirm."

The smartgun operator swung her tracker and her rifle in a wide arc. The last place she pointed both of them was directly behind her. The portable sensor let out a sharp beep.

"Hudson may be right."

Ripley and Hicks exchanged a glance. At least they wouldn't have to stand around anymore waiting for something to happen.

"It's game time," the corporal said tightly.

Ripley called to the pair of troopers. "Get back here, both of you. Fall back to Operations."

Hudson and Vasquez started to backtrack. The comtech's eyes nervously watched the dark tunnel they were abandoning. The tracker said one thing, his eyes another. Something was wrong.

"This signal's weird. Must be some interference or something. Maybe power arcing unevenly somewhere. There's movement all over the place, but I don't see a thing."

"Just get back here!" Ripley felt the sweat starting on her forehead, under her arms. Cold, like the pit of her stomach. Hudson turned and broke into a run, reaching the door a moment before Vasquez. Together they pulled it closed and locked the seal-tight.

Once inside, they began sharing out the remnants of their pitifully small armory. Flamethrowers, grenades, and lastly, a fair distribution of the loaded pulse-rifle magazines. Hudson's tracker continued to beep regularly, rising in a gradual crescendo.

"Movement!" He looked around wildly, saw only the silhouettes of his companions in the shadowed room. "Signal's clean. Can't be an error." Picking up the scanner, he panned the business end around the room. "I've got full range of movement at twenty meters."

Ripley whispered to Vasquez. "Seal the door."

"If I seal the door, how do we get to the dropship?"

"Same way Bishop did. Unless you want to try to walk out."

"Seventeen meters," Hudson muttered. Vasquez picked up her handwelder and moved to the door.

Hicks handed one of the flamethrowers to Ripley and began priming the other for himself. "Let's get these things lit." A moment later his sprang to life, a small, steady blue flame hissing from the weapon's muzzle like an oversize lighter. Ripley's flared brilliantly as she nudged the button marked IGNITE, which was set in the side of the handgrip.

Sparks showered around Vasquez as she began welding the door to the floor, ceiling, and walls. Hudson's tracker was going like mad now, though still not as fast as Ripley's heart.

"They learned," she said, unable to stand silence. "Call it instinct or intelligence or group analysis, but they learned. They cut the power and they've avoided the guns. They must have found another way into the complex, something we missed."

"We didn't miss anything," Hicks growled.

"Fifteen meters." Hudson took a step away from the door.

"I don't know how they did it. An acid hole in a duct. Something under the floors that was supposed to be sealed but wasn't. Something the colonists added or modified and didn't bother to insert into the official schematics. We don't know how up-to-date those plans are or when they were last revised to include all structural additions. I don't know, but there has to be something!" She picked up Vasquez's tracker and aimed it in the same direction as Hudson's.

"Twelve meters," the comtech informed them. "Man, this is one big signal. Ten meters."

"They're right on us." Ripley stared at the door. "Vasquez, how you coming?"

The smartgun operator didn't reply. Molten droplets singed her skin and landed, smoking, on her suit. She gritted her teeth and tried to hurry the welder along with some choice imprecations.

"Nine meters. Eight." Hudson announced the last number on a rising inflection and looked around wildly.

"Can't be." Ripley was insistent, despite the fact that

the tracker she was holding offered the same impossible readout. "That's inside the room."

"It's right, it's right." He turned his instrument sideways so she could see the tiny screen and its accompanying telltales. "Look!"

Ripley fiddled with her own tracker, rolling the fine-tuning controls as Hicks crossed to Hudson's position in a single stride.

"Well, you're not reading it right."

"I'm not!" The comtech's voice bordered on hysteria. "I know these little babies, and they don't lie, man. They're too simple to screw up." He was staring bug-eyed at the flickering readouts. "Six meters. Five. What the fu—?"

His eyes met Ripley's, and the same realization hit them simultaneously. Both bent their heads back, and they angled the trackers in the same direction. The beeping from both instruments became a numbing buzz.

Hicks climbed onto a file cabinet. Slinging his rifle over his shoulder and clutching the flamethrower tightly, he raised one of the acoustical ceiling panels and shined his flashlight inside.

It illuminated a vision Dante could not have imagined in his wildest nightmares, nor Poe in the grasp of an uncontrollable delirium.

XIII

The serviceway between the suspended acoustical ceiling and the metal roof was full of aliens. More aliens than he could quickly count. They clung upside down to pipes and beams, crawling like bats toward his light, glistening metallically. They covered the serviceway as far back as his light could shine.

He didn't need a motion tracker to sense movement behind him. As he snapped light and body around, the beam picked out an alien less than a meter away. It lunged at his face. Ducking wildly, the corporal felt claws capable of rending metal rake across the back of his armor.

As he tumbled back into Operations the army of infiltrating creatures detached en masse from their grips and claw holds. The flimsy suspended ceiling exploded, raining debris and nightmare shapes into the room below. Newt screamed, Hudson opened fire, and Vasquez gave Hicks a hand up as she let go with her flamethrower. Ripley scooped up Newt and stumbled backward. Gorman was at her side in an instant, pumping away with his own rifle. No one had time to notice Burke as the Company rep bolted for the only unblocked corridor, the one that connected Operations to Medical.

Flamethrowers brightened the chaos as they incinerated one attacker after another. Sometimes the burning aliens would stumble into one another, screeching insanely and adding to the confusion and conflagaration. They sounded much more like screams of anger than of pain. Acid poured from seared bodies, chewing gaping holes in the floor and adding to the danger.

"Medical!" Ripley was backing up slowly, keeping Newt close to her. "Get to Medical!" She turned and dashed for the connecting corridor.

The walls blurred around her, but at least the ceiling overhead stayed intact. She was able to concentrate on the corridor ahead. She caught a glimpse of Burke just as the Company rep cleared the heavy door into the lab area and slid it shut behind him. Ripley slammed into it and wrenched at the outside latch, just as it clicked home on the other side.

"Burke! Open the door! Burke, open the door!"

Newt tugged on Ripley's pants as she slipped behind her, pointing down the corridor. "Look!"

An alien was striding up the passageway toward them. A *big* alien. A shaking Ripley raised her rifle, trying to recall in an instant everything Hicks had taught her about the powerful weapon. She aimed the barrel straight at the middle of the glistening, skeletal chest and squeezed the trigger.

Nothing happened.

A hiss came from the advancing abomination. The outer jaws parted, slime splattering on the floor. Calm, calm, don't lose it, Ripley told herself. She checked the safety. It was off. A glance revealed a full magazine. Newt clung desperately to her leg and began to wail. Ripley's hands were trembling so violently, she nearly dropped the gun.

It was almost on top of them when she remembered that the first high-powered round had to be injected into the breech manually. She did so, jerked convulsively on the trigger. The rifle went off in the thing's face, hurling it backward. She turned away and covered her face as best she could in what had by now become an instinctive defensive gesture. But the energy of the shell impacting on the alien's body at point-blank range had thrown it back with such force that the spraying acid missed them completely.

The dampened recoil was still strong enough to send her off-balance body stumbling into the locked door. Her sight had been temporarily wiped by the nearness of the explosion, and she blinked furiously, trying to bring her eyes back into focus. Her ears rang with the concussion.

In Operations, Hicks looked up just in time to fire at a leaping outline, the force of the pulse shell hurling his assailant backward into a blazing cabinet. By this time the combined efforts of the flamethrowers had activated the fire-control system, and the overhead spinkler jets deluged the room. Water cascaded around the corporal, drenched the other soldiers. Some of it penetrated the central colony computer, ruining it for future use. But at least it didn't pool up around their legs. By now there were enough acid holes to drain it off. The fire siren wailed mindlessly, making it difficult for the combatants to hear each other and rendering any thought of unifed tactics impossible.

Hudson was screaming at the top of his lungs, his shrill tone audible over the siren's moan. "Let's go, let's go!"

"Medical!" Hicks yelled to him. He gestured frantically as he retreated toward the corridor. "Come on!"

As the comtech turned toward him the floor panels erupted under his feet. Clawed arms seized him, powerful triple fingers locking around his ankles and dragging him down. Another towering shape fell on him from behind, and he was gone in seconds, swallowed by the subfloor crawlway. Hicks let loose a rapid-fire burst in the direction of the cavity, hoping he got the comtech as well as his abductors, then turned and ran. Vasquez and Gorman were right behind him, the smart-gun operator laying down a murderous arc of fire as she covered their retreat.

Ripley was fumbling with the door handle when Newt pulled on her arm to attract her attention. The girl pointed silently to where the bleeding, half-blown-away alien was trying to rise to advance on them again. Flinching away from the blast and glare, Ripley drilled it a second time. The pulse-rifle's muzzle jerked ceilingward, and Newt covered her ears against the roar. This time the nightmare stayed down.

A voice sounded behind them. "Hold your fire!" Hicks and the others materialized out of the smoke and dust. They were grime-streaked and soaking wet. She stepped aside, gestured at the door.

"Locked." It wasn't necessary to explain how. Hicks just nodded.

"Stand clear." From his belt he removed a cutting torch that was a miniature of the one Vasquez had used earlier to seal first the fire-tunnel door and then the one leading into Operations. It made short work of the lock.

Inhuman shapes appeared at the far end of the corridor. Ripley wondered how they could track their prey so efficiently. They had no visible eyes or ears, no nostrils. Some unknown, special, alien sensing organ? Someday maybe some scientist would dissect one of the monstrosities and produce an answer. Someday after she was long dead, because she had no intention of being around when it was attempted.

Vasquez passed her flamethrower to Gorman and unslung her rifle. From a pouch she extracted several small egg-shaped objects and dumped them into the underslung barrel of the M-41A.

Gorman's eyes widened as he watched her load the grenades. "Hey, you can't use those in here!" He backed away from her.

"Right. I'm in violation of close-quarter combat regulations ninety-five through ninety-eight. Put me on report." She aimed the muzzle of the gun at the oncoming horde. *"Fire in the hole!"* She pumped up a round and let fly, turning her head slightly as she did so.

The blast from the grenade staggered Ripley and almost knocked Vasquez off her feet. Ripley was sure that she could see the smartgun operator smiling as the light from the explosion illuminated her battle-streaked face. Hicks wavered, the blue-hot flame of his torch shooting wildly upward for a moment. Then he straightened and resumed cutting.

The lock fell away from the door a moment later, clattering inside Medical. He reholstered the torch, stood up, and kicked the door open. Molten droplets went flying. Hicks and his companions ignored them. They were used to dodging spraying acid.

He turned just long enough to shout back at Vasquez. "Thanks a lot! Now I can't hear at all!"

She affected a look of bewilderment that was as genuine and heartfelt as her gentle nature, cupping a hand to one ear. "Say what?"

They stumbled into the ruined Med lab. Vasquez was the last one through. She turned, slid the heavy door halfway closed behind her, and in rapid succession fired three grenades through the resultant gap. An instant before they went off, she shut the door the rest of the way and ran. The triple boom sounded like a giant gong going off. The heavy metal security door was bent inward off its track.

Ripley had already crossed to the far side of the annex to try the door. This time she wasn't surprised to find it locked. She worked on it as Hicks used his torch to seal the bent door they'd just come through.

In the main lab Burke found himself backing across the dark floor. This time there would be no discussion of hypothetical iniquities, no polite give-and-take. He would be shot on sight. Maybe Hicks would hold off, and Gorman, but they would be unable to restrain Hudson or that crazy Vasquez woman.

Gasping, he crossed to the door that led out into the main complex. If the aliens were wholly preoccupied with his former colleagues, he might have a chance, might pull it off in spite of everything that had gone so dreadfully wrong. He could slip back into the colony proper, away from the fight, and make a roundabout run for the landing field. Bishop was amenable to argument and reason, as any good synthetic ought to be. Maybe he could convince him that everyone else was dead. If he could manage that small semantic feat and disable the android's communicator so that the others couldn't contact him to dispute the assertion, they'd have no choice but to take off immediately. If the directive was delivered with enough force and with no one to counter it, Bishop should comply.

His fingers reached for the door latch, froze without touching the metal. The latch was already turning, seemingly by itself. Almost paralyzed with fear, he staggered backward as the door was slowly opened from the *other* side.

The loud crack of a descending stinger was not heard by those in the annex.

Vasquez's grenade party had cleared the corridor long enough for Hicks to get the door sealed. It assured them of a few secure minutes, a holding gesture and no more. Now the corporal backed away from the doorway and readied his rifle for the final confrontation as something whammed against the barrier from outside, dimpling it in the middle. A second crash made metal squeal as the door began to separate from its frame.

Newt tugged insistently at Ripley's hand. Finally the adult took notice, forcing her attention away from the failing door.

"Come on! This way!" Newt was pulling Ripley toward the far wall.

"It won't work, Newt. I could barely fit in your hideaway. The others have armor on, and some of them are bigger. They won't be able to fit in there at all."

"Not *that* way," the girl said impatiently. "There's another."

Behind a desk an air vent was a dark rectangle against the wall. Newt expertly unlatched the protective grille and swung it open. She bent to duck inside, but Ripley pulled her back.

She glanced petulantly up at the adult. "I know where I'm going."

"I don't doubt that for a minute, Newt. You're just not going first, that's all."

"I've always gone first before."

"I wasn't here before, and you didn't have every alien on Acheron chasing you before." She walked over to Gorman and swapped her rifle for his flamethrower before he could think to protest. Pausing just long enough to tousle Newt's hair affectionately, she dropped to her knees and pushed into the shaft. Darkness unknown confronted her. At the moment it felt like a comforting old friend.

She looked back past her shoulder. "Get the others. You stay behind me."

Newt nodded vigorously and disappeared. She was back in seconds, diving into the duct to crowd close to Ripley as the older woman started forward. The girl was followed by Hicks, Gorman, and Vasquez. Between their armor and the big pulse-rifles they were hauling, it was a tight squeeze for the soldiers, but everyone cleared the opening. Vasquez paused long enough to pull the grille shut behind them.

If the tunnel narrowed down ahead or split off into smaller subducts, they'd be trapped, but Ripley wasn't worried. She had a great deal of confidence in Newt. At worst they'd have time to exchange polite farewells before drawing straws, or something similar, to decide who got to deliver the final coup de grace. A glance showed that the girl was right behind her.

Closer than that. Used to moving through the labyrinth of ducts at a much faster pace, Newt was all but crawling up Ripley's legs.

"Come on," the girl urged her repeatedly, "crawl faster."

"I'm doing the best I can. I'm not built for this, Newt. None of us are, and we don't have your experience. You're sure you know where we are?"

"Of course." The girl's voice was tinged with gentle

contempt, as though Ripley had just stated the most obvious thing in the world.

"And you know how to get to the landing field from here?"

"Sure. Keep going. A little farther on and this turns into a bigger tunnel. Then we go left."

"A bigger duct?" Hicks's voice reverberated from the metal walls as he spoke to Newt. "Girl, when we get home, I'm going to buy you the biggest doll you ever saw. Or whatever you want."

"Just a bed will be fine, Mr. Hicks."

Sure enough, another several minutes of rapid crawling brought them into the colony's main ventilation duct, right where Newt said it would be. It was spacious enough to allow them to rise from a crawl to a low crouch. Ripley's hands and knees screamed in relief, and their pace increased markedly. She kept banging her head on the low ceiling, but it was such a relief to be off all fours that she hardly noticed the occasional contact.

Despite their increased speed, Newt kept up easily. Where the adults had to bend to clear the top of the duct, she was able to stand and run. Armor clattered and banged in the confined tunnel, but at this point it was agreed that speed was more important than silence. For all they knew, the aliens had poor hearing and located them by smell.

They were coming up on an intersection where two main ducts crossed. Ripley slowed to fire a preventative blast from the flamethrower, methodically searing both passageways.

"Which direction?"

Newt didn't have to think. "Go right here." Ripley turned and started up the right-hand tunnel. The new duct was somewhat smaller than the colony main but still larger than the one they'd used to flee Medical.

Behind her and Newt, Hicks was addressing his headset pickup as they scuttled along. "Bishop, this is Hicks, do you read? Do you read, Bishop? Over." Silence greeted his initial query, but eventually his persistence was rewarded by a static-distorted but still recognizable voice.

"Yes, I read you. Not very well."

"Well enough," Hicks told him. "It'll get better the closer we come. We're on our way. Taking a route through the colony ductwork. That's why the bad connection. How are things at your end?"

"Good and bad," the synthetic replied. "Wind's picked up a lot. But the dropship's on its way. Just reconfirmed drop and release with the *Sulaco*. Estimated time of arrival: sixteen minutes plus. I've got my hands full trying to remote-fly in this wind." An electronic roar distorted the end of his sentence.

"What was that?" Hicks fiddled with his headset controls. "Say again, Bishop. Wind?"

"No. The atmosphere-processing station. Emergency venting system is approaching overload. It'll be close, Corporal Hicks. Don't stop for lunch."

In the darkness the soldier grinned. Not all synthetics were programmed for a sense of humor, and not all those that were knew how to make use of it. Bishop was something else.

"Don't worry. None of us are real hungry right now. We'll make it in time. Stand by out there. Over."

Preoccupied with his communication, he almost ran over Newt. The girl had halted in the duct. Looking beyond the girl, he saw that Ripley had stopped in front of her.

"What is it, what's wrong?"

"I'm not sure." Ripley's voice was ghostly in the darkness. "I could swear I saw—there!"

At the extreme limit of her flashlight Hicks made out a moving, obscene shape. Like a ferret, the alien had somehow managed to flatten its body just enough for it to fit inside the duct. There was additional movement visible beyond the intruder.

"Back, go back!" Ripley yelled.

Everyone tried to comply, jamming into each other in the confined tunnel. Behind them the sound of a grating being torn apart echoed through the duct. The grating collapsed with a sharp *spanggg*, and a deadly silhouette flowed through the resultant opening. Vasquez unlimbered her flamethrower and bathed the tunnel behind them in fire. Everyone knew it was a temporary victory. They were trapped.

Vasquez leaned to one side and stared upward. "Vertical shaft right here. Slick, no handholds." Her tone was clipped, matter-of-fact. "Too smooth to try a chimney ascent."

Hicks broke out his cutting torch, snapped it alight, and began slicing through the wall of the duct. Molten metal spattered his armor as sparks filled the confined tunnel with lurid light. Vasquez's flamethrower roared again, then sputtered out.

"Losing fuel." From the other direction the column of aliens continued to close on them, their advance slowed by their need to squeeze through the narrow walls.

Hicks had three-quarters of an exit cut in the side of the tunnel when the portable torch flickered and went out. Cursing, he braced his back against the opposite wall of the duct and kicked hard. The metal bent. He kicked again and it gave way. Without pausing to see what lay on the other side, he grabbed his rifle and dove through the opening...

... to emerge into a narrow serviceway thick with pipes and exposed conduits. Ignoring the still-hot edges of the cavity, he reached back inside to pull Newt to safety. Ripley followed, turned to aid Gorman. He hesitated at the opening long enough to see Vasquez's flamethrower run dry. The smartgun operator dumped it aside and drew her service revolver.

There was movement above her as a grotesque shape dropped down the vertical overhead duct. As the alien landed in the tunnel she rolled clear and let fly with the automatic pistol. The alien tumbled toward her as the small projectiles ripped into its skeletal body. Vasquez snapped her head to one side just in time to avoid the stinger. It buried itself into the metal wall next to her cheek. She kept firing, emptying the pistol into the thrashing form as she kicked at the powerful legs and quivering tail.

A gush of acid finally cut through her armor to sear her thigh. She let out a soft moan of pain.

Gorman froze in the tunnel. He glanced at Ripley. "They're right behind me. Get going." Their eyes met for as long as either of them dared spare. Then she turned and raced up the serviceway with Newt in tow. Hicks followed reluctantly, staring back at the opening he'd cut in the ventilation duct. Hoping. Knowing better.

Gorman crawled toward the immobilized smartgun operator. When he reached her, he saw the smoke pouring from the hole in her armor, shut out the gruesome smell of scarred flesh. His fingers locked around her battle harness, and he started dragging her toward the opening.

Too late. The first alien coming from the other direction had already reached and passed the hole Hicks had made. Gorman stopped pulling, leaned forward to look at Vasquez's leg. Where armor, harness, and flesh had been eaten away by the acid, bone gleamed whitely.

Her eyes were glazed when she looked up at him. Her voice was a harsh whisper. "You always were stupid, Gorman."

Her fingers seized his in a death grip. A special grip shared by a select few. Gorman returned it as best he was able. Then he handed her a pair of grenades and armed another couple for himself as the aliens closed in on them from both ends of the tunnel. He grinned and raised one of the humming explosives. She barely had enough strength to mimic the gesture.

"Cheers," he whispered. He couldn't tell if she was grinning back at him because he had closed his eyes, but he had a feeling she was. Something sharp and unyielding stroked his back. He didn't turn to see what it was.

"Cheers," he whispered feebly. He clicked one of his grenades against one of Vasquez's in the final toast.

Behind them, the serviceway lit up like the sun as Ripley, Newt, and Hicks pounded along full tilt. They were a long way from the opening the corporal had cut in the wall of the duct, but the shock wave from the quadruple explosion was still powerful enough to rock the whole level. Newt kept her balance best and broke out in front of the two adults. It was all Ripley and Hicks could do to keep up with her.

"This way, this way!" she was shouting excitedly. "Come on, we're almost there!"

"Newt, wait!" Ripley tried to lengthen her stride to catch up to the girl. The sound of her heart was loud in her ears, and her lungs screamed in protest with every step she took. The walls blurred around her. She was dimly aware of Hicks pounding along like a steam engine just behind her. Despite his armor, he probably could have outdistanced her, but he didn't try. Instead he laid back so he could protect against an attack from behind.

Ahead the corridor forked. At the end of the left-hand fork a narrow, angled ventilation chute led upward at a steep forty-five degrees. Newt was standing at its base, gesturing frantically.

"Here! This is where we go up."

Her body grateful for a respite no matter how temporary, Ripley slowed to a halt as she examined the shaft. It was a steep climb but not a long one. Dim light marked the end of the ascent. From above she could hear the wind booming like air blowing across the lip of a bottle. Narrow climbing ribs dimpled the smooth sides of the shaft.

She looked down to where the chute punched a hole in the floor and disappeared into unknown depths lost in darkness. Nothing stirred down there. Nothing came climbing toward them. They were going to make it.

She put her foot onto the first climbing rib and started

up. Newt followed as Hicks emerged from the main corridor behind them.

The girl turned to wave. "Just up here, Mr. Hicks. It's not as far as it looks. I've done it lots of tim—"

Rusted out by seeping water, worn through by the corrosive elements contained in Acheron's undomesticated atmosphere, the rib collapsed beneath her feet. She slipped, managed to catch another rib with one hand. Ripley braced herself against the dangerously slick surface of the chute, turned, and reached back for her. As she did so, she dropped her flashlight, watched it go skittering and bumping down the opening until its comforting glow faded from sight.

She strained until she was sure her arm was separating from her shoulder, her fingers groping for Newt's. No matter how far over she bent, they remained centimeters apart.

"Riiipplleeee . . ."

Newt's grip broke. As she went sliding down the chute Hicks made a dive for her, laying himself out, flat and indifferent to the coming impact. He slammed into the floor next to the chute, and his fingers dug into the collar of the girl's oversize jacket, holding the material in a death grip.

She slipped out of it.

Her scream reverberated up the chute as she vanished, plummeting down into darkness.

Hicks threw the empty jacket aside and stared at Ripley. Their eyes met for just a second before she released her own grasp and went sliding down the chute after Newt. As she slid, she pushed out with her feet, braking her otherwise uncontrolled descent.

Like the corridor above, the chute forked where it intersected the lower level. Her flashlight gleamed off on her right, and she shifted her weight so she would slide in that direction.

"Newt. Newt!"

A distant wail, plaintive and distorted by distance and intervening metal, floated back to her.

"Mommy—where are you?" Newt was barely audible. Had she taken the other chute?

The shaft bottomed out in a horizontal service tunnel. Her undamaged flashlight lay on the floor, but there was no sign of the girl. As Ripley bent to recover the light the cry reached her again, bouncing off the narrow walls.

"Moommmeee!"

Ripley started down the tunnel in what she hoped was the right direction. The wild slide down the chute had completely disoriented her. Newt's call came again. Fainter? Ripley couldn't tell. She turned a circle, panic growing inside her, her light illuminating only grime and dampness. Every projection contained grinning, slime-lubricated jaws, every hollow was a gaping alien mouth. Then she remembered that she was still wearing her headset. And she remembered something else. Something the corporal had given her that she'd given away in turn.

"Hicks, get down here. I need the locator for that bracelet you gave me." She cupped her hands to her mouth and shouted down the serviceway. "Newt! Stay wherever you are. We're coming!"

The girl was in a low, grottolike chamber where the other branch of the chute had dumped her. It was crisscrossed with pipes and plastic conduits and was flooded up to her waist. The only light came from above, through a heavy grating. Maybe Ripley's voice had also, she thought. Using the network of pipes, she started to climb.

A large, bulky object came sliding down the chute. Hicks wouldn't have found the description flattering, but Ripley was immensely relieved to see him no matter how rumpled he looked. The mere presence of another human being in that stygian, haunted tunnel was enough to push back the fear a little way.

He landed on his feet, clutching his rifle in one hand, and unsnapped the emergency location unit from his battle harness. "I gave *you* that bracelet," he said accusingly, even as he was switching the tracker on.

"And I gave it to Newt. I figured she'd need it more than I would, and I was right. It's a good thing I did it or we'd never find her in this. You can bawl me out later. Which way?"

He checked the tracker's readout, turned, and started off down the tunnel. It led them into a section of serviceway where the power hadn't been cut. Emergency lights still brightened ceiling and walls. They switched off their lights. Water dripped somewhere nearby. The corporal's gaze rarely strayed from the tracker's screen. He turned left.

"This way. We're getting close."

The locator led them to a large grate set in the floor—and a voice from below.

"Ripley?"

"It's us, Newt."

"Here! I'm here, I'm down here."

Ripley knelt at the edge of the grating, then wrapped her fingers around the center bar and pulled. It didn't budge. A quick inspection revealed that it was welded into the floor instead of being latched for easy removal. Peering down, she could just make out Newt's tear-streaked face. The girl reached upward. Her small fingers wriggled between the closely set bars. Ripley gave them a reassuring squeeze.

"Climb down off that pipe, honey. We're going to have to cut through this grate. We'll have you out of there in a minute."

The girl obediently backed clear, shinnying down the pipe she'd ascended as Hicks fired up his hand torch. Ripley glanced significantly in its direction, then met his eyes as she lowered her voice.

"How much fuel?" She was remembering how Vasquez's flamethrower had run out at a critical moment.

He looked away. "Enough." Bending, he began cutting through the first of the bars.

From below Newt could watch sparks shower blindingly as Hicks sliced through the hardened alloy. It was cold in the tunnel, and she was standing in the water again. She bit her lip and fought back tears.

She did not see the glistening apparition rising silently from the water behind her. It would not have mattered if she had. There was nowhere to run to, no safe air duct to duck into. For a moment the alien hovered over her, motionless, dwarfing her tiny form. Only when it moved again did she sense its presence and whirl. She barely had enough time to scream as the shadow engulfed her.

Ripley heard the scream and the brief splashing below and went completely berserk. The grating had been half cut away. She and Hicks wrenched and kicked at it until a portion bent downward. Another kick sent the chunk of crumpled metal tumbling into the water. Heedless of the red-hot edges, Ripley lunged through the opening, her light clutched in one hand, its beam slashing over pipes and conduits.

"Newt! Newt!"

The surface of the dark water reflected the light back up at her. It was placid and still after having swallowed the section of grille. Of the girl there was no sign. All that remained to show that she'd ever been there was Casey. As Ripley looked on helplessly, the doll head sank beneath the oily blackness.

Hicks had to drag her bodily out of the opening. She struggled blindly, trying to rip free of his embrace.

"No, noooo!"

It took all his strength and greater mass to wrestle her away from the opening. "She's *gone*," he said intensely. "There's nothing you or I or anybody else can do now. Let's go!" A glance showed something moving at the far end of the corridor that had led them to the grating. It might be nothing more than his eyes playing tricks on him. Eye tricks on Acheron could prove fatal.

Ripley was sliding rapidly into hysteria, screaming and

crying and flailing her arms and legs. He had to lift her clear of the floor to keep her from diving through the gap. A wild plunge into the water-filled darkness below was a short course to suicide.

"No! No! She's still alive! We have to—"

"All right!" Hicks roared. "She's alive. I believe it. But we gotta get moving. Now! You're not going to be able to catch her that way." He nodded at the hole in the floor. "She won't be waiting for you down there, but they will. Look." He pointed, and she stopped struggling. There was an elevator at the far end of the tunnel.

"If there's emergency power to the lights in this section, then maybe that's functioning too. Let's get out of here. Once we're up top, we can try to think this through where they can't sneak up on us."

He still had to half drag her to the elevator and push her inside.

The movement he'd detected at the far end of the tunnel coalesced into the advancing outline of an alien. Hicks practically broke the plastic as he jammed a thumb on the "up" button. The elevator's double doors began to close—not quite fast enough. The creature slammed one huge arm between them. As both humans looked on in horror, the automatic safety built into the elevator doors buzzed and began to part. The machine could not discriminate between human and alien.

The drooling abomination lunged toward them, and Hicks blew it away, firing his pulse-rifle at point-blank range. Too close. Acid sluiced between the closing doors to splash across his chest as he shielded Ripley with his armor. Fortunately none of the acid struck the elevator cables. The elevator began to ascend, clawing its way toward the surface on lingering emergency power.

Hicks tore at the quick-release catches on the harness as the powerful liquid ate through the composite-fiber armor. His plight was enough to galvanize Ripley out of her panic. She clawed at his straps, trying to help as much as she could.

Acid reached his chest and arm, and he yelled, shucking out of the combat armor like an insect shedding its old skin. The smoking plates fell to the floor, and the relentless acid began to eat through the metal underfoot. Acrid fumes filled the air inside the elevator, searing eyes and lungs.

After what seemed like a thousand years, the elevator ground to a halt. Acid ate through the floor and began to drip onto the cables and support wheels.

The doors parted and they stumbled out. This time it was Ripley who had to support Hicks. Smoke continued to rise from his chest, and he was doubled over in agony.

"Come on, you can make it. I thought you were a tough guy." She inhaled deeply, coughed, and inhaled again. Hicks choked, gritted his teeth, and tried to grin. After the foulness of the tunnels and ductways the less-than-idyllic air of Acheron smelled like perfume. "Almost there."

Not far ahead of them the sleek, streamlined shape of Dropship Two was descending erratically toward the landing grid like a dark angel, side-slipping as it fought its way through the powerful wind gusts just above the surface. They could see Bishop, his back to them, standing in the lee of the transmitter tower as he struggled with the portable guidance terminal to bring the dropship in. It sat down hard and slid sideways, coming to a halt near the middle of the landing pad. Except for a bent landing strut, the inelegant touchdown appeared to have left it undamaged.

She yelled. The synthetic turned to see the two of them stumbling out of a doorway in the colony building behind him. Putting the terminal down carefully, he ran to help, getting one powerful arm under Hicks and helping him toward the ship. As they ran, Ripley shouted to the android, her words barely audible over the gale.

"How much time?"

"Plenty!" Bishop looked pleased. He had reason to be. "Twenty-six minutes."

"We're not leaving!" She said this as they were staggering up the loading ramp into the warmth and safety of the ship.

Bishop gaped at her. "What? Why not?"

She studied him carefully, searching for the slightest suggestion of deception in his face and finding none. His question was perfectly understandable under the circumstances. She relaxed a little.

"Tell you in a minute. Let's get Hicks some medical and close this sucker up, and then I'll explain."

XIV

Lightning crackled around the upper rim of the failing atmosphere-processing station. Steam blasted from emergency vents. Columns of incandescent gas shot hundreds of meters into the sky as internal compensators struggled futilely to adjust temperature and pressure overloads that were already beyond correction.

Bishop was careful not to drift too close to the station as he guided the dropship toward the upper-level landing platform. As they approached, they passed over the ruined armored personnel carrier. A shattered, motionless hulk outside the station entryway, the APC had finally stopped smoking. Ripley stared as it slipped past beneath him, a monument to overconfidence and a misplaced faith in the ability of modern technology to conquer any obstacle. Soon it would evaporate along with the station and the rest of Hadley colony.

About a third of the way up the side of the enormous

cone that formed the processing station, a narrow landing platform jutted out into the wind. It was designed to accommodate loading skimmers and small atmospheric craft, not something the size of a dropship. Somehow Bishop managed to maneuver them in close. The platform groaned under the shuttle's weight. A supporting beam bent dangerously but held.

Ripley finished winding metal tape around the bulky project that had occupied her hands and mind for the past several minutes. She tossed the half-empty tape roll aside and inspected her handiwork. It wasn't a neat job, and it probably violated twenty separate military safety regulations, but she didn't give a damn. She wasn't going on parade, and there was no one around to tell her it was dangerous and impossible.

What she'd done while Bishop was bringing them in close to the station was to secure Hicks's pulse-rifle to the side of a flamethrower. The result was a massive, clumsy siamese weapons package with tremendous and varied firepower. It might even be enough to get her back to the ship alive—if she could carry it.

She turned back to the dropship's armory and began loading a satchel and her pockets with anything that might kill aliens: grenades; fully charged pulse-rifle magazines; shrapnel clips; and more.

Having programmed the dropship for automatic lift-off should the landing platform show signs of giving way, Bishop made his way aft from the pilot's compartment to help Hicks treat his injuries. The corporal lay sprawled across several flight seats, the contents of a field medical kit strewn around him. Working together, he and Ripley had managed to stanch the bleeding. With the aid of medication his body would heal. The dissolved flesh was already beginning to repair itself. But in order to reduce the pain to a tolerable level, he'd been forced to take several injections. The medication kept him halfway comfortable but blurred his vision and slowed his reactions. The only support he could give to Ripley's mad plan was moral.

Bishop tried to remonstrate. "Ripley, this isn't a very efficacious idea. I understand how you feel—"

"Do you?" she snapped at him without looking up.

"As a matter of fact, I do. It's part of my programming. It's not sensible to throw one life after another."

"She's *alive*." Ripley found an empty pocket and filled it with grenades. "They brought her here just like they brought all the others, and you know it."

"It seems the logical thing for them to do, yes. I admit there is no obvious reason for them to deviate from the pattern they have demonstrated thus far. That is not the point. The point is that even if she is here, it is unlikely that you can find her, rescue her, and fight your way back out in time. In seventeen minutes this place will be a cloud of vapor the size of Nebraska."

She ignored him, her fingers flying as she sealed the overstuffed satchel. "Hicks, don't let him leave."

He blinked weakly at her, his face taut with pain. The medication was making his eyes water. "We ain't going anywhere." He nodded toward her feet. "Can you carry that?"

She hefted her hybrid weapon. "For as long as I have to." Picking up the satchel, she slung it over one shoulder, then turned and strode to the crew door. She thumbed it open, waiting impatiently for it to cycle. Wind and the roar from the failing atmosphere processor rushed the gap. She stepped to the top of the loading ramp and paused for a last look back.

"See you, Hicks."

He tried to sit up, failed, and settled for rolling onto his side. One hand held a wad of medicinal gauze tight against his face. "Dwayne. It's Dwayne."

She walked back over to grab his hand. "Ellen."

That was enough. Hicks nodded, leaned back, and looked

satisfied. His voice was a pale shadow of the one she'd come to be familiar with. "Don't be long, Ellen."

She swallowed, then turned and exited, not looking back as the hatch closed behind her.

The wind might have blown her off the platform had she not been so heavily equipped. Set in the station wall opposite the dropship were the doors of a large freight elevator. The controls responded instantly to her touch. Plenty of power here. Too much power.

The elevator was empty. She entered and touched the contact switch opposite C-level. The bottom. The seventh level, she thought as the elevator began to descend.

It was slow going. The elevator had been designed to carry massive, sensitive loads, and it would take its time. She stood with her back pressed against the rear wall, watching bars of light descend. As the elevator descended into the bowels of the station the heat grew intense. Steam roared everywhere. She had difficulty breathing.

The slow pace of the descent allowed her time to remove her jacket and slip the battle harness she'd appropriated from the dropship's stores on directly over her undershirt. Sweat plastered her hair to her neck and forehead as she made a last check of the weaponry she'd brought with her. A bandolier of grenades fit neatly across the front of the harness. She primed the flamethrower, made sure it was full. Same for the magazine locked into the underside of the rifle. This time she remembered to chamber the initial round to activate the load.

Fingers nervously traced the place where marking flares bulged the thigh pockets of her jumpsuit pants. She fumbled with an unprimed grenade. It slipped between her fingers and fell to the floor, bouncing harmlessly. Trembling, she recovered it and slid it back into a pocket. Despite all of Hicks's detailed instructions, she was acutely aware that she didn't know anything about grenades and flares and such.

Worst of all was the fact that for the first time since

they'd landed on Acheron she was alone. Completely and utterly alone. She didn't have much time to think about it because the elevator motors were slowing.

The elevator hit bottom with a gentle bump. The safety cage enclosing the lift retracted. She raised the awkward double muzzle of rifle and flamethrower as the doors parted.

An empty corridor lay before her. In addition to the illumination provided by the emergency lighting, faint reddish glows came from behind thick metal bulges. Steam hissed from broken pipes. Sparks flared from overloaded, damaged circuits. Couplings groaned while stressed machinery throbbed and whined. Somewhere in the distance a massive mechanical arm or piston was going *ka-rank*, *ka-rank*.

Her gaze darted left, then right. Her knuckles were white above the dual weapon she carried. She had no flexible battle visor to help her, though in the presence of so much excess heat its infrared-imaging sensors wouldn't have been of much use, anyway. She stepped out into the corridor, into a scene designed by Piranesi, decorated by Dante.

She was struck by the aliens' presence as soon as she turned the first bend in the walkway. Epoxy-like material covered conduits and pipes, flowing smoothly up into the overhead walkways to blend machinery and resin together, creating a single chamber. She had Hicks's locator taped to the top of the flamethrower, and she looked at it as often as she dared. It was still functioning, still homing in on its single target.

A voice echoed along the corridor, startling her. It was calm and efficient and artificial.

"Attention. Emergency. All personnel must evacuate immediately. You now have fourteen minutes to reach minimum safe distance."

The locator continued to track; range and direction spelled out lucidly by its LED display.

As she advanced, she blinked sweat out of her eyes. Steam swirled around her, making it difficult to see more than a short distance in any direction. Flashing emergency lights lit an intersecting passageway just ahead.

Movement. She whirled, and the flamethrower belched napalm, incinerating an imaginary demon. Nothing there. Would the blast of heat from her weapon be noticed? No time to worry about maybes now. She resumed her march, trying not to shake as she concentrated on the locator's readouts.

She entered the lower level.

In the inner chambers now. The walls around her subsumed skeletal shapes, the bodies of the unfortunate colonists who had been brought here to serve as helpless hosts for embryonic aliens. Their resin-encrusted figures gleamed like insects frozen in amber. The locator's signal strengthened, leading her off to the left. She had to bend to clear a low overhang.

At each turning point or intersection she was careful to ignite a timed flare and place it on the floor behind her. It would be easy to get lost in the maze without the markers to help her find her way back. One passageway was so narrow, she had to turn sideways to slip through it. Her eyes touched upon one tormented face after another, each entombed colonist caught in a rictus of agony.

Something grabbed her. Her knees sagged, and the breath went out of her before she could even scream. But the hand was human. It was attached to an imprisoned body, surmounted by a face. A familiar face. Carter Burke.

"Ripley." The moan was barely human. "Help me. I can feel it inside. It's moving..."

She stared at him, beyond horror now. No one deserved this.

"Here." His fingers clutched convulsively around the grenade she handed him. She primed it and hurried on. The voice of the station boomed around her. There was a rising note of mechanical urgency in its tone.

"You now have eleven minutes to reach minimum safe distance."

According to the locator, she was all but on top of the target. Behind her the grenade went off, the concussion nearly knocking her off her feet. It was answered by a second, more forceful, eruption from deep within the station itself. A siren began to wail, and the whole installation shuddered. The locator led her around a corner. She tensed in anticipation. The locator's range finder read out zero.

Newt's tracer bracelet lay on the tunnel floor, the metal fabric shredded. The glow from its sender module was a bright, cheerless green. Ripley sagged against a wall.

It was over. All over.

Newt's eyes fluttered open, and she became aware of her surroundings. She had been cocooned in a pillarlike structure at the edge of a cluster of ovoid shapes: alien eggs. She recognized them right away. Before they'd been carried off or killed, the last desperate adult colonists had managed to acquire a few for study.

But those had all been empty, open at the tops. These were sealed.

Somehow the egg nearest her prison became aware of her stirrings. It quivered and then began to open, an obscene flower. Something damp and leathery stirred within. Transfixed by terror, Newt stared as jointed, arachnoid legs appeared over the lip of the ovoid. They emerged one at a time. She knew what was going to happen next, and she reacted the only way she could, the only way she knew how—she screamed.

Ripley heard, turned toward the sound, and broke into a run.

With horrible fascination Newt watched as the facehugger climbed out of the egg. It paused for a moment on the rim, gathering its strength and taking its bearings. Then it turned toward her. Ripley came pounding into the chamber as it poised to leap. Her finger tensed on the pulse-rifle's trigger. The single shell tore the crouching creature apart.

The flash from the muzzle illuminated the figure of a mature alien standing nearby. It spun and charged the intruder just in time for twin bursts from the rifle to catapult it backward. Ripley advanced on the corpse, firing again and again, a murderous expression on her face. The alien jerked onto its back, and she finished it with the flamethrower.

While it burned, she ran to Newt. The resinous material of the girl's cocoon hadn't hardened completely yet, and Ripley was able to loosen it enough for Newt to crawl free.

"Here." Ripley turned her back to the girl and bent her knees. "Climb aboard." Newt clambered up onto the adult's hips and locked her hands around Ripley's neck. Her voice was weak.

"I knew you'd come."

"So long as I could still breathe. Okay, we're getting out of here. I want you to hang on, Newt. Hang on real tight. I'm not going to be able to hold you, because I've got to be able to use the guns."

She didn't see the nod, but she felt it against her back. "I understand. Don't worry. I won't let go."

Ripley sensed movement off to their right. She ignored it as she blasted the eggs with the flamethrower. Only then did she turn it on the advancing aliens. One almost reached her, a living fireball, and she blew it apart with two bursts from the rifle. Ducking beneath a glistening cylindrical mass, she retreated. A piercing shriek filled the air, rising above the pounding of failing machinery, the wail of the emergency siren and the screech of attacking aliens.

She'd have seen it earlier if she'd looked up instead of straight ahead when she'd entered the egg chamber. It was just as well that she hadn't because, despite her determination, she might have faltered. A gigantic silhouette in the ruddy mist, the alien queen glowered above her egg cache like a great, gleaming insectoid Buddha. The fanged skull was horror incarnate. Six limbs, two legs and four taloned arms, were folded grotesquely over a distended abdomen. Swollen with eggs, it comprised a vast, tubular sac that was suspended from the latticework of pipes and conduits by a weblike membrane, as though an endless coil of intestine had been draped along the supporting machinery.

Ripley realized she'd passed right beneath part of the sac a moment earlier.

Inside the abdominal container countless eggs churned toward a pulsating ovipositor in a vile, organic assembly line. There they emerged, glistening and wet, to be picked up by tiny drones. These miniature versions of the alien warriors scuttled back and forth as they attended to the needs of both eggs and queen. They ignored the staring human in their midst as they concentrated with single-minded intensity on the task of transferring newly deposited eggs to a place of safety.

Ripley remembered how Vasquez had done it as she pumped the slide on the grenade launcher: pumped and fired four times. The grenades punched deep into the flimsy egg sac and exploded, blowing it to shreds. Eggs and tons of noisome, gelatinous material spilled over the floor of the chamber. The queen went berserk, screeching like a psychotic locomotive. Ripley laid about with the flamethrower, methodically igniting everything in sight as she retreated. Eggs shriveled in the inferno, and the figures of warriors and drones vanished amid frenzied thrashing.

The queen towered above the carnage, struggling in the flames. Two warriors closed in on Ripley. The pulse-rifle clicked empty. Smoothly she ejected the magazine, slammed another one home, and held the trigger down. Her attackers vanished in the homicidal hail of fire.

It didn't matter if it moved or not. She blasted everything that didn't look wholly mechanical as she ran for the elevator, setting fire to equipment and destroying controls and instrumentation together with attacking aliens. Sweat and steam half blinded her, but the flares she'd dropped to mark her path shone brightly, jewels set among the devastation. Sirens howled around her, and the station rocked with internal convulsions.

She almost ran past one flare, skidded to a halt, and turned toward it. She staggered on as if in a dream, her lungs straining no longer. Her body was so pumped up, she felt as though she were flying across the metal floor.

Behind her, the queen detached from the ruined egg sac, ripping it away from her abdomen. Rising on legs the size of temple pillars, she lumbered forward, crushing machinery, cocoons, drones, and anything else in her path.

Ripley used the flamethrower to sterilize the corridor ahead, letting loose incinerating blasts at regular intervals, firing down side corridors before she crossed them to keep from being surprised. By the time she and Newt reached the freight elevator, the weapon's tank was empty.

The elevator she'd used for the descent had been demolished by falling debris. She hit the call button on its companion and was rewarded by the whine of a healthy motor as the second metal cage commenced its slow fall from the upper levels. An enraged shriek made her turn. A distant, glistening shape like a runaway crane was trying to batter its way through intervening pipes and conduits to reach them. The queen's skull scraped the ceiling.

She checked the pulse-rifle. The magazine was empty, and she was out of refills, having spent shells profligately while rescuing Newt. No more grenades, either. She tossed the useless dual weapon aside, glad to be rid of the weight.

The cage's descent was too slow. There was a service ladder set inside the wall next to the twin elevator shafts, and she scrambled up the first rungs. Newt was as light as a feather on her back.

As she dove into the stairwell a powerful black arm shot through the doorway like a piston. Razor-sharp talons slammed into the floor centimeters from her legs, digging into the metal.

Which way now? She was no longer fearful, had no time

to panic. Too many other things to concentrate on. She was too busy to be terrified.

There: an open stairwell leading to the station's upper levels. It rocked and shuddered as the huge installation began tearing itself to bits beneath her. Behind her, the floor buckled as something incredibly powerful threw itself insanely against the metal wall. Talons and jaws pierced the thick alloy plates.

"You now have two minutes to reach minimum safety distance," the sad voice of the station informed any who might be listening.

Ripley fell, banging one knee against the metal stairs. Pain forced her to pause. As she caught her breath the sound of the elevator motors starting up made her look back down through the open latticework of the building. The elevator cage had begun to ascend. She could hear the overloaded cables groaning in the open shaft.

She resumed her heavenward flight, the stairwell becoming a mad blur around her. There was only one reason why the elevator would resume its ascent.

At last they reached the doorway that led out onto the upper-level landing platform. With Newt still somehow clinging to her, Ripley slammed the door open and stumbled out into the wind and smoke.

The dropship was gone.

"*Bishop!*" The wind carried her scream away as she scanned the sky. "Bishop!" Newt sobbed against her back.

A whine made her turn as the straining elevator slowly rose into view. She backed away from the door until she was leaning against the narrow railing that encircled the landing platform. It was ten levels to the hard ground below. The skin of the heaving processing station was as smooth as glass. They couldn't go up and they couldn't go down. They couldn't even dive into an air duct.

The platform shook as an explosion ripped through the bowels of the station. Metal beams buckled, nearly throwing her off her feet. With a shriek of rending steel a nearby cooling tower collapsed, keeling over like a slain sequoia. The explosions didn't stop after the first one this time. They began to sequence as backup safety systems failed to contain the expanding reaction. On the other side of the doorway the elevator ground to a halt. The safety cage enclosing the cargo bay began to part.

She whispered to Newt. "Close your eyes, baby." The girl nodded solemnly, knowing what Ripley intended as she put one leg over the railing. They would hit the ground together, quick and clean.

She was just about to step off into open air when the dropship rose into view almost beneath them, its hovering thrusters roaring. She hadn't heard it approach because of the howling wind. The ship's loading boom was extended, a single, long metal strut reaching toward them like the finger of God. How Bishop held the vessel steady in the rippling gale Ripley didn't know—and didn't care. Behind her, she could just hear the voice of the station. It, like the installation it served, had almost run out of time.

"You now have thirty seconds to reach . . ."

She jumped onto the loading boom and hung on as it retracted into the dropship's cargo bay. An instant later a tremendous explosion tore through the station. The resultant wind shear slammed the hovering craft sideways. Extended landing legs ripped into a complex of platform, wall, and conduit. Metal squealed against metal, the entanglement threatening to drag the ship downward.

Inside the hold Ripley threw herself into a flight seat, cradling Newt against her as she strapped both of them in. Glancing up the aisle, she could just see into the cockpit where Bishop was fighting the controls. As they retracted, the sound of the landing legs pulling free echoed through the little vessel. She slammed home the latches on her seat harness, wrapped both arms tightly around Newt.

"Punch it, Bishop!"

The entire lower level of the station vanished in an expanding fireball. The ground heaved, earth and metal vaporizing as the dropship erupted skyward. Its engines fired hard, and the resultant gees slammed Ripley and Newt back in their seat. No comfortable, gradual climb to orbit this time. Bishop had the engines open full throttle as the dropship clawed its way through the blighted atmosphere. Ripley's back protested even as she mentally urged Bishop to increase the velocity.

As they left blue for black, the clouds lit up from beneath. A bubble of white-hot gas burst through the troposphere. The shock wave from the thermonuclear explosion rattled the ship but didn't damage it, and they continued to climb toward high orbit.

Within the metal bottle Ripley and Newt stared out a viewport, watching as the blinding flare dissipated behind them. Then Newt slumped against Ripley's shoulder and began to cry quietly. Ripley rocked her and stroked her hair.

"It's okay, baby. We made it. It's over."

Ahead of them the great, ungainly bulk of the *Sulaco* hung in geo-synchronous orbit, awaiting the arrival of its smaller offspring. On Bishop's command the dropship rose until docking grapples snapped home, lifting them into the cargo bay. The outer lock doors cycled shut. Automatic warning lights swept the dark, deserted chamber, and a warning horn ceased hooting. Excess engine heat was vented as the cavernous hold filled with air.

Within the ship Bishop stood behind Ripley while she knelt beside the comatose Hicks. She glanced questioningly at the android.

"I gave him another shot for the pain. He kept insisting that he didn't need it, but he didn't fight the injection. Strange thing, pain. Stranger to me still, this peculiar inner need of certain types of humans to pretend that it doesn't exist. Many are the times I'm glad I'm synthetic."

"We need to get him to the *Sulaco*'s medical ward," she replied, rising. "If you can get his arms, I'll take his feet."

Bishop smiled. "He is resting comfortably now. It will be better for him if we jostle him as little as possible. And you are tired. For that matter, *I'm* tired. It'll be easier if we get a stretcher."

Ripley hesitated, looking down at Hicks, then nodded. "You're right, of course."

Picking up Newt, she preceded the android down the aisle leading to the extended loading ramp. They could have a self-propelling stretcher back for Hicks in a few minutes. Bishop continued to talk.

"I'm sorry if I gave you a scare when you emerged onto the landing platform and saw the ship missing, but the site had simply become too unstable. I was afraid I'd lose the ship if I remained docked. It was simpler and safer to hover a short distance away. Close to the ground, the wind is not as strong. I had a monitor on the exit all the time so that I'd know when you arrived."

"Wish I'd known that at the time."

"I know. I had to circle and hope that things didn't get too rough to take you off. In the absence of human direction I had to use my own judgment, according to my programming. I'm sorry if I didn't handle it the best way."

They were halfway down the loading ramp. She paused and put a hand on his shoulder, stared evenly into artificial eyes.

"You did okay, Bishop."

"Well, thanks, I—" He stopped in mid-sentence, his attention focused on something glimpsed out of the corner of one eye. Nothing, really. An innocuous drop of liquid had splashed onto the ramp next to his shoe. Condensate from the skin of the dropship.

The droplet began to hiss as it started to eat into the metal ramp. Acid.

Something sharp and glistening burst from the center of his chest, spraying Ripley with milky android internal fluid. An alien stinger, queen-size, driving straight through him from behind. Bishop thrashed, uttering meaningless machine noises and clutching the protruding point of the spear as it slowly lifted him off the landing ramp.

The queen had concealed herself among the landing mechanism inside one strut bay. The atmospheric plates that normally sealed the bay flush with the rest of the dropship's skin had been bent aside or ripped away. She'd blended in perfectly with the rest of the heavy machinery until she began to emerge.

Seizing Bishop in two huge hands, she ripped him apart and flung the two halves aside. Rotating warning lights flashed on her shining dark limbs as she slowly descended to the deck, still smoking where Ripley had half fried her. Acid dripped from minor wounds that were healing rapidly. Sextuple limbs unfolded in unhuman geometries.

Breaking out of her paralysis, Ripley lowered Newt to the deck without taking her eyes off the descending nightmare.

"Go!"

Newt bolted for the nearest cluster of packing crates and equipment. The alien dropped to the deck and pivoted in the direction of the movement. Ripley backed clear, waving her arms and shouting, making faces, jumping up and down— doing anything and everything she could think of to draw the monster's attention away from the fleeing child.

Her decoying action was successful. The giant whirled, moving much too quickly for anything so huge, and sprang as Ripley sprinted for the oversize internal storage door that dominated the far end of the cargo hold. Massive feet boomed on the deck behind her.

She cleared the door and flailed at the "close" switch. The barrier whirred as it complied with the command, moving much faster than the doors of the now vanished station. An echoing *whang* reverberated through the storage room as the alien struck the solid wall an instant too late.

Ripley didn't have time to stand around to see if the

door would hold. She moved rapidly among bulky, dark shapes, searching for a particular one.

Outside, the queen's attention was drawn from the stubborn barrier to visible movement. A network of trenchlike service channels protected by heavy metal grillwork underlaid the cargo bay deck like the tributaries of a river system. The channels were just deep enough for Newt to enter. She'd dropped through one service opening and had begun crawling, scurrying toward the other end of the cargo bay like a burrowing rabbit.

The alien tracked the movement. Talons swooped, ripped up a section of grillwork just behind the frantic child. Newt tried to move faster, scrambling desperately as another piece of grille disappeared right at her heels. The next to go would be directly above her.

The alien paused in mid-reach at the sound of the heavy storage room door grinding open behind her. In the opening stood a massive, articulated silhouette.

Riding two tons of hardened steel, Ripley strode out in the powerloader. Her hands were inside waldo gloves while her feet rested in similar receptacles attached to the floor controls of the safety cab. Wearing the loader like high-tech armor, she advanced on the watching queen. The loader's ponderous feet boomed against the deck plates. Ripley's face was a mask of maternal fury devoid of fear.

"Get away from her, *you!*"

The queen emitted an inhuman screech and leapt at the oncoming machine.

Ripley threw her arm in a movement not normally associated with the activities of powerloaders or similar devices, but the elegant machine reacted perfectly. One massive hydraulic arm slammed into the alien's skull and threw it back against the wall. The queen reacted instantly and charged again, only to crash into a backhand that literally landed like a ton. She fell backward into a pile of heavy loading equipment.

"Come on!" Ripley wore a frenzied, distorted smile. "Come on!"

Tail lashing with rage, the queen charged the loader a third time. Four biomechanical arms swung at the loader's two. The great stinger stabbed at the flanks and underside of the loader, glancing harmlessly off solid metal. Ripley parried and struck with sweeping blows of the steel tines, backing up the loader, then advancing, pivoting to keep the machine's arms between her and the queen. The battle moved across the deck, demolishing packing crates, portable instrumentation, small machinery, everything in the path of the fight. The cargo bay echoed with the nightmarish sounds of two dragons battling to the death.

Getting the two powerful mechanical hands around a pair of alien arms, Ripley clenched her own fingers tight inside the waldoes, crushing both biomechanical limbs. The queen writhed with outrage, the talons of her other hands coming within inches of penetrating the safety cage to tear the tiny human apart. Ripley raised her arms, lifting the queen off the deck. The loader's engine groaned as it protested against the excessive weight. Hind legs ripped at the machine, denting the safety cage protecting its operator. The alien skull inclined toward her, and the outer jaws began to part. Ripley clung grimly to her controls.

The inner striking teeth exploded toward her. She ducked, and they slammed into the seat cushion behind her in an explosion of gelatinous drool. Yellow acid foamed over the hydraulic arms, crawling toward the safety cage. The queen tore at high-pressure hoses. Purple fluid sprayed in all directions, machine blood mixing with alien blood.

As it lost hydraulic pressure on one side the loader crumpled and fell over. The queen immediately rolled to get on top of it, avoiding the crushing metal arms, trying to find a way to penetrate the safety cage. Ripley hit a switch on the loader's console, and its cutting torch came to life, the intense blue flame firing straight into the alien's face. It screamed

and drew back, dragging the loader with it. As she fell and
the world was turned upside down around her, Ripley's safety
harness kept her secured to the driver's seat.

Together machine, biomechanoid, and human rolled into
the rectangular pit of the loading dock. The loader landed on
top of the alien, crushing part of its torso and pinning it
beneath its great weight. Acid began to seep in a steady flow
from the badly damaged body.

Ripley's eyes widened as she fought with the loader's
controls. The dripping acid spread out over the airlock doors
and began to smoke as it started eating its way through the
superstrong alloy. Beyond the outer lock lay void.

As the first tiny holes appeared, she struggled to unstrap
herself from the driver's seat. Air began to leave the *Sulaco*
as the insatiable emptiness of space sucked at the ship. A
rising wind tore at Ripley as she stumbled clear of the loader.
Jumping a puddle of smoking acid, she grabbed at the bottom
rungs of the ladder that was built into the wall of the airlock.
One hand slapped the inner door's emergency override. Above,
the heavy inner airlock doors began rumbling toward each
other like steel jaws. She climbed wildly.

Beneath her, the first holes widened, were joined by
others as the acid did its work. The flow of escaping air
around her increased in volume, slowing her ascent.

Newt had emerged from the network of subfloor channels to hide among a forest of gas cylinders. When the
powerloader, Ripley, and the alien had tumbled into the airlock, she'd slipped out for a better look.

Now the suction from below pulled her legs out from
under her and dragged her, kicking and screaming, across the
smooth deck. Bishop, or rather his upper half, saw her coming. He grabbed a support stanchion with one hand. With the
other he reached out, and thanks to perfect synthetic timing,
just managed to get his fingers entwined in the girl's belt as
she slid by. She hung there in his grasp, floating in the in-
tensifying gale like a Newt-flag as the wind sucked at her.

Ripley's head emerged above deck level. As she tried to kick up and out with her right leg, something caressed her left ankle and latched hold. An experimental tug almost tore Ripley's arms from their sockets. Desperately she threw both arms around the ladder's upper rung, which was mounted a foot away on the deck. The inner airlock doors continued rumbling toward one another. If she didn't pull herself clear or drop back down within a couple of seconds, she'd end up looking just like Bishop.

Below, the acid-weakened outer lock doors groaned. A portion of the inner reinforcing collapsed. The interlocked powerloader and alien queen settled a few centimeters. Ripley felt her arms giving way as she was dragged down, but it was her shoe that came away first. Her leg was free.

Summoning strength from unknown depths, she dragged herself onto the deck just as the inner airlock doors slammed shut. Beneath her, the alien queen uttered another scream of rage and exerted all her incomprehensible strength. The heavy loader squealed as she began to push it aside.

It was half off when the outer doors, honeycombed by acid, fell apart, sending chunks of metal, bubbles of acid, the queen, and the powerloader spilling out into space. Ripley rose and stumbled to the nearest viewport. The queen's efforts were enough to propel her clear of the *Sulaco*'s artificial gravity field. Still screaming and tearing at the powerloader, the queen tumbled slowly back toward the inhospitable world she'd recently fled.

Ripley stared as her nemesis faded to a dot, then a dim point, and was at last swallowed by the rolling clouds. Within the cargo bay turbulent air eddied and settled as the *Sulaco*'s cyclers worked to replenish the atmosphere that had been lost.

Bishop was still holding Newt with one hand. His bisected torso trailed artificial inner organs and sparking conduits. His eyelids fluttered, and his head sometimes jerked unpredictably, bumping against the deck. His internal regulators had managed to shut off the flow of android blood, fighting a holding action against the massive injury. White encrustation sparkled along the edge of the tear.

He managed a small, grim smile as he eyed the approaching Ripley. "Not bad for a human." He regained control of his eyelids long enough to give her an unmistakable wink.

Ripley stumbled over to Newt. The girl looked dazed. "Mommy—mommy?"

"Right here, baby. I'm right here." Sweeping the girl up in her arms, she hugged her as hard as she could. Then she headed toward the *Sulaco*'s crew quarters.

Around them, the big ship's systems hummed reassuringly. She found her way up to Medical and returned to the cargo hold with a stretcher in tow. Bishop assured her that he could wait. With the stretcher's aid she gently loaded the sleeping Hicks and trundled him back to the hospital ward. His expression was peaceful, content. He'd missed the whole thing, luxuriating in the effects of the injection Bishop had given him.

As for the android, he lay on the deck, his hands crossed over his chest and his eyes closed. She couldn't tell if he was dead or sleeping. Better minds than hers would determine that once they got back to Earth.

In sleep Hicks's face lost much of its macho Marine toughness. He looked much like any other man. Handsomer though, and certainly more tired. Except that he wasn't like any other man. If it hadn't been for him, she'd be dead, Newt would be dead, all dead. Only the *Sulaco* would have lived on, an empty receptacle awaiting the return of humans who would never come.

She thought of waking him, decided against it. In a little while, when she was sure that his vital signs were stabilized and the repairs to his acid-scarred flesh well under way, she'd place him in one of the empty, waiting hypersleep capsules.

She turned to inspect the sleeping chamber. Three capsules to prep. If he still lived, Bishop wouldn't need one.

The synthetic would probably have found hypersleep confining.

Newt looked up at her. She held two of Ripley's fingers as they strode together up the corridor.

"Are we going to sleep now?"

"That's right, Newt."

"Can we dream?"

Ripley gazed down at the bright, upturned face and smiled. "Yes, honey. I think we both can."

"So it is my company which you prefer, after all."

Lord Dare spoke sensuously in her ear.

Elaine pulled away from his grasp. "You are all about in your head, my lord. And how dare you touch me in such a familiar manner."

"But you've chosen an ideal trysting place, my dear," he pointed out reasonably. "Secluded enough for me even to venture a kiss." His teasing smile increased her unease.

"You wouldn't dare!" she exclaimed.

He gave a sudden shout of laughter and said, "Sometimes it's truly a pleasure to live up to my reputation!"

And with that his mouth swooped suddenly on hers in a suffocating kiss. Elaine struggled, but to no avail. A wave of heat seemed to sweep over her as his demanding mouth pressed against her lips. Suddenly Lord Dare released her.

"It seems," he said, rather breathlessly, "that we are to be interrupted. So I shall bid you good evening until next time, my dear."

"There will be no next time," Elaine almost shouted, but found herself speaking to air. Lord Dare had disappeared.

Books by Jean Reece

HARLEQUIN REGENCY ROMANCE
16–THE PRIMROSE PATH

THE DEVIL'S DARE
DARE

JEAN REECE

Harlequin Books

TORONTO • NEW YORK • LONDON
AMSTERDAM • PARIS • SYDNEY • HAMBURG
STOCKHOLM • ATHENS • TOKYO • MILAN

Published September 1989

ISBN 0-373-31110-9

Printed in U.S.A.

CHAPTER ONE

"I TELL YOU, MISS, I've heard it again, and it's nigh on driving me distracted!" Cook declared petulantly.

Miss Elaine Farrington eyed her in exasperation. "But this is some farrago of nonsense, Mrs. Beale, surely. Ghosts? In the middle of London? And in the fashionable area, at that? You must be all about in your head. It is too absurd."

Cook stood by her guns. She was a stout lady, and standing thus with her arms akimbo, she seemed a formidable challenge to any possible supernatural manifestation. Unfortunately, she was so cow-hearted as to threaten her employer with immediate notice!

"You may call it what you please, Miss, but it's as I say. I heard it last week, and I heard it again just a moment ago. Knock, knock, knocking. It's more than a body can bear!"

Elaine decided to humour the poor woman, who was clearly seriously put out. "Just where did these ghostly sounds come from, Mrs. Beale?"

"From the walls theirselves!" she declared portentously.

The effect fell sadly flat. Elaine shook her head in pity. How depressing to have to puncture the woman's illusions. "But, Mrs. Beale, surely you must realize that a more logical explanation exists for these sounds than ghosts.''

Cook wrinkled her nose, obviously loath to listen to logic. After a prolonged pause, she said, ''Yes? And what may that be, Miss?''

''Rats,'' Elaine declared bluntly.

''Rats!'' the woman repeated, horrified.

''Rats.'' Elaine was inexorable.

Mrs. Beale shook her head violently. ''I've heard rats afore, Miss. And these ain't rats. Rats make scratching noises: scratch, scratch, scratching.'' She took a deep breath, ready to expatiate on the matter at some length. ''Now these noises was far different. Knocking noises I say they were....''

Impatiently Elaine cut her off. ''Yes, I know. Knock, knock, knocking.'' She sighed. ''Why don't you show me just where you think they came from?''

Cook was delighted to do so.

She promptly led Elaine down the stairs into the nether regions of the house.

Elaine had been virtual mistress of this house on South London Square since her mother's death some eight years before, so she was no stranger to the servants' region. Nor was she unfamiliar with the odd flights of fancy to which some servants were given. But because she was a kind mistress, ever ready to consider the feelings of others, she was unwilling to make short shrift of Cook's obvious delusions.

Now Nicholas, her brother, would have had no patience with this sort of thing. He would have summarily dismissed Cook and then left it to his long-suffering sister to arrange a replacement. On the other hand, Elaine thought indulgently, Nicholas might just have accepted Cook's declarations as the sort of mad lark he relished, and he might have investigated them with gleeful enthusiasm.

The women soon entered the kitchen. It was remarkably clean and well cared for, and Elaine did not hesitate to compliment the Cook on her housekeeping.

Mrs. Beale swelled with gratification. "Well, I do take pride in my work," she acknowledged with a becoming show of humility. "And if I could just make Becky polish the pots and pans with less back talk, I'd have things well in hand here."

Becky was the second kitchenmaid, who was given to flirtation with the night watchman and the street hawkers, as well as with visiting tradesmen. Being a favourite of these fellows, she had consequently a somewhat inflated opinion of both her charms and her position in the house. But Elaine had heard all this before. She only smiled and stood expectantly, listening.

After a moment, she said, "Well, Mrs. Beale, I'm afraid I do not hear these vaunted knockings of yours."

Cook frowned. "I heard them, I tell you, Miss. Right where I'm standing, I heard them. Not more than fifteen minutes ago."

Elaine waited again, for perhaps ten seconds. Then she smiled and said brightly, "Well, Mrs. Beale, I'm afraid you've disappointed me sorely. I was so looking forward to seeing a ghostly spectre floating about the pots and pans. I expected your ghost to be some antique serving woman who lost her heart to the butler and who, because of unrequited affection, cut her throat with the best carving knife and subsequently took to haunting the place of her suffering.''

''That's all very well,'' Cook said grimly, her thin mouth tightening. ''But I heard it. Knock, knock, knocking.''

''Have you been visiting the wine cellar a trifle too often, Mrs. Beale?'' Elaine asked teasingly.

The woman puffed with indignation. ''Well, I never,'' she huffed. ''Not in all my born days...''

Elaine quickly held up a placating hand. ''Please forgive me, Mrs. Beale. I couldn't resist teasing you. I know perfectly well that you and my grandfather's Madeira are complete strangers.''

''Aye, and so we are. But I'm beginning to wonder, Miss, whether the two of you are!''

Elaine chuckled. ''Why, Mrs. Beale, you ought to be dismissed without a character for casting such an aspersion upon your mistress.'' The severity of her words was belied by the distinct twinkle in her large blue eyes.

''As though you would,'' the woman muttered. ''But I warn you, Miss, if I hear that knocking again, I'll give you my notice.''

''Have no fear, Mrs. Beale. If you hear that knocking again, I'll retire you with pension. A few years in a sunny cottage may restore your sanity.''

With this Parthian shot she turned to leave, and then stopped, her head turning abruptly at a sudden sharp tapping.

Mrs. Beale shrieked in terror, throwing her apron over her head.

"Be quiet!" Elaine commanded. But too late. The tapping noises had ceased as suddenly as they had begun.

"Is that what you've been hearing?" Elaine demanded in an undertone.

"Yes," Cook replied feebly, her head still covered.

"Why, that's not a knocking noise. It's a tapping noise," Elaine said accusingly.

Cook was unimpressed by this subtle distinction. "I heard it, and you heard it, and that's all that concerns me," she declared in a slightly stronger voice, as she peered momentarily from behind her apron.

"Well, that's not all that concerns me," Elaine replied briskly. "I did hear it, and I want to know the cause of it!"

"I *told* you the cause of it," Cook exclaimed, flapping her apron to its proper place in exasperation.

Elaine stared at her.

"Ghosts!"

Elaine made a noise perilously approaching a snort. "You are demented," she declared with conviction. "A ghost in the middle of London? Impossible. It is more likely to be a housebreaker."

"A housebreaker!" Cook repeated, her militant impulses instantly aroused. "Just let anyone try to break into this house," she threatened, reaching menacingly for a large cleaver.

Elaine smiled. "I only hazard that as a guess, Mrs. Beale. But I can't wholly believe it. For one thing, it's rare for a housebreaker to make attempts at a house in broad daylight."

Cook considered this. "Aye, so it is."

"Especially a house so well guarded by the male sex," Elaine pursued.

"You mean by Mr. Nicholas?" Cook scoffed.

"No, I mean by Becky's numerous suitors."

Cook greeted this facer with silence. Finally she said, "Well if it ain't ghosts, and if it ain't a house-breaker, then what is it?"

"I don't know, but I intend to find out."

"Lawks, Miss, what are you meaning to do?" Her eyes widened in trepidation as she watched Elaine move stealthily about the room.

"I mean to hunt down the source of that noise," Elaine replied stoutly, her head slightly tilted as she tried to fix the direction from which the sound had come.

"Do no such thing, Miss! If it's a ghost, it'll spirit you away."

"If it's a ghost, Mrs. Beale, it'll have no opportunity to spirit me away, for I assure you that I'll faint away first."

Mrs. Beale protested loudly at this, but Elaine paid no heed. As far as she could tell, the tapping seemed to have originated in the wine cellar, and yet the sound had seemed closer to them than the depth of the cellar would suggest.

She continued to walk about the room, frowning in concentration. The logical approach, she decided, would be to search all the adjoining rooms. She picked up a tallow candle from a sideboard and quickly lit it from the fires burning in the stove.

Without hesitation, she opened the door into the cellar and stepped down the stairs. She heard Cook give another shriek at her sudden disappearance and turned around to see her shrinking hesitantly in the doorway.

Elaine waved her away. "If you wish to be of service to me, Mrs. Beale, find Seaton, or better yet, young Ben."

Cook considered the soundness of this advice for a moment. "But I don't want to leave you alone," she ventured meekly.

Elaine quelled an impulse to snap. "Well, the sooner you find them, the sooner you may return to bear me company," she pointed out reasonably.

Accepting the force of this argument, Cook turned and rushed out of the room. Elaine could hear her calling shrilly for both the butler and the footman. Her voice faded as Elaine went farther into the cellar. To her growing puzzlement, however, she found nothing suspicious: no one lurked behind the casks of porter; no one hid behind the bottles of port, claret, and canary; no one skulked beside the kegs of Malaga.

Undeterred, Elaine retraced her steps to the kitchen. Another door opened onto an alleyway outside. Although the walls of the house were too thick for the tapping sounds to have originated outside, Elaine thought it only right to explore all possibilities. Carefully she opened the door, then peered cautiously from behind it.

She saw a hawker pausing to sharpen his tools before stepping back onto the square to call out his wares. A few empty baskets and barrels lay higgledy-piggledy against the wall. A wagon was poised to turn into the roadway, while its driver considered the narrowness of the course. Nothing could have occasioned the noise she had heard.

Elaine started to close the door behind her, then froze as she noted a movement behind one of the barrels. Her eyes narrowed as she tried to distinguish the shape in the shadows. A man was hiding there.

Decisively, she stepped forward. "What do you think you're doing lurking about my house in this havey-cavey fashion?" she demanded in rather more forceful language than was her wont.

Elaine's irritation rose when there was no answer.

"Come out!" she demanded angrily. "Come out and show yourself."

But again silence was the only response.

"All right!" Elaine declared in exasperation. She strode forward, determined to expose him herself.

Her indignation carried her onward and she paid no attention to the ground. She forgot that the butler continually complained about the pitted, deeply rutted surface of the alley. There were a number of old underground conduits in South London Square, and many householders had problems with subsidence. Elaine was forcibly reminded of this fact when the very ground beneath her suddenly gave way. Unable to save herself, she pitched forward into a surprisingly deep hole. Grasping vainly at the air, she gave a startled scream.

She landed with a hard thud and lay still a moment, both stunned and winded. What had happened? She blinked confusedly at the sudden blackness.

She had fallen into a hole, she concluded, caused by that ground-shifting she had heard about.

With a moan, she struggled to her knees. If Seaton knew that the ground about the house was weak, then he should have seen to it that something was done. She would tell him so in no uncertain terms as soon as she escaped from this pit. But that, she thought, looking about, was not going to be easy. The sides were surprisingly steep and offered few handholds. Even if she could clamber out, would not such an effort merely bring more earth down on top of her?

This is absurd, she thought in frustration and not a little anxiety. Never again would she chase after intruders. Leave intruders to the butler and the footman, she adjured herself. After all, when Cook and the others discovered she was not in the cellar, they were bound to search elsewhere for her. She had only to wait. But Elaine revolted at the thought of spending a moment more than necessary in this wretched hole. "Help! Someone please help me!"

She staggered to her feet and stretched her arm as far toward the top of the hole as she could. To her surprise, she felt someone take her hand in a strong and steady grip.

"Seaton?" she inquired doubtfully.

"No, it is not Seaton," a deep voice replied. "Here, give me your other hand."

She waited, unaccountably hesitant. Then she mentally shook herself and put up her other hand. It, too, was firmly seized, and she was lifted easily into the open air. She seemed to rise upward, until her eyes were level with those of her rescuer. She had a glimpse of dark, almost black eyes, twinkling with undisguised amusement. Then she felt herself set gently upon the ground.

Ruffled by the expression in those eyes, Elaine averted her gaze, busying herself with brushing the dirt from her gown with rather violent swipes until she regained her composure.

"I hope you have suffered no injuries, my dear," he inquired politely.

She raised a disdainful eyebrow. Then with a last shake of her skirts, she lifted her head and extended a hand in her best formal manner.

The stranger took it, bowing and then favouring her with his disturbing glint of a smile. As he straightened up, Elaine found herself studying him with irresistible curiosity.

The man was a veritable Adonis. Well over six feet tall, he was blessed with the widest shoulders she had ever seen. His face was amazingly handsome, for he had dark eyes set under arching eyebrows, a perfectly straight nose, a classically moulded mouth and an iron jaw. His athletic physique was effectively set off by a natty dark blue coat, buckskins, and gleaming Hessian boots.

Disconcerted by the results of her study and by the undue interest she felt she had shown, she demanded sharply. "Why were you hiding in this alley?"

The man had been eyeing her with a similar close scrutiny. He was apparently far from annoyed by her appearance. Admiration replaced the amusement in his eyes and he smiled slightly. "I might as easily ask what you were doing in that hole."

"I fell into that hole!"

He twitched a comically mobile eyebrow. "I daresay that is a new and fashionable practice of young ladies of quality," he observed politely.

"What do you mean?"

"Why, falling into holes when they are completely alone, unattended by either a groom or a maidservant."

She could hardly miss the innuendo in this remark or the warmth of his gaze, which dwelt on her figure with undisguised pleasure. "I am neither alone nor unattended," she said, stiffening.

"I see." He nodded affably. "Has your groom fallen into that hole as well?" he asked in an interested tone. "I don't believe I saw him, but then I don't believe I was looking for him. I should have realized, however, that young ladies rarely fall into holes alone."

She gasped in outrage. "You dare suggest . . ." she began with dangerous calm.

He held up his hand. "But, my dear, I suggested nothing. You yourself said you were not alone."

She dearly wished to box his ears. "I meant that I have several servants in my house."

He nodded again, his solemn expression belied by the mischievous glint in his eyes. "That is usually the case."

She bit her lip, suddenly assailed by an attack of the giggles, as the absurdity of the situation overcame her.

"That's much better," he said with approval.

Quickly she repressed her unbecoming mirth. With dignity she declared, "You are impossible. I should perhaps have mentioned that this is my house." She pointed.

He jerked suddenly forward. "What! You live in *that* house?" he demanded.

She eyed him with some surprise but replied coolly, "Yes, at Farrington Place. I am Elaine Farrington."

She thought this announcement had somehow shocked him, yet the expression on his handsome face had been so fleeting, Elaine could not be sure of its meaning.

"I am most honoured to make your acquaintance, Miss Farrington." He bowed again after a moment.

"I am in no mood for such punctilio, sir. It comes a little behindhand. Who are you, and why were you in this alley?"

"I am in this alley, my dear girl, because I heard your cries for help. As I can never resist a female in distress, I hurried to lend you whatever assistance I could."

She frowned uncertainly at him. "You mean you were not in the alley before I cried for help?"

His eyes opened wide. "Before you cried for help?" He gazed about at the rather squalid surroundings. *"Here?"*

"That's all very well," Elaine conceded, studying him searchingly and resisting the impulse to return his smile. "But you still have not told me who you are."

"Why, I am Dare, Charles Thane, you know."

She almost flung up her hands in horror. Lord Dare. The Devil's Dare! The wild Devil's Dare. Lud, of all people to render her assistance, she thought to herself, trying to ignore the humour of the situation. He had certainly lent a number of demimondaines his assistance in a variety of scandalous ways, if his reputation were to be believed. He was a veritable rakehell whose mad pranks were the talk of London. A reckless Corinthian ever ready for a bout of fisticuffs or a daredevil curricle race, he was also a noted gamester, who had lost and won several fortunes at the green baize tables.

There was nothing, in short, that gossip claimed he would not do on a dare. Why, had he not walked backward all the way to Brighton on Lord Axminster's challenge? Dressed as a highwayman, he had even held up the Prince's own coach on Finchley Common. He had even managed to come unscathed from that escapade, for Lord Dare and Prinny were bosom chums, who often vied to outdo each other in drinking, gaming, racing, or other amusements of the ton.

Sternly Elaine quelled her impulse to ask him if several of the tales told of him were true. As a well-bred young lady, she suspected she should not even have heard such stories.

Lord Dare had watched her changing expressions with considerable appreciation. As he smiled down at her he said with the utmost readiness, "My dear, they are all true, even those that are entirely unknown to you, as they are unfit for the delicate ears of a young lady of quality."

She almost blushed at this sally. How dared he tease her in this ungentlemanly fashion? She lifted her chin. "I am amazed at your audacity in so confronting such a female," she said coldly, then turned to march away. She stopped, though, as he cleared his throat.

"Well, my dear, I could hardly tell from your cries that you were one," he pointed out reasonably.

Indignantly she began, "Are you implying—"

"I imply nothing," he interrupted hastily, giving her his glinting smile. "I am merely attempting to exculpate myself." He paused, then gave her an arch look, his dark eyes resting again on her charming figure. "And to make my intentions known to you."

She stiffened. "Your intentions!" she repeated. "You may have all the intentions you please, but I'll tell you now that I at least have no intention of succumbing to your well-known if dubious charms."

Again she started to fling away only to stop as he once more cleared his throat.

"I am afraid that you misunderstand me." His tone became saintly. "My intentions were to render a lady in distress whatever assistance I could. I trust I gave no offence in this purely innocent intent."

She made a choking sound then chuckled. "You, sir, are incorrigible."

His smile widened. "Such is my reputation."

"And I see you have no difficulty in living up to it." He merely shrugged, apparently refusing to rise to this bait. "And I'm afraid I, too, have been infected by your behaviour. It was very remiss of me not to thank you for helping me."

"Yes, so I thought," he agreed blandly. "But I did not think it my place to point this out to you."

"I admire your restraint, sir."

One eyebrow flew up, as he said somewhat regretfully, "Yes, and so do I admire my restraint. You did say that you have several servants close at hand."

Elaine was just now wondering what could have happened to Mrs. Beale and her colleagues. She nodded absently in affirmation, then realized the significance of his question and took two hasty steps away from him. "Yes, I *do* have servants close at hand. Several!" she declared rather breathlessly.

"What a pity." He gave a sigh. He plucked up immediately, however. "Oh, well, I daresay I shall find another opportunity."

She nearly put up her hand to still her palpitating heart. What a fool she was to behave in this missish fashion. She was no girl just out of the schoolroom; rather, she was a lady well able to take care of herself. To prove this fact, she curled her lips in a scornful smile and asked in a mildly interested tone, "An opportunity for what, Lord Dare?"

He was far from being overwhelmed by her apparent disinterest, as he looked deeply into her blue eyes. "For responding to your challenge, my dear."

"What challenge?"

"Why your challenge that I couldn't make you succumb to my, er, dubious charms, of course."

She blinked at the man in utter amazement. His audacity was beyond belief. "Let me tell you, my Lord Dare, that you will be at *point non plus* if you think to cut a wheedle with me."

He held up a cautionary finger, his expression tinged with slightly mocking reproach. "I serve you no Spanish coin, my dear, for I am quite sincere. And quite determined."

With that, he gave her one final, flourishing bow and sauntered away, leaving Elaine rooted to the ground, seething with indignation.

She swung on her heels and marched back into her house. How dared that man speak to her in that fashion? He *was* a devil! Just let him make an attempt upon her virtue or her heart. She would enjoy giving him a crushing snub.

When she ascended the stairs and stepped into the breakfast parlour, she found Mrs. Beale cowering behind the heavy sideboard. She glared at the chicken-hearted cook. "And what are you doing here, Mrs. Beale?"

The woman squirmed, much discomfited at being found out in her defection. "Why, uh, why, I was looking for a weapon, Miss Farrington, so I was. Some blunt instrument to attack the intruder with, I promise you."

"Were you, indeed? Of course, this sideboard must have proved rather unwieldy. You were contemplating the china plates, I collect?"

Mrs. Beale straightened herself. "There's no need for sarcasm, Miss. I was only doing my best."

Her best to protect herself, thought Elaine grimly. Oh, well, what was the use of remonstrating? If Seaton or the footman had been on the scene, she might have been spared Lord Dare's attentions, but there was no use in making a fuss about what had already passed.

"Mrs. Beale," she said in a quieter tone. "If you hear that knocking noise again, I want you to come to me directly, is that understood?"

The woman nodded. "Was it an intruder, then?"

Elaine frowned. "I don't know what it was."

Mrs. Beale threw up her hands in horror. "Then it *was* a ghost! Oh, heavens preserve us."

"No one will preserve you, Mrs. Beale, if you continue talking such nonsense. In fact, I'll turn you off without hesitation."

Mrs. Beale sniffed, too assured both of Elaine's kind nature and of her position in the Farrington household to take this threat seriously. "And without a character, either, to be sure."

Elaine smiled reluctantly. "That would be impossible," she acknowledged. "Only remember to fetch me directly upon hearing any strange noise."

Mrs. Beale nodded and then returned to her basement domain with a pronounced air of martyrdom.

Elaine watched her, a pensive expression on her face. If she were of a fanciful nature, no doubt she would expect to be murdered in her bed this very night after having caught a glimpse of a figure in the shadows of the alley. But as she was not, she would not leap to any hasty and probably farfetched conclusions.

How could she be certain that the figure she had espied had any connection with the knocking? Also, how could she be certain that the figure was really that of a man? She shook her head dismissively. The only

thing of which she *could* be certain was that she had
broken through some of the weakened ground beside
her house. And that the cavity could prove hazardous
to others if not filled in. Seaton must see to it immediately. She tugged the bellpull.

As she waited for the butler, she wondered whether
or not to tell Nicholas of the afternoon's events. He
was a headstrong youth on whom she was not wont to
place too much dependence. She loved him dearly, of
course, but she had no doubt that if she were to tell
Nicholas of Lord Dare's insults, Nicholas would
gladly challenge him to a duel, meet him upon some
heath in the dawn, and probably get his head blown
off.

And if she were to tell him the more innocuous tale
of the knocking she had heard, he would no doubt
keep everyone in the house, including Aunt Augusta,
up all night for a week in hope of laying a trap for a
perhaps nonexistent intruder.

She was being somewhat cynical, she told herself,
but eighteen years' experience of her brother's dispo-
sition gave force to her reflections. She would not tell
Nicholas a thing.

Of course she was accustomed to seeing to matters
on her own. Their parents had died when Elaine was
still in the schoolroom and Nicholas was still in long-
coats. The orphans had been left to their Aunt Augusta's care, if care was the proper word for it. Perhaps keeping was closer to the truth. For Aunt
Augusta had kept them clothed, fed, and educated,
but she had not cared for them one jot. The only thing
she had been known to take care of—and great care,

at that—was her own uncertain health. She was a hypochondriac of the highest degree, rarely leaving the safety of her couch and the sanctity of her room.

As Elaine was of a far less retiring nature, she had gradually taken over the duties of the household, simply for want of something to do. She soon became *de facto* mistress of the house, looked to by everyone, including Aunt Augusta and Nicholas, and responsible for all arrangements both trivial and important.

She had had her own come-out, of course, when she turned eighteen. Aunt Augusta had been induced to solicit her friend Lady Somercote's patronage for Elaine's attendance at all the balls, routs and assemblies of the Season. To be sure, Lady Somercote, who had herself no daughters, was still Elaine's chaperon at all social functions when Nicholas was so boorish as to refuse. Though, Elaine thought wryly, she had been out for two years now and was fast becoming thought of as already on the shelf.

It was not that she was averse to marriage. Quite the contrary. She felt she would make a good wife, if only she could find a gentleman who struck her as having the makings of a good husband. So far, no aspirant for her hand had measured up to her expectations, and she was content to survey the hopefuls for another year or so before making any irrevocable choice.

Indeed, there were many suitors in her pocket, for she was not only a considerable heiress, but she was also something of a beauty. She had received many odes dedicated to her *beaux yeux*, to her golden hair, to her cherry lips; so many, in fact, that she was now rather contemptuous of her much-vaunted beauty. Of course she looked like a golden princess; of course she had a fairy figure. But these attributes meant very little to her. She would rather be a fashionably dark beauty with Junoesque proportions, perversely giving little value to her own Dresden doll perfection.

She wondered idly if Lord Dare had been attracted to her face. She glanced into a pier-glass upon the thought and burst into sudden laughter. Her hair looked as though it had been pulled about by a windstorm, and her face was smirched with dirt. Quite a picture she made, to be sure. Enough to cause a stir in any man's heart. She giggled, caught again by the absurdity of the situation. Lord Dare had been making game of her, no doubt.

According to his reputation, he made game out of life itself. A jolly way to waste one's time, was it not? He was always ready to pick up any carelessly thrown gauntlet or deliberately dropped handkerchief. But she had thrown neither her handkerchief nor her cap at him, and he had insulted her beyond permission. Yet, catching her reflection in the glass again, she could not help but find his behaviour amusing. She might as well have been a harridan or a hag, for obviously nothing mattered to him but the challenge itself. No wonder the beau monde called him the Devil's Dare.

But wasn't it an odd coincidence for him to be so close as to lend her assistance in her sudden predicament? While South London Square was in the fashionable part of London, Farrington Place was at the end of one side and pedestrian traffic was not heavy. Perhaps Lord Dare had been visiting an acquaintance in the vicinity. She fell to cudgelling her brain, wondering who amongst her neighbours could be considered a crony of Lord Dare. None sprang to mind.

Her thoughts were interrupted by Seaton's entrance. Before she could instruct him to see to the danger in the alley, her attention was sought by the posy of violets upon a silver salver, which Seaton now proffered to her with a bow.

Her eyebrows went up. "But what is this? It is rather late for callers, is it not?"

"Yes, Miss," Seaton replied deprecatingly. "But the, er, gentleman only stopped to leave you this."

"Indeed. How irregular. Did the gentleman deign to leave a message with this pretentious tribute?"

Seaton cleared his throat, too well-trained to evince any reaction to Elaine's comments. "No, Miss. But he did leave a card."

Elaine picked it up and found herself frowning darkly at the name printed with a flourish in bold script. It was Lord Dare's.

CHAPTER TWO

THE NEXT MORNING, Elaine received a caller who was more properly respectful of etiquette. Not only did he send in his card at a more conventional hour, but he also waited in the salon for Elaine to hurry in to greet him. And hurry she did, for the visitor was her cousin, Lord Elcho.

He was standing before the Adam mantlepiece, his long, loose-limbed form erect. His rather narrow back was almost rigid, as he did not deign to rest even an arm along the mantle. He was complete to a shade in a blue coat and yellow pantaloons. His face, though, was also rather rigid, particularly the tight mouth. It was a somewhat lined face, despite the fact that he was only in his late thirties. And he had curiously light blue eyes, which were always bright and wide open, giving his countenance a perpetually earnest, almost fervent, expression.

He was now intently studying the posy resting upon the mantlepiece. He turned at Elaine's entrance.

"Have I a new rival?" he demanded without preamble.

She sailed past him, taking the posy in her hands and holding it gently. "But of course," she replied, a lilt in her voice. "Don't I manage to acquire a new suitor every week?"

His thin lips curled in a perfunctory and humourless smile. "On the average, yes. Whom have you managed to snare now?"

She tilted her pretty chin, considering. "You know, Simon. I think the boot is on the other leg for once. I believe this gentleman is attempting to snare me."

His eyes managed to widen even more at this. "Then he is not a gentleman at all," he declared. His mouth hardened as her eyes twinkled. "Who, may I ask, is this audacious scoundrel?"

"As you have characterized him to a peg by calling him audacious, I believe you may well be able to identify him yourself."

He shook his head, impatiently. "Cut the faradiddles, Elaine. Who is he?"

She was taken aback by his curtness. Although he had oft times professed affection for her, she had never taken these sentiments very seriously, believing him to be merely teasing her in a cousinly fashion. Indeed, she thought of him not as an aspirant to her hand, but as a close friend. Since she preferred to keep him as such, she forced herself to smile before returning a flippant answer.

"Why, I am surprised by your lack of perception, Simon. It is Lord Dare, of course."

Elcho's hand clenched. "Lord Dare," he grated. "That man!"

Elaine stared at him in real consternation. Why, he had turned as pale as whey. Although she knew that

Lord Dare's reputation was deplorable, she had hardly expected quite this reaction.

"Don't look so put about, Simon," she soothed. "I assure you, I was funning. You need pay no attention to Lord Dare."

"He is not a fellow worthy of your notice! You must cut him from your acquaintance. I demand it!"

She surveyed her seething cousin with disdain. Drawing herself up, she said quellingly, "Simon, recollect you have no right to make any demands upon me."

He bit his nether lip and muttered under his breath, turning uncomfortably red.

To assuage the harshness of her words, she smiled kindly upon him again. "You must allow me to use my own judgement in such matters as this, Simon," she pointed out reasonably. There was a tense pause. "Now," she said gaily, "let us turn our conversation to a subject which I know to be very dear to your heart."

He seemed inattentive, his head averted, absorbed in his own thoughts.

"What news from Scotland?" she asked in a cajoling tone.

He was evidently abstracted, for he replied absently, "They're drawing up a commission to inspect the Scottish Regalia, to be headed by Walter Scott, of all people. Then Scotland will know how true the Prince Regent has been to his word."

Elaine knitted her brow. "True to his word?" she repeated, puzzled.

His head turned sharply, his thoughts suddenly arrested by her question. Once again, he seemed alert. "What did I just tell you?"

Bemused by this behaviour, she replied in her most reassuring voice, "That a commission has been formed to inspect the Scottish Regalia." Comprehension dawned, and she asked more excitedly, "Oh, do you mean the ancient Regalia that have been tightly locked in a chest and kept in a close-guarded cell to ensure their remaining in Scotland? The sword and the sceptre engraved with oak leaves that are older than the English crown jewels and that are never to leave Scotland?"

"Yes!" He nodded eagerly. "But some Scots fear that they *have* been removed from Scotland! They believe the Prince Regent had them carried off!"

Elaine was horrified, and she shook her head in disbelief. "Oh, no. He couldn't have done such a thing. Why, it would be madness!"

Elcho's face became very serious indeed. "It would be grounds for breaking the union between Scotland and England."

His portentousness tickled her sense of humour and she could not believe he was serious. "Oh, Simon," she chuckled, "what a jokesmith you are."

"I would hardly joke about such an important subject. Some Scots still chafe under the union, I hope I need not remind you. They think that by joining us with England, the union has forced a slave's yoke on us. And I understand their discontent. We've lost our independence. We've lost our very character as a nation."

"I, too, can understand their discontent. We are cousins, after all, and I share your Scottish blood through my mother. But I must say, Simon, that although I deplore the loss of many of Scotland's traditions, I feel that Scotland has benefitted both economically and socially from its union with England."

"After the Scottish Regalia Commission, my dear Elaine, that may become a question for bitter and bloody debate."

"I think you exaggerate the matter," she persisted.

Elcho looked her steadily in the eye. "If the commission discovers that the Regalia have been stolen from Scotland, then that will be a matter for war."

"But what if the Regalia have not been removed? You say that the Scottish populace only suspects. This must be a mere speculation. Evidently they have no proof."

"They hope to verify their suspicions when the commission opens the gaol gates in three weeks' time."

"Do you seriously believe that they will find them gone?"

Again he looked at her, a guarded expression on his face. A rather forced smile thinned his lips. "Of course, I cannot answer that question. We must wait upon the event. And pray that rebellion will not ensue."

Elaine laughed uncomfortably. Her attempt to turn the conversation into more peaceful channels had proved remarkably ineffective. She decided on another attempt. "Do you attend Vauxhall Gardens tonight, Simon?"

He frowned at this question, obviously considering Vauxhall a concern as remote to him as the Antipodes. "Vauxhall?" he repeated.

"Yes," she answered indulgently. "Nicholas has got up a party, you must know."

"You are not going to accompany him, are you?" he demanded, as though she had got a maggot in her head.

"Yes," she replied shortly, a dangerous light in her eyes.

"What a madcap affair that will be," he sneered. "A party got up by young Nicholas. I daresay it will include all the rakehells in town."

"Do you, indeed?" she said coldly. "I would rather think that there must be more than just two rakehells residing in London. Then perhaps you are more optimistic than I."

He opened his mouth to snap a rejoinder but stopped at the forbidding look in her eyes. Elaine would brook no criticism of Nicholas, justified though it might be. "Well, I know that the greatest rakehell in London is Lord Dare, and he seems to be making up to you." This attempt at lightness quickly ended, for unable to repress his feelings, he exclaimed, "Elaine, do you not see the bad lot Nicholas has fallen in with?"

"Both Lord Dare and Nicholas are my concern, Simon, not yours. It was very kind of you to visit this morning. Please do so again soon."

The intention behind these words was unmistakable. Immediately, Elcho swung round on his heels and stalked to the door. Upon reaching it, he half turned and began to say something but closed his mouth again. He nodded curtly then left.

How like Simon to throw her into a temper, Elaine thought. But how dared he criticize Nicholas? He must have known she would fly up into the boughs at that. And her awareness that his criticism was well-deserved made it no more palatable.

Ever since Nicholas had become a member of the Great Go, Elaine had harboured many fears about his town doings. He had taken to drinking Blue Ruin, once even boxing the Watch before ending the night in Tothill Fields. However, these were mere pranks compared to his newest activities. His cronies now included Lord Mandeville and men of his kidney, all loose fish who went out raking every night, roving from the green baize tables at Great Go to the barques of frailty at Madame Bertha's love boat. She worried that Nicholas would fall into some disgraceful scrape and do himself serious harm.

And of course all her remonstrances were in vain. She succeeded only in making him itch for wilder pranks. But tolerance was her only recourse, tolerance and keeping a close watch over him so that she would always be at hand to help him if he needed her. Forbidden pleasures were always more alluring than those indulgently permitted. Perhaps Nicholas would lose interest in his rakish ways if she took them as tame stuff he would soon grow out of.

But enough fruitless introspection, she thought, and continued with her household duties, stopping by Aunt Augusta's sitting room to learn if she had any specific directions for Elaine to give the housekeeper.

Aunt Augusta was reclining upon a deeply cushioned sofa, pulled close to the fire, which was shaded by a purple screen. Nevertheless, her eyes were firmly closed, her usual pained expression on her face. She was a fragile woman, thin and frail, with pale cheeks and perfectly white hair. A paisley shawl was wrapped about her feet, and an array of medicaments—from vinaigrette, hartshorn and water, pastilles, and asafetida drops to more drastic measures such as valerian and camphorated spirits of lavender—stood within easy reach upon a marquetry table. As Elaine peeped around the door, she saw Aunt Augusta struggle to open one eye.

"Good morning, Aunt Augusta," she said in cheerful rallying tones.

Her aunt winced. "Not so loudly, my dear," she moaned. "Please have some pity."

As Elaine was quite inured to Aunt Augusta's invalidism, she vouchsafed no reply to this, merely asking, "Do you have any special requests for dinner tonight? Nicholas and I will be dining out, you know."

Aunt Augusta appeared overwhelmed at this disclosure. "What temerity, my dear, what temerity!" she expostulated feebly. "Dining where? You will do your constitution permanent damage, I have no doubt."

Elaine bit her lips. "Vauxhall's rack punch is much vaunted, I know, but I will take your warning seriously. I promise you that I shall not touch a drop of the stuff."

Aunt Augusta shuddered. "Vauxhall," she repeated, horrified. "Oh, I will have a fit of the spasms.

Going to Vauxhall tonight and to your godmother's
ball later this very week!'' Her hand groped wildly for
her vinaigrette. She clutched it tightly and put it up to
her nose for a resounding sniff. "My dear, you are
cruel, too cruel! I will have nightmarish visions for the
rest of the day. Vauxhall! The crowd, the lights, the
music. Oh!''

These were the very reasons which caused Elaine to
anticipate tonight's party so eagerly. She refrained
from informing Aunt Augusta of this fact, however,
contenting herself with nodding sympathetically. "It
fills me with apprehension, Aunt. How kind of you to
put me on my guard.''

"And the damp gardens," Aunt Augusta reminded her as one in duty bound. "Don't go traips-
ing about the gardens, or you will do your lungs
serious harm.''

Elaine blinked at this injunction and was forced to
bite back a laugh. "Oh, you are too good, Aunt. I
won't move an inch from my chair the whole night
through, I promise you. I'll stop my ears to the music
of the Pandean band, and I'll close my eyes to all the
frequenters of the place.''

"And promise not to eat any of the food!''

"And I'll close my mouth to all refreshments,"
Elaine promised blithely. "Now I can look forward to
my evening with unimpaired enjoyment.''

"Yes." Aunt Augusta sighed weakly, her mind obviously relieved. "So you can. As for myself, all I will
want is some barley water and biscuits.''

Elaine nodded, blew her aunt a kiss, and left the
room. Interpreting biscuits in a generous spirit, she

soon instructed the housekeeper to prepare some chicken, kidney pie, buttered carrots, and a syllabub.

Although Elaine had had no intention of adhering to her aunt's strictures, when the impassive butler informed her that Lord Mandeville, Nicholas's most recently acquired crony would be one of the party, the news effectively deprived her of all appetite and anticipation.

Nicholas Farrington's party reached Vauxhall that evening by the land entrance. Upon alighting from the carriage, Mandeville punctiliously took Elaine's arm, leading her with almost exaggerated gallantry to their supper box in the Crescent.

Vauxhall Gardens was a fairyland park, comprising groves, colonnades, and walks, all lit by thousands of sparkling lights. Music could be heard wafting from the Rotunda at the centre of the principal grove; fountains were playing amid various coloured lights. All was light, colour, and gaiety.

After entering their supper box, the party settled down to an evening's pleasure. Elaine's enjoyment, however, was quite cut up by a close inspection of her brother. He seemed already to be red in the gills, no doubt due to some deep drinking. He was all of eighteen years old, blond like his sister, with very merry eyes and a laughing mouth. But recently his eyes had acquired a few lines of dissipation, his mouth a somewhat set cast, and his countenance a constant flush. Indeed, tonight his complexion was downright hectic.

"So, my darling sister," Nicholas assayed gaily. "Shall you dare taste Vauxhall's famous burnt rack punch?"

Mindful of her aunt's strictures, Elaine dutifully declined this refreshment, pronouncing herself to be satisfied with lemonade.

Nicholas grimaced. "Vile stuff, I assure you. You'll maudle your insides with it, if you are not careful."

Elaine cast a deprecating glance at Lord Mandeville, but this gentleman paid little heed to Nicholas. Rather, he sat with his long nose very high in the air, an expression of disdain upon his thin, pointed face. Elaine gave a mental shrug. Rather high in the instep, was he not?

Of course he was a regular roaring-boy. Indeed, he modelled himself after the Prince Regent, not only in his heavy drinking and womanizing but also in the prodigality with which he gambled and collected art treasures.

Worse, he also had pretensions to the Dandy set. Beside the wasp waist and padded shoulders, the pomaded hair à la Brutus, and the numerous fobs and seals that made him appear a caper merchant, Lord Mandeville also displayed the air of contemptuous disregard for the rest of the world so much favoured by the London Dandies. It was not a set for which Elaine held any partiality.

"You may insist upon being damnably straitlaced, my dear, but I shan't join you in your abstemiousness. Bring us a round," Nicholas directed the obsequious waiter.

Elaine clasped her hands together. She forced herself to listen with the appearance of absorbed attention to the music from the Rotunda, or, as it was referred to by many, from the Umbrella. She also occupied herself with admiring the many twinkling lights, the cascades, and the tasteful statues scattered about.

Nicholas and Lord Mandeville, however, occupied themselves with more lively sport. There was a bevy of gaudily dressed females in the next box. Nicholas dug his elbow into Lord Mandeville's ribs, winking broadly.

Mandeville lifted his quizzing glass and stared at the bits of muslin, taking in the low-cut clinging gowns that displayed to advantage their opulent figures. Following her brother's gaze, Elaine observed their painted, leering countenances with a shudder.

Having received his glass of punch from the waiter, Nicholas lifted it in a salute to a Junoesque female with a headdress of waving ostrich plumes.

It then became apparent that these beauties were not without an escort. A stout gentleman who had had his back to Nicholas slewed around suddenly. He glared ferociously as the ostrich-plumed belle tittered behind her fan, then kissed her fingers in Nicholas's direction.

The stout gentleman's displeasure mounted as Nicholas made a great show of catching this kiss and bestowed it tenderly in his inner breast pocket.

Elaine turned away in disgust. "Nicholas, do strive for a little conduct, if you please."

Nicholas's attention, however, was wholly riveted on his latest flirt. He waggled his eyebrows at her and nodded meaningfully. Before she could respond in kind, the stout gentleman took her roughly by the arm and loudly demanded that she accompany him for a stroll about the gardens.

Her painted red lips pouted, but she rose to her feet readily enough and set off, clinging to his arm and pressing herself closely against him. Elaine watched their departure with relief, for she had noted that the gentleman, though stout, was unusually large and broad shouldered. It would not do for Nicholas to arouse his ire.

Nicholas frowned at his Cyprian's defection, and turned back to his punch. He downed his drink with one flick of the wrist, a practice much applauded by Lord Mandeville, who seemed willing to join Nicholas in turning their evening into a drinking bout.

After the first set of the concert, a bell rang, informing the audience that the time for the Grand Cascade had arrived. Hoping to divert Nicholas from his intended debauch, Elaine spoke to him. "Oh, do please accompany me to the Grand Cascade, Nicholas. I vow I haven't seen it for this age."

"Oh, that's tame stuff, Elaine," Nicholas replied with a disastrous lack of gallantry. "Wait until the fireworks go off. I'll take you to that."

"How inconsiderate you are. I declare, I shall go off to see it without any escort at all."

Nicholas smiled at this sally, and even Mandeville was moved to twitch his pursed lips in supercilious acknowledgement.

A voice from behind her made Elaine spin around in surprise. "I had no idea you were so daring, Miss Farrington," it said.

It was Lord Dare! How long had he been standing there, studying them? she wondered, irrationally irritated.

Nicholas rose promptly, if somewhat unsteadily, to his feet. Mandeville made do with a slight lifting of his thin eyebrows.

"How-de-do, sir," Nicholas greeted him with careless grace. He squinted at Dare's tall and nattily dressed form. "Do I know you?"

A humorous expression flickered over Dare's face. "You probably know *of* me," he said with a twisted smile. "I am Dare."

Nicholas's jaw dropped in surprise, and he bent forward to scrutinize Dare more closely. "Are you indeed?" he gasped. "Famous! Capital! I've been wanting to meet you this age. Ever since I learned it was you who broke Prinny's record in the curricle race to Brighton."

Dare flung up a quick hand, as though hoping to be spared a glowing account of such past misdeeds. "And I have been wanting to meet you, Mr. Farrington," he said smoothly, "ever since I learned that you are Miss Farrington's brother."

Not ever before having deemed this fact a mark of distinction, Nicholas was much struck by Lord Dare's words. He puffed out his chest a bit and exclaimed, "Why, so I am. I am much honoured to have come to your notice, my lord."

Lord Dare bowed and glanced down at Elaine's wooden countenance. "I wonder if your sister is feeling similarly honoured."

Nicholas gave a snort. "Oh, Elaine. She don't know enough about you to appreciate the circumstances properly. She rarely listens to *on dits*," he whispered in piercing accents behind his hand. "She's a high stickler, you must know."

"Thank you for this information." Dare bowed, his solemn tone belied by the mischievous light in his eyes. "I hope it will prove of use to me."

"Well, I have no use for it."

"I had somehow guessed as much."

Nicholas laughed good-naturedly. "Sit down, sit down, my lord, and join us for a round."

Lord Dare glanced again at Elaine. "But are you not forgetting that Miss Farrington has expressed a desire to see the Grand Cascade?"

Nicholas blinked.

"I no longer wish to see it," Elaine said forcefully.

"Well, don't look like such a long meg, then, Elaine. Have some punch, Lord Dare."

Dare ignored him, still looking intently at Elaine. "Ah, how pleasant it is to keep my illusions. It had surprised me to hear Miss Farrington desire to be so daring as to walk about Vauxhall Gardens or to take a close look at the Cascade. Many a duenna would frown at such impropriety."

"Why, there's nothing improper about viewing the Cascade," Elaine exclaimed, much put out.

"Then, why are you afraid to do so, now that I am here to accompany you?"

Nicholas absorbed this leveller with widening eyes. "There's much in that. If Lord Dare is to escort you, then why do you hesitate?"

Elaine cast him a fulminating look. "I am afraid of nothing," she said coldly.

Nicholas nodded, reassured. "That's what I thought. Always said you could throw your heart over any fence. Game as a pebble, that's what."

Lord Dare lifted his quizzing glass and studied Elaine through it interestedly. "Is she, indeed? She's not living up to her reputation now, though."

Elaine choked down a laugh. "But you are certainly living up to yours," she declared roundly. Then she capitulated and rose gracefully to her feet. "Let us go then."

He bowed low over her hand. "You do me great honour." As he lifted his head, the smile lurking deep in his eyes made her heart give a decided leap.

"The boot's on the other leg," Nicholas put in. He tugged Elaine's sleeve. "Have him tell you all about his curricle race. He's a great goer."

"Of that I have no doubt," Elaine said with a sniff, as she preceded Lord Dare out of the Crescent toward the Rotunda.

The curtain of the Grand Cascade rose to reveal a rural scene, containing in miniature a cascade, a water mill, a bridge, and such various vehicles as coaches, wagons, and carts, which moved across the stage. This marvel, accompanied by such realistic sound effects as creaking wheels and rushing water, however, paled into insignificance, as far as Elaine was concerned, beside Lord Dare. She was more interested in him than in the stage before her.

Unable to resist the impulse, she turned to him. "I daresay you have a veritable collection of tales that would make me round-eyed in astonishment,'' she murmured provocatively.

He turned slightly, gazing into her beautiful blue eyes. He seemed to consider her words seriously for a moment. Then he sighed, shrugged, and lightly replied, "I never relive the past, my dear. The present is too engrossing. Especially a present which includes someone as lovely as yourself.''

"Well, it won't include me for long!''

"You should stop offering me challenges, my dear. You see, I'm bound to take you up on them.''

Disconcerted by these words, Elaine fidgeted with her embroidered reticule. Swiftly, Lord Dare reached out and grasped her hand. Almost as though she had suffered a sudden burn, she jerked her hand away. She felt strangely breathless. She waited a moment to calm her racing heart before saying bitingly, "Lord Dare, I find your attentions distasteful.''

His eyes flashed, and he leaned forward to assure her calmly, "That is because you are not accustomed to them. But you will grow used to them in time.''

The man was an accomplished flirt! Her hand itched to slap his smiling face. "No, I shan't,'' she declared hotly. "I wish you would refrain from such complete nonsense.'' He started to respond, but she interrupted him. "I wish to return to my brother.''

He stared at her, then his strong jaw clamped shut as he submitted with a stiff bow. And so they returned to the Crescent. And found it in uproar. Apparently Nicholas had made good use of Elaine's short absence. He stood by the table in the next box, in hot dispute with the stout gentleman. At this very moment, that gentleman swung his fist and caught Nicholas full on the chin with a flush hit.

Elaine stopped dead in her tracks. Nicholas reeled at the blow but made a quick recovery. He took a snowy handkerchief from his coat sleeve and delicately wiped the blood from his face. He crumpled up the handkerchief, let it drop to the ground, and without further ado, leaped toward his opponent and delivered a resounding right hook.

"A regular set-to," Lord Dare observed, his voice shaking with laughter. "What a young rapscallion your brother is."

The attendant females set up a series of shrieks and squawks, drawing the attention of the occupants of the other boxes. Lord Mandeville hovered about the fighting pair, vainly remonstrating and waving his hands.

Elaine hurried to Mandeville's side. "Can't you make them stop?" she demanded urgently.

"No, I cannot," he replied petulantly, his face alarmingly red. He closed his eyes as Nicholas dealt his opponent another punishing right. "The wretched boy pays me no heed. I wash my hands of him."

Indeed, Nicholas ignored Mandeville completely, nor did he mind his sister's anxious pleas for him to bethink himself. At the beginning of this bout he had seemed to have the advantage, due to his quickness and expertise, but the stout gentleman's greater strength told as the fight progressed. He dealt Nicholas a cross-buttock which threw him abruptly to the ground. Dazed, Nicholas shook his head, but gamely struggled to his feet, only to receive a right hook that sent him staggering back.

"Won't someone please stop this?" Elaine begged in a despairing voice to the growing crowd of onlookers.

Lord Dare promptly responded to this plea. "With pleasure," he said, gripping her shoulder reassuringly. With his usual sangfroid, he stepped forward from the crowd that had formed a circle around the fighters.

He waited till Nicholas was again thrown down in complete disorder. Dare then tapped the stout gentleman on the shoulder. The man whirled round, his fists raised. Almost casually Lord Dare slipped inside his guard and dropped him with a single punch.

By this time Nicholas had risen to his feet. He stood blinking at his unconscious opponent. "Did I do that?" he asked bemusedly.

Lord Dare hid a smile, pretending to flick a speck of dust from his coat. "You were the one fighting him, were you not?"

"So I was." He wiped his hands in satisfaction. "Told the fellow to keep his nose out of my affairs, or I would flatten it for him."

"You would appear to have kept your word."

"So I have." He smiled and turned eagerly to the Cyprian who had originally won his attentions. "And now..."

But Lord Dare prevented further intercourse. He took Nicholas firmly by the arm and propelled him to where Elaine was standing. She glared disdainfully at the lingering onlookers, who quickly dispersed, disappointed at the bout's sudden close. She glowered at the singularly unrepentant Nicholas. Then she turned to catch Lord Dare smiling quizzically at her.

"I return him to you, Miss Farrington, safe and sound," he said with a bow.

Unaccountably, her real gratitude changed to rising resentment. "Well, Lord Dare, you seem to have become the family's guardian angel. While your services have, of course, been appreciated, I do assure you that we shall manage quite well without your assistance."

He lifted an eyebrow at her. But instead of taking instant affront, he looked down at her with an understanding expression. Then his mouth twisted. "As you know, I am no angel. My actions are far from altruistic. I shall expect recompense for any service I do you. Of that you may have no doubt."

Elaine responded to the less provoking part of this speech. "I assure we have no further call for any service of yours."

He gave her a sidelong glance, his eyes enigmatic. "That depends upon what you mean by service."

"By Jove, that's a point," Nicholas put in suddenly. "For instance, sister, what I would consider a service, you might consider an ill-turn."

Elaine looked at him in exasperation. "Just so, Nicholas," she snapped.

Nicholas brightened at this unexpected agreement, but Lord Dare quickly disillusioned him. "Don't take her at her word, Farrington. You can see from the way her beautiful eyes sparkle that she is in something less than complete agreement."

"If you mean I approve my brother's lamentable tendency to fall into disgraceful exhibitions, you are quite right; however, I have no intention of raking him down in so public a place."

"She'll wait till you get home," Dare whispered loudly into Nicholas's ear. Mr. Farrington nodded resignedly.

Elaine started hotly to deny this, but she admitted that such, indeed, was her intention. She bit back a laugh, shaking her head in amused chagrin.

Lord Dare observed these signs with interest. He gave a slow smile. "Were you about to speak, Miss Farrington?"

"You are insufferable!"

"Very true. But as I told you before, you will grow to accept it with time." He then bowed abruptly, disappearing before Elaine could say another word.

Finding herself staring at empty air, Elaine took a deep breath and with controlled calm asked her brother if they now could return home. Officiously, Nicholas took both Elaine and Mandeville by the arm and shepherded them to the land entrance where their carriage awaited them.

On the ride home, he entertained them with an exhaustive description of his recent triumph. He dwelt extensively on his opponent's manifold weaknesses and his own magnificent prowess. Gentleman Jackson, he declared, would have been proud of him. Far from being proud of him, Elaine still seethed with indignation over the scene; in Mandeville's presence she restrained her tongue.

When they reached Farrington Place, Nicholas escorted Elaine to the door and then promptly took the wind out of her eye by announcing his intention to accompany Mandeville to the Great Go. She had to swallow a hot rejoinder, for Seaton opened the door and stood waiting for them. She could not comb her brother's head with a footstool right under the butler's nose. And so she bade Nicholas good-night in a stifled voice.

She marched up to her bedroom where her maid was waiting to undress her. Mary chatted inconsequentially as she helped Elaine into her nightdress and plaited her golden hair. The girl's murmuring voice did much to soothe Elaine's jangled nerves.

She dismissed Mary with a pleasant smile and her thanks. She tied the ribbons of her nightcap under her chin, then climbed into bed, pulling the bedclothes cozily about her ears. She lay awake a few moments, reviewing the evening's events.

Lord Dare was certainly proving far more assiduous in his attentions than she had anticipated. And she had to admit to herself that she was grateful to him for intervening in that reprehensible affair in the Crescent. Nevertheless, his winning ways would serve him not at all. She had no intention of succumbing to Lord Dare's charms. And she would tell him so, to his face—when next they met.

CHAPTER THREE

AND SHE MET LORD DARE again that very week at her godmama's. Lady Somercote's ball signalled the true opening of the Season. Even Nicholas agreed to accompany Elaine for he could not miss this annual gathering of the haut ton.

No expense was spared for this magnificent event. Red carpets lined the entranceways. Banks of flowers and potted palms decorated the huge ballroom. Waiters darted about, carrying trays laden with champagne in tall crystal glasses and silver baskets of lobster patties and Chantillies.

To do the ball justice, Elaine chose her prettiest gown, a confection all in white with a Russian bodice and inserts of blue satin down the front. Mary arranged her hair into a riot of ringlets à la Medusa, tenderly placing a white rose in their midst. Long white gloves, secured with two sparkling diamond-and-aquamarine bracelets, and an ivory frosted fan finished the toilette.

Floating down the staircase, Elaine found Nicholas, dressed in silk pantaloons and a dark coat, awaiting her. Since he looked interestingly pale, Elaine had no doubt that his previous evening had been yet another revel-rout.

"Nicholas," she said before she could restrain herself. "You'll drink yourself into your grave."

Fortunately, he refrained from biting her nose off. He contented himself with a merry, if slightly sheepish, smile and said, "Considering the poisonous stuff I was served last night, I have no doubt you are quite right. Tothill Fields," he explained. "Blue Ruin. Vile stuff."

"I shall have to take your word for that, dear brother."

Seaton opened the door, and Nicholas escorted Elaine to the carriage that was pulled up in front of the house. They had said good-night to Aunt Augusta earlier that evening and did not disturb her again. After all, the thought of her charges venturing into the dangerous night air could only bring on one of her spasms.

"I am so glad you have come," Lady Somercote exclaimed as they greeted her. "Now I can feel that my ball is a real success."

Elaine smiled affectionately at her. Lady Somercote was a favourite of hers. She was a pretty, fluttering creature, with pale yellow hair and bright blue eyes. She was generous to a fault and had quite the kindest heart of anyone Elaine had ever met. She kissed her hostess, then gazed smilingly about her.

The ballroom was already filled to overflowing. Elaine knew Lady Somercote had invited more than five hundred guests, a number calculated to achieve the accolade desired by every hostess: to have her ball declared a lamentable crush.

"I don't think you need *our* presence to assure you that your ball is a resounding success, dear God-mama Lavinia," Elaine said quizzingly.

Lady Somercote coloured in pleasure. "How kind of you to say so," she murmured. She pressed Elaine's hand affectionately and waved her forward into the ballroom. She knew that several smarts and beaux were eagerly awaiting her goddaughter's entrance.

It was a beautiful ballroom with painted ceilings, shining mirrors, sparkling chandeliers, and colourful banks of sweetly scented flowers. And it was made even more beautiful by its occupants. They were a kaleidoscope of colour. The ladies shimmered in silks, satins, and brocades of all shades, and their jewels sparkled in the candlelight. The gentlemen wore knee-breeches or pantaloons of satin, complemented by magnificent waistcoats, flowing cravats, and glinting fobs and seals.

The most beautiful guest in the room, or so he evidently hoped, was a dear friend of both Elaine and Nicholas: Lord Darlington. He was a slender young gentleman, of average height and graceful carriage. His face was perfectly round and rather cherubic, his curly brown locks providing a suitable halo. Though his person might be unremarkable, his dress certainly was not. Lord Darlington aspired to the Dandy set, and as he possessed a handsome fortune, he could indulge his every whim. This evening he was arrayed in shades of orange and yellow. His waisted coat with exaggeratedly long tails was of pale orange; his satin knee-breeches were yellow; both his waistcoat and his stockings were striped orange and yellow.

Elaine and Nicholas greeted this vision with unfeigned delight, for they had long ago realized that Darlington's outlandish attire covered an exceptionally good-natured soul.

He returned their greeting distractedly, for he had just discovered that his coat was marred by an infinitesimal wrinkle. His face puckered with disquiet, he sighed. "And this is the first time I've ever worn it. Fainall will certainly have to be brought to book for its condition."

"What a catastrophe," Elaine clucked. "But your valet can hardly be held accountable. No one, not even Fainall, has quite your eye for detail, Darlington. Perhaps no one else will notice it since it's such a small wrinkle."

"One can scarcely see it," Nicholas said placatingly.

"There's no such thing as a small wrinkle," Darlington explained in all seriousness. "Either on your face or on your clothes." He sighed. "I must ask Alvanley if he thinks I should leave the ball immediately."

Lord Alvanley, a Corinthian with a most prosaic turn of mind, could be trusted to relieve Darlington of all anxiety, so Elaine and Nicholas encouraged this intent, smiling and nodding as Darlington tottered off to the gaming room in search of his friend.

Her attention was almost immediately claimed by her cousin, Lord Elcho. He was standing near the wall, making painstaking conversation with a dowager sitting in a bergère chair.

"My dear Elaine," he exclaimed, his light-coloured eyes brightening. "How wonderful it is to see you."

Elaine took his hand and made her brother's presence known to Elcho. The two shook hands, Nicholas in a rather mechanical fashion, for he was obviously chafing to get away. He bowed, then indicated his desire to follow Lord Darlington to the gaming room on the first floor, but Elaine detained him by the simple expedient of gripping his coat sleeve.

"Careful, dear sister, or you'll give my coat such a wrinkle that I, too, will have no choice but to flee from the ballroom." Nicholas playfully slapped away her hand.

"Oh, no, you don't, Nicholas." Elaine eyed him steadily. "It doesn't become you to poke fun at Darlington. And you must do the pretty, for a change. Dance with a young lady of quality. It is not a painful exercise, and you might just enjoy it. And," she added meaningfully, "Lady Somercote will expect it."

Nicholas grimaced. He lifted his quizzing glass and halfheartedly peered about him. Elaine began to hope when she saw him give a sudden smile. Unfortunately, this smile was meant only for the approaching Mandeville. Incorrigible boy, Elaine thought with a reluctant chuckle.

Mandeville sauntered toward them. He was dressed exquisitely, displaying a profusion of rings, pins, fobs, chains and seals. His hair was pomaded, and he waved a languid handkerchief at them. The handkerchief suddenly stilled and dropped, when Mandeville caught sight of Elcho. He actually checked his approach, and stood there, apparently debating whether or not to beat a hasty retreat!

Elaine blinked and looked at Lord Elcho, her eyebrows lifting. Then her puzzlement increased, for Elcho was frowning direly at Mandeville, his manner distinctly menacing, his brow creased and darkling.

To Elaine's astonishment, she saw Mandeville swing on his heel and hasten away, without a backward glance. Nicholas's mouth fell open, and he gasped, "Well, I must say! The cut-direct. I never would have believed it of him."

Although she was far from sharing his chagrin, Elaine commiserated with him for a moment. She then indicated a shy young thing cowering beside her mama, and without a partner for the next set. Nicholas sighed and shrugged his shoulders. Then rather militantly he approached the dab of a girl—who appeared less than gratified by his alarming attention—and led her onto the floor.

Elaine returned to Lord Elcho, who was still frowning heavily. After a moment's silence, she commented, "I thought you and Mandeville were bosom chums. Have you had a falling-out?"

His eyes flickered impatiently, then his face became masklike. "A falling-out?" he repeated.

"Yes. I couldn't help but notice Mandeville's reluctance to greet you."

There was another pause. Then he noisily cleared his throat. "I did have a minor discussion with that…that fellow," he confessed reluctantly, his eyes shifting under her gaze. "I no longer count him amongst my acquaintance. And I told him to avoid Nicholas in the future. I feel he is a bad influence.''

Elaine's eyes kindled dangerously. "That was mighty officious of you, my lord. No doubt I should express my gratitude. Unfortunately, it is something quite the contrary that I now feel.''

He turned red and pulled at his suddenly constricting collar. "I know it was not my place. But surely you know the concern I feel for you . . . and your brother, of course.''

"Your solicitude is overwhelming. And quite unnecessary. You have no right to interfere in our affairs.''

"I wish you would give me that right," he began, his eyes becoming overbright.

She stopped him abruptly, bowing coldly and striding away. And she came face-to-face with Lord Dare. He was looking fine as fivepence in an elegant black coat and pantaloons and a plain white waistcoat. A single fob hung at his waist, a single diamond glinted within the folds of his neckcloth, and one golden ring adorned his hand. Lord Darlington ought to take sartorial hints from him, Elaine thought suddenly, for he took the shine out of every other gentleman in the room.

His smile glinted down at her. "May I have this dance?" he asked.

Without hesitation, she nodded and marched onto the floor. She was still angry. Elcho was too encroaching by half, she told herself. She was stiff and unyielding in Lord Dare's arms, and she all but ignored her partner.

They had made several revolutions about the floor before Lord Dare ventured to speak. "And I've always thought that music soothes the distraught spirit," he commented wistfully. "No doubt I have been shamefully misled."

Elaine tried not to grit her teeth.

Lord Dare spoke with spurious sympathy. "I daresay you are fighting your chagrin at having so easily capitulated to my charms," he said, the expression in his eyes positively seraphic.

In her surprise, she missed a step and was momentarily sustained by Dare's strong arms. Her heart began to beat uncomfortably loudly, and she swallowed with difficulty. "I beg your pardon?"

His eyes danced as he nodded. "Yes! Why, you accepted my hand for this dance without the slightest demur."

"Well, that had nothing to do with *you*!"

For a moment, he seemed profoundly taken aback. Then with a crestfallen air that Elaine did not at all believe, he said sadly, "I see. Your dancing with me has nothing to do with me. I collect that it was the music, after all, that your soul craved."

That won a reluctant grin from her. But as she had no intention of discussing personal matters with Lord Dare, she did not explain that it was distance from Lord Elcho she had actually craved. Her cousin was becoming insufferable. How dared he take it upon himself to decide upon Nicholas's friends! She looked about the dance floor with half a mind to tell Lord Mandeville to pay no attention at all to Lord Elcho.

Dare recalled her wandering attention by politely clearing his throat. "Are you looking for someone?"

"Lord Mandeville," Elaine disclosed without thinking.

Lord Dare stiffened, then his shoulders shook with silent laughter. Elaine looked quickly up at his face and watched him try to summon a pained expression. "Oh, shall I ever recover my reputation? Is he my rival, then?"

As if he could ever have a rival where a lady was concerned, she thought fleetingly. Then she gave herself a mental shake. "Don't be nonsensical. He's a friend of Nicholas."

"Ah, yes," he said, nodding wisely. "I see that I'm not the only one who has observed that the way to your heart is through your brother."

"Don't talk such nonsense. I tell you, he's just one of Nicholas's cronies."

"Ah, yes," he repeated. "But nevertheless, he's not impervious to feminine charms." His face became wistful. "And neither, I find, am I."

"I don't know what you mean."

"I don't know myself. You see, I've never been a squire of dames. So I am unfamiliar with the signs."

"Don't try to gammon me, my lord. I know very well that you're a veteran in the petticoat line."

He gave his twisted smile and said, most improperly, "You see, I've had very little traffic with carefully nurtured females. *Chères amies* are another matter altogether. One can set up a particular with amazing ease."

Elaine gaped at this response. Yet it did not offend her; rather, she was amused at his outrageousness. "I must bow to your experience, my lord. But have you found no time in your life for more serious attachments?"

His dark eyes were hooded. "Why, no. I've been preoccupied with other matters."

"As well I, and all of London, know. You've been preoccupied with setting the town on its ear and throwing the scandal-mongers into a pelter, have you not? I've heard that you even held a curricle race inside Carlton House."

He frowned slightly, and his eyes scanned her face searchingly. "Such pranks seem to you unaccountable, I imagine."

"Why, no. I collect your reckless, care-for-nobody nature must account for them. Otherwise, there could indeed be no reason for them."

His nostrils flared, his expression almost blazing. Then his face tightened to immobility. "No. No reason at all. And for no reason at all, I seem to be falling a victim to your beauty. As is also Mandeville."

"Neither of you cares a snap for my beauty," she disclaimed hotly, her cheeks glowing. "Why, Mandeville sees nothing beyond his own very long nose."

"I don't think you could convince Miss Iona Poole of that. Mandeville's taking a real interest in her charms also, as she will soon discover."

Elaine eyed him suspiciously. "Miss Iona Poole?"

"Yes. Mandeville holds quite a number of Poole's vowels. And Miss Poole believes she can induce him to tear up all those pretty little IOUs. The poor simple girl has gone into the conservatory to discuss the matter with him."

"How do you know all this?"

"I know about all sorts of things," he murmured inscrutably.

"And you believe Mandeville will take advantage of Miss Poole?" she asked, horrified. Dare gave what seemed to her a callous shrug. "Why don't you do something about it?" she demanded.

As the music came to a finish, Dare led Elaine to the wall before speaking. "There will come a time when I wish to interfere with Mandeville's doings," he said in a voice of indefinable menace. "But that moment has not, as yet, arrived."

She almost stamped her foot with indignation. "So you will do nothing?"

His eyes narrowed, and his expression remained impassive. "I'm afraid," he said coolly, "I have misled you in your recent experiences. I must remind you that I am no guardian angel. Miss Poole's virtue is no concern of mine."

"You are insufferable!" she snapped. Without another word, she went in search of Nicholas.

She came upon her brother just as he was about to make a surreptitious exit from the ballroom on his way to the gaming room. At sight of her, he flushed and looked just like a guilty schoolboy.

"Nicholas!" Elaine cried impetuously. "You must help her."

Nicholas's eyes widened in astonishment. "Help whom?" he demanded.

"Miss Iona Poole!"

"I never heard of the girl." He shook his head and started to whisk away. However, curiosity got the better of him, and he stopped and asked, "Save her from what?"

"Mandeville. He's taken her to the conservatory."

"I had no idea there was anything dangerous in that room. What is it, a loose chandelier?"

Elaine made a face at his funning. "This is serious, Nicholas. It is your long-nosed friend whose intentions are dangerous."

Nicholas stared. "Do you mean Mandeville?"

"Yes, that's exactly who I mean!"

"Pooh. You don't think he's going to ravish the girl in the middle of a ball, do you?"

"I can't be sure," Elaine said darkly. "All I know is that you're wasting precious time." She gripped his sleeve tightly and pulled him forward. "Come along."

Protesting, he followed her to the conservatory. It was a large room, leading off the ballroom, with a high-vaulted ceiling and leaded-glass doors.

As they were about to open these doors, they were suddenly transfixed by the scene within. A young girl was struggling in Mandeville's arms, trying desperately to evade his kisses.

Nicholas sprang forward, pushed through the doors, and laid a heavy hand on Mandeville's shoulder.

Breathing raggedly, Mandeville swung around to face his accoster. "You!" he gasped. "What the devil do you want here?"

Nicholas ignored him. He looked only at the shaken girl. "I believe this dance is ours," he said gently, holding out his hand.

Miss Poole shuddered. Her pretty childlike countenance was flushed, and her dark hair was slightly dishevelled. She looked as though she might faint, but she managed to pull herself together. Without a word or glance to Mandeville, she took Nicholas's hand and they left the conservatory.

Mandeville started to protest, but as he passed, Nicholas warned him, "Have a care, Mandeville, have a care!"

Mandeville's face darkened. His mouth opened and shut, and his cheeks puffed out, but he did not speak again.

Resisting the impulse to snap her fingers under Mandeville's long nose, Elaine hurried forward to soothe Miss Poole. She helped her rearrange her dress and tidy her hair, all the time assuring her her absence had not been noticed. Then she looked in admiration at her brother. His face was set, and his eyes were still bright.

"Well done, Nicholas," she exclaimed. "That was very well done of you."

The three now came flush against Lord Dare, who had apparently witnessed the entire encounter. He had his quizzing glass to his eye, and he studied Nicholas. "Yes. Very neat," He commented.

Nicholas appeared highly gratified. He put up his hand in modest disclaimer.

Miss Poole then added her mite. "Indeed," she said warmly. "It was exceedingly well done of you. I don't know how to thank you."

He looked suddenly down at the sound of her soft, shy voice, an arrested expression on his face. He seemed to be seeing her for the very first time.

They stood so, almost frozen in time, staring into each other's eyes. A slight blush crept into Miss Poole's cheeks, but she made no attempt to avert her eyes.

"It makes one feel a trifle *de trop*, doesn't it," Lord Dare remarked to Elaine.

She could have kicked him, for his words seemed to bring the pair to their senses. Nicholas blinked, bit his lips, then without saying a word he bowed and stalked away.

Lord Dare watched his exit with interest. "An intriguing young cub, is he not? There is more to him than I had thought. I believe I shall cultivate his acquaintance."

"Really?" Elaine asked, her voice dripping with sarcasm. "Do you think you'll have the time? I thought you intended to cultivate mine."

He smiled, his dark eyes gleaming appreciatively. "Jealous? You have no need. I'll always have time for you, my dear."

She turned her shoulder on this attempt at levity and smiled reassuringly at Miss Iona Poole. "I'm sure you'll wish to rejoin your mama. Do you know where she is?"

Miss Poole pointed to a tiny birdlike creature roosting in a rout chair along the wall. Elaine nodded

and led the girl to her mother. After a few brief re-
marks she tactfully left them together.

She was soon joined by Lord Elcho, who hastened
to her side. "Elaine," he exclaimed, "what has happened? You look quite done-up."

She looked him up and down, frowning. "You seem
to take an inordinate interest in what does not concern you," she retorted before she could stop herself.

He stiffened, outraged. "If my own cousin does not
concern me, then I don't know what should!"

The justice of his words only made her the angrier.
"There are limits, however, to cousinly affection."

"Is he annoying you?" a voice politely inquired. It
was Lord Dare, once more standing at her elbow.
"What was it Nicholas said in order to extricate Miss
Poole from Mandeville's clutches? Ah, yes, I remember. I believe this dance is ours, is it not?" And he
grandly held out his hand to Elaine, bowing with a
flourish.

She stepped back from him. "How dare you class
my cousin with Mandeville?"

He looked at her through half-closed eyes, his
mouth curling. "They seem to have a great deal in
common. More, perhaps, than you know." His eyes
opened suddenly, and he stared directly at Elcho. "Do
you not agree, my lord?" His words held a distinct
threat.

Lord Elcho seemed badly discomposed. He paled,
and his shaking hand went involuntarily to his cravat.

Dare's words put Elaine all on end. "You are mistaken, my lord. It is you who have most in common
with my Lord Mandeville, not Lord Elcho."

"I see," Dare said, his brows snapping together and his mouth closing in a thin line. "Then you are quite happy in his company?"

"Happier in his than in yours."

He bowed stiffly. "Then I shall leave you to it."

She watched his departure with a smouldering gaze. Before she could speak, however, Lord Elcho exclaimed, "That devil! I can't abide him!"

Although Elaine shared his sentiments, she was still not in sympathy with her cousin. Therefore, she said in a repressive voice, "I don't believe I care to discuss your opinion of him, Simon. I think we have said enough to each other this evening, so I wish you goodnight."

His fists clenched, and he ground his teeth. Yet he managed a creditable bow as Elaine nodded and turned away, once more to search for her brother.

She had no doubt that he had headed for the gaming room. She, therefore, descended the grand staircase, smiling politely at various acquaintances as she passed. The ball had been so fraught with unpleasant incident that she thought it wise to retire.

She waited at the base of the stairs until a footman in a dark blue livery appeared. "Please ask my brother, Mr. Farrington, to come out to me," she directed him, knowing no lady of quality could enter a gaming room herself.

He bowed obsequiously, then scuttled off down the marble hallway. Elaine stepped back into a shallow alcove, which had been, for this evening of festivity, transformed into a veritable bower, with a gigantic potted palm and a multitude of flowers.

She was admiring a particularly beautiful orchid when the sound of a step made her turn with a smile, hoping to see Nicholas. She learned her mistake, however, when she turned straight into Lord Dare's arms. To her astonishment, he grasped her slim waist tightly.

"You have left Lord Elcho," he observed exultantly. "So it is *my* company that you prefer, after all!"

Elaine pulled away from his grasp. "You must be all about in your head, my lord. And how dare you touch me in such a familiar manner?" She sounded missish, but with him so very close to her, she felt decidedly unsure of herself.

"But you've chosen such an ideal trysting place, my dear," he pointed out reasonably. "Secluded enough for me even to venture a kiss." His teasing smile increased her unease.

"You wouldn't dare!" she exclaimed.

He gave a sudden shout of laughter. A look of real delight illumined his face. Then, with a strange mixture of glee and sympathy, he said, "Sometimes, it's truly a pleasure living up to my reputation!"

And with that, his mouth swooped suddenly on hers in a suffocating kiss. Elaine struggled but to no avail. A wave of heat seemed to seep over her as his demanding mouth pressed against her lips. His arms felt like iron bands about her. Her head swam, and she had begun to feel positively dizzy, when she was suddenly released.

She gasped for breath and could neither speak nor move. Dare kindly turned her half-around so that she could see her brother approaching.

"It is Nicholas," Lord Dare whispered in Elaine's ear, himself sounding strangely breathless. Then his voice quivered with suppressed laughter. "He certainly is spoiling sport tonight, isn't he? But there will be other opportunities."

"There will not!" Elaine began, but she found herself speaking to air. Lord Dare had disappeared.

CHAPTER FOUR

ONCE SAFELY ENSCONCED in their carriage, Elaine was hard-pressed not to complain vociferously to Nicholas. However, embarrassment caused her to hold her tongue, embarrassment and another emotion she did not examine too closely.

Nicholas, however, took notice of her kindling eyes, commenting, "Dancing agrees with you, my dear. Why, it gives you quite a sparkle."

She glared at him a moment, then sighed and shook her head. "Yes. If you were more attentive to the art, then you, too, would benefit from its advantages."

"Oh, pooh. Dancing's dull stuff. Not at all in my line."

Elaine smiled in amused acknowledgment. To soothe her lacerated sensibilities, she began to tease Nicholas gently for his night's work.

"How disappointed Miss Iona Poole will be to learn that. You made quite an impression on her, you know," she said, a slightly malicious gleam in her eye.

Nicholas scowled at her, remaining silent for an appreciable length of time. He even commenced to pull at his lower lip, a sign of perturbation from his early childhood. Then he waved his hand airily before snapping his fingers in Elaine's face. "I care not a whit for Miss Iona Poole, nor, for that matter, for any other presentable female.''

Surprised by the home hit she had scored, she pursued the matter. She nodded slowly. "I see. You cherish *tendres* only for unpresentable females.''

He attempted a careless shrug. Then he twirled a gold fob that hung from his waistcoat, seemingly engrossed in the play of reflected moonlight. "I've never been one for romance, as you know,'' he replied finally, his tone a nice mixture of pride and regret.

"I know only too well, dear brother. Riots and rumpuses are more in your line. Therefore, it will no doubt crown your evening when I tell you that you made quite an impression on the Devil's Dare.''

Nicholas brightened perceptibly. "You don't say! You aren't bamming me, are you?''

She shook her head at him, laughing in consternation. "My, what a reprehensible character you are. To think of experiencing transports of delight because you won the approval of the Devil's Dare.'' Her words were particularly bitter, for she still felt Lord Dare's lips hot against hers. How she wished she could wipe that unsettling experience from her memory as thoroughly as she had, rather schoolgirlishly, wiped her own lips after Lord Dare had released her.

Nicholas was serenely oblivious to her tone, having promptly flown *aux anges*. "The Devil's Dare approves of me,'' he breathed wonderingly. His breast began to swell and his eyes to sparkle. "I must say, I find that highly gratifying. Come, cut line, Elaine. Tell me all that he said.''

He was like a puppy begging for a treat. But she was extremely loath to give it him. If only she had not mentioned Lord Dare, she thought to herself in despair. Grudgingly she replied, "He merely said that there was more to you than he had thought and that he felt he should, as he put it, cultivate you."

Nicholas went into high alt. "Cultivate me," he exclaimed, his face glowing at the prospect. "What a world of experiences this opens up to me. You don't know what this means to me."

Elaine could only regard him with a jaundiced eye. If Nicholas knew what kind of experience Lord Dare had introduced *her* to this very evening, he might think less of his hero. As it was, Nicholas's exultation would no doubt completely gratify Lord Dare. He had probably, she thought grimly to herself, expected an equally enthusiastic response when he proposed winning her affections. Well, she vowed militantly, he must now know how very fair and far off he was there!

When the carriage pulled up before Farrington Place, Elaine was left to the care of a prompt and well-trained footman, who assisted her from the carriage, for Nicholas made no move whatsoever to quit his seat. Instead, he leaned forward and quickly shut the carriage door behind her before signing the driver to continue on. Deserted so unceremoniously on the flagway, Elaine watched the retreating vehicle with increasing misgiving. She had no doubt that Nicholas intended to offer himself forthwith to the Devil's Dare as a most willing protégé. She bitterly reproached herself as she went inside. She should have bitten out her tongue before she had uttered a syllable to Nicholas of Lord Dare's interest in him.

She should, rather, have informed him of Lord Dare's interest in her. Then he could have called Dare to book for her. That devil should pay for insulting her! When she asked herself exactly why she had refrained from disclosing Dare's iniquitous behaviour, she decided that she had found herself unable to put the experience into words. Indeed, just thinking of it cast her again into emotional turmoil.

Pulled out of her pucker by Seaton's solicitous inquiries, Elaine looked up to tell him that she would need no further services for the evening and that he could tell Mary not to wait up for her. With that, she stepped into the salon, determined to await Nicholas's return.

She was certain that Nicholas would approach Lord Dare hoping for a night's raking. But she would put a spoke in his wheel by lying in watch for him. Indeed, she felt it to be her duty to do so. He must be made aware of Lord Dare's perfidy. As matters now stood, Nicholas was the proverbial lamb in the jaws of a wolf.

For Lord Dare *was* a wolf, as she well knew. Why, he was worse than Lord Mandeville, for Mandeville had only attempted to kiss Miss Iona Poole. Lord Dare had succeeded in his reprehensible endeavour.

Elaine's cheeks burned at the memory. A man had never kissed her full on the lips before. She had previously received chaste pecks on the cheek and experienced only the occasional surreptitious arm about her waist. However, these encounters had but little prepared her for Lord Dare's kiss. Did all such kisses

cause the blood to race so violently and the heart to
beat so riotously? Or perhaps it was just in Lord
Dare's power alone.... She caught herself up at the
thought. Forget it, she admonished herself, else she
would never again be able to look Lord Dare straight
in the eyes.

To banish him entirely from her thoughts, she decided she should spend her hours of vigil in reading.
She had left a novel by the great Walter Scott on a little Pembroke table, ready to be taken up again at the
first opportunity.

Therefore, she seated herself in the comfortable
wing-backed chair beside the fireplace, noting with
pleasure that a fire was crackling steadily away. As she
began to turn the pages of *Waverley*, she remembered
Lord Elcho's telling her that Scott was to lead the Regalia Commission. It was an office he would no doubt
take very seriously, for much of his writing concerned
the history of Scotland and its ancient traditions.

He had indeed won for Scotland much prestige,
evoking in his novels the glory of its powerful clans,
its fierce Highlanders, its ancient bards. By gaining
respect for Scotland, he hoped consequently to gain
for it better treatment. He had succeeded so well that
the Prince Regent had undertaken a personal Scottish
tour. He had arrived in Edinburgh wearing a full
Highland costume.

Scott had also tried to win Scotland's respect for
England's regent. But Elaine doubted that he would
ever succeed in this enterprise. Prinny was a far from
inspiring figure. In fact, while in Edinburgh, he had
essayed the famous Highland fling. A heroic effort,

considering his great weight, but on that ended ingloriously: the Prince had slipped, twisting his ankle. He had taken to his bed for two weeks, emitting therefrom such rending cries of pain and suffering that all Edinburgh had feared his total mental collapse. Indeed, Prinny's brother, the Duke of Cumberland, had declared that his brother's illness was higher than the foot and that a blister on the head might be more efficacious than a poultice on the ankle.

Even without such valid cause for discontent, Elaine knew that staunch Jacobites would always exist who would refuse their loyalty to the Prince, who would never submit to England's sway, who would never cease to plan for rebellion.

If the Prince Regent had indeed removed the Scottish Regalia from their legal resting place... Elaine shuddered at the possible ramifications. Prinny was a renowned collector of art treasures. Carlton House was filled with the ornate furniture, bronzes, porcelain, gold and silver plate that he had collected from the greatest artists in Europe. The Scottish Regalia, therefore, must sorely tempt him. She knew that the sword of state was a most beautiful piece of workmanship, a present from Pope Julius II to James IV, and that the sceptre, wrought in oak leaves, was of layered gold.

These ancient treasures had been safeguarded by the Scots throughout their turbulent history until the union, at which time England had agreed to keep them safe in Edinburgh under lock and key, where they would remain as perpetual emblems of Scotland's history and greatness.

She hoped fervently that the Regalia Commission would find the ancient Scottish Regalia secure in their storage chest. For their loss would prove a powerful pretext for a dangerous and perhaps bloody rupture between Scotland and England.

Sighing, Elaine turned to her book, losing herself by degrees in the pleasures of Scott's novel. So she whiled away the hours until Nicholas's return.

And there were many hours indeed, until he finally appeared, looking extremely well-to-live. He sauntered into the salon, making straight for the brandy decanter on the sideboard. He turned as Elaine delicately cleared her throat and squinted at her through obviously bleary eyes. He waved his arm in greeting, smiling muzzily. Then he was so gracious as to bestow upon her a wet and smacking kiss.

"Greetings, dear sister of my heart," he exclaimed. This endearing salutation might have been more effective had Nicholas not immediately returned his attention to the brandy decanter. He poured himself a most generous libation.

"I see you are fast degenerating into a model pupil," Elaine observed dryly. "Lord Daré must be quite proud of you."

At the mention of his idol's name, Nicholas fairly burst with satisfaction. "By Jove, he is a veritable inspiration."

Elaine made a wry face. "Yes, but he inspires me only with a desire to slap his face."

Nicholas waved an airy hand. "I daresay that is because you have not seen him in his element."

"And just where is that, pray?"

"At a gaming-hell, of course!"

"Well, I could hardly be expected to be allowed past those sacred portals, now could I?" Elaine demanded.

The sarcasm was wasted on Nicholas. He patted her shoulder in lively commiseration. "True enough. You don't know what you're missing." He rubbed his hands with relish. "The fellow's an inspiration."

"You said that already."

"Yes, but Barrymore was so sure of himself. He wagered five thousand pounds on just one turn of the cards."

"And Dare accepted that wager?" Elaine asked, aghast.

Nicholas blinked at her in surprise. "Why, of course! He *had* to. He has a reputation to uphold, you must know. They don't call him the Devil's Dare for nothing."

Elaine fully agreed with him. "He lost, of course."

"He did not!" declared Nicholas triumphantly. "He won! And his expression never changed. What a cool hand he is, to be sure."

Elaine could not share in his rejoicing. She would have preferred to hear that Dare had rolled himself up.

"And then he challenged everyone present—on *my* suggestion, if you please—to a drinking bout, declaring that since he had five thousand pounds, he was determined to spend it all that very night."

Elaine's mouth fell open. The man must be mad. "Did everyone take him up on it?" she inquired feebly.

"Why, of course. It was the only thing we could do, Miss Woolly-crown!"

Elaine nodded. "Of course, I see that that is true. And did he succeed in this gargantuan challenge?"

"He jolly well did," Nicholas exclaimed eagerly. Then he caught himself up, his cheeks reddening. "At least, I expect he did. You see, I was a trifle top-heavy, and I don't quite recall . . ." His voice trailed off.

Elaine gave a peal of laughter. "I'm surprised that you're able to hold a conversation. Did you sleep it off, dear brother?"

"I believe I may have dozed off," he said with great dignity. "But I awoke once I was in the fresh air."

"Carried out, were you?"

Nicholas descended from his unwonted heights and laughed like the boy he was. "Yes. Lord Dare, or Charles, as he so kindly begged me to call him, had the waiters carry me to his curricle, and he drove me home."

"How very kind of him," Elaine said bitterly.

"I certainly appreciated it. He is a top-of-the-trees sawyer. Drives to an inch, he does."

"I'm surprised that you were in any condition to observe his driving."

"Told you. The fresh air revived me."

As he said this in a voice that was becoming increasingly drowsy, Elaine could only smile. Nicholas's eyelids were drooping, and she had no doubt that he would soon be asleep. "Perhaps you had best retire for the evening," she suggested kindly.

He thrust out his chin at this, as though she had cast an aspersion on his ability to hold his liquor. "I am *not* sleepy."

Elaine nodded. "Quite so." Without further ado, she rose to her feet and tripped from the room. If he fell asleep on the settee, she decided that it would do him no great harm. In fact, it might be a salutory lesson for him to awake with a stiff neck. And if he did not awaken before the night was through, she had no doubt that his valet would hasten down the stairs to retrieve him. At least Nicholas had survived the night. This knowledge provided her with a modicum of comfort, and that must content her. And with that Elaine went up to her room and prepared for sleep.

She was not allowed, however, the felicity of a peaceful night's repose. Suddenly Elaine awoke, her heart beating wildly. She looked about her in some confusion, wondering what it was that had awakened her. She listened intently, and to her gathering horror, she heard running feet and a shout. Then there was a tremendous crash, and the sound of moans.

Elaine threw back the bedclothes with shaking fingers and struggled into her wrapper. Her maid was standing in the doorway, her eyes dilated with fear and the taper in her hand shaking so miserably that the light flickered eerily about.

"Here, Mary," Elaine said shortly. "Give that to me." She took the taper and cupped her hand over the flame. Then she flew down the staircase. At its base, she was met by Seaton and two footmen, all agog.

Elaine did not linger to ask them any questions but followed the sound of the moaning, trying to control her fears.

She entered the back salon to see Nicholas lying full-length on the floor, a buhl table overturned, several pieces of Sèvres china shattered, and a branch of candles broken and spluttering on the carpet.

"Nicholas!" Elaine screamed. She knelt beside him. "Are you all right?"

"Of course I'm not all right," he replied a trifle testily. "I've got a bruised leg, and a bump on my head the size of a hen's egg."

"Oh, let me see!" She started to put out her hand to touch it, but Nicholas cringed away. "Seaton, bring some cold compresses quickly. And some sal volatile."

"Oh, is Seaton there?" Nicholas inquired weakly. "Not sal volatile. Brandy."

Seaton forgot to bow in his agitation but immediately ran out of the room to fetch the requirements.

"But what happened, Nicholas? Were you walking in your sleep?"

"Don't be a clunch. Of course I wasn't walking in my sleep!" Nicholas struggled to sit up, assisted by Elaine. He paused a moment, holding a hand to his head, obviously waiting for his vision to clear. "I was chasing after an intruder! I almost had him, too. But I fell over this table. What in the world induced you to place this table right in the middle of the floor, I'll never know," he said bitterly.

"I was foolish beyond permission," Elaine could not resist saying. Then the gravity of the situation sobered her. "But Nicholas, you must be bamming me. An intruder, here? How do you know it was an intruder?"

He looked at her a moment, clearly unable to find words. "What do you mean how did I know it was an intruder? The fellow was knocking on the walls! That's what woke me up!"

"Knocking on the walls?" Elaine repeated.

"I thought it might be a servant just up from the basements, so I called out to him. But the fellow took off like a shot. Of course, I chased after him. And I almost had him, too, but..." and he glared at Elaine.

"But you fell over the table, I know." She nodded absently. "Who was it?" she demanded.

"How the devil could I know that? It was dark, remember? I couldn't see his face."

"What was he doing knocking on the walls?"

"Searching for a secret panel, of course," Nicholas said. "Good Lord, use your head. How can I possibly know why he was knocking on the walls?"

Although he had spoken sarcastically, his words caused Elaine to narrow her eyes, suddenly deep in thought. She remembered Cook's complaints of a knocking noise. Had the knocker returned tonight?

Her mind seething with conjecture, Elaine soothed Nicholas as best she could, eventually leaving him to the restorative effects of the brandy. If she weren't what Nicholas termed a high-stickler, she, too, might have resorted to the decanter to settle her disordered nerves.

What was it all about? she demanded of herself. Why should an intruder persist in entering Farrington

Place? Various possibilities each more outlandish than the others sprang to mind. But even after careful consideration, she succeeded only in bringing a headache upon herself.

She was a much put-upon female, she decided darkly. First Lord Dare, now this. She remembered suddenly that Dare had driven Nicholas home. And that he had been conveniently nearby to help her out of the subsidence she had fallen into while first investigating the tappings. Was it possible that Lord Dare was the intruder?

He had already cut up her serenity with his romantic attentions. If she had to endure his attentions in another form—as a housebreaker, in fact—she would be thrown permanently into high fidgets. However, he hardly seemed a likely candidate for such a role. All his escapades were both noisy and notorious. He could scarcely have taken up burglary.

She let Seaton and the footmen assist Nicholas to bed. For herself, she doubted she would be vouchsafed a moment's peaceful slumber, for her brain was in far too much of a whirl.

Passing Aunt Augusta's maid on the way to her own room, she was pleased, though not surprised, to learn that her aunt had slept throughout the night's rumpus. But Aunt Augusta alway slept a deep untroubled sleep, so her delicate constitution had not, therefore, been endangered by the excitement of the night.

Once in her room, Elaine rejected the impulse to invoke sleep with the aid of laudanum drops. Instead, she climbed back into her bed, her brain filled with knocking noises, midnight intruders, and Lord Dare.

The next morning, Elaine attempted to relieve her taut nerves and anxiety by cantering through Hyde Park, accompanied by her groom. The fair spring weather had induced a number of the ton to take an airing. Upon passing through the park's wrought-iron gates, Elaine observed that Rotten Row was quite congested with high-perched phaetons, elegant chaises, and showy mounts. Chafing to escape the sluggish traffic, Elaine was detained by the greetings of several passersby.

The gregarious Lady Pennington, who was sporting a modish hat with a remarkably high crown and a huge upstanding poke front, which forced her continuously to duck her head against the wind so that she looked afflicted with the palsy, stopped her outright in order to have a pleasant gossip. She directed Elaine's attention to several beaux who were flirting outrageously with pretty damsels, each dressed to perfection in striped spencers and cambric walking dresses. Then she pointed to Lord Ambersey, who, obviously repairing the ravages of the night's carouse, was fast asleep in his phaeton. He was reclining against its squabs, his mouth wide open, his head rolling with every jolt incurred by his impassive driver. And finally there was Lady Cork, whose latest freak was to drive her chariot accompanied neither by tiger nor groom but by a live monkey.

"How indelicate of her," Lady Pennington clucked. "Just look at the way the little creature clings to her neck."

Elaine murmured a faint expostulation—to the effect that she hoped the monkey would not choke Lady Cork. But she was quite unable to muster any interest in such vagaries. She finally freed herself from Lady Pennington's grasp only to fall victim to the importunate and flirtatious Lord Carlysle who demanded, in rather petulant tones, why she had not saved a waltz for him last night at Lady Somercote's ball.

Lady Somercote's ball. It seemed ages past, to be sure. Smiling apologetically, she managed at length to disengage herself from Lord Carlysle without further offence.

Now at last, she was able to spur her horse forward to a deserted path, her groom keeping a discreet distance behind. While cantering briskly along, she reviewed once more the recent disturbances: the tapping noises, the intruder. What did it all mean? Why should Farrington Place be the subject of such attentions? And did Lord Dare have a place in these mysteries? She had no answers. She could only determine to keep a close watch on all events about Farrington Place.

As she reached this resolve, she simultaneously reached the Achilles statue at the marble gates on the other side of the Park. Halted beside it was the Devil's Dare, himself looking very much like the classic Greek hero: broad-chested, broad-shouldered, and devastatingly handsome. This morning he was driving an appropriately classical high-perch phaeton with gold-painted wheels. However, unlike Achilles, he was dressed à la modality in buckskin and top-boots, and a tan coat of superfine cloth.

Still at points with him over his previous night's outrage, Elaine pulled her horse up immediately, hoping to wheel it about in order to beat a hasty retreat.

"I always knew that I had a magnetic effect on females," Lord Dare commented smoothly, bringing his horses into an easy trot beside hers. He ignored her stiff back and red unwelcoming face, and regarded her with a lurking smile.

"You must confuse me, sir, with some barque of frailty or some young rakeshame," she said repellingly. "Such characters, I believe, are indeed drawn to you."

"Young rakeshames like your brother, Nicholas?" he asked quietly, his quirking eyebrow lifting.

She bit her lip. He was a regular nail, he was, she thought to herself, fuming. "My brother, Nicholas, is not a rakeshame," she averred in stifled tones. "Only a very much misguided youth."

"Yes, indeed," he agreed, nodding tolerantly. "A regular young trump, full of pluck. Well, I'm going to take him in hand for a space of time, so you need no longer fear for his guidance."

She froze with terror at the prospect and flung him a look of burning reproach. His lips curled in a distinctly sardonic manner, as though he were mocking himself. Her eyes widened. "Are you trying to bait me?" she demanded.

"Not at all," he responded promptly, an edge to his voice. "I have every intention of taking Nicholas under my aegis so that all your qualms may be allayed." His eyes flickered, as though he were looking inwardly. "Yes," he continued. "With my guidance, Nicholas will turn out a pattern-card youth, I have no doubt of it. He could ask for no better hand on the leading strings than mine, you know."

She knew nothing of the sort. "You have windmills in your head," she declared roundly.

"Ah." He held up his white hand. "But consider, you must know that I myself have a model of the first order to follow in bringing Nicholas to the right about."

"Who?" she asked suspiciously.

"My own sire."

She was surprised and continued looking at him, curious and interested, waiting for him to elaborate.

He opened his eyes wide in mock surprise. "What? My father is unknown to you? I can scarcely credit it. And I thought he had been well-known to all of London. He was a notorious member of the Hell-fire club, you must know," he disclosed calmly.

Elaine gasped in real shock, almost recoiling. The Hell-fire Club! The sect of pseudo-monks who honoured their idols with unspeakable rites and, it was rumoured, even human sacrifice. They drank blood out of skulls. And worse, they preyed on innocent virgins!

His mouth hardened at the look of horror on her face. "Just so," he said, nodding with grim satisfaction. "Truly a parent to emulate, eh? One to look up to and be guided by, was he not? With real pride, I determined to follow in his footsteps." His voice was tinged with bitter irony. "Especially after he had reduced my mother to a state of abject shame and misery by his treatment of her. He took real delight in cruelty, I assure you.''

"But you're not like that. I'm sure of it!'' she blurted out before she could stop herself.

He looked quickly at her, a light springing in his eyes. Then he turned his face away and forced a shrug. "His contemporaries called him the Damnable Dare. And as I am known as the Devil's Dare, you can see how I've succeeded in my ambition.'' His expression seemed to deny any pleasure in this triumph. "I may not be positively cruel, but I care not a whit for anyone. I'm a care-for-nobody, as you said yourself. I risk all on a dare. And for no reason at all.'' Then he said in a soft undervoice, "Except that I want to live down my father's memory.''

Her ears pricked up at this. "Live down?'' she repeated, confused.

"Did I say live down? I mean, outshine my father's memory with exploits of my own, of course.''

For a long moment, she studied him, trying to gauge the precise meaning of his words. But his face was so enigmatic that she gave it up as a hopeless endeavour. Finally, she commented shyly, "Well, you've certainly had enough adventures. Too many to make you a safe mentor for Nicholas. He's ripe for any spree as it is. And your guidance will have, I fear, a far from salutary effect on him. Your careful advice put him into a drunken stupor last night.''

His face relaxed into a look of real amusement. "Ah, but what a game youth he is. Quite a notion of his—to down five thousand pounds' worth of spirits. He has real potential.''

"Yes. He is a youth of rare qualities," she agreed. "You have no idea how much your approval of him gratifies me."

"Is that all about me which gratifies you, my dear? My talents are far more varied than you seem to think."

She felt her face grow suddenly hot. "I've no doubt," she replied coldly. Casting about for a safe topic, she noticed, with odd relief, how well he managed his restive pair of horses. Quite an impressive charioteer, she decided. So straight and powerful. Clearing her strangely constricted throat, she managed, "Well, I do approve of your driving skills. You, my Lord Dare, are, as Nicholas declares, a top-of-the-trees sawyer. You have good hands, light and steady."

He countered with a compliment of his own. "You have a very good seat yourself," he observed, his eyes sweeping her trim figure. Her riding habit of emerald-green velvet with its high-standing collar trimmed with lace displayed her figure to extreme advantage, and his eyes warmed as they dwelt upon it.

Elaine felt acutely uncomfortable under his gaze; nevertheless, she adhered to her determined course. "Nicholas has expatiated at tiresome length on your manifold driving skills. He said he couldn't hold a candle to you. You *did* drive Nicholas home last night, did you not?" She watched his face closely, but it remained smiling and at ease.

"Yes, I did. No doubt he would have driven himself into the Thames if left to his own devices. Why do you ask so pointedly? Were you disappointed that I left the house without making my presence known to you?''

Had he done so? she asked herself anxiously. Or had he been the one who... After a slight hesitation, she said repressively, ''It would have been most improper for you to make your presence known to me at that time of night.''

''That depends upon what purpose I might have had,'' he replied.

These words unnerved her considerably. ''And what purpose *could* you have at that time of night?'' she demanded, her mouth dry.

He shrugged flippantly. ''The worst, of course. If you always think the worst of me, then you'll be awake on all my suits. I am not my father's son for nothing, my dear.''

The worst of him? Slowly she shook her head in disbelief. ''You are coming it much too strong, my lord, pitching such tales. Why should you take your father's misdeeds so much to heart?''

His mouth twisted oddly. ''It's very kind in you to credit me with a heart.'' He glanced at her with veiled eyes. ''I used not to think I had one anymore. But, as I said last night, I'm beginning to believe that I may have been wrong!''

Elaine's own heart beat strongly at these words.

''You have no idea to what depths of degradation my father—'' He stopped, his voice hardening. ''I was a witness to one of their satanic masses, you see. It initiated me rather early to the ways of the world. Or of the underworld, you might say. I learned then that a heart just gets in one's way.''

Elaine's own heart now seemed to be in her throat. "And that's indeed why you're such a care-for-nobody?"

He took a deep breath and held it a long moment. He seemed on the verge of telling her something, but he stopped himself, catching his nether lip. He bent his head, twisting the leaders in his hands. "There! You've plumbed my depths, my dear," he said in a harsh voice. "Now you see why nothing moves me save challenges. They alone make me feel anything."

"But what will you do, my lord, if one day you should lose one of those so important challenges?"

His eyes glinted dangerously. "But, my dear, I never lose. At anything. Neither at cards, nor at love!"

She could hardly fail to comprehend the thrust of these words. And they made her as mad as fire. How could she have been such a gudgeon? He had merely been flirting with her again, hoping to gain her interest with his Banbury tales! Before she could administer a blistering snub, however, she was interrupted by a shout from Nicholas.

"And look what the turn of cards has brought me now," Lord Dare murmured, as Nicholas's phaeton approached.

Nicholas greeted the pair gaily, looking especially gratified at seeing Lord Dare. "What bang-up luck to meet up with you, Charles," he exclaimed. "I was feeling rather solitary after having ordered Darlington home. His coat! He had it dyed chestnut to match his horse." Nicholas exploded with laughter. "I told him to return home immediately because the combination was so distracting that he might cause accidents."

"Speaking of accidents, Nicholas," Lord Dare suddenly put in. "Your sister has been discussing your driving skill with me."

Nicholas puffed with affront. "Why, I can drive to an inch," he declared stoutly. "I've driven through the narrowest gate back and forth without once scraping the varnish of my carriage."

Lord Dare pooh-poohed this vaunt. "What difficulty does an immobile gate pose, I ask you? Real skill, however, is required to confront moving obstacles."

Nicholas stuck out his lower lip, then his eyes narrowed speculatively as he studied the congested Rotten Row. Nodding, he suddenly pointed toward the traffickers on the Row and exclaimed recklessly, "Just watch this!"

Without further ado, he urged his pair toward the Row, then cleft the surge of traffic, driving straight against its current. The traffic broke and scattered as if it had struck a wall. Horses shied, drivers cursed, pedestrians shouted. Lord Deering veered clumsily to the right, barely missing one of the poplar trees which lined the Row. Lady Shoreham shrieked hysterically, covering her face with her lace-trimmed parasol. And Lord Ambersey's carriage, turned aside by its panic-stricken groom, swayed so violently that it brought Lord Ambersey wide awake just in time to experience the carriage's overturning. Entirely unscathed, Nicholas drove straight on, ruthlessly navigating these rough waters just like the captain of a speeding vessel.

Paralyzed with shock, Elaine could only stare speechlessly after her brother. Turning at the sound of Lord Dare's voice, she saw that his eyes were brimful with laughter.

He shook his head ruefully. "Quite an excellent start I've made with the boy," he commented. Then he tipped his beaver hat and drove off in Nicholas's wake.

Elaine remained dumbfounded. What next? Was Nicholas completely dead to all sense of propriety or indeed of danger?

"I see the Devil's Dare has made his mark on your brother," a voice suddenly observed. It was her cousin, Lord Elcho. Acknowledging the truth of his words, she tightened her hands with anguish on her reins.

CHAPTER FIVE

LORD ELCHO CLEARED his throat and shifted uneasily in the saddle. Noting how uncomfortable he seemed, perched precariously upon his mount, she realized for the first time that he looked ridiculous atop a horse. What a contrast he made to the Devil's Dare, she thought.

"I *warned* you against the Devil's Dare," he said with grim satisfaction, indicating the havoc in Rotten Row. "He is a most dangerous rake."

"I wonder how you could imagine any warning of yours would hold any weight with me, Lord Elcho?" Elaine snapped impulsively, her eyes blazing.

He frowned and his hands twitched spasmodically. "Let us cry truce, shall we, cousin? I know you think me a meddlesome fool, but let me assure you that my concern for you—and for Nicholas, of course—is very deep!"

She felt herself relenting at his plaintive tones. "I apologize," she said more warmly. "You know me, my lord. I fly too easily into such miffs."

"But you have no need to do so with me," he pointed out humbly. "I'm only thinking of you, you must know."

His words mollified her further. "Well, cousin," she started, readmitting him to the ranks of her relations, "don't let us brangle. While I appreciate your concern, I cannot permit you to criticize my acquaintances."

He leaned forward suddenly, startling his horse into dancing nervously. "I am only trying to help you!" he exclaimed, panting at the exertion of controlling his horse. "You must be careful of the Devil's Dare. He would do almost anything for the mere game of it."

Elaine became suddenly still. Almost anything! The words seemed to fall into her mind like stones. She caught a last glimpse of Lord Dare's phaeton. Well, he was certainly cutting up her serenity—and all seemingly just for a dare. And he had told her himself that he was trying to outshine his father with his own exploits. She shook her head, blinking, and turned to find Lord Elcho watching her with a strange smile playing on his face. The smile annoyed her, and her lips narrowed.

"When I need your advice, cousin," she said, "I'll certainly ask you." With that, he would have to be content.

Nicholas returned to Elaine within a few minutes, looking much heated and flushed with triumph. He glowed with satisfaction. "Charles has pronounced me a first-class whip. A real out-and-outer." He was near to bursting with pride.

The enormity of his misbehaviour overcame her. "Are you quite insane, Nicholas? You must have windmills in your head to have behaved so madly in Hyde Park!" she stated.

He nodded. "You have a point. I should have performed my feat on the King's Highway, where I would have had more intrepid drivers to contend with."

"But Nicholas!" She persevered against all odds. "Don't you realize what a humdudgeon you've created?"

"Gave them quite a show, eh? Why, Lord Stokes stopped right in his tracks to watch my driving."

"I'm sure he had no choice but to do so if he valued his life," Elaine observed despairingly.

"Yes. Charles said that I put him quite to shame. But he'll come about again, I've no doubt. Pity Stokes and the other traffickers won't be able to see it happen tonight."

Elaine stared at him with sudden misgiving. "Tonight?" she repeated in failing accents. "And what, may I ask, is to occur tonight?"

"Oh, merely a bout of cards," he replied cheerfully. "I thought it only right to give Charles a chance at a riposte, so I invited him to our Tuesday evening. I intend to engage him in a game of whist."

"Nicholas, you cannot have done so!"

He smiled euphorically. "Yes, it is rather a triumph, I must say. Charles doesn't lend his presence to many at-homes. We must consider ourselves highly fortunate that he believes he has a score to settle with me!"

"You are all about in your head!" Elaine declared. "Not many hostesses *desire* so notorious a guest. Indeed, I find the whole idea of his presence extremely undesirable."

"So do I." Lord Elcho stuck in his oar. "I think you quite heedless, subjecting your sister to the Devil's Dare!"

"Well, she can devote her attention to our other guests," Nicholas replied with aplomb. "I believe Lord Darlington will be attending. And surely some of her female friends, as well."

Dearly though she wished to ring a peal over his head, Elaine knew she would be wasting her energy. She tried a different tack. "I would like, I think, to make a friend of Miss Iona Poole," she said in a deceptively innocent voice. "She seems a charming girl." She saw a telltale blush creep up Nicholas's cheeks. "I wonder if she also could be induced to attend our Tuesday?"

Nicholas did not speak, looking as though he mistrusted his ability to utter his sentiments in a reasonable tone.

"Miss Poole is a most unexceptionable female," Lord Elcho remarked, fortunately filling in the silence with his judicious words. "However, I doubt she would wish to pursue a friendship with you, Elaine, if she were to meet Lord Dare at Farrington Place."

"Perhaps so. Another time, do you think, Nicholas?"

Nicholas swung away, only to espy the very Miss Poole, sitting in a barouche beside her tiny mama. She looked excessively pretty in sprigged muslin with a pink tiffany sash, a pink silk coat, and a delightful hat tied under her heart-shaped chin with pink ribbons. Nicholas was held spellbound by the vision.

As they watched, Lord Mandeville approached the barouche, doffing his curly-brimmed beaver with a great display of punctilio. Although Miss Poole visibly cringed, her mama smiled benignly and welcomed him.

"What the devil!" Nicholas ejaculated under his breath. Elaine watched with interest as Nicholas impetuously spurred his horse forward, apparently with every intention of cutting Lord Mandeville out, as though they were on a dance floor rather than on Rotten Row.

Realizing Nicholas's purpose, Mandeville signed the Poole groom to whip up while he himself kept abreast of the carriage on his mount. He obviously hoped to shake off the worrisome youth. But as they disappeared round the curve of the road, Nicholas was gaining steadily, holding firm in his aim of displacing Mandeville and rescuing the lovely Miss Poole. Elaine sighed and turned her own mount homeward.

The Farringtons' Tuesdays at-home were a long-established custom; these were pleasant informal evenings on which Elaine and Nicholas gathered together old and new friends for relaxing conversation, tea, quadrille, and occasional games of commerce or rubbers of whist.

Aunt Augusta had not, however, accustomed herself to these evenings. And so for some years, Elaine and the upper servants had conspired to keep her entirely ignorant of Tuesday's approach. Yet with uncanny instinct, Augusta always sensed the approach of her ordeal.

"And what plans have you for tonight, my dear?" she asked in deceptively abstracted tones this Tuesday morning when Elaine entered her room to inquire of any special household orders.

Aunt Augusta had recently discovered in herself a tendency to wheeze slightly. That, coupled with palpitations of the heart, indicated a condition of such extreme seriousness that she resorted to several doses of camphorated spirits. These draughts had, not surprisingly, made her feel in truth as sick as a cushion.

Elaine tucked an additional paisley shawl—there were three already—about her aunt's tiny feet and answered soothingly. "Nothing to put yourself into a pucker about, my dear. A quiet evening at home, I assure you."

Aunt Augusta sat bolt upright at this, eyes staring. "Another at-home!" she almost shrieked. "Oh, no. I shall never endure it!"

"You've endured quiet evenings at home for as long as I can remember. And you've survived them every one."

"What a callous nature is yours," Aunt Augusta returned, groaning heavily, one hand covering her heart, the other groping frantically for the sal volatile. "Have you no pity for my sufferings?"

"Nothing about tonight will cause you any suffering at all," Elaine replied patiently. But to prove her compassion, she uncorked her aunt's vinaigrette and held it under that afflicted lady's nose.

Aunt Augusta sniffed deeply. "It's Tuesday." She shuddered. "Don't deny it. You and Nicholas persist in subjecting me to these Tuesdays."

"Nicholas and I have nothing to say about the existence of Tuesdays. They were occurring long before either of us was born."

"Don't hedge, my dear. The house is going to be invaded. Your friends. Nicholas's friends. I don't know how I shall endure it."

Elaine patted her thin hand. "You may safeguard yourself by the simple expedient of locking your door."

"*My* door!" She flung up her hands. "You must lock up the entire house!" she declared as forcefully as she could. The exertion caused her to collapse against her couch.

"I will certainly lock up the house," Elaine promised her. "After the guests have all arrived, that is. We want them to be safe, too."

Aunt Augusta cast her a look of bitter reproach before achieving a prolonged moan and taking refuge in her vinaigrette. Elaine kissed her and went to make her own preparations.

Although this Tuesday should have been no different from any other, Elaine found herself taking special care with her toilette. She spent quite half an hour soaking in her hip-bath, the water scented with ambergris. And she deliberated at unwonted length over the merits of her jonquil crepe and her cerulean blue sarcenet before choosing a newly made-up gown of pomona green satin with tiny puff sleeves, its bodice and hem picked out with gold embroidery. Her hair was done up becomingly à la Sappho, a diamond spray placed artistically in its midst. And she looked, as her maid breathlessly told her, as fine as could stare. This tribute gave her pause as she stood before the cheval glass adjusting the clasp of a diamond-and-emerald bracelet. Then she put up her chin defiantly. She *always* looked as fine as could stare. And so she would tell Lord Dare, should he have the audacity to comment upon her appearance. In this mood, she went downstairs.

The evening's entertainment began innocuously enough. Lord Darlington had brought in tow his crony Lord Alvanley, a tall, straightforward fellow whom his friends affectionately referred to as Spidershanks. A Stanhope crop and a dark coat cut by Stultz declared his Corinthian allegiance as surely as Lord Darlington's ruffled shirt, highly starched collar-points projecting to his cheekbones, neckcloth of awe-inspiring dimensions, and nice array of fobs, seals, and rings declared his Dandy aspirations. To all these, Darlington had disastrously added a pair of striped pantaloons, completed by a matching pair of boots. He hoped, he informed Elaine, that he might start a new fashion.

"They would have caught the eye of Beau Brummell himself," she declared, with perfect truth.

His round, pleasant face turned quite pink with gratification. "What say you to a matching striped cane, my dear?" he demanded suddenly. "Do you think it would become all the go?"

She blinked. "It certainly would complete the ensemble," she said cautiously, valiantly striving to subdue a bubble of laughter.

Nicholas, who had overheard Lord Darlington's question, unhesitatingly vetoed the plan. "I tell you,

Darlington," he declared frankly. "You'd look exactly as if you'd grown a third leg."

Elaine greeted Lord Dare with cool civility. Far from being crushed by her formality, he nearly put her out of countenance with his glinting smile and the tender kiss he bestowed on her hand. His lips felt as though they had seared her flesh, and she hastily passed on to greet her next guest.

To her surprise, this guest proved to be Lord Mandeville. Watching him slowly mount the stairs to the drawing-room, Elaine turned to Nicholas. "I thought Mandeville was in your black books," she murmured.

Nicholas shrugged unconcernedly. "Oh, it doesn't do to stand upon bad terms with him, you know. From Hyde Park, Mandeville made straight for White's. Of course, I followed him, and we cried truce over two glasses of daffy. And when he heard that I had bagged the Devil's Dare for our at-home, he naturally begged an invitation."

Elaine eyed Mandeville's expressionless countenance with some misgiving. But when she saw Dare watching, she greeted him with studied affability. Mandeville responded with a conventional bow, so she then favoured him with a pleasant smile before she and Nicholas accompanied him to the card table. Casting a quick glance behind her, Elaine noted with satisfaction that her actions had had the desired effect. As he followed them, Lord Dare's brows furrowed in a black frown.

"And how did you find Miss Iona Poole this afternoon?" she blandly inquired of Mandeville as the gentlemen seated themselves at the table.

"Otherwise engaged," he replied shortly. Despite the exaggerated padding of his coat's shoulders and his extremely puffed shirtfront, he looked somewhat deflated, deep in the sullens.

"Ah, yes? Then I imagine she is getting rather more attention than she is used to. She seemed to be particularly in demand at Lady Somercote's ball," she observed irrepressibly.

"Rather too much so, I agree." He eyed Nicholas with barely concealed resentment.

"You mustn't object to having a rival," Lord Dare advised, abruptly entering their conversation. He was lounging negligently in a chair, his muscular legs crossed at the ankle, and his slim hand idly twirling his quizzing glass. "Flirtations require excitement to render them palatable, eh? Tame stuff unless a challenge exists." And he turned his dark eyes suddenly to Elaine.

Instinctively she responded to the gleam in his eyes, her lips curving in an answering smile. But then she caught herself, remembering that word *flirtation*. He was a practiced hand at that game, indeed, he was. She imagined that few ladies—gently nurtured or otherwise—could resist that smile of his. And he had confidently prophesied that she, too, would succumb to his charms. Determined to prove him wrong, she turned her eyes coolly to her other guests. Besides Darlington and Alvanley, these included her lifelong friends, Anna and Maria Bishop. She beckoned them over and soon engaged the four in a lively game of Speculation at the next table. She attended to this game assiduously, trying to ignore the near presence of Lord Dare.

He, however, appeared to be completely engrossed in his game of whist with Nicholas, as Mandeville looked on.

This exemplary behaviour, however, failed to win her approbation. Why should he find a game of cards so interesting? she wondered. Nicholas was no worthy opponent, since he had a deplorable tendency to make his discards too rashly. Lord Dare, on the other hand, seemed capable of reading Nicholas's cards with alarming accuracy. His own discards were precisely considered, and Nicholas went down in the first game heavily.

Elaine suddenly asked herself why she should find the whist game so interesting. After some thought, she decided her major emotion was concern for her brother. She disliked seeing him in Lord Dare's toils. As to her own feelings—she shrugged impatiently. She was not the first female to feel his attraction, and she had no doubt that she would not be the last.

The separate games continued until the footmen appeared with trays of cakes, jellies, trifles, and puptons of fruit. But both Nicholas and Dare declined refreshments without a glance up from their cards. The fact that a crucial play had just been made did not mollify Elaine at all.

Soon afterward, Anna and Maria Bishop took an early leave, claiming a morning's engagement at the Botanical Gardens with their current beaux. Elaine put

aside the box of counters and fishes she was holding
to accompany them to the head of the stairs. After
their departure, she directed Seaton to bring the
gentlemen more spirituous refreshments. After all, she
reflected dryly, they had unanimously repudiated the
tea-table.

About to return to the drawing-room, Elaine found
herself suddenly confronting Lord Dare. He smiled at
her in his disconcerting way.

"Why, my dear Miss Farrington," he murmured,
his dark eyes caressing her. "How perceptive of you
to guess that I wanted to be alone with you. Shall we
step into the back salon here where we can be certain
of some privacy?"

Elaine pulled herself together and declared blight-
ingly, "I have no wish to be alone with you, sir, in the
back salon or elsewhere."

His eyebrow lifted. "You were thinking perhaps of
another room?" And his eyes followed the staircase to
the upper floors.

Elaine gasped in outrage. "You—you—" she sputtered, too angry to speak coherently.

"Ah, I'm being too precipitate." He nodded un-
derstandingly. "You had intended to wait until your
guests left. Admirably discreet." He stopped, his face
becoming suddenly serious. "In fact, I feel I am alone
with you, even though in the midst of a crowd." His
eyes narrowed. "Perhaps it is because I've shared a
confidence of sorts with you." His nostrils quivered as
he forced out, "About my father, I mean. I rarely talk
about him, you must know. Does sharing a confidence with another create a feeling of intimacy, or

does a feeling of intimacy lead one to share a confidence? An unanswerable question, I fear. Whatever the cause, I feel we're close to each other. Do you not?''

Waves of warmth swept over Elaine, but she ignored them, though with difficulty, and responded coldly, ''Leave off your wheedling, my lord. We are indeed close to each other because this is a very narrow hallway. But I hardly would call it a sound basis for an intimate relationship.''

Although he stared at her blankly for a moment, the Devil's Dare was far from having been tipped a settler. His face relaxed and he said agreeably. ''Ah, so you *do* intend to wait until later.'' He audaciously pinched her chin, and then winked at her. ''I, too, can be patient.'' Without another word, he bowed and returned to the drawing-room.

Elaine shook herself. She had not got the better of that encounter. In fact she was thoroughly weak in the pins. She would not speak to Lord Dare again tonight—she would not even set eyes on him.

At this moment Seaton reentered the hallway, bearing a heavy silver tray laden with crystal decanters. Elaine beckoned him over. ''Seaton! I find that I have developed the headache and must retire immediately. Pray convey my apologies to the gentlemen.''

Seaton nodded and continued on his way, and Elaine fled up the stairs to the safety of her bedchamber. Mary, who had been waiting her return, helped her into her night-wear. Elaine then dismissed her and sat at her dressing table to brush out her long golden hair with sadly unsteady hands.

There was no impropriety Lord Dare would not commit. How well he lived up to his sobriquet—and to his ambition to outshine his father!

But, worse than that, he was a regular Banbury man, claiming a special feeling of intimacy with her. He was just trying to turn her up sweet. She did acknowledge she felt a pull of attraction whenever he was near. But that, no doubt, was because he was a handsome and accomplished flirt.

He had, of course, claimed he had no serious involvements, not with ladies of quality. Then she resolutely shook her head. His only interest in her was that challenge that she had so ill-advisedly offered him. A challenge, she knew to her cost, he would never refuse!

On this realization, she leaped to the door. She turned the lock with a sharp snap. Breathing a sigh of relief, she suddenly recalled Aunt Augusta. Well, at least her aunt would approve. She cared not a jot what the Devil's Dare thought.

Why should she? He was ne'er-do-well, *worse than* his father, for he acknowledged the faults in which he persisted. But if she didn't stop thinking of him, she would not get a wink of sleep all night.

Climbing into bed, she pulled the bedclothes about her neck. She managed to fall into a fitful sleep; nevertheless, images of the handsome Devil's Dare flitted through her dreams.

But even this uneasy rest was destined to be rudely interrupted. There was a sudden concerted shout. Elaine flung out of bed, grasping hurriedly at her wrapper.

The house was now silent. Tiptoing stealthily down the staircase, she stopped midway and crouched so that she could peer into the drawing-room from behind the banister.

The gentlemen had used the time to good advantage, she observed, taking due note of the empty decanters lining both the card table and the sideboard.

"I'm sick of London life!" Lord Alvanley was declaring vociferously. "I prefer the outdoors. I'm a Melton man myself. Keep a hunting-box in the country. Wish I were there now. Because London's too insipid in the extreme. There's no sport to it."

Nicholas shook his head mournfully, a doleful expression on his rather flushed face. "How right you are, Alvanley. No sport at all. I daresay not even Charles could find us some outdoor sport here in London." With difficulty, he lifted his head to glower challengingly at the Devil's Dare.

Dare regarded him inscrutably for a moment. His hand closed tightly over his glass, and he downed his drink with one flick of the wrist. "I'll give you some outdoor sport," Elaine heard him respond. She froze. What would the Devil's Dare mean by *sport*?

"We'll give Alvanley his fox hunt," he said, mischievously regarding his staring friends.

"Take a damper," Lord Darlington recommended.

"Quite unnecessary," he returned politely. "Can't let young Nicholas down. He made me a challenge, and I *must* meet it. I've a prize notion, and you shall soon know it."

"But there's no hunting now," Nicholas objected. "Besides, we can't leave town in the middle of the Season."

"We shan't, but we shall have our hunt all the same." Dare's animation grew.

"Pray, how may that be?" Alvanley interposed. "No foxes in London."

"Yes. How?" Nicholas tapped Lord Dare on the shoulder. "How can we hunt without a fox?"

His eyes kindling, Dare smiled broadly. "But we *do* have a fox."

Nicholas cocked his head. "Tare an' hounds. Where is it? Have we had it all this time, and I never knew?"

Elaine suppressed a choke of laughter. She thought she saw what Dare was about!

Lord Dare nodded.

Nicholas began peering under chairs, and behind curtains. "But cut line, man, where have you hid the beast?"

"He stands before you."

Nicholas stopped. He walked close to Lord Dare and gave him a dazed scrutiny. "Do you mean you?" he asked at length.

"None other."

"Most irregular," Nicholas muttered. He shook his head and sat down on the sofa next to Alvanley. "Don't you think it most irregular?"

Alvanley considered. "Pon rep," he cried out finally in a delighted voice. "I find it vastly suitable. Always thought Dare was a wily fox."

His face flushing with triumph, Lord Dare bowed.

Elaine realized that it now behooved her to inter-fere. But she must be discreet. She stepped cautiously down the staircase and crept up to the drawing-room door. She must not be seen in such improper attire. Lord Darlington stood with his back to the doorway. She reached round and tapped him on the back.

He jumped and swung round to glare at her. "Don't do that!" he objected automatically. "You'll wrinkle my coat!"

"How careless of me, Lord Darlington," Elaine apologized.

Lord Darlington stared at her, a puzzled frown wrinkling his white forehead. "I thought you had gone to sleep." Then he stepped forward and stared round the door. "But Miss Farrington," he exclaimed in dismay. "That rose-coloured silk don't suit your complexion at all!"

She bit her lip. After a brief struggle with herself, she said, "I will engage never to be seen wearing it in public again, I promise you."

He patted her shoulder comfortingly. "I think that would be best."

She turned as Nicholas suddenly raised his voice. He was confronting Alvanley, his face red. "It can't be done, I tell you. It's impossible."

"I don't see why. We give him a ten minute start, let blow the horn, then off we go."

"Let blow the horn and go where?" Lord Darling-ton demanded, trying to catch up.

Nicholas answered shortly, "After the fox, of course."

"Oh, to be sure, after the fox." Lord Darlington nodded.

Elaine shrank farther behind the door. They were deeper in their cups than she had thought.

"These gentlemen are planning to hold a hunt," Lord Darlington whispered in her ear.

She tried to respond calmly. "Oh? I had no idea it was the season. When is the hunt to be held?"

"Now."

"Now?" She put a hand to her brow. What would they think of next? Again she decided to try the reasonable approach. "They intend to rush off to the country in the middle of the night and hold a hunt?"

"I'm afraid you labour under a misapprehension, Miss Farrington." Lord Darlington smiled sympathetically. "They intend to hold the hunt here."

"In this house?"

"They talk of horses, so I expect the hunt will be in the streets."

She gave a short laugh. Good God! A mad hunt through London. She looked curiously at Lord Dare—he appeared entirely at his ease.

Nicholas's face, however, had turned purple, and he was gesturing wildly. "The fox will have an unfair advantage!"

"Oh, don't be ridiculous, Farrington. What can you mean?" Alvanley said reasonably.

Nicholas sniffed.

"Mandeville and Darlington will both be mounted, so how can the fox have an advantage?" Alvanley went on.

"He'll have an advantage over me! My horse isn't saddled and waiting as is yours."

Alvanley snorted, and Lord Dare serenely ignored Nicholas.

Alvanley then turned to Lord Dare, clapping his hands. "So, is all settled then, o wily fox?"

Lord Dare nodded, his eyes flashing.

"You have a ten minute start, and whoever runs you to ground first is declared Huntsman of the Season."

Nicholas eyed him balefully. "You sound as though you expect to run the fox to ground first."

"But of course."

"Well, it is quite unfair! You have a horse, and I shall have to be content with a chair, of all things."

Alvanley paused, clearly swayed by this argument, for the flunkies who carried chairs were notoriously slow. Then he snapped his fingers. "Tell you what," he cried. "You can start off five minutes before the rest of us."

Nicholas's eyes brightened. "Five minutes?" he repeated, pulling at his lower lip. "Might do."

Elaine cast an imploring look at Lord Darlington. "Couldn't you try to stop them?"

He looked doubtful, but reluctant to refuse a lady's request, he turned to Lord Dare. "I say, Dare, perhaps we should reconsider this madcap scheme, eh?"

Lord Dare's look of mock-surprise was answer enough.

Darlington shrugged. "No use."

Elaine realized the truth of his words. Indeed, she knew that remonstrances with Nicholas would also have no force whatsoever. And in her present state of *déshabillé*, she was loath to confront the other gentlemen. She remained in agonized silence.

Nicholas tugged the bellpull violently. Seaton came in, and Nicholas ordered the guests' horses to be brought round and a chair called. Impassive as always, Seaton bowed and retired.

"Well, then, my fox," Alvanley said, rubbing his hands. "Off with you now, and know that we shall be hard on your heels." He cast a glance at the gold-and-crystal clock on the mantle.

Obviously eager to be off, Dare quickly shook each gentleman's hand and wished them all the best of luck. Then with extraordinary speed, he dashed out the door, surprising poor Seaton, who was bearing a tray of glasses. The evening's last toasts went flying.

Intent on his purpose, Dare did not slow down but raced down the stairs with Nicholas trotting behind.

"He's getting on his horse now," Nicholas called out. "He's off!"

"Ah, what adventure!" Alvanley was heard to exclaim as he rushed to the door, with Mandeville and Darlington following. Elaine crept forward in the dark hall. The men crowded together on the front steps.

Alvanley was forcibly restraining Nicholas. "Hold to," he gasped, gripping him by the shoulders. "Your time's not yet come."

"It has, it has. Let go, damn it. I must be after the fox."

Finally, Alvanley released Nicholas. He shot forward and burst onto the street. Seeing the chair, he jumped into it with such violence that the chairmen tottered, the poles tilted precariously, and the whole chair turned over and collapsed on the ground. Nicholas was tossed incontinently into the street.

"Dash it all," he cried. "I've been thrown!"

"Off with you now," Alvanley shouted. "The fox will be lost if you do not hasten, my friend."

Nicholas scrambled up from the ground, muttering, and gave the chairman nearest him a sound rap on the head. "Steady this time!"

The chairmen braced themselves for the shock of Nicholas's reboarding. Once safely inside, he leaned out the window and shouted, "Tally ho! After the fox!" And the chairmen rushed headlong into the night.

Alvanley waited until Nicholas was out of sight. Then he leaped upon his horse. "Tantivy, tantivy, and off we go!" he shouted, waving his hat.

Quickly Darlington and Mandeville followed suit. Speechless, Elaine watched as the horsemen vanished and the hunting calls died away.

And so the hunt began.

Abandoning her post at the door, Elaine sank into a hall settle. She could just imagine the havoc they must be wreaking on the busy streets of London, forcing wagons into ditches, causing horses to shy, and waking blameless citizens from their rest. She only hoped that Nicholas would not end the night in a watch house, or worse, with a broken neck.

What could she have done to prevent this madness? she demanded of herself. Never have let the Devil's Dare cross her threshold, was the inevitable answer.

Well, she would prevent any such recurrence, she determined. She would use every means possible to bring Nicholas safe out of Dare's toils. That is, if he survived this evening's lunacy.

She gave a long sigh. She doubted she would get a wink of sleep the entire Season, for this night, too, must be spent awaiting Nicholas's return.

Pulling her rose silk wrapper tightly about her, she went back to the drawing-room. She sat where she could frown relentlessly at the delicate little mantle clock, and remained in this brown study until a sudden tapping noise sent the blood rushing to her head. She leaped from the chair. There it was again!

This time, she decided, she would solve the mystery. Listening intently, she headed toward the kitchen and the source of the sound.

She stood a moment before the kitchen door. She took a deep breath, then flung the door wide open.

There, sitting on the wooden bench, his Hessian boots propped up against the large oak table, was Lord Dare, munching on a chicken leg.

He peered at Elaine rather owlishly for a moment. His face was unusually flushed, and he was breathing somewhat heavily. But he swiftly regained his composure and placed the piece of chicken on a plate, carefully wiping his hands on a napkin. "You've certainly taken your time, my dear. I, like the wily fox I am, have sent everyone off on a false scent. Now we may have our long-postponed tête-à-tête!"

CHAPTER SIX

ELAINE GAPED AT HIM, rooted to the floor. "What...what are you doing here?" she demanded in as forceful a voice as she could muster.

His mouth twitched, but he quickly checked a laugh. He sipped again from his goblet of wine. Rising to his feet, he graciously bowed, waving his hand at the table. "Whiling away the time with a midnight repast, my very dear Miss Farrington."

This explanation was so nonsensical that Elaine almost lost her temper. "Could you not have done that at your own home, Lord Dare?" she asked ironically.

"Ah, but there I would have missed the tastiest morsel of all." With obvious relish, he surveyed her silk-clad form. "Don't I deserve something, after waiting so patiently?"

"If you received your just deserts, Lord Dare, you'd be run through with a sword!" she declared hotly. Her words were brave enough, but that look in his eyes set her heart to pounding rapidly. She looked about for the bellpull. But naturally enough, the servants' regions lacked this urgently needed convenience.

"There's a butcher's cleaver within easy reach," Lord Dare helpfully informed her. "You might use that instead. And there are several sharp knives available should you wish further to defend your honour.''

She gulped convulsively. But her ready sense of the ridiculous got the better of her, and she had to suppress a most unsuitable giggle. After a long moment she asked, ''Need I defend my honour, my lord?''

''I would think it a wasted effort, when you could use your energies to so much better effect.''

These words, and their accompanying look, did not reassure Elaine. She moved away from him, her hand reaching behind her for the kitchen door.

Lord Dare observed these signs of maidenly panic through his upraised quizzing glass. He shook his head admonishingly. ''You are too previous, my dear,'' he chided, his eyes dancing as he advanced upon her. ''After your having come all the way down to the kitchen to meet me, it seems rather anticlimactic for you to leave again before I've even kissed you.''

''But I didn't come down to the kitchen to meet you,'' she exclaimed. Her hand finally encountered the door latch. She gripped it as if it were a lifeline.

At first he looked dubious, then he raised one eyebrow. ''You mean that you've indeed come upon me as an unlooked-for pleasure?'' He opened his arms wide.

''A pleasure?'' she gasped. ''What conceit! Your presence here, my lord, at this time of night, is not a pleasure but an offence.''

''But such a mild one. You must first let your imagination run over the full gamut of possible offences before you condemn me out of hand.''

The more
you love romance . . .
the more
you'll love this offer

FREE!

Mail this heart today!
(See inside)

Join us on a Harlequin Honeymoon
and we'll give you
4 free books
A free bracelet watch
And a free mystery gift

248 CIH 4AJC (U-H-RG-09/89)

IT'S A
HARLEQUIN HONEYMOON—
A SWEETHEART
OF A FREE OFFER!
HERE'S WHAT YOU GET:

1. **Four New Harlequin Regency™ Novels—FREE!**
   Take a Harlequin Honeymoon with your four exciting romances—yours FREE from Harlequin Reader Service®. Each of these hot-off-the-press novels brings you the passion and tenderness of today's greatest love stories...your free passports to bright new worlds of love and foreign adventure.

2. **A Lovely Bracelet Watch—FREE!**
   You'll love your elegant bracelet watch—this classic LCD quartz watch is a perfect expression of your style and good taste—and it is yours FREE as an added thanks for giving our Reader Service a try.

3. **An Exciting Mystery Bonus—FREE!**
   You'll be thrilled with this surprise gift. It is elegant as well as practical.

4. **Money-Saving Home Delivery!**
   Join Harlequin Reader Service® and enjoy the convenience of previewing four new books every other month delivered right to your home. Each book is yours for only $2.49*—26¢ less per book than the cover price. And there is *no* extra charge for postage and handling. Great savings plus total convenience add up to a sweetheart of a deal for you! If you're not completely satisfied, you may cancel at any time, for any reason, simply by sending us a note or shipping statement marked ''cancel'' or by returning any shipment to us at our cost.

5. **Free Insiders' Newsletter**
   It's *heart to heart*®, the indispensible insiders' look at our most popular writers, upcoming books, even comments from readers and much more.

6. **More Surprise Gifts**
   Because our home subscribers are our most valued readers, when you join the Harlequin Reader Service®, we'll be sending you additional free gifts from time to time—as a token of our appreciation.

START YOUR HARLEQUIN HONEYMOON TODAY—JUST
COMPLETE, DETACH AND MAIL YOUR FREE-OFFER CARD

Get your fabulous gifts
ABSOLUTELY FREE!

MAIL THIS CARD TODAY.

PLACE
HEART STICKER
HERE

GIVE YOUR HEART
TO HARLEQUIN

YES! Please send me my four Harlequin Regency™ novels FREE, along with my free bracelet watch and free mystery gift. I wish to receive all the benefits of the Harlequin Reader Service® as explained on the opposite page.

NAME _____
(PLEASE PRINT)

ADDRESS _____ APT. ____

CITY _____ STATE _____

ZIP CODE _____ 248 CIH 4AJC (U-H-RG-09/89)

OFFER LIMITED TO ONE PER HOUSEHOLD AND NOT VALID TO CURRENT HARLEQUIN REGENCY™ SUBSCRIBERS.

HARLEQUIN READER SERVICE® "NO RISK" GUARANTEE
—There's no obligation to buy—and the free books and gifts remain yours to keep.
—You pay the low members-only discount price.
—You may end your subscription anytime by sending us a note or shipping statement marked "cancel" or by returning any shipment to us at our cost.

PRINTED IN U.S.A.
© 1989 HARLEQUIN ENTERPRISES LIMITED

START YOUR
HARLEQUIN HONEYMOON TODAY.
JUST COMPLETE, DETACH AND MAIL YOUR
FREE OFFER CARD.

If offer card is missing, write to: Harlequin Reader Service® 901 Fuhrmann Blvd
P.O. Box 1867 Buffalo NY 14269-1867

DETACH AND MAIL TODAY!

Her imagination needed no prompting from Lord Dare. Her body was quivering with a strange mixture of apprehension and excitement, just at his physical proximity. He must have sensed her emotion, for he stood watching her intently, his mouth beginning to tighten and his eyes to narrow.

She lifted the latch with shaking fingers, but before she could pull open the door, Lord Dare pounced on her.

His hands closed over her shoulders. His breathing was ragged. "You've become impatient with me," he murmured, his face uncomfortably close to hers. "I will waste no more time with words, I promise you."

She twisted out of his hold, anger lending her unexpected strength. "You go too far, my lord," she cried. "Don't touch me again, else, I'll scream loudly enough to bring the entire household down here."

A look of admiration flickered over his face. "Then it will be bellows to mend with me, eh, what?" he asked wryly. "But why notify the entire household of a rendezvous you've taken so much trouble to keep secret? How foolhardy."

"A rendezvous?" she snorted. "With you? You must be all about in your head."

"If not with me, then with whom?" he demanded, his voice suddenly harsh.

"With no one. I heard a noise, and I thought that Nicholas might need my help!"

His mouth pursed thoughtfully as he studied her for a moment. Then he gave a short laugh. "Nicholas. I should have known. What an exceptionally good sister you are, my dear," he commented dryly. He looked at her with a slight smile. "Don't you ever spare *yourself* a thought?"

His look held her, and she found it difficult to reply, or to tear herself away. He seemed to mesmerize her.

He shook his head, as though at himself. "It seems so odd. I can hardly spare a thought for anything *but* you, despite all else that demands my attention." He moved even closer to her, so close that she could feel the warmth of his breath on her face. His eyes seemed to burn into hers. "You are so beautiful," he breathed. His hands reached out to grasp her shoulders again, and his lips lowered almost to hers.

"What a very touching scene, to be sure." A new voice shattered the spell. Elaine gave a start and swung around to see Lord Mandeville!

Blinking, she realized that he had apparently just entered the kitchen from the street entrance. He looked extremely disheveled: his coat was wrinkled, his cravat loose, his hair tangled. But it was his expression that made her stare. His face was white as a tucker, and a muscle at the corner of his mouth twitched spasmodically.

"Lord Mandeville!" she exclaimed. "What are *you* doing here?"

"Chasing the fox, of course," he sneered. "I had no idea, however, that the fox was pursuing his own game."

Inured to such surprises, Lord Dare studied Mandeville with mocking eyes. "But I'm always after some sport," he explained kindly. He bent his head to smooth a crease in his cravat. Then he raised his eyes in a look that seemed to bore right through Mandeville. "I thought you knew that." His words held a veiled significance that escaped Elaine but that caused Mandeville's thin body to stiffen.

Before Mandeville could reply, Lord Dare turned to Elaine. His face was hard, and his eyes refused to meet hers. "No wonder you were not pleased to find me. You had an assignation with Mandeville here. Therefore, I was decidedly *de trop*.

"How dare you suggest such a thing!" She glared angrily at him.

He brightened hopefully. "Well, what else am I to think?" he demanded. "Here is Mandeville, and here are you. Can it be a coincidence?"

"You are decidedly at outs! I heard strange noises in the kitchen. Naturally I came to investigate. I certainly had no expectation of meeting either you or Lord Mandeville!"

He shot a piercing look at Mandeville, who was beginning to look very red about the gills. Then his mouth curled in a slow malicious smile. He returned his gaze to Elaine, and he regarded her a moment with softened eyes. But it wasn't long before an expression of real mischief crept over his face. "A very likely story," he said with a sniff. "And quickly thought of. I commend you on your acuity."

"How dare you cast aspersions on this lady's name?" Lord Mandeville hissed, unexpectedly coming to Elaine's defence. He seemed to harbour an inexplicable dislike of Lord Dare. To Elaine's astonishment, he declared pugnaciously, "You shall be called to book for this, I promise you."

Lord Dare's eyes contemptuously swept Mandeville's slight form. "By you?" he asked in a soft voice, lifting his dark eyebrows.

The menace in that soft voice chilled Elaine's blood.

"Yes, by m-me," Mandeville stammered.

"Do you dare?" Lord Dare pressed, stepping threateningly close to his opponent.

Dare towered over Mandeville, his tall, powerful form dwarfing Mandeville's. Elaine felt it paramount that she intervene. "Gentlemen! Please try to remember that you are gentlemen. To quarrel in the presence of a lady is not at all the thing."

"But that it is a lady before whom we are quarrelling is the very question we are trying to decide," Dare explained to her kindly, speaking as though she were a backward child.

Elaine felt as though she had been struck full in the face; she was far too angered to note the light dancing in his eyes.

Much tried, Mandeville turned on her as a less formidable opponent. "That is so, after all. What were you doing here alone with Lord Dare? Embracing! I saw you with my own eyes."

"You shall answer for that!" A third gentleman's voice ripped across the room.

Almost dizzy with surprise, Elaine swung around to face Lord Elcho! What was he doing here? He had apparently just entered the kitchen through the door off the staircase. This kitchen was becoming as crowded as Rotten Row during the Grand Strut!

Lord Elcho was dressed in evening attire, and looked precise to a pin—which was entirely characteristic of him. His next action, however, was so uncharacteristic that Elaine almost reeled in shock. Elcho glared balefully at Mandeville. Then he snarled, rushed forward, and without further ado, fastened his hands around Mandeville's neck in a murderous grip.

Mandeville clutched frantically at the choking hands. He made odd gagging noises, and his mouth opened and shut like a fish's.

"Ah," Lord Dare observed in amusement. "Now here is Lord Elcho to join us. My dear Miss Farrington, you were planning a veritable orgy, were you not?"

For a moment Elaine envied Lord Elcho, for she herself felt like wringing Lord Dare's neck! And yet Lord Elcho was indeed choking the life out of Mandeville. It was too fantastical!

Obviously possessing far greater presence of mind, Dare sauntered forward and tapped Lord Elcho on the shoulder. "That is no way to settle an affair of honour, Elcho."

Unfortunately, Lord Elcho paid him not the slightest heed at all.

"Stop them!" Elaine gasped to Lord Dare.

His mouth pursed, and he puffed out his cheeks. "But why should I?" he asked. "Elcho's killing two birds with one stone," he added cryptically.

Elaine could not ponder this remark. They must be stopped! Glancing around, she hoisted a large ewer of water and flung it full over the pair of them.

They staggered back, spluttering at the water's impact. Elcho released Mandeville's neck to wipe the water from his eyes.

"Very good," Lord Dare said approvingly, laughter in his voice. "That should dampen their ardour."

"You, sir, are detestable. I never want to see or to speak to you again!" she declared in a shaking voice.

His withers were obviously unwrung. "Oh, yes." He nodded with spurious understanding. "You are wanting to be alone with these two gentlemen." He extricated an enamelled snuffbox from his pocket and flicked it open with a graceful twist of his wrist.

All three of them glared at Lord Dare. Elaine clenched her fists, striving to subdue her wrath.

Neither Mandeville nor Elcho, however, practiced such restraint. Rather, they regarded Dare with a hostility that made the room fairly crackle. They seemed, irrationally, to have transferred their ire to him. And Elaine, much bewildered, could not understand the undercurrents here.

"You shall pay for those words, my Lord Dare!" Elcho snarled, still panting from his altercation with Mandeville and from the shock of water in his face. His light hair was plastered to his narrow head, and his always prominent eyes seemed ready to pop out of their sockets.

"To be sure, he will," asseverated Lord Mandeville, behaving much more bravely now that he had a second to support him.

"I'm quite willing to pay. And at this very moment, and against both of you at once!"

"You must all be addle-brained." Elaine wrung her hands. How she wished she had never left the safety of the drawing-room. "What are you about?"

Dare flicked her a look alive with meaning. "I'm trying to satisfy these two gentlemen. And to settle the matter as quickly as possible so as not to inconvenience you. I would be loath to disrupt your evening's plans further."

He shot this last remark at Elcho and Mandeville, seemingly intent on fanning the flame of their anger. He was succeeding only too well, though, for if Elaine had been a man, she, too, would gladly have joined forces with them.

"Please, please bethink yourselves," she implored them, all but shaking Lord Dare by the shoulders. "This is madness! And all this from an evening's sport!"

He laughed out loud at that. "Exactly! I *knew* you had plans."

She stamped her foot. "I was referring to your mad fox hunt, and you know it. I heard you and the others planning it." She turned to Lord Mandeville. "Be reasonable, I beseech you. Lord Dare was merely trying to avoid the hounds by hiding in the kitchen when you ran him to ground. And—" she turned pacifically to Lord Elcho "—Mandeville merely misconstrued Lord Dare's behaviour toward me. Such a kick-up. I don't see why you're refining so much upon the incident!"

"Nonsense," Elcho said roughly. "This fellow has insulted you, and he must be made to pay for it."

"He has also insulted me," Mandeville put in. "And I demand satisfaction for that, too."

"But, gentlemen, I'm ready to satisfy you this very instant. Surely you must know that. Choose your weapon. As I earlier informed Miss Farrington, there are any number of knives, cleavers, and skewers available.''

Elaine shrieked and started to flee from the kitchen. Lord Dare instantly blocked the door with his powerful form. "We do not need your servants as seconds, my dear, though that was very kind in you to think of." He took her by the shoulders and planted her firmly in a chair. "Sit you there safe and out of harm's way," he directed in an urgent undervoice.

She tried to struggle loose from his grasp, but he was too strong for her. She fell back against the chair, exhausted.

"Now, gentlemen. Shall we proceed?" He saw that they had made no move whatsoever. "What, no weapons? Shall it be fisticuffs, then?" He shrugged unconcernedly. "So be it. I shall meet your challenge in any way you choose, of course."

Both Mandeville and Elcho were apparently ready to oblige him. The latter started to swing at him, but Lord Dare stopped him by holding up an imperious hand.

"Wait. I must even the odds. Let me see." He rubbed his jaw thoughtfully.

Elaine interposed desperately. "You cannot mean to fight with both of them."

"But, it is their challenge, my dear girl," he explained. "Of course I must accept them. It is my way, as you no doubt have learned by now." He snapped his fingers. "I have the very thing." And with that, he quickly snuffed out the flames of the candles that lit the kitchen.

Darkness suddenly filled the room. Elaine stared into the blackness. What on earth was happening?

She jumped at the sound of a crash and a loud thud. Desperately though she strained, she could see nothing. Feet scuffled, and someone groaned as a hard blow was struck.

Murder could be happening right here in her kitchen. But it was too dark for her to see it!

But that groan galvanized her. She stood up and screamed for help. She groped her way toward the door, fearing a blindly striking fist would find her.

The noise increased. Pans clattered to the floor, dishes shattered, and wood cracked. Elaine was almost frantic. As she reached the door, she put her hand out to the latch, but she was grasped by an unseen assailant.

"Give them up. Or you'll be sorry!" a voice hissed in her ear.

She tried to clutch at the whisperer but she caught only thin air. "Who is it? What are you talking about?" she cried. She shook her head, trying to make sense of the words. Give them up to the authorities, that must be what was meant! Call the night watch. And so she would!

She slipped out of the kitchen and rushed out into the street, searching frantically for Becky's beau, the night watchman.

THE NEXT MORNING, Nicholas descanted upon the glories of his fox hunt at tiresome length. "What a lark it was!" he crowed, spearing a slice of beefsteak with his fork. "We careered from one end of the town to the other."

Elaine surveyed him with a jaundiced eye. "And did you run your fox to ground?" she asked. She shuddered as he gulped down his porter. She herself could only manage a few bites of toast dipped in tea.

"Well, no," Nicholas admitted. Then his eyes twinkled wickedly. "I did, however, manage to win a spectacular prize."

His words filled her with foreboding. "Dear heaven," she said feebly. "And what, may I ask, was that?"

"The Golden Ball's hat!"

"Whaaat?"

"You know, Lord Appleby, the fabulously rich Golden Ball!" Nicholas closed his eyes with delight at the memory. "There he was, sauntering down St. James's Street, dressed in a coat of pink silk damask all covered with spangles and French embroidery, if you can credit it. And on his head reposed this enormous hat, complete with two rows of diamond beads and loops of gold. All cocked in the newest military style, too. Well, the moment he saw me, dashing headlong down the street, he threw up his hands and ran wildly in the opposite direction."

Elaine choked. "Wh-what did you do, Nicholas?" she demanded, fascinated.

He smiled gleefully. "Well, I knew I had a prize within my grasp, so I swooped down and snatched his hat from off his head. I waved it three times triumphantly over my own head and was off before Golden

Ball could even utter a curse." He whooped and slapped his knee.

Elaine couldn't help but laugh. And yet the laughter soon died away as she considered the night's events. "Nicholas," she said urgently. "You must avoid Lord Dare from now on. He's an evil influence!"

"Pooh!" Nicholas spurned this sisterly advice. "I'm not going to keep the hat, you know. I'll send off a footman to restore it to Golden Ball. It was all just a bit of fun. Nothing to throw you into the dismals, I promise you."

"Nicholas, listen to me," Elaine insisted. "You never found your fox, did you?"

"Why, no," he acknowledged. "But that didn't affect the pleasure of the sport."

She would not turn from her purpose. "Nicholas, I'll tell you why you didn't run your fox to ground."

"Why?" he demanded.

"Because he was safe and snug, hiding away in your own kitchen!"

Nicholas shook his head in awed admiration. "Dare's a wonder, I tell you. What a brilliant ploy. The last place in all of London that I would have looked."

"It wasn't brilliant. It was reprehensible! Nicholas," she said awfully, "when I confronted him last night, he insulted me!"

Nicholas frowned. "I doubt that, sister. Why should he? What did he do, anyway?"

"He tried to kiss me!"

Nicholas laughed. "He didn't! What a rascal. There we were racing through the streets, and he was pursuing a flirtation."

"He was *not* pursuing a flirtation," Elaine contradicted icily. "He insulted me."

"Stuff and nonsense. He was complimenting you, no doubt. You don't realize what a condescension it was on his part."

"Condescension!"

"Yes," he averred. "Dear sister, you just don't appreciate him properly." And with that, he rose from the table and took his leave of her.

She didn't know about appreciating Lord Dare, but she did know that she and Nicholas were looking at him through very different pairs of spectacles. She almost despaired when she thought of the further escapades into which the Devil's Dare might lead Nicholas. That man was such a heedless care-for-nobody that he would ruin Nicholas without the slightest compunction.

Her thoughts went back over the night's events.

She had failed to locate the night watchman. However, the noise had roused Seaton and the footmen. Elaine had returned to the kitchen to find them staring aghast at the chaos before them. The oak table had been overturned; several chairs had splintered into pieces; plates and silver lay scattered over the floor. But the room was totally deserted. Elaine assumed that Mandeville and Elcho had fled in terror from the Devil's Dare. She did not attempt an explanation, merely directing the servants to retire and leave everything till next day.

When morning came, Mrs. Beale surveyed the havoc that had been wrought in her domain. She had no hesitation at all in identifying its source.

"Ghosts!" she screamed. "Them naughty, nasty ghosts! Look what they did to my kitchen."

Elaine could only shake her head in silent sympathy. Let the servants believe that the house was infested with ghosts. It was better than their knowing that it had been infested with madmen.

She shook her head again, still somewhat bemused. Whatever had induced her cousin, Lord Elcho, to behave in such a violent way? Jealousy? She devoutly hoped not. And Mandeville. The man was clearly unhinged, or so puffed up with his own consequence that he could not bear an insult to his person. Their behaviour was utterly unaccountable.

Elaine sighed, feeling decidedly down-pin. Indeed, this morning, she had toyed with the idea of following Aunt Augusta's lead and remaining safely on her couch all day, if not the rest of the week! She might that way at least catch up on some of her lost sleep. She had actually resorted to some burnt feathers, solicitously prepared for her by Mary, to restore her spirits.

However, she was made of resilient stuff, and she had to see to her household duties. She began mechanically sifting through the morning's correspondence, which Seaton had brought into the breakfast parlour on a silver salver. No, she couldn't understand what maggots had gotten into Elcho's and Mandeville's heads.

But despite Nicholas's assertion, she thought with a darkening face, she *could* understand Lord Dare's character. He alone of the three was adhering to his normal behaviour, which was characteristically despicable.

Among the various letters and invitation cards, Elaine discovered the ostentatious, gilt-edged invitation card the Prince Regent used to announce dinner parties and balls. With widening eyes, Elaine realized that she and Nicholas had been invited to one of Prinny's notorious dinners, to be held tomorrow evening!

These dinners were veritable bacchanalia. Why, Prinny was known to serve up as many as thirty-six entrées! Added to these was a torrent of wine culminating in unlimited Madeira and port. Prinny's dinners were calculated to render his guests either bilious or stupefied.

It was highly irregular to receive the invitation so hard upon the event. No doubt this was Lord Dare's work. Although she and Nicholas had gone to several Carlton House balls, they had never before been invited to one of the dinners. She knew Lord Dare to be a close crony of Prinny's. Apparently, Lord Dare intended to introduce poor Nicholas into all the more scandalous circles.

She could not contemplate refusing the invitation as that would constitute a solecism of mammoth proportions. But, she could keep a very close eye on Nicholas. Also, she must resign herself to the unpleasant task of speaking with Lord Dare.

She had intended, of course, never to speak to him again. He had insulted her, treating her as if she were one of his Cyprians! And then he had turned her house into bedlam itself. However, it was of supreme importance that she persuade him to renounce her brother as a companion. She couldn't stand by and let Dare ruin Nicholas's life. She would have to swallow her righteous indignation—for her brother's sake.

The last letter on the salver was a missive written in a strange hand. She broke the seal and spread open the vellum sheet. Frowning in puzzlement, she read over the message twice. "Give them up. Or you'll regret it!" The letter was unsigned, but she recognized the words instantly.

Last night in the kitchen, some one had whispered them in her ear.

Then she had thought they meant that she should give the three gentlemen in her kitchen up to the authorities. What did they mean now? Give what up? And to whom? The message was entirely incomprehensible. She stared at it with a growing sense of consternation. What did it mean?

CHAPTER SEVEN

LATER THAT MORNING, much to her chagrin, Elaine received a call from Lord Elcho. She would as lief not have seen him, for she doubted her ability to treat him civilly. Nevertheless, *she* would honour proprieties, even if her guests did not!

As she entered the blue salon, she studied her cousin from under her eyelashes, curious to see what damage had been wrought during the bout of fisticuffs. She observed, not without a modicum of disappointment, that he had suffered neither a black eye nor a bruised jaw. He appeared, on the contrary, surprisingly unscathed.

But while his person appeared unharmed, his pride had suffered a severe blow. She noted with dour satisfaction how stiffly he bowed to her and how curtly he refused the seat she indicated. She seated herself on a Pembroke chair, folding her hands on her lap. Then she looked expectantly at Elcho.

"I came to explain my behaviour of last night," he said in a voice devoid of all emotion. "It was reprehensible in me to fight before you. I have no idea what came over me."

"Do not fall into the mopes over it, my dear cousin. I fear you have merely succumbed to the influence of the Devil's Dare."

His eyes kindled dangerously. "As have you?"

She stared at him before saying coolly, "I don't know what you mean."

He seemed to swell with suppressed anger. "Lord Mandeville swears he saw you and Lord Dare embracing!"

"You have discussed the matter with him? After you had left my kitchen—in shambles, I might add. I had thought, foolishly perhaps, that you had taken him into too much aversion ever to speak with him again."

He reddened, and he ran his hand under his high starched collar. "I felt it necessary to know why he had attacked Lord Dare."

"It's a pity that you didn't take such a reasonable course earlier in the night. Then, you spurned the use of words and resorted instead to violent action!"

His mouth twitched, and he began to pace about the room. "You are evading my question!" he burst out. "Tell me, were you and Lord Dare embracing? Had you invited him to your home for a clandestine meeting?"

"I *beg* your pardon!" she exclaimed, her eyes snapping.

He stopped before her, his breathing laboured. "Then what was he doing here?" he asked grimly. "At such a time of night? I happened to be passing when I saw his horse tethered at the post. Understandably I was filled with conjecture. Indeed, I could hardly believe my eyes.''

"And so you took it upon yourself to burst unbidden into my house! You are going far beyond permission, cousin.''

He shrugged his sharp shoulders, unabashed. "But what was he doing here unless you had invited him?''

"I do not know what he was doing here. He claimed he was leading the hounds on a false scent. In the same case, I do not know what Mandeville was doing here. And likewise, I do not know what you were doing here.''

He bit his lip. "I told you. I was concerned for your safety.''

"That's as paltry an excuse as either Lord Dare's or Mandeville's.'' Her eyes narrowed at a sudden suspicion. "Was it you who whispered in my ear last night?''

He looked wholly bewildered by her words. "Did what?''

"Whispered in my ear,'' she repeated.

"Whispered what?'' he demanded, obviously striving to make sense of her question.

She turned away, reluctant to mention the words or the note. Whoever had sent the note had been in the kitchen with her last night. It must have been one of the three combatants. Her brain whirled at this realization.

Why should they choose to communicate with her in this way? More seriously, why should they threaten her? What did they want of her?

"What is it you want of me?" she repeated, scarcely aware she spoke aloud.

"What do I want of you?" Elcho appeared dazed. He stepped forward and took her nerveless hand in his. "I want your trust. Please give it me."

Her trust? That was the one thing that, at this moment, she felt herself entirely unable to give. Yet she did not wish to wound Elcho's feelings unnecessarily.

"Please, cousin, let us cease pulling caps. I understand you were concerned for my safety. Let us leave it at that."

"But why was Lord Dare here?" Elcho insisted, his voice rising. His interest seemed almost obsessive.

She became very still. Why *was* Dare here last night? She remembered that she had heard that strange tapping before finding Lord Dare in her kitchen. And Dare had been there when she fell into the subsidence. Again, Lord Dare had been present when Nicholas surprised the intruder. Was there a connection between the tapping and Lord Dare? The evidence seemed to be mounting.

"Stop belabouring the matter so." Irritated, she shook her hand loose from Elcho's. "I can't think why you should be in such a taking. Indeed, it is I who should ring a peal over your head for behaving so violently last night in my kitchen. But, I will endeavour not to speak of it again—on the condition that you do not do so, either.

He opened his mouth, then closed it in a thin line, letting his breath out in a long sigh. "So be it."

Next evening Elaine prepared herself for the Carlton House dinner, victim to an almost paralyzing mixture of emotions. While she feared Nicholas's introduction into the Carlton House set, she could not help but be thankful for the diversion the dinner offered her. The question of the mysterious letter plagued her almost to tears.

What could it mean? she asked herself again and again. Give up what? Could it be some prank? Or some mistake? But no matter how she cudgelled her brain, she could produce no convincing explanation.

Since the dinner was such an important social event, Elaine felt she must inform Aunt Augusta of the party. Therefore, at her usual morning conference, she broached, in a deceptively casual voice, the matter of Prinny's invitation.

"Carlton House?" Aunt Augusta repeated querulously, instinctively reaching for her vinaigrette.

Elaine had it ready. "Yes, dear Aunt, Carlton House."

"But, my dear, one of Prinny's gorges! Ugh!" She fell back against her pillows. "I believe he brings whole roasted pigs to the table. Such a sight would give me a spasm."

"I have no doubt," Elaine agreed. "However, I promise neither to look at nor to eat a whole roasted pig."

Aunt Augusta revived momentarily. "You do?" she asked weakly. "Perhaps you will survive it, then." Colour returned to her ashen cheeks at a sudden thought. "Oh, I recollect now. To attend a party at Carlton House is a most salubrious experience."

"Is it, indeed?" Elaine asked, a tremor in her voice.

"But yes," Aunt Augusta averred. "Only bethink yourself. Prinny keeps fires burning in all the grates, especially during these months, since he considers spring breezes dangerously unhealthy."

Since it was the end of May, the prospect of attending a party heated by endless burning fires failed to win Elaine's approbation.

"And," her aunt continued, "he keeps all the windows tightly closed, so that no fresh air can possibly enter the rooms." Aunt Augusta abandoned the vinaigrette, becoming increasingly more bobbish. "And with the extraordinary number of guests he invites, the rooms become a veritable steambath. Nothing could be better."

"It'll be more effective than taking a trip to a watering place," Elaine agreed in a failing voice.

"So it will." She bestowed a sunny smile on her niece, then she disposed herself comfortably on her couch, ready for a gentle doze.

A WHOLE ROASTED PIG was not placed directly before Elaine at Prinny's dinner table. However, she had a very clear view of the Prince Regent, and she could hardly be blamed if the porcine image lingered in her mind. Prinny was quite the most rotund gentleman she had ever seen. She had heard that when he undid the stays of his Cumberland corset, Prinny's stomach was so large as to reach his knees. She was pleased to perceive that report had not wronged him.

She had the good fortune of being placed near the head of the table; in fact, her table partner was none other than the Devil's Dare himself, who was always placed within conversational distance of Prinny.

Elaine was looking her very best that evening, as was Nicholas. By odd coincidence, both were wearing white. Elaine had chosen white satin cut in a simple Grecian style. A delicate gold thread ran through it, and it was edged with gold braid. Over her shoulders she draped a richly embroidered scarf of spangled gold. Gleaming gold chains and armbands finished her costume. Nicholas had told her before they left home that she looked just like Diana, the huntress.

"You have hunting on the brain," she had replied, a humorous twist to her mouth. "But tell me, how do you like my hair?"

Nicholas stepped back to admire it. A wide white ribbon was wound round her hair, and her golden curls tumbled unrestrained over it. He nodded his approval, much to Elaine's gratification.

His own hair, pomaded, perfumed, and glistening, was styled in the Windswept manner. His coat was of white satin like that of his sister's dress, and it, too, was trimmed with gold. He even sported a waistcoat of snowy white brocade.

"If only Miss Poole could see you now," Elaine had said with a soulful sigh.

"You deserve I should box your ears, my dear sister."

They both laughed, anticipating an evening of unmixed pleasure. Or, at least Nicholas had anticipated such an evening. Elaine could not feel entirely at ease, knowing she was going to enter the notorious Carlton

House, and that she would meet there the Devil's Dare.

Carlton House was also a Palace of Art. It was a magnificent palace, not a spot without some ornament, often gold upon gold. Prinny had crammed it with priceless furniture, bronzes, Sèvres porcelain, paintings, tapestries, and countless other treasures.

Passing through its fine Corinthian-porticoed entranceway, brother and sister had been greeted by the Prince, awaiting his guests at the head of a graceful double staircase. He himself looked most magnificent in the uniform of a field marshal. It was a particularly splendid one, too, Elaine observed, for even the seams of the coat were heavily embroidered.

He was much impressed by the picture the Farringtons made, and expressed his appreciation to Lord Dare, standing beside him.

"They look like a matched set," he observed, lifting his quizzing glass to survey them more closely.

Lord Dare's eyes widened, and he caught his breath at sight of Elaine. His whole face glowed for a moment. Then he turned his head slightly at Prinny's words. "Very true, Prinny. But—" and his eyes danced with mischief "—they are far from being matched in temperament. The sister, I'm afraid, is rather straitlaced."

Prinny's face fell ludicrously. "Oh, dash it all, what a pity. The boy, I take it then, is a young hellion?" He cocked an inquiring eye at Lord Dare, who nodded. Prinny sighed gustily. "Wish it were the other way round."

"Oh, so do I," Lord Dare agreed sweetly. He shot a gleaming eye at Elaine who, responding despite herself, had to bite back a sudden laugh.

"Who knows? You may prove a beneficial influence upon her." Prinny all but leered and poked Lord Dare's ribs with his elbow. "I've placed her beside you at the dinner table, so take advantage of all your opportunities."

"I always do," Dare assured him, a quiver of laughter in his voice. Elaine had to avert her eyes, else she knew they would both be in the whoops. They seemed to share an unspoken communication, as if they were, indeed, closely linked. It must be, she thought, that they shared a common sense of humour. She knew they both delighted in the ridiculous. However, she knew also that Lord Dare delighted in setting her all on end. And Prinny's words did little to soothe her. Indeed, such a preamble led her to fear that the dinner conversation would be a trifle *risqué*.

Once seated beside the Devil's Dare, however, she found that nothing could have been more innocuous. Prinny's thoughts, apparently, dwelt on affairs of state, not the least of which was the affair of the Scottish Regalia Commission.

"Dash it, Charles," the Prince spoke familiarly to Lord Dare, "Scott is getting damned hoity-toity about it." He shook his head ponderously, downing a drink with one toss.

Lord Dare shrugged his broad shoulders in patent unconcern. "But what is Scott to you, my Prince? A mere scribbler."

Elaine bridled with indignation at hearing her favourite author stigmatized so disparagingly. She listened closely, though, recalling her discussion with Elcho concerning the Regalia.

"He's more than that, and you know it." Prinny frowned significantly at his friend.

Lord Dare shrugged again, then addressed his attention to a joint of beef. The table was laden heavily enough to have seriously tried Aunt Augusta's fortitude. Indeed, it might even have altered her views on Prinny's wholesome surroundings, Elaine observed.

The supper table itself filled the two-hundred-foot length of the Gothic conservatory. In front of the Regent's seat was a large circular basin, which fed a stream that meandered between banks of flowers to the end of the table, offering flashing glimpses of gold and silver fish. The tureens, dishes, and plates were all solid silver. And the table itself boasted such masterpieces as *turbot à l'anglaise*, *filets de volaille*, and *poule à l'indienne*. In addition to other wines, there was iced champagne for everybody. Peaches, grapes, pineapples, and other fruits were piled up everywhere. And Prinny spiced it all by airing his complaints against Scott and the commission.

"Must you harp continuously on that string?" Lord Dare now asked audaciously.

"But *you* know how very important a matter it is," Prinny declared, though in increasingly slurred accents. "You *must* be impressed with a true sense of the danger we face."

Lord Dare yawned delicately. That set up Prinny's bristles sufficiently for him to gesture wildly and shout, "Dasset!"

A footman in a green-and-gold uniform materialized immediately at his side. "Yes, Your Highness?" He bowed.

"Bring me that damnable letter from that damned Scott fellow." Prinny continued muttering to himself, as he downed several glasses of wine.

The letter duly appeared, and Prinny groped for his quizzing glass. He squinted, holding the paper at arm's length, obviously trying to focus his vision but to no avail. In exasperation, he thrust it toward Lord Dare. "Read it. That damned mushroom."

Since this epithet was fortunately cast at the absent Walter Scott, Lord Dare took the epistle without a demur. He scanned it briefly.

"Aloud, Charles, if you please," Prinny commanded.

Lord Dare kindly obliged him, settling himself back comfortably in his chair. In his deep, rich voice, he read, "'I thank Your Highness for granting a petition to the officers of state and to me to institute a search after the Regalia of Scotland. The spirit of the Scots has always clung fondly to these emblems. To soothe their anxiety, it was specially provided by an article of the union, that the Regalia should never be removed, under any pretext, from the kingdom of Scotland. Accordingly, they were deposited, with much ceremony, in a strong chest, secured by many locks, and the chest itself placed in a strong room, which again was carefully bolted up and secured, leaving to national pride the satisfaction of pointing to the barred window with the consciousness that there lay the Regalia of Scotland. But this gratification has become strangely disturbed by a rumour that the Regalia have been sent to London under Your Highness's own secret warrant! Should this indeed prove to be the case, I cannot answer for my fellow countrymen, who will, I believe, defend their rights with their arms and their lives. Ever Your Highness's truly faithful Walter Scott.' ''

Elaine felt stirred by these words, caught up by their spirit and dignity. She knew that her cousin, Elcho, too, would applaud their sentiment.

Lord Dare started to return this weighty correspondence to his equally weighty Regent, but discovered to his amusement that the Prince had dozed off during its reading.

Elaine choked a laugh, and Lord Dare turned to her with a quizzical expression on his handsome face. "You see how overpowered he is by it all."

She laughed out loud, but quickly covered her mouth, for the sound caused Prinny to stir and once again to open his eyes. Relentlessly—and remarkably—he took up the thread of conversation where he had dropped it.

"Well, Charles, don't you see?" he demanded. "What are you going to do about it? You *will* do something, won't you?"

Prinny's obvious dependence on Dare puzzled Elaine. Observing Dare closely, she saw him give an infinitesimal frown and shake of his head, a movement that managed somehow, much to Elaine's mystification, to quiet Prinny. Dare polished his own quizzing glass with a lawn handkerchief before looking up. "Of course," he said insouciantly, "I will do something, Your Highness. I always meet my challenges, you must know that." The force with which he said this last phrase brought a pleased smile to his prince's rather fat lips, but caused Elaine to knit her brows. "I shall endeavour to distract Your Highness's attention with some sport."

Prinny waved a dismissive hand. "Ah, what sport can be had at formal dinner party and ball, I ask you?"

Lord Dare grinned. "There's *always* sport to be had," he promised.

Prinny brightened and readied himself for Dare's sport by becoming foxed in the extreme.

Elaine cocked an anxious eye at Nicholas, only to discover that he was eagerly drinking in Lord Dare's words. The delicious *gâteau glacé aux abricots* she was eating turned to ashes in her mouth.

Having endured just yesterday an example of Lord Dare's sport, she felt wholly incapable of witnessing another. But she could hardly drag her brother to the safety of their carriage. Therefore, when the guests were released to the ballroom, she decided at least to dispose herself safely. She made straight for one of the bergère chairs that lined the wall, determined to spend the evening there in the unalarming company of dowagers and widows. There, surely, no harm could reach her.

As these beturbaned ladies had nothing more interesting to discuss than the latest style in dresses or the most recent *crim. con.* scandals, Elaine felt fortunate indeed to be soon joined by Lord Darlington.

He entered the ballroom attired in such magnificence as to rival its dazzling mirrors and sparkling chandeliers. He was dressed entirely in cloth of gold, even sporting a spangled gold waistcoat. Elaine blinked as he approached her.

"Good evening to you, Miss Farrington," he greeted her with a delighted bow. The dowagers and widows all but shielded their eyes against his brilliance.

"Is it indeed evening?" Elaine teased. "I beg to doubt you, my lord, for I do believe the very sun, at its blazing noon, has entered the ballroom."

Lord Darlington looked much gratified by this compliment. "Too kind, too kind," he said, blushing. "I was beginning to have my doubts, when I could induce no link-boy to guide me into the palace with his torch. However, you much reassure me."

Elaine lifted her fan to hide a smile. "Perhaps the link-boys believed you needed no torch, your costume being brighter than any light they could offer."

He seemed much struck. "Why, that's so! You could be right." His face settled into a complacent beam. He turned to look about him. Garlands of roses, palm trees, and hundreds of candles decked the ballroom, providing a splendid background for its guests. The dance floor was filled to overflowing with twirling dancers, who also glittered and sparkled, but with colour and gaiety rather than with cloth of gold. He smiled benevolently. "How pretty everything looks. But why aren't you dancing, my dear? Don't tell me you lack for partners."

"I know it's indelicate for me to admit this, Lord Darlington, but I'm filled to such repletion by Prinny's dinner that I hesitate to risk dancing."

His mouth rounded in understanding. "My poor child. How could Prinny inflict one of his dinners upon you? What a beast he is."

Her blue eyes kindled at this. "He's not the beast. It's Lord Dare. He wanted, no doubt, to be certain Nicholas attended the evening's festivities." The bitter note in her voice indicated to Lord Darlington that she was less than pleased by this circumstance.

"He has taken quite a liking to Nicholas," Lord Darlington observed, stroking his round chin. He eyed Elaine speculatively. "And to other members of your family, as well."

She sat bolt upright. "I beg your pardon?"

"Forgive me, my dear Miss Farrington, I forget myself," Lord Darlington hastened to apologize.

Elaine frowned at him suspiciously for a few moments, but his expression remained singularly innocent. She sniffed and shrugged her shoulders.

"Where *is* Nicholas, by the way?" Lord Darlington asked idly. "Lord Alvanley went off to search for him a while ago and has not returned."

Elaine closed her eyes and suppressed a shudder. "He's with Lord Dare, I have no doubt."

"I wonder what they could be doing?"

At his very words, a sudden rumble was to be heard over their heads. As it became a veritable thundering, Elaine and all the dowagers and widows stood up, aghast. The chandeliers hanging from the ceiling began to sway precariously, creaking and rattling. And the mirrors on the walls began to vibrate so that they seemed in imminent danger of shivering into a thousand pieces.

"Lord Darlington, what is it?" Elaine gasped. "An earthquake?"

He did not answer but instead took her hand in order to guide her out of the ballroom to a more safely situated room.

As they reached the double staircase, Elaine heard shouts and cheers from the Long Gallery above. She stood stock-still. Then she tugged Lord Darlington's hand. "It's from up there!"

"Yes, I know. That's why I want us to go out there." He indicated the Sienna marble entrance.

She broke loose from his hold. "But Nicholas has to be up there. I must see what's the to-do!" She hurried up the stairs, followed by the clucking Lord Darlington.

The sight which met her eyes at the entrance to the Long Gallery was so shocking as almost to deprive her of her senses. A troop of horses was tearing pell-mell down the gallery. Upon closer inspection, Elaine realized that there were only three riders—the mirrors on the wall had served terrifyingly to multiply their images. These riders were Prinny, Alvanley, and Nicholas. Lord Dare was on the sidelines, grandly officiating. Each of the riders was whooping and waving his arms above his head, trying to outjockey his opponents.

Paintings were tilting, and footmen ran to and fro, frantically grasping marble busts, china figurines, and gilded clocks.

As the riders reached the end of the hall, they pulled up their mounts, causing them to fall upon their haunches, then swung them around and went tearing off in the opposite direction, the footmen running hard behind, determined to preserve the art treasures at the other end of the room.

As this mob dashed headlong toward them, both Elaine and Lord Darlington screeched with terror and scrambled madly for the door. At the sound of a feminine scream, the Prince Regent pulled his horse to an abrupt halt. As his girth was greater than his gentlemanly intentions, he promptly tumbled off his horse's back and fell to the floor with a heavy thud. The sound of a crash of glass beneath them left Elaine in no doubt that one of the crystal chandeliers in the ballroom had succumbed to its fate.

Four footmen rushed to assist their royal master to his feet. The other riders promptly abandoned their race, dismounting in a trice.

Prinny bent his gaze upon Elaine. He squinted, bringing her into focus. "It's the straitlaced sister!" he exclaimed in the liveliest dismay. "How we must have lacerated her sensibilities!" He tottered forward, his arms outstretched. "My dear maiden, I kiss your feet in apology. Please forgive us for frightening you so. Let me kiss your feet!"

Elaine used her feet to better purpose by taking to her heels and scurrying down the stairs. She was followed by all the gentlemen in the room. And she could hear Prinny repeating, "But let me kiss your feet!"

As she reached the base of the stairs, she halted, wondering how she could escape Carlton House as quickly as possible. A respite was afforded by Lord Alvanley's grasping Prinny's shoulder and inquiring boisterously, "But why her feet? She has pretty ankles, I admit. But her mouth, ah, that is much more desirable."

"*Every* lady's mouth is desirable," Prinny declared, puffing.

Nicholas, decidedly red in the face from his exertions, looked revolted. "But you can't possibly go about kissing the mouth of every lady you see."

"Of course he can," Lord Dare interpolated with a chuckle. "You forget, he's the Regent."

"I can?" Prinny all but rubbed his hands with glee.

"No, he can't," Nicholas contradicted adamantly. He cast a challenging look at his idol. "And neither, my dear Charles, can you." He awaited with shining eyes the effect of these words.

Elaine wished to heaven that Nicholas had held his peace. For no sooner was this challenge issued than Lord Dare, urged on by the gentlemen surrounding him, ruefully laughed, then came swooping down the stairs, determined to kiss the mouth of every woman in the ballroom. Prinny followed, ready to do the same.

Elaine ran into the ballroom, hoping to warn the ladies in time, but within seconds the place was in uproar. Shrieks were sent up. And the crowd in the ballroom surged and billowed like waves at high tide, as the women desperately tried to evade Prinny's and Lord Dare's embraces.

CHAPTER EIGHT

SEVERAL HYSTERICAL LADIES rushed out of the ballroom. Lady Porth, who had been keeping an eagle eye on her young daughter just out of the schoolroom, found herself in dire need of protection, as Prinny was cutting a swath in her direction. Miss Porth, with great temerity, propelled her mother into a bank of potted palms, where they both cowered under cover. The Duchess of Berwick, thrown into a high fidget, gathered up her train of purple satin and showed a good deal more of her ankles than was seemly as she made a dash out of the room. And several swooning ladies were carried out by solicitous swains. Gracious heavens, thought Elaine to herself. What a rare rumpus this is!

She was herself more properly in the briars than she had at first realized, for it soon became apparent that Prinny had her within his sights. She saw him circle warily about her, strategically manoeuvring to win his prize. As horrified as if she had seen a lion about to attack, Elaine backed up, only to come to an abrupt halt against the wall. Beleaguered, she cast frantically about the room, hoping to see either Nicholas or Lord Darlington.

But assistance came from a far more astonishing quarter. Just as Prinny started to fling his arms about Elaine in order to plant a kiss full on her mouth, the Devil's Dare intervened.

He stepped between the Prince and the cringing Elaine as smoothly as if he had interrupted a waltz rather than an amorous advance. "But, my Prince," he expostulated reproachfully. "You have already favoured this young lady with your attentions."

Prinny goggled. Then he closed his eyes, wagging his head. "Have I?" he demanded dubiously, opening his eyes again.

Maintaining an admirably straight face, Lord Dare nodded. "But how could you forget? Of course you have. Look at her face—how becomingly flushed with pleasure it is. Doesn't she look as if she's just been kissed?"

Elaine's face was indeed bright red, but not with pleasure. Moreover, her eyes were round with amazement. To think of the Devil's Dare coming to her rescue in such a way!

"She does look overheated," Prinny agreed, after subjecting her countenance to a vague scrutiny. "Oh, well, then. I haven't the time to kiss each lady twice this evening. There're too many of them." And with that, he swung on his heels and waved his fat arms. "Heigh-ho! I'm out for blood!" And off he went in hot pursuit of poor Lady Ancaster, whose generous proportions and breathtakingly low décolletage had just that moment caught his eye.

Elaine's elbows were gripped hard, and she was impelled with surprising force out of the room. Before she knew what was about, she was outside Carlton House, thankfully breathing in the cool delicious night air.

She turned to confront Lord Dare with clenched fists, hardly able to wait while he bespoke her carriage, before demanding in a breathless voice if his head had gone to let.

He gave a short laugh. "You do have unusual ways of expressing gratitude," he observed, his mouth twisting.

"Gratitude!" Elaine huffed. "Outrage, more like."

"What, do you mean you wanted to be kissed by Prinny?" Lord Dare demanded in the liveliest surprise. "I wonder how I came to make such a mistake. And you were looking so beset, too." He sighed, rubbing his square jaw thoughtfully, only his dancing eyes at odds with his serious demeanour. "Well, I'm reluctant to oblige you, considering I have always thought you a gently nurtured female—in fact, the *only* gently nurtured female to number amongst my acquaintance—but I suppose it can still be arranged."

He was doing it much too brown to suit Elaine. She pursed her mouth primly. "If you think me a gently nurtured female, I wonder how you dare speak to me as you do."

"How I *what*?"

There was a long pause, then Elaine burst out with the laugh she had endeavoured vainly to hold back. "Oh, do be serious," she begged. "Last night you didn't think me a gently nurtured female. On the contrary, you accused me of being quite other." Her breast heaved at the recollection.

He watched it appreciatively. "How I wish that were true," he said soulfully, sighing and shaking his head.

How provoking he was. He always managed to appeal to her sense of humour, effectively taking the wind out of her eye. Although he had magically robbed her of all sense of rancour, she couldn't help but ask, "If you didn't believe it to be true, then why did you accuse me of having an assignation with both Mandeville and Elcho?"

His face became suddenly very grave, and he contemplated her through half-closed eyelids. Twisting a heavy gold signet ring about his finger, averting his head, he commented, "What other explanation suffices for their presence in your kitchen last night? What wonder if I was jealous?"

"Jealous," she repeated, beginning to prickle all over with anger again.

He held up a peremptory hand. "Besides, my dear, those accusations had nothing to do with you. I was merely trying to put Mandeville and Elcho in a rage."

"And what possible motive could you have for doing so?"

"I'm ruthless with my rivals, you must know."

"*And* with the object of your affections! You certainly brought them to daggers-drawing. But you also made me as mad as fire. What a rare set-about. Have you no sense of propriety?"

He shook his head mournfully. "Such is not my reputation."

She snorted. As the carriage drew up before them, she suddenly bethought herself of a way to bring him to *point non plus*. "You must be slipping, then," she said with a sigh of false sympathy.

He looked mildly surprised. "I?" he asked suspiciously.

"Why, yes. You certainly failed to win your dare tonight, haven't you? It must be for the first time."

He stared at her, an arrested expression in his face.

As he did not speak, Elaine let loose another shaft. "And you even prevented Prinny from winning his. You must be turning over a new leaf."

His eyes gleamed with admiration as he acknowledged this hit. For a moment he seemed positively captivated. Then his face clouded as he brooded over something. "Perhaps I am. You obviously think this a consummation devoutly to be wished. But I wonder if you really know me as well as you think you do," he exclaimed, as though the words were wrung out of him.

She felt her pulse begin to race at his tone. "So do I wonder, my lord," she tried to reply flippantly, but she managed only a small voice.

"And yet, you know me better than most."

"Do I?"

He leaned toward her, his face tense. He opened his mouth, and Elaine waited on tenterhooks. But he clamped his mouth shut again, giving his head a vicious shake. "I cannot dishonour his confidence in me," he ejaculated under his breath.

"Whose confidence?" she demanded, justly exasperated.

He looked down, his face suddenly immobile. Achieving a careless shrug, he replied, "Why, your brother's, of course. He'd be most disappointed in me if I really turned over a new leaf. He thinks me game for all suits."

"Well, what I think you, my lord," she steamed, "is a...a—"

"A rakeshame?" he supplied politely. "A reckless ne'er-do-well?"

She choked. "A bamboozler!"

He grinned. "Well, what I think you is a darling. If anyone could make me turn over a new leaf, it would be you."

"What a delightful prospect!" She couldn't help but gurgle with laughter.

He looked at her wonderingly, his whole face alight. He helped her into the carriage but retained his grasp of her hand, holding it so tightly that Elaine felt herself begin to quiver.

He lifted her hand and, with great solemnity, kissed it. The warmth of his lips made her feel slightly dizzy. She met his steady gaze with difficulty, and realized from his disturbing expression that it was clearly unsafe to be alone with him. "My dear," he said in a caressing voice, "you are a far greater prize than all the treasures in Prinny's palace."

She felt her heart leap in response to this! But she caught herself. This was coming it too strong. What flummery! He was merely conducting his usual flirtation with her, and well she knew it. "Well," she snapped, "you haven't won me yet!"

He bowed, though looking far from shattered, and closed the carriage door, signing the coachman to be off. As the horses' hooves clattered away, Elaine heard him shout after her, "And don't put yourself in a pucker, my dear. I shall send Nicholas home to you tonight safe and sound."

Elaine leaned back against the squabs, feeling strangely overwhelmed. What an odd taking to be in, she chided herself weakly. One would think she was missish.

She was worse than that, she decided after a few minutes, during which time she managed to regulate her breathing and to calm her palpitating heart. She was an air-dreamer. She meant nothing to Lord Dare. She was but a citadel he was determined to storm. A challenge, merely. Just another exploit that would allow him to outshine his dastardly father. And the sooner she dismissed Dare from her thoughts, the better it would be for her.

Nicholas was far more deserving of her attention than was Lord Dare. And yet she had left him not only to his own devices, but worse, to Lord Dare's. How could she have deprived herself of yet another night's peaceful rest? She sighed disconsolately as the carriage neared Farrington Place.

Guided into the salon by the two footmen, Elaine told Seaton to bring her a glass of ratafia. She was in sore need of a reviving draft. Sinking into the comfortable deep-winged chair before the fireplace, Elaine closed her eyes in exhaustion. Each encounter with Lord Dare seemed to drain her both emotionally and physically.

Seaton brought the ratafia to her in a Waterford crystal glass on a heavily embossed silver salver. A silver barrel filled with biscuits was beside it. Placing this repast on a tiny tripod table, he bowed his leave-taking.

Elaine lifted the glass by its stem, twirling it idly. She took slow meditative sips, wondering how she could dismiss Lord Dare not only from her thoughts but also from her society. Yet everything in her seemed to rebel against this necessity. To strengthen her resolve, she marshalled evidence against him. He seemed, she told herself with truth, to be behind every disturbance she had recently endured. And he most certainly was leading Nicholas into dangerous excesses. She, therefore, must persuade him to detach Nicholas from his allegiance.

No matter how humiliating such a course would be, she must make a push to protect Nicholas. At the first opportunity, she would request an interview with Lord Dare. She would subdue her own aversion to him, for Nicholas's sake.

Elaine shook her head at herself, far from being deceived. Nevertheless, this decision relaxed her. And the ratafia was more effective than she had anticipated, for within moments, her eyelids dropped, and she fell into a comfortable doze.

But again her sleep was of a lamentably short duration. She awoke suddenly. She was dreaming. She had to be! Her whole body went taut. It was the knocking, again, and she wasn't dreaming.

This time she rang the bellpull for Seaton. Her heart pounded uncomfortably as she awaited him, but rather than stir from this chair and expose herself to heaven knew what dangers, this time she would send off Seaton and the footmen to investigate the noise!

Seaton entered, looking harassed. Obviously he, too, had heard the noise.

She caught his eye in silent inquiry. After a moment, he bowed. "I will see to it, Miss Farrington."

Elaine nodded. Then when he had left she felt quite sick with suspense. She devoutly hoped they would find only a nest of rats. But she feared the origin of the sounds was more serious than rodents.

She bounded in the chair, so startled was she when Nicholas kicked open the salon door. "Good heavens!" she squealed. "How you frightened me!" She noted that his neckcloth was loosened and that his carefully styled hair was now in natural riot.

He frowned at her. "Dear sister," he said, shaking his head. "You must learn to control your nerves." He clucked regretfully. "If it hadn't been for you, I should have won this evening's race!"

Elaine was far from repentant, feeling other matters took precedence over Nicholas's loss. She began to protest, but he shook his head again. "Really, sister, I had no idea you were so fidgety. Even Lord Dare said you were more nerves than flesh!"

"He did, did he? Well, all I can say is that you've more hair than wit! What were you thinking of, behaving in such an outrageous way? You could have broken your neck!"

"No such thing." Nicholas impatiently dismissed the suggestion. "The floor was well-carpeted, so the horses' hooves couldn't have slipped. Else I'm sure that Charles—endeavouring to cheer up the Prince with some sport, you know, as was his challenge—would never have suggested the race. Prinny found the idea extremely diverting and immediately ordered the footmen to bring up the horses. And you must know that the mounts in Prinny's own stables are extremely well-trained. The only mishap that occurred was through your doing. You shouldn't have interrupted us. I am sure that Charles was within an ace of declaring me the winner." He moaned, sinking in a chair, covering his face with his hands.

"Well, at least you're alive to try again another day," Elaine replied sardonically. She had other matters to occupy her mind, which prevented her from paying much attention to Nicholas.

Yet her facetious words consoled him, for when she turned her head to look at him, she found him smiling radiantly. This smile fully gained her attention. What did it presage?

"Your words are truer than you know, dear sister," he exclaimed, elated. "Charles has promised me another chance."

"He has?"

"Yes! I complained bitterly to him as he drove me home—"

Elaine interrupted him. "He drove you home?" she asked urgently.

Nicholas nodded in simple pride. "I felt all the go, too. Lord, it isn't every young blood who gets taken up twice in Charles's curricle."

"So I should imagine," she said in a hollow voice.

"Well, that's by the by. I tell you, dear sister, Charles is bang up to the echo. Upon finding me so disappointed at having the race curtailed, he assured me there would be other races to win in the future. Well, this seemed to me an open lead, so I immediately issued him a challenge to another race. And, of course, as I knew he must, he accepted!"

"Another race? And where will this one be held? In Almack's Assembly Rooms?"

Such awful irony failed to puncture Nicholas. He laughed. "By Jove, what a lark that would be. No, no, it's a curricle race to Brighton, if you must know. We leave at the crack of dawn Saturday."

With that, he patted her heartily on the shoulder and bade her a cheerful good-night. He stopped at the door. "This has been a most eventful night for me, all things considered." He paused, blushing slightly. "Do you know that I even managed to win a kiss from Miss Poole, who most fortunately happened to be attending Prinny's ball? Well—" he ducked his head "—so did Prinny and Alvanley, but she liked my kiss the best." This declaration sent him out of the room, smiling like a veritable moonling.

A curricle race to Brighton. The thought of it made Elaine's blood run cold. She had heard how dangerous such races could be. The Brighton road was a busy highway, always crammed with coaches, wagons, and other large vehicles. And Nicholas would be bound to drive recklessly in hope of beating Lord Dare to flinders. She knew he would meet with some terrible accident.

Her thoughts were ruthlessly interrupted by Seaton's abrupt entrance. She shook herself, trying to recall her senses. "Seaton," she gasped. "What did you find?"

Without a word, he held out to her a gold-topped ebony cane. Elaine stared at it as if it were a serpent.

"Is it Nicholas's?" she managed to ask.

"His valet says that it does not belong to Mr. Nicholas."

"Where did you find it?"

"In the wine cellar." Seeing that Elaine was not about to take the walking stick from him, Seaton placed it, with great care, upon the mantlepiece. Then he bowed, and clearly feeling that he had discharged his duty, he left the room.

And Elaine was left subject to wild conjectures. She went rigid as one explanation struck her like a blinding light. Something must have been concealed in the house! And now someone must be either keeping an eye on it or trying to retrieve it. Worse, she had an appalling premonition that she knew just what it was.

Her first impulse was to run in terror from the house. Her next was to call in the Bow Street Runners! The house must instantly be searched. If what she suspected were indeed true, then the matter was too grave to leave in the hands of Seaton or the footmen. And it certainly could not be left to Nicholas. He would probably convert the search into a mad treasure hunt.

But she could not bring Bow Street Runners into the house. Such a measure would not only set the ton in a bustle, but it would also drive poor Aunt Augusta distracted. Further, it might alert the perpetrator of this act.

Preferring action to thought, Elaine quitted her chair, compelled to investigate the wine cellar. She was uncertain what she might find there, but it must be the proper area to search, since there the cane had been discovered.

Taking with her naught but a silver candlestick, Elaine descended the stairs into the cellar. Now it seemed a cold, damp place, made more eerie by a continually whistling wind.

Slowly she pulled the wooden door shut behind her. The only illumination was that from her own candle, as the windowless chamber itself afforded no light.

Peering closely about her, she noted, as if seeing it for the first time, that both the floor and walls, which were of perfectly smooth stone, provided no convenient nook or crevice for a useful hiding-place. The cellar was devoid of those cabinets, chests, or cupboards Mrs. Radcliffe's novels and other works of lurid fiction had led her to deem necessary for secreting valuable goods.

Against the wall reposed only one huge barrel, containing porter. But as it was in constant use, Elaine doubted its practicability as a secure hiding-place. The wooden racks laden with crusted wine bottles were narrow and open; they, too, seemed utterly useless for the purpose.

Refusing to be daunted, Elaine began tapping the walls, hoping to hear a hollow sound. She also hoped that Mrs. Beale was fast asleep. Otherwise the cook would be certain that the plaguey ghosts were busy again.

Elaine tapped and tapped for what seemed an eternity—all to no avail. The walls were disappointingly solid and secure. Baffled and beginning to feel frustrated, she sat down beside the large wooden barrel, too distracted to mind the dust which was besmirching her white ball gown, and tried to think.

Perhaps, after all, she had leaped to an absurd conclusion. Perhaps another explanation could account for the tapping noises, the intruder, the threats, and the cane. But no other conclusion presented itself. Something had to be hidden in the cellar. But where?

At that moment, the candle flame leaped and sputtered, causing Elaine to turn her head to look at it. She must have been in the cellar for well over an hour, since the candle had burnt so low; indeed, it must now be nearing dawn. The candle guttered in its socket, and before Elaine could pick it up, it went out.

To her surprise, the cellar was not immediately plunged into complete darkness. Her eyes widened, and she stared, puzzled, at the shaft of light rising through a crack beneath the large wooden barrel.

Could that be possible? How could light, faint though it was, shine up through a cellar floor?

She ran her hand over the barrel and its base. There was something havey-cavey about this barrel, and she was determined to discover what it was. But she found its planks were solid and hard. Its iron bands, too, were secure. She began to feel utterly confounded, when, after a great deal of this careful probing, one of the nails in the base sank at her touch, and before she knew what was afoot, the barrel slid aside on a hidden groove, revealing a large, gaping hole in the ground!

Elaine could hardly credit her eyes. Yet there it was: a large hole. This must be the source of the light beneath the barrel. It must lead to some sort of tunnel which opened, somewhere, into the light of day.

Instantly, Elaine resolved to search its length. Trying to calm her fast-beating heart, she eased herself down through the hole and found herself within a long, narrow passageway stretching before her.

Her head bowed, and her hands touching the walls, Elaine slowly made her way along the tunnel. She found that it was perfectly round, and that at even distances it branched off into other tunnels. It must once have been a drain or conduit of some sort, Elaine realized. She had heard of several such drains in South London, but she had not thought one had been attached to her very own cellar.

She had also heard of chalk-mine tunnels in South London, and at the thought, she remembered the hole which had suddenly opened up beneath her and through which she had fallen days before in the alley. That must have been a subsidence from this very tunnel! Chalk mines, she knew, caused bizarre land movement. Why, she had heard once of a cart-horse actually being swallowed whole when the ground fell away beneath it. And yet this couldn't be a mine, since it utterly lacked supports. No, it was just a stupid old drain! But then why had someone secured a secret entranceway to it?

She was beginning to feel stifled in the tunnel's closeness. But she refused to stop. The tunnel's only reasonable origin, she concluded, must have been as an escape route for someone in the past. She imagined all sorts of people who could have made use of such an escape route, from priests and political fugitives to rakehells and recluses.

She began to feel as though she were moving in a dream, or a nightmare, more like, as she continued to follow the pale light before her. But her mental and physical meanderings were suddenly brought up short as she found herself reaching the end of the tunnel. Looking up, she saw that the light fell through an iron grid which seemed to frame the blue sky above. Putting up her hands, she shoved at this grid, gasping as dirt fell upon her face. She shook it away and exerted all her strength to lift the grid. When it moved at last, Elaine pushed it quickly aside. Then she cautiously stuck her head up through the hole, curious to learn where the tunnel led.

It must have been shorter than she had thought, for it ended in the square garden just across the road in front of Farrington Place! She must have seen this square garden a hundred times every day of the year. And yet she had never suspected that she had her own private tunnel to it. It was too incredible! Why would anyone wish to attach the wine cellar entrance to this garden?

She knew that Prinny's Brighton Pavilion boasted an underground passageway to an adjacent house. But as it facilitated his midnight visits to his mistress, Mrs. Fitzherbert, who lived in that house, it seemed eminently practical. This passage seemed, on the other hand, not only impractical but also absurd.

As she stood thus, her head sticking straight out of the ground like the enchanted head in *Don Quixote*, Elaine suddenly had the oddest sensation of prickling at her neck. Turning completely around, she found herself being stared at aghast by a burly, bewhiskered fellow she had no difficulty in identifying as the gardener. In fact, he had apparently just finished weeding a flower bed, for he still held his hoe. He dropped this tool, clearly amazed at the apparition before him.

Elaine looked at him a moment, then she was overcome by all the possible explanations for her sudden appearance before the gardener. Mrs. Beale, no doubt, would declare that she was a ghost. At the thought, she quoted, "Earth to earth, ashes to ashes," in a sepulchral voice, then promptly dropped back into the tunnel! Quickly replacing the grid, she closed her ears to the horrified gasp and vociferous curses the poor gardener immediately fell to uttering.

Stooping once more, she retraced her steps, but this time she moved even more slowly. She would now explore not the tunnel but its contents. She did not recall seeing any object on the floor during her first passage, but since she had been so engrossed in the tunnel itself, such a failure did not surprise her.

Now she scanned each inch of the ground very carefully, hoping to discover some hidden hoard. She stopped, frozen, when just at the turn of one of the side tunnels, she spied some rocks piled together in a sort of cairn.

Her hands began to tremble, and her breathing became shallow. Kneeling quickly, she grasped the stones. Large and heavy, they proved difficult to move, but with some effort, Elaine managed to push them aside. Revealed beneath them was a large oblong box wrapped in an oilskin.

She unfolded the oilskin with shaking hands, then discarded it, her attention riveted on the wooden box beneath. It was roughly made, its catch of tarnished brass.

Her throat felt painfully dry, and her eyes burned with excitement. Biting her lip, she hurriedly lifted the catch, then stared at the contents.

The box held a sword and a sceptre!

Both were beautiful pieces of workmanship; both were of obvious antiquity. The golden scabbard was richly decorated with silver filigree, double-gilded, representing oak leaves and acorns. The golden sceptre, too, was ornamented with leaves and acorns. Even in the faint light, the treasures shone like torches.

Elaine closed her eyes and released her breath. She had found the ancient Regalia of Scotland!

CHAPTER NINE

THOUGH HER EYES BEHELD the gold and her fingers touched the cool metal, Elaine couldn't quite accept that she had actually found the ancient sword and sceptre.

Why were they here and not in their rightful resting place in Edinburgh? They *must* be returned before the commission discovered their absence. If it were generally known that the Regalia no longer rested securely in Edinburgh, then a cry of such outrage would arise that a bloody rebellion would erupt! The Scots were a formidable and deadly foe. During the last rebellion, the Highlanders had marched almost to London before being repelled.

At this thought, Elaine hastily recovered the wooden box and recoiled from it as though it were a fire-hot brand. She darted pell-mell through the tunnel to the safety of the wine cellar and hastily pushed the barrel back to its proper place. Then she sought the refuge of her bedroom, numb with fright and confusion.

Safe in bed—or at least she profoundly hoped that she was safe—the bedclothes pulled tightly about her neck, she realized, however, that she must think clearly and logically. At least, she told herself, she now had the explanation of the recent disturbances. Someone had been either keeping an eye on the Scottish Regalia or trying to steal them from their hiding-place!

This conclusion did not provide her with a particle of relief. For although she had discovered the cause of these events, she had still to learn the identity of their perpetrator.

Why would someone hide away the Regalia? she asked herself. To cause a Scottish-English incident, to have the time to find a buyer—or to win a dare?

She bit her lip in dismay as she remembered the first time she had met Lord Dare, when she had fallen into the tunnel's subsidence! Had he been there to check on the Regalia?

Someone had been searching the house, too. She had the gold-topped ebony cane in her possession to prove it. Whoever owned that cane was the midnight intruder, and knew the Regalia were connected with Farrington Place. And, her eyes widening with dawning comprehension, she knew that the intruder must be one of Elcho, Mandeville, or Lord Dare. One of these three gentlemen had demanded, both by whispering in her ear and by writing that note, that she give up the Regalia to him.

How could she help but suspect Lord Dare? Then she remembered how the Prince Regent himself had complained so bitterly to the Devil's Dare about the Scottish Regalia. He had even demanded of Lord Dare what he was going to do about them! Did Prinny know the Regalia had been stolen? Was he hinting to the thief that they be returned?

And yet she could not accept that Lord Dare was capable of a deed so serious in its ramifications. Something in her cried out against the thought. She remembered the warmth of his smile. The clear look in his dark, brilliant eyes. And his spirit, which seemed too frank and candid for such hole-in-the-corner behaviour as this.

Doubt nagged her, nevertheless. She knew she was far from being objective where Lord Dare was concerned. Indeed, she could be certain of nothing—except that the owner of the gold-topped ebony cane must be connected with the Scottish Regalia.

But, she thought suddenly, the cane was her trump card. No one knew she had seen the Regalia. She could use the cane to flush out the culprit.

Perhaps she could avoid the scandal of having the Regalia found in the tunnel from her wine cellar—which she thought was still the safest place in which to keep them—if she were to frighten the intruder into revealing himself. Perhaps he could then be induced to return the Regalia to their rightful place before the commission unlocked the gaol gates. She must do something to prevent the terrible consequences—both national and personal—of the Regalia's having been hidden in her tunnel.

After much pondering, Elaine decided to act this very evening. It was Wednesday, and tonight an Assembly would be held at Almack's. Since these affairs were habitually attended by almost every member of the beau monde, she could be tolerably sure of seeing there all three of her suspects.

She scrambled out of bed and set the bell ringing to summon Mary. Within minutes, she was able to confront her brother with a demand that he squire her that evening to Almack's.

He gaped at her a moment, obviously trying to decide whether or not he had heard her aright. Noting her unusually pale countenance, his brow wrinkled with real concern. "Are you feeling a trifle out of sorts, my dear?"

She started to declare that she felt extraordinarily out of sorts, then caught herself up and asked baldly, "Why?"

"Don't think you could be feeling quite the thing, demanding I take you to Almack's, of all places. In fact, you must be burnt to the socket."

Silently agreeing with this assessment, she asked in as reasonable a tone as she could muster, "And what possible objection could you have?"

"I have a number of them," he promptly replied. He lifted his slender hand to count them off his fingers. "The place is too damned stuffy by half. They never offer champagne or a civilized drink but maudle your insides with tea or orgeat. The card games are all limited to shillings play. And worst of all, I have to wear knee-breeches!"

"And what is wrong with knee-breeches?"

"They make me feel like a damned flunky, that's what," he flashed triumphantly.

That won a reluctant smile and a nod of the head from Elaine. Yet she was not going to be so easily defeated. "If you attend Almack's, then you may chance to see Miss Poole."

These words caused Nicholas to bite his lower lip, deep in thought.

"Perhaps you might even win a waltz with her." Elaine ruthlessly dangled this carrot before him.

His eyes glistened at the possibility. "Do you think so, indeed?" he asked.

"I have no doubt of it. Who could resist you, dear brother of mine? Especially in knee-breeches."

He gave a dignified sniff. "Well, if you're so determined, then I will be so very obliging as to cancel all my other engagements just to play your cicerone at Almack's."

"Nicholas, you are too good to me."

That evening, Elaine paid only half a mind to her preparations for Almack's. She was engrossed in preparing methods of unveiling the thief. Mary, however, made certain that her mistress was dressed in the first style of elegance. Elaine's gown was of pink jaconet muslin fastened down the centre with diamanté rosettes over a petticoat of white satin. Diamonds sparkled round her throat and in her hair, done up à la Medusa. A rose-embroidered fan and long white gloves completed her ensemble.

Almack's was a famous hunting-ground, where young débutantes set their caps at eligible beaux. Indeed, it was cynically referred to as the Marriage Mart. Elaine had entered its sacred portals countless times since her début, but she had never done so before with the intention of literally hunting down a gentleman.

The Assembly Rooms were the most exclusive and the most important supper and dancing club in the whole of London. They were ruled by a group of patronesses, including Lady Jersey, Lady Cowper, and the Princess de Lieven, who wielded great power. They set arbitrary and unalterable rules, such as that no young lady could waltz without first having received permission to do so from one of the patronesses and that no guest could be admitted after the hour of 10:00 p.m.

Elaine made certain that she and Nicholas were inside the spacious rooms of Almack's well before that hour. He had protested at her haste, wishing to take time to make sure he looked his best. Unlike his sister, he had been painstaking in his appearance—dressing in the *de rigueur* black satin knee-breeches, a white waistcoat, striped stockings, and a waisted coat with very long tails. He hoped, no doubt, to make a most favourable impression on Miss Poole.

Scanning the rooms upon their entrance, Elaine found them crowded in the extreme. Dancers, moving to the music played by a hidden orchestra, filled the dance floor. Dowagers, seated on little gilded chairs, lined the sides of the room. And roués and rakes gossiped in tight little knots as they eyed the young débutantes. Elaine discovered almost immediately that each of her candidates was in attendance.

Now, to sport.

She was kindly greeted by the Princess de Lieven, who with her usual finesse introduced Elaine to Mr. Stanton. This thin blond gentleman promptly led her out on the floor, as the musicians struck up the notes for a country dance. Elaine moved through the set, paying very little mind to her partner. Rather, she kept her eyes on the nearest of her suspects, Lord Mandeville.

At the set's close, she pleaded a dreadful thirst. Mr. Stanton obediently trotted off to obtain some iced lemonade. Elaine had made certain that she was left to wait beside the pillar at which Lord Mandeville was stationed.

He had his back to her, his attention on a group of young bucks vociferously discussing the respective merits of the Osbaldistone and the Mailcoach neckties.

She reached out and tapped Mandeville peremptorily upon the shoulder with her fan.

As he swung round, plainly offended at this familiarity, she stood very straight, coolly meeting his look. "Have you not an apology to make me, my Lord Mandeville?" she demanded.

He stiffened. His head, held already high to avoid having his eyes poked out by his collar-points, went even higher. "I beg your pardon?"

"That's the dandy, my good fellow. It could perhaps have been said with more enthusiasm, but I'm sure Miss Farrington will accept the deed for the will."

Elaine turned to see Lord Dare at her elbow. He was dressed in a long-tailed coat of fine blue cloth, which set off his strong shoulders to perfection. And his tight black knee-breeches revealed a pair of muscular legs.

Mandeville glared at him. His hands clenched, and he swelled with anger. "You are offensive, sir," he hissed.

"Not yet. But if you give me enough time, I believe I may be very offensive indeed." His words, though calmly spoken, contained that same veiled menace which he seemed to reserve especially for Mandeville.

"We have business to finish between us, my lord," Mandeville said wrathfully.

"Yes, and you may have no doubt that it will be finished," was Dare's maddeningly unmoved reply.

Elaine intervened. "Really, gentlemen, must you be at daggers-drawn again? It becomes tedious."

Dare bent the beam of his dark gaze upon her. His eyes began to twinkle. "Don't tell me you are bored with us, Miss Farrington," he exclaimed in mock dismay. "That puts me on my mettle, it does. It's a challenge, indeed. I shall *have* to contrive a way to enliven your evening."

Such a promise was far from being reassuring. She regarded him warily. "I beg you not to trouble yourself, my lord. I can brush along adequately well without your help."

"Do not fear, Miss Farrington," he said with a smile, wilfully misinterpreting her words. "I will not fail you."

Briefly, Elaine contemplated fleeing from Almack's forthwith. However, she must first lay her bait. Therefore, she steeled herself to smile, as though with real pleasure. "You are too kind, my lord."

"Are you going to put on a scene in Almack's as shocking as the one I beheld the other night?" Mandeville demanded in a pelter. "Is that how you intend to enliven her evening?"

"It is a suggestion I will consider, Mandeville."

"Then you *were* embracing." A third gentleman's voice startled Elaine, causing her to turn in astonishment to Lord Elcho. He was breathing rather rapidly, disarranging the folds of his snowy neckcloth with each breath. His jaw worked, and his prominent eyes blazed. "As Miss Farrington's cousin, I demand satisfaction!"

"Really, Simon," Elaine exclaimed in horror, "you go too far!"

"No! It is this damned rakeshame who goes too far. He cannot insult you and remain unpunished."

"Don't you think, however, that I am best qualified to determine whether or not I've been insulted?" she demanded with hauteur.

He bit his lip and stared down at her, nonplussed.

"Yes," Lord Dare agreed with disastrous alacrity. "He is being awfully encroaching, isn't he? Especially since the correct person to call me to account is not your cousin but your brother." His voice became as smooth as velvet. "As I don't believe Nicholas Farrington will call me out, I must conclude that you wish to pick a quarrel with me, Elcho."

Lord Dare's words caused Elcho to struggle visibly with himself. His hands clenched so tightly that his knuckles whitened. "I wish, merely," he said in a strangled voice, "to protect Miss Farrington from your attentions."

"I thought you wished to protect her from my insults. Now it's my attentions. Really, Elcho, you must make up your mind."

Elaine swung upon Lord Dare, her temper rising. "I would appreciate it, my Lord Dare," she exclaimed, twisting her embroidered ivory fan between her hands, "if you would hold your tongue. You are too provoking. I had hoped that tonight I could cry truce between us. Now let us not brangle any more. Lord Mandeville, I do, however, demand an apology for your behaviour the other night. It was entirely unwarranted and unacceptable.''

"I suggest you come to terms with her," Lord Dare recommended gently, constituting himself her knightly protector. "Else you will have to come to terms with me!"

Elaine felt a thrill of excitement, acknowledging to herself that the role suited him perfectly. However, she knew that she must pretend to take it in bad part and started to remonstrate with him. She was interrupted by Lord Mandeville. He tugged in agitation at a gold fob hanging from his waist, then flung up his hands and muttered ungraciously, "Oh, very well. I apologize."

"Very unprettily said," Lord Dare commented sweetly.

Elaine frowned him down. "Thank you, my lord." She stopped and moistened her lips. In as even a voice as she could muster, she continued, "Now I have some good news for one of you. I have your gold-topped ebony cane. Seaton found it. One of you must have left it behind after your scuffle."

Her eyes moved swiftly from one gentleman to the next, avidly observing their expressions. To her growing dismay, she found each of them completely impassive. She lifted her eyebrows, questioning. "Am I mistaken? Does the cane not belong to one of you?"

Her question was met with absolute silence.

She could have shaken her fists in frustration. How could they be so cool? She studied each closely in turn but found nothing in their wooden countenances. "Seaton brought it to me just last night, having found it in the wine cellar, of all places. I thought it must have rolled down there from the kitchen. However, if none of you claims it, then I assume it was left there by some strange intruder. I shall have to take it, therefore, to the Bow Street Runners." She paused and surveyed the effect of these words. There was none. She took a very deep breath. "Perhaps the cane will have some distinguishing marks which will identify its owner. The Bow Street Runners can trace him down. If it belongs to an intruder, then they can bring him to justice."

Again, absolute silence greeted her words. She was vexed almost to tears. Bowing her head, she desperately tried to think of something else to say. She looked up eagerly as Lord Dare cleared his throat.

"A very wise resolve, Miss Farrington. I believe every young lady of quality should number a couple of Bow Street Runners amongst her acquaintance."

She didn't know whether to be disappointed or diverted. For the purpose of her ploy, she thought it would be wiser to appear to be diverted. "Oh, la, my Lord Dare. Acquaintance with you has made me audacious."

His lips twisted a smile, a look of admiration stealing into his face. Then his black eyebrows lifted at a sudden idea, and his eyes gleamed with amused speculation. "Has it, indeed? If that is so, then I'm sure we can put your audacity to useful purpose in helping alleviate the tedium of this evening at Almack's."

With that, he bowed and made straight for a group of the patronesses gathered together in an alcove.

Elaine watched his departure in chagrin. How could he be so very nonchalant?

Elcho leaned forward and whispered urgently in her ear, "I suggest you leave this place at once, else the Devil's Dare will embroil you in some misadventure. He's dangerous, you must know."

She felt inordinately irritated at these words. She did not know if Dare was dangerous. Indeed, the dangerous suspect could be either Mandeville or even Elcho himself. She was disappointed in the extreme that her ploy had succeeded so ill. There had been no blanched countenance, no starting eye, no twitching lip to reveal the cane's owner. So she still remained in doubt, subject to all manner of suspicions and conjecture.

She forced herself to look rather scornfully at Lord Elcho before saying, "I am not as cow-hearted as you think me. There's very little that the Devil's Dare can do in the middle of Almack's, you know."

"I would beg to differ."

She turned her shoulder on him and, just to be safe, sought for Nicholas amidst the crowd of merry-makers. Should Lord Dare succumb to his besetting sin and try to set Almack's on its ear, she must make a hasty exit, and she would need her brother close at hand.

Elaine surveyed the happy throng all engaged in dancing, gossiping, drinking, or just plain ogling! She wished she were as carefree as they! But she had her task. It was her duty to discover the identity of the midnight intruder.

To her pleased surprise, she found Nicholas dancing with Miss Iona Poole. The girl looked very fetching this evening in orange-blossom sarcenet. Her soft brown eyes were regarding Nicholas in evident adoration. His own gaze was equally bemused.

Elaine was momentarily diverted by this sight. Her brother had finally signed up for a life's lease, she thought. Nicholas, leg-shackled! It was too exquisite for words. Impulsively, she turned to Lord Mandeville, who was still standing glowering at her side. "Oh, Mandeville, I must thank you for the service you have done my brother."

Mandeville, who was certainly not in the habit of doing anyone a service, drew his thin eyebrows together in silent inquiry.

"Yes," Elaine said, nodding and indicating the dancing pair with her fan. "You brought Miss Poole to my brother's notice. I have no doubt that they will make a match of it. Have you?"

There had been no malicious intent behind these words. Yet Lord Mandeville looked as though she had struck him in the face with her ivory fan. He lifted his quizzing glass in order to survey Nicholas and Miss Poole as they progressed through their dances. The truth of Elaine's words must have been apparent, for he snarled, "That damned young jackanapes! He thinks he has ousted me from Miss Poole's affections. What effrontery. He'll soon discover his mistake if he tries to interfere between me and mine."

"Yours? I think it is you who are guilty of effrontery, my lord. You are not engaged or related to Miss Poole. Neither she nor my brother needs care one jot for you and your threats."

"We shall see, Miss Farrington. We shall see!" He did not even bother to bow but marched away.

Well! thought Elaine to herself. He certainly was puffed up with his own consequence. Nicholas was worth a thousand of him, and she was glad that Miss Poole had recognized this fact.

But now her own concerns resurfaced. She nodded distantly to Lord Elcho, then withdrew in the bluest megrims to a gilded cabriolet chair along the wall. She flicked her fan open and shut and stared blindly before her.

She had failed miserably. Not one of her suspects had risen to the fly she had cast. She had been so certain that the cane would prove irresistible. But now matters were becoming desperate. She must think of something! Dejectedly she propped her chin on her hands, closed her eyes, and tried to determine what she should do next. Her eyes flew wide open as she heard someone clucking his tongue.

"Tsk-tsk. It is worse even than I thought," Lord Dare said, a quiver of laughter in his voice as he shook his head.

He was speaking not to Elaine but to the Princess de Lieven. Tall and dark with mischievously dancing eyes, the patroness looked most impressive this evening in a dress of purple grosgrain and magnificent diamond necklace with a matching tiara. She was regarding Elaine now in mock-dismay. "But yes, far worse. I'm afraid Almack's has become to her dull stuff, indeed."

Elaine sat bolt upright at this.

"But what does Almack's offer, I ask you? Dancing, merely." Lord Dare dismissed it grandly with a wave of his white hand.

"Very pretty dancing, you must allow," the Princess de Lieven objected with an answering sweep of her bejewelled arm. "The music is very stirring, especially when the band strikes up a waltz. And it is always exciting to be held in a man's arms for a waltz!"

Elaine could only stare at her in fascinated horror.

"Well, why do you need music for that, I ask you? If the whole point of the waltz is to be held in a man's arms, then music would seem to be rather superfluous."

The Princess de Lieven tilted her head, then nodded at the truth of Dare's words. "But without music the waltz would be just a shocking display of animal attraction, wouldn't you say?"

"Exactly so!" Lord Dare exclaimed triumphantly.

The Princess de Lieven laughed and slapped his arm playfully. "You are wholly lacking in proper feeling, my lord."

"Proper feeling, yes. I am *never* proper."

Her eyes widened, and she regarded Lord Dare with something akin to awe. "You wouldn't do such a thing. You couldn't!"

His eyes seemed to kindle with barely suppressed excitement.

The Princess de Lieven drew herself up with all her dignity, which was considerable. "You wouldn't dare! Not here."

Elaine wished to heaven that she could sink into the ground. She waited in suspense for the inevitable blow.

"I wouldn't *what*?"

The Princess de Lieven looked him up and down, obviously striving with herself. She lost the struggle and burst again into a peal of laughter. "But my Lord Dare! You couldn't find a partner. No young lady would wish so to expose herself."

"You don't know Miss Farrington as well as *I* know her," he responded instantly, a thrilling note in his voice. "I've never before encountered a woman of such spirit." His dark eyes then turned compellingly to Elaine's. She felt as though a cord of communion between them had suddenly been pulled taut. She leaned toward him as he bent toward her.

"Don't fail me," he whispered.

His look was irresistible. Her surroundings receded as Elaine focused entirely on Dare. She stood up and took his hand, moving as if she were in a dream. Indeed, she felt like a sleep-walker, for she had no will of her own. She was entirely in his power.

She felt his arm slowly encircle her waist, his touch causing her to tremble with uncontrollable excitement. Then he whisked her out onto the dance floor, twirling her about so fast and so inexorably that she felt quite dizzy.

They moved in perfect unison. Indeed, Elaine felt that they were one. She was completely enthralled by her partner, by the sensations he stirred within her.

Nothing existed save Lord Dare. She could see only his dark eyes burning into hers. And their expression set her heart to beating rapidly. Her breath became shallow, and she knew that if his strong arms weren't supporting her, she would be in danger of swooning away like a girl in a novel.

And although Dare accorded hardly at all with her idea of a perfect romantic hero, with all sorts of preposterous virtues, she knew that she was deeply in love with him! This realization effectually brought her to her senses, and she jerked herself out of Lord Dare's arms.

They both stood stock-still. His eyes were fixed on her face. He had seemed, during the dance, to have undergone an enlightenment so blinding as almost to deprive him of his senses. And she could only stare back, herself wholly unable to move.

Their trance was ruthlessly shattered by what seemed a torrent of whispers sweeping over the Assembly Rooms. Elaine found herself the cynosure of all eyes. She must have been mad. She staggered back a few paces, only to be embraced by the chuckling Princess de Lieven.

"My dear Miss Farrington," she cooed. "Lord Dare was right about you. Exquisite. Exquisite. You put us all to shame."

Elaine was too dazed to make any sense of the words. She was immediately surrounded by two other of the patronesses, Lady Sefton and Lady Jersey. These two looked outraged, and they attacked the Princess de Lieven like angry lionesses.

"What do you mean, she puts us all to shame?" Lady Jersey demanded. She was a thin, ethereal woman with a restless manner, and she waved her hands accusingly at the Princess. "She puts herself to shame!"

"Au contraire," replied the Princess smoothly. She gave Elaine's nerveless hand a reassuring squeeze. "She was helping Lord Dare win a challenge I made him. She succeeded admirably, do you not think?"

Lady Sefton regarded Elaine out of her wide blue eyes. She was quite the kindest of the patronesses, and she had no desire to see Miss Farrington disgraced. She patted Elaine's cheek, then shook her finger at Lord Dare. "I should have known this was all your doing," she reproached him.

"But it was all *my* doing," the Princess de Lieven promptly interposed. "I made him a challenge that he couldn't refuse! Besides, you know very well that a young lady can waltz at Almack's only with our permission. Well—" her dark eyes flashed "—I gave her permission to waltz."

"Between sets? While no music was playing?" cried Lady Jersey.

Elaine had *thought* she heard no music. But she had been so entranced by Lord Dare that she probably could not have heard music even if it had been played.

The Princess de Lieven gave a careless shrug. "If she has my permission, then she can waltz—with or without music. Are we not law here?"

Both Lady Jersey and Lady Sefton seemed struck by this. "Why, yes, we *are* law!" the former agreed suddenly with decision. She gave Elaine a sunny smile. "A nice, docile girl you are." She flicked Elaine's chin with a teasing finger. "We are most pleased with your behaviour."

At this pronouncement, another gale of whispering swept the room, then a loud cheering and clapping was set up. No doubt, the ton was congratulating Lord Dare on his triumph. It was not every day that they were treated to such high entertainment as witnessing the Devil's Dare win a challenge.

Nicholas hurried to embrace his sister. "Well done, Elaine!" he shouted. "I knew you was game as a pebble."

Her look spoke volumes. Before Nicholas could rush forward to clap Lord Dare on the back, Elaine gripped his hand. "Please take me home," she begged in a stifled voice.

His mouth dropped. "What? Before you've been duly congratulated by all? Really, Elaine, you mustn't deprive yourself."

"Please," she insisted, tears pricking at her eyes.

Nicholas gulped with acute discomfort at sight of her tears. "To be sure, Elaine. Of course. Instantly. Only please don't turn into a watering-pot!"

She nodded, fighting back her tears. Curtseying quickly to the patronesses, she hurried out of the Assembly Rooms, followed by Nicholas, who enthusiastically accepted the congratulations of various persons they passed.

Elaine did not trust herself even to look at Lord Dare. She was afraid of revealing too irrevocably her feelings for him.

The carriage ride back to Farrington Place was accomplished in complete silence. Finding his sister such poor company, Nicholas led her into the drawing-room, then promptly took his leave of her.

Elaine barely noticed his departure. She sank onto a red-and-gold brocaded settee, overcome by her emotions. She *did* love Lord Dare! She had been falling in love with him ever since she met him. Now she knew her feelings were deep and abiding.

She couldn't say why she loved him. Except that he was handsome beyond dreams, fascinating beyond words, and exciting beyond resistance! But, more than that, she felt strangely drawn to him, as though they were indeed kindred souls.

Nevertheless, she was not blind to his faults! He was a heedless, reckless care-for-nobody. His one ambition in life, as he had told her, perhaps in all seriousness, was to emulate his almost satanic father! And yet, she had sensed hurt behind this vaunt of his. He must have been deeply shamed by his father.

Perhaps it was bravado that made him behave so carelessly. But whatever the cause, he had upset her existence since the day she had met him. He had embroiled both Nicholas and her in his outrageous escapades. And tonight's waltzing episode seemed to cap this heedless career. He hadn't cared that he had exposed her to comment and censure. He had cared only about winning his dare.

Her heart sank at the thought. If he could so easily endanger her, then could he not as easily endanger all of England? Could he not steal the Regalia—to win one of his precious dares?

She stood up and began to pace restlessly about the drawing-room. She refused to believe it! She could not believe Lord Dare capable of so dastardly a deed. Suddenly she was brought up short by a loud clattering noise and Seaton's voice raised in vociferous surprise in the next room.

Elaine went quickly into the blue salon to investigate. The sight which met her stopped her in her tracks. It was young Jeremiah, Nicholas's tiger. Seaton had him tightly by the ear, and the small boy was dancing in anguish. But he seemed to be dancing on a veritable pile of canes!

"What is this all about?" she demanded.

Seaton straightened up immediately, regaining his wonted dignity. He made Jeremiah also stand up straight before his mistress. "This young lad," he said in an emotionless voice, "was coming down the stairs. With these." He indicated with a stately inclination of his head the pile of canes on the floor. "Of course, I stopped him to ask him what he thought he was about. I regret the noise disturbed you, Miss Farrington."

Elaine's eyes flew to the mantlepiece. She breathed a sigh of relief. The gold-topped ebony cane was still there!

She turned back to the boy. He was beet-red, and he was panting slightly, but he met his mistress's eye bravely enough. "I was doing nothink wrong, Miss, the gen'leman said so."

Her heart in her throat, she gasped, "What gentleman?"

"I dunno. It was his groom what spoke to me."

"Spoke to you?" Elaine repeated.

"He promised me a gold guinea from his master if I brought him every cane in the house. He said there was no harm in it. He said his master was playing a hoax. For a dare."

CHAPTER TEN

ELAINE BROODED IN SILENCE almost the entire next morning, refusing the bed tray Mary so solicitously brought her. She even refused to have the curtains of her room opened. The dreary darkness of the shadows aptly suited her humour.

If the discovery of the Scottish Regalia hadn't been enough to overset her nerves, the discovery that she loved the Devil's Dare certainly had. And there was the suspicion, seemingly borne out by last night's escapade with the canes, that the Devil's Dare was responsible for the appearance of the Scottish Regalia in her wine cellar tunnel.

Yet by late afternoon she managed to recover sufficiently to quit her bedchamber. Weak and listless herself, she discovered that Nicholas, by contrast, was in high alt. He had spent his day in a whirlwind of activity, preparing for the curricle race to Brighton. He had had his racing curricle brought out, chosen his fastest team of horses, and assigned his tiger the task of blowing the yard of tin at all toll-gates.

The evening before, Elaine had questioned Jeremiah closely, but she had become convinced that he would not recognize the groom even if he were lucky enough to see him again. So she had sent him off to bed with a scold and a command never again to accept commissions from strangers. Then she had directed Seaton to return all the canes to Nicholas's room, commenting grimly that Nicholas might need them should he break his leg in his curricle race to Brighton.

When Lord Dare called later in the evening to invite Nicholas to White's, Elaine immediately requested an audience with him. After all, she owed him a bear-garden jaw for his treatment of Nicholas. She didn't know whether to be gratified or annoyed by the alacrity with which he accepted her invitation. He entered the salon, looking quite eager, his eyes alight.

He was also looking extremely handsome, dressed in a dark coat, intricately tied cravat, and pale pantaloons. His black locks, brushed à la Brutus, shone, as did a diamond glittering in his snowy cravat.

His expression quickly changed as he scanned her face. "Why, my dear Miss Farrington, you look as sick as a cushion. What's amiss?"

Despite the tenderness with which it was spoken, this far from gratifying description brought a sharp retort to her lips. But she bit it back. She must not let her tongue run wild, else she would blurt out her knowledge of the Scottish Regalia, and her suspicion of his complicity in its theft. She must not broach the matter at all while she was still uncertain of his guilt. Indeed, she thought to herself with a tiny shake of the head, the only thing she knew him to be positively guilty of was of turning her into a sighing miss, lovesick and forlorn.

She twisted a fine cambric handkerchief in her hand and swallowed with difficulty. "Lord Dare," she managed after a long pause, "of course I'm a bit out of sorts."

He leaned forward, a sharp, questioning look in his eyes. "But why 'of course'?"

Her handkerchief fluttering, she motioned him to sit down. He stood a moment, looking down at her, then seemed to force himself to relax. He sat down beside her on the satinwood scroll-backed sofa, turning a little to the side, and stretching his arm along the sofa's back so that he could study her profile.

She burst out, "I am sick with apprehension, my Lord Dare."

He looked surprised, as though this was not at all what he had expected. "About what, may I be so bold as to ask?"

She gave him a sidelong glance, taking note of the tightness of his beautifully moulded lips. Casting frantically about, she gasped, "About the curricle race!"

His face twitched with disappointment, then he shook his head and laughed ruefully to himself. "Your brother. I should have known." After a moment he ventured to give her shoulder a quick, sympathetic squeeze.

She fought a strong impulse to relax against him. "Don't be so callous, my lord. I think your influence over Nicholas reprehensible! I'm agonized by the possibility that Nicholas may come to some dreadful harm."

"But to what harm could he come, my dear Miss Farrington? I think you are flying into a grand fuss for nothing."

His casual unconcern galled her. "Oh, do you so, indeed?" she fired up. "Well, I think you are a heartless beast!" She spoke with a deal more violence than was her wont, as she suddenly released her pent-up emotions.

He was greatly taken aback. He blinked and sat a little away from her. "Don't eat me, my dear. I was only trying to reassure you."

She vouchsafed only a sniff.

"But you can't expect me to cry off from the challenge, now, can you?"

She flung wide her arms. "Well, you cried off from Nicholas's kissing challenge," she reminded him reasonably.

Much discomfited, he extricated his *grisaille* snuff box from his pocket. Opening it with a mechanical flick of his thumb, he inhaled then dusted his coat carefully before answering in a controlled voice, "Very true, Miss Farrington." He shot her a keen look. "And you now believe that you can induce me to do the same with this curricle race?"

"Yes."

A very odd expression swept over his handsome face, one half of resignation, half of hope. "Perhaps you can, after all."

She gasped with relief. She smiled at him, brimming with gratitude. "You are too good, Lord Dare. I knew you couldn't be so very bad as your reputation claims."

His eyes flickered as though he had suffered a blow. "You wrong me, Miss Farrington." His mouth twisted. "And I was beginning to think you knew me so well. Stupid of me. I am *very* bad. Indeed—" his face hardened from an unspoken disappointment "—so very bad that I must first hear what inducements you are going to tempt me with before I agree to cry off."

"I-inducements?" she stammered.

"Yes."

"What can you be thinking of?"

He snorted a laugh at that. "Really, Miss Farrington. You're not just out of the schoolroom, you know. Surely you don't need me to be explicit."

She all but tore the handkerchief in her hand to shreds. Oh, the man *was* a devil!

Her silence goaded him to prompt, "Would you be willing to oblige me, if I were willing to oblige you?"

She lifted her gaze to the ceiling, as though to seek guidance from some higher source. He was offering her a *carte blanche*, of course. He was too improper to offer anything else. He was just intent on winning the challenge between them, after all! She was so bitterly disappointed in having Lord Dare confirm her worst suspicions that she hardly knew what she was saying when she said through stiffened lips, "Yes."

Astonishment held him very still for a moment. Then he seemed to shake from head to toe with barely suppressed excitement. His arms shot out, as though closely to embrace her. But he caught himself, and he slowly reached out his hand to take her by the chin and to turn her face toward his.

"Then, my dear," he said in a strangled voice, "your Nicholas will be safe."

She tried to push away his hand, but it held firm. In a miserable voice, she said, "You don't know how happy you make me."

He stood up then bowed. As he straightened, she saw that his expression was very serious, his eyes burning. "And you don't know how happy you make me." With that, he swung around on his heels and left her.

Elaine knew that her next course of action should be to contact the Bow Street Runners and to turn Lord Dare over to the authorities. He must be brought to justice. Undeniably he was the source of every sinister event connected with the Regalia. And Elaine now had proof positive that he did not shrink from the grossest offence.

But to call the Bow Street Runners and to have them find the Regalia in her house! The scandal would be enormous. She and Nicholas would never again be able to hold up their heads in society. And Aunt Augusta would surely be undone.

Yet she had to admit to herself that it was not for her own sake she hesitated. She felt deep concern for Lord Dare. As a traitor—even a madcap one—he would be very severely punished.

Thus she wavered. For a moment she was tempted to behave as though she'd never found the Regalia. But she dismissed this craven impulse. She had found them. And she knew that their loss to Scotland and the political implications were too important to be ignored.

But for all her agonizing she found no solution either during the day or the long, weary night.

The next morning, in the breakfast parlour, she waved away all solid nutriments, nursing instead her cup of hot chocolate. She told the impassive Seaton that she was not hungry now and doubted that she would ever be hungry again. The necessity of reaching a decision concerning Lord Dare still plagued her.

Silently, Seaton proffered her another tray, this one carrying a wafered note.

Elaine started to take it, then stopped. "Did the runner wait for a reply?" she asked suspiciously.

"No, Miss, he did not." Seaton continued to hold the salver before her.

"Thank you, Seaton." Waiting until he had left the room and closed the panelled door behind him, Elaine gingerly broke the wafer.

"Miss Farrington," the note read. "You have something of mine. And I have something of yours. If you restore to me my gold-topped ebony cane this evening when I call on you, then I will restore to you your brother, Nicholas."

Her first impulse was to call not only for the Bow Street Runners but also for every constable in the city of London. But she must think of Nicholas's safety.

Her second impulse, instantly to confront Lord Dare, must wait until evening. It must be Lord Dare who had sent that note. It was he Nicholas had left with last night—to go to White's, indeed!

Oh, yes, she thought bitterly, he had told her Nicholas would be safe. He had failed to explain, however, his true intent: to keep Nicholas in his own safekeeping until he had retrieved his wretched cane!

Poor Nicholas! Was he really safe? Could Dare be trusted to keep his word? Or— As the horrible possibility dawned on Elaine, she felt hysterical tears gathering behind her eyes. But she must maintain her calm and wait for the promised arrival of the Devil's Dare.

The day wore on and Elaine vacillated between hope and despair. Her nerves were frayed almost to breaking point when the disapproving Seaton at length announced the Devil's Dare. Elaine stood up from the sofa, as stiff as an effigy. "You here, my Lord Dare? Should you not be readying yourself for your curricle race to Brighton? You leave at dawn, I collect."

He frowned down at her. He was unusually pale, and his face was taut. "But I told you that Nicholas would be safe."

Then it was true! He *had* spirited away poor Nicholas!

"What do you want?" she demanded, gripping her hands together agitatedly. How could she satisfy Lord Dare's demands? Her brother's life or England's peace? The decison was impossible.

He moved toward her suddenly, as though released from a spring. "But I *told* you what I want." He moistened his obviously dry lips and watched her, half-fearfully. "Do you think you can satisfy me?"

She flung a tormented look at him, scanning his face for some token of mercy. To her growing horror, she saw that he was as tense as a panther poised for attack. His hands were tightly clenched, and a muscle at his square jaw jumped. His tension increased Elaine's despair. Oh, she could not let him harm Nicholas. Her instincts were to sacrifice anything in order to save her beloved brother. "Yes," she whispered, her shoulders drooping. She felt strangely faint, and she would have collapsed without further ado had Lord Dare not caught her immediately in a crushing embrace.

His dark face swam before her eyes, and she tried to push him away. But his mouth swooped down hard on hers, kissing her ruthlessly.

A wave of excitement crashed through Elaine as his arms tightened around her, almost squeezing the breath out of her. She half-yielded, carried away on the tide of his passion.

He lifted his head after a long moment, a gasp like a sob breaking from him. His eyes seemed to burn through her. "My God," he murmured shakily, his voice husky. Elaine could feel his heart racing beneath her hands. He seemed to be struggling with himself. "I'm sorry," he began, then he stopped. Surrendering again, he brushed his lips hot against hers. She quivered uncontrollably as he rained kisses upon her neck, cheek, and brow.

He stopped himself again, taking a deep breath, trying to control the emotions that threatened to overpower him. He stared into her eyes. "I want even more than this from you, Elaine."

Her brain whirled, and she clung to him for support. "More?" she whispered. What more could he possibly want in exchange for Nicholas's safety than her virtue and his incriminating gold-topped ebony cane?

"I want you to be mine. Entirely my own."

Elaine tore herself away from his demanding hands and burning lips. She turned around frantically. Her hand shot out and closed quickly over the gold-topped ebony cane still on the mantlepiece. She swung the cane over her head and brought it crashing down upon his own. The impact made a sickening thud, and Lord Dare's eyes closed as he fell against her and slid down her rigid body to the floor. He lay there, crumpled, unconscious.

Elaine stared down at him in shock. Her hands were shaking miserably. Gracious heavens, what had she done? She had certainly let him have his cane but in a quite unexpected manner!

She knelt and found that his head, thankfully, was not bleeding. But she had dealt him a very heavy blow. Now what must she do?

At this opportune moment, Seaton ushered another gentleman into the room.

"Mandeville!" Elaine gasped. She wished she were as unconscious as Lord Dare. "What, by all that's wonderful, are you doing here?"

Lord Mandeville stood absolutely still, arrested by the sight of the unconscious Lord Dare. After a moment he found his voice. "I—I hoped to find Nicholas. I w-wanted to dissuade him from taking part in the curricle race against—" and he stopped, pointing significantly at Lord Dare.

Her hand went to her forehead. "I beg your pardon?" she whispered, feeling a sudden attack of nausea.

Mandeville closed the drawing-room door tightly and leaned against it. Breathing raggedly, he said,

"Yes. But I see that you have taken more forceful measures to prevent the race."

"I beg your pardon?" she repeated, trying to shake off her confusion.

His Adam's apple bobbed. "Lord Dare can hardly race against Nicholas while he is thus unconscious, now, can he?"

"Oh, Mandeville," she almost sobbed. "You must think me a veritable shrew. But, I had to do something."

Mandeville's face was as pale as whey, yet he nodded approvingly. "I've always deplored Dare's inordinate influence over Nicholas and felt that something should be done to curtail it." He gave a ghost of a smile. "But I must admit that I hadn't expected you, Miss Farrington, to take such drastic measures."

"Well, I have taken them," she replied. "It was over before I really knew what I was about. This cane was in my hand. And then it was on Lord Dare's head."

At sight of the gold-topped ebony cane, Mandeville looked as though Elaine had struck *him* on the head with it. His eyes narrowed, and his mouth tightened to a line. But he quickly managed to retrieve his air of equanimity. "A most appropriate place for it, my dear," he assured her. "Please keep it close at hand in case you need it again."

"Again?"

"Why, yes. He may regain consciousness before you've had time to dispose of him."

"Dispose of him!" Elaine shrieked. "What can you mean?"

Mandeville sighed. "Nothing quite so murderous as you so obviously imagine."

She sighed. She really must control herself, else, Mandeville would think she was quite mad. "Well, what *do* you mean?" she asked in a more temperate manner.

"Why, that we must make certain of him until past dawn tomorrow. Nicholas cannot race against an absent opponent."

Elaine felt light-headed with relief. Yes! They could secure him. And then they could threaten to turn him over to the Bow Street Runners unless he told them where Nicholas was!

She looked at Mandeville, her eyes bright. "What shall we do?"

Something very like triumph flashed in his face. "Why, nothing could be easier. We stow him away in a quiet place for the necessary few hours."

"But where?"

He shrugged, at a loss.

"In the wine cellar?" Elaine supplied, finding it an ironically fitting choice.

He nodded slowly, his pale eyes gleaming. "Very good. A most appropriate place."

Elaine opened the door, peering about to see if the hall was deserted. Fortunately, the servants all appeared to be snug in their beds for the night.

She turned to find that Lord Mandeville had pulled the cravat from around his neck. He rolled Lord Dare on his side and also untied Dare's cravat. Her heart leaped to her throat, as Dare stirred and murmured. But Mandeville quickly snatched up the ebony cane and brought the hilt down hard on Dare's neck. The prisoner relapsed into unconsciousness with a moan. Mandeville threw the cane from him. Elaine stared at him, horrified and yet too afraid to protest. Apparently oblivious to her presence, he wrapped the cravats about Dare's wrists and ankles. The Devil's Dare was now trussed up right and tight.

With great difficulty, Mandeville managed to hoist Lord Dare over his shoulder, then he motioned with his arm for Elaine to precede him. She took up a branch of candles, then hurried forward, her hand at her throat. She felt certain that at any moment one of the servants would surprise them, and oh, then wouldn't the fat be in the fire!

They descended the stairs to the basements, Mandeville gasping from the exertion. He deposited Lord Dare roughly on the floor and then propped him up against the great porter barrel.

"Let him rest there for a moment. I must return to the drawing-room to be certain that we have left all in order." Elaine followed him almost out of the room, but he stopped her with his hand. "You remain here to keep watch over Lord Dare. I shall return immediately."

Elaine watched his retreating form. Then she slowly descended the stairs again. Dear me, she thought to herself, what a tangle! And how will we unravel it?

A stifled moan brought her round to find the Devil's Dare glaring at her. His eyes were ablaze, and his mouth formed the grimmest line.

She bent to help him sit up more comfortably. She had to stifle a sudden nervous giggle because he looked so strangely unkempt, his normally immaculate hair all tousled. He was clearly in a rage.

"I do hope you aren't feeling too ill," she said now solicitously.

"Damn you, I feel abominable," he snapped. He looked as if he would like to shake her, and he struggled furiously with his bindings.

"You will not be able to release yourself," she said tartly. "So you might as well stop your struggling."

He ground his teeth. "I suppose it would be ridiculous to inquire why you have done this." He mustered a surprising amount of dignity, considering his position. And though his head must have been hurting him, he held it up proudly.

Elaine shook her head at him in reproach.

A bitter smile even began to twist his lips. "Despite all my hopes, you truly *do* think badly of me, don't you?" His voice was hard. "I'll have you know, Elaine, that I was *not* offering you a slip on the shoulder, as you so obviously thought. I was making you a perfectly honourable proposal."

"Honourable!"

His eyebrows lifted and his lips curled as he nodded in grim satisfaction to himself. "Why, yes." He took a deep breath and in a voice devoid of all emotion, he said, "And I'm still willing to make it. It can be a wedding across the anvil for all I care. Just so long as there *is* a wedding."

Elaine stared down at him in the deepest dudgeon. How dared he be so flippant? He was a callous monster! And, oh, *how* could she be so much in love with this monster?

However, her attention was distracted by the returning Mandeville. He re-entered the cellar, carrying the gold-topped ebony cane.

"Well, my dear," he said, standing before Elaine, "we have succeeded."

"Ah! So you *are* in on it together," Lord Dare suddenly grated.

Mandeville sneered at him, showing his small white teeth. "As you will see," he murmured. "Your persistent curiosity about my doings will at last be gratified." He turned back to Elaine. "And now there's nothing for it except for you, my dear Miss Farrington, to show me where is the hiding-place."

His words baffled her completely. She blinked at him. "The hiding-place?" she repeated in bewilderment.

"Don't play the green girl, Miss Farrington! Where are the Scottish Regalia?"

Her eyes widened. "What?"

His thin brows snapped together. "Cut line, girl. You try my patience too far. Where are the Regalia!"

She desperately tried to regain her senses. "If you know of the Regalia, then surely you also know their whereabouts."

"Of course I don't know their whereabouts. Do you think I'd have been haunting this place every night searching for them if I did?"

"Then it was your cane I found!"

He lifted the hand which held the cane. "Yes. This cane belongs to me. So I know its secret." He pulled at the shaft of the cane and unsheathed a sword-stick!

It flashed in the light of the candles so that Elaine flinched.

Mandeville held it aloft, smiling at it. "I brought it along in case I needed protection during my nightly ferretings. After the brush I had with Nicholas one evening, I thought it advisable."

"You were the intruder?"

He lifted his long nose disdainfully. "Surely you've grasped that by now."

So Mandeville was the intruder! He had been the cause of the knocking noises. He had whispered in her ear. He had sent her the threatening note.

"But if you know about the Regalia, then why don't you know their whereabouts?" she demanded.

"Because your cousin, Lord Elcho, wouldn't tell me, that's why. I suppose he doubted my loyalty. And rightly so, damn his eyes."

Elaine reeled. "Simon!"

He curled his lips in a mirthless smile and waved the sword-stick airily. "Didn't you guess, Miss Farrington? Who else of your acquaintance feels as deeply about Scotland as does your cousin?"

Elaine was wholly incapable of replying.

"Yes. Since we are such cronies, he approached me with his plan soon after Prinny toured Scotland. He knew that the Prince had expressed an interest in the Regalia, and that's when he devised his plan to steal them. If the Regalia were to disappear, then the Scots would blame the Regent. Elcho believed, quite mistakenly as it happens, that I, too, wished to win Scotland's independence. My real intention, however, was to win myself a fantastic fortune."

Elaine clasped her hands tightly together, listening to his disclosures in growing amazement.

"And so we spirited the Regalia out of the gaol, with the help of one of the guards, whom we bribed."

"You and Simon?"

"Yes. But after we'd stolen the Regalia, Elcho tucked them away in a secret hiding-place he knew of at Farrington Place—only hinting to me that it was somewhere in the basements of the house."

Elaine's eyes flew involuntarily to the large porter barrel. Mandeville's hand shot out to grasp her roughly by the arm, twisting her toward the barrel. "Is it here?" he hissed. He pointed the sword-stick threateningly.

"I don't believe Simon would have anything to do with such a dastardly plot!" She pulled away from him.

"You'd be wrong," he said grimly. He pressed the point of the sword-stick threateningly close to her throat. "Wrong, too, if you further resist me."

Elaine winced at the sharp pain and stood immobile. Resolutely, she closed her mouth.

"You forget, my dear, that I have another weapon. Nicholas. Don't you want him safely returned to you?"

Her vision blurred so that she felt quite weak with dizziness. Nicholas! Of course, it was Mandeville who had abducted Nicholas, demanding the cane in exchange for his safety. Nicholas was in danger every moment he was in this madman's power. Seeming of its own volition, her hand rose and pointed numbly at the nail in the barrel's base. "There's a tunnel beneath this barrel,'' she said, her breathing as irregular as if she'd been running.

Mandeville's eyes flashed, and he nodded. "Very wise, my dear."

She pulled loose from his grasp and started to shrink toward the door.

"Far too previous, Miss Farrington. I must yet secure you as tightly as I've done the Devil's Dare. You will both be harmless hidden away in this tunnel here. And I shall have time to flee the country with my prize!"

Instinctively, she continued backing toward the door.

"Don't try to resist him!" Lord Dare's voice ripped across the room to her. "He's ruthless."

Lord Dare's words had the opposite effect to the one intended. She did not stop; she ran up the stairs into the kitchen. She heard Mandeville clatter up the stairs after her. Reaching the large oak table, she caught hold of a plate of broiled tongue resting upon it, and threw it down the stairs. It caught him on the shoulder, then dropped to the ground, and he spun round, almost losing his balance. Elaine ran to the door which led to the street. She had her hand on the latch when Mandeville grasped her by the shoulder and flung her backward. She rolled down the stairs, landing in a heap, the breath knocked hard out of her.

From his pocket Mandeville whipped a cord of rope which he had obviously taken from the drawing-room curtains. Still stunned by her fall, Elaine was tied at the wrists before she could recover.

Mandeville was breathing heavily, his eyes glittering. He pulled Elaine roughly to her feet, and she staggered forward. Deftly, he pressed the nail at the barrel's base so that the large wooden barrel slid aside.

Lord Dare rolled out of its way, then lay perfectly still. Elaine caught his eye. He seemed so calm and unafraid that she, too, was reassured. And there was also something in his look which caused her heart to give a great leap. At least she knew that Lord Dare wasn't a traitor! This realization filled her with a glow of happiness.

Mandeville disappeared into the tunnel to deposit the branch of candles there. Then he returned, and stepped menacingly toward her. "Descend quickly. I shall secure you first, then return for Dare."

Elaine stumbled awkwardly down the steep incline, Mandeville close behind her. With the flat of his hand, he shoved her foward.

They were almost at the centre of the tunnel when their progress was suddenly interrupted. Mandeville pushed her to her knees. "Listen. I hear something!" he exclaimed.

He rushed forward, and Elaine struggled to her feet and followed him.

"Elcho!" Mandeville snarled, enraged at the sight of Elcho standing protectively before the box containing the Regalia.

The two men faced each other. Elcho, pale, tense, and grimed with the dirt from the square garden entrance to the tunnel, smiled mirthlessly. His light hair stood on end, and his fists were clenched. "You thought me a complete air-dreamer, didn't you,

Mandeville. But I'm no cloth-head. I'm up to all your rigs, believe me. I long suspected your loyalty, but I knew positively of your duplicity when Elaine informed us she'd found your damned cane in the wine cellar."

"Simon!" Elaine gasped. "You did steal the Regalia, after all? I didn't want to believe it."

He hardly looked at her. "You've always known my sentiments," he pointed out with strange calm. His prominent eyes shone unnaturally in the light of the flickering candles. "You thought me worse than an air-dreamer; you thought me a mere bagpipe. Well, I saw my chance for my country, and I took it! I've known since childhood of the secret tunnel here. I discovered it before ever you and Nicholas came to live at Farrington Place, but I kept the knowledge to myself. I knew even then it might prove useful to me in my lifelong desire to gain Scotland's independence, to free Scotland from the unbearable yoke of English rule."

"But England is your country, too," she said, trying to reason with him.

"England!" He spat out the words. "It is a land for slaves. Save your breath, dear cousin. When Scott and the other officers open the Regalia chest, they will find it empty! And the day for rebellion will have at last arrived!"

His face was rapt. The hair on her scalp rising, Elaine realized that it was useless to remonstrate with him. She twisted her tied hands desperately so that the cord chafed at her wrists. The ramifications of Elcho's actions were terrible to contemplate.

Mandeville was circling Elcho warily, searching to see if he carried any weapons.

"You *are* worse than an air-dreamer," he hissed. "You are a fool. I used you to get the Regalia undetected out of Scotland. I planned all along to steal them, to win the treasure for myself. And now I have it. The Regalia are mine!"

"Damn you!" Elcho shouted. "I won't let you take them."

Elaine watched, paralyzed, as Elcho leaped upon Mandeville. The impact was so great that Mandeville was overset.

They landed on the ground apart from each other. "I *will* have the Regalia," Mandeville vowed. He scrambled about the ground, frantically trying to regain the sword-stick, which had been flung from his hand in the fall.

He found it and struggled to his feet. The flash of its blade in the dim light caused Elaine to run as fast as she could back to the wine cellar. She must get help!

Behind her she heard scuffling, grunting, and the thud of blows. Before very long, the sound of a terrible scream spun her instantly round. She saw Elcho clutch at his shoulder, his face contorted with pain. Blood was seeping through his fingers. Then he dropped in a swoon.

She must have gasped involuntarily, for Mandeville, readying himself to deliver the fatal blow, stopped and turned round. At the vicious look on his face, she screamed and ran hard again.

She staggered up the incline, her bound hands making it almost impossible to keep her balance. But she gained the wine cellar once more. However, Mandeville was close on her heels.

She ran toward the door, risking a glance over her shoulder. Mandeville had emerged from the tunnel. But it was another figure that caused Elaine to stand stock-still, frozen in amazement.

As Mandeville started toward her, Lord Dare, now loosed from his bonds, tapped him on the shoulder. Mandeville jumped around and, astounded, threw up his hands, so that the bloodied sword-stick dropped with a clatter to the floor.

Lightning quick, Lord Dare bent and snatched it up. "My, how careless of you."

Mandeville snarled and leaped upon the Devil's Dare, throwing his weight against him so that they both toppled over. As Elaine watched, sick with fear, Mandeville tightened his hand over the gold-topped hilt, trying to wrest it from Dare. The two rolled on the floor, struggling in deadly earnest. Suddenly the Devil's Dare kicked Mandeville from him and flung the sword-stick across the floor. Then he quickly scrambled to his feet. Before Mandeville could also rise, Dare seized him by the collar, holding him before him. His left fist contacted Mandeville's chin so that the force of the blow lifted Mandeville off the ground. He groaned, fell backward, and lay still.

Darlington and Nicholas, calling loudly, burst from the kitchen down into the cellar. Nicholas started toward Elaine, his hands waving, he tripped over Mandeville's body. His chin hit the ground in a resounding blow. He put his arms out and blinked. Beholding on the ground before him a large red tongue, he cried, "Dear God, I do believe I've bitten my tongue off!"

Darlington, who had been busy untying Elaine's wrists, gave a loud laugh. He assisted Nicholas to his feet and carefully dusted off his coat. "Nary a bit, my friend. You've only winded yourself." Then he surveyed Mandeville. "But I do believe that you have sent Mandeville into oblivion."

Nicholas gasped in dismay, and they both bent to revive Mandeville.

Elaine rushed forward, not to assist in reviving Mandeville, but to greet her brother with heartfelt relief.

Her progress was arrested by Lord Dare, who gripped her arm and pulled her to him so violently that her breath was knocked out of her. He folded her tightly in his arms. Breathing shakily, he buried his face in her neck and murmured, "Thank God you're safe!"

EPILOGUE

WHEN SHE WAS RELEASED and allowed to come up for air, Elaine gave Lord Dare a very flushed smile. "Yes, I'm safe. And so, I see, is Nicholas." Because she felt strangely shy of Lord Dare, she pulled herself away and went over to the busy Darlington and Nicholas.

"But how did you escape from Mandeville?" she demanded eagerly.

Nicholas straightened himself quickly, and with a great show of brotherly affection he buffeted her on the shoulder. "Don't fly into the high fidgets, Elaine," he recommended in a loud voice. "I didn't exactly escape from Mandeville. I was released."

"By whom?"

He rolled his eyes and grinned widely. "By Miss Poole, the enchanting darling that she is!"

Elaine closed her eyes, overcome by both this disclosure—and by the reek of his breath. Somewhere, Nicholas had stopped for refreshments. "B-but how..." she stammered.

"The fellow never really had me, you must know. He did get me just a trifle top-heavy from drink at White's, so that I didn't object to going to his house. But I didn't stay there for long."

"No?" she managed to ask, regarding her brother with something akin to awe.

He shook his head. "No, my dear sister. You see, the fellow had been fool enough to threaten to dispose of me as his rival to Miss Poole. You know, he always was too consequential by half." Nicholas shook his head pityingly. "In any case, he had certainly set Miss Poole in a bustle. She lives on Green Street near Mandeville, you know, so when she saw me, top-heavy as I was, being spirited away into Mandeville's house, why, she quite promptly called in the assistance of the Bow Street Runners."

Elaine's mouth dropped in amazement. Miss Poole's temerity cast Elaine's hesitation quite in the shade. In point of boldness, Elaine mournfully realized that she could hardly hold a candle to her prospective sister-in-law.

"Fancy her caring that much for my safety," Nicholas marvelled. "That would indicate that she cherishes a partiality for me, wouldn't it?" The look in his bleary eyes was not unhopeful.

Elaine choked down a laugh. "Most decidedly."

"And Darlington, here, happened to be strolling down Green Street when the Runners were storming Mandeville's house. He must have got caught up in the spirit of the thing, because he joined them and stormed the house, too!"

Elaine could hardly imagine Darlington storming anything, but she turned to him in grateful admiration. "My, how hardy of you that was," she said, sighing.

Darlington blushed. "Well, I thought it was rather brave," he remarked, innocent of satire. "Especially since I was wearing a brand-new coat of puce Bath Webbing cut by Weston. And look! The sleeve's been ripped." He held his war wound up for inspection, and she shook her head in sympathy.

"Yes, poor Darlington was quite unmanned from the exertion," Nicholas cut in. "So we came straight to the wine cellar here to recoup our strength. And we found the Devil's Dare lying on the floor all tied up. Of course, we released him. It was only polite for us to do so." He swayed a moment on his feet, assailed by a sudden qualm. "I hope we did the right thing. Of course, I don't know why he was all trussed up like that."

"Your sister knocked me unconscious, then tied me up," Lord Dare informed him calmly.

Nicholas stared at him like a gapeseed. "But why? Why would she do such a thing?"

"Because I wanted to marry her."

Elaine stole a look at Lord Dare, her throat tight. He was staring at her unwaveringly. Their eyes met, and Lord Dare smiled at her, a warm, loving smile. He took two steps toward her, and she felt a sudden thrill as his hand reached out to touch hers.

Nicholas looked revolted. "You must be bamming me. You can't really be meaning to marry my sister."

With a determined set to his face, Lord Dare declared, "Well, I am."

Elaine caught her breath. She lifted her face to his great height, and he bent his head so that their lips almost touched. "I am," he breathed solemnly. Then he closed his eyes, and as if in answer to all her prayers, he touched her lips with a kiss.

Nicholas clucked audibly. "No wonder she tied you up. Probably thought you were touched in your upper works. Only fit to be tied."

Dare lifted his head with a jerk. His hands held tightly to Elaine's shoulders, and his whole face seemed to be alight. His eyes twinkled into hers before he cast a sapient look at his prospective brother-in-law. "Hadn't you better inform Miss Poole that you are no longer Mandeville's prisoner? You should relieve her mind, you know. Take Darlington along to corroborate your story."

"By Jove!" Nicholas exclaimed with delight. "What a very good idea." He nodded eagerly and nearly stumbled over Mandeville again as he rushed through the door. Darlington hurried behind.

Elaine started to follow, but Dare pulled her back to him. "Now that I have you, you are not easily going to escape me, my dear."

Since he was such a very large gentleman, Elaine decided the safest course would be to humour him. She even went so far as to protect herself by squeezing him very tightly about the neck.

In a shocking return to reality Elaine suddenly recalled Elcho's presence in the tunnel. Quickly calling for Seaton and the footmen, she ordered them to retrieve him.

As she shot orders to the housemaids—for bandages and basilicum powder with which to dress Elcho's wound and for sal volatile with which to revive Mandeville—Lord Dare coolly sent off a runner for several officers who had standing orders to be ready to take Mandeville and Elcho into their custody. These two traitors would be brought to justice.

The activity of the servants, as well as the arrival of several persons of large and not very genteel aspect, had created such a commotion that Aunt Augusta took the unprecedented course of quitting her room to investigate firsthand their cause.

She staggered to the base of the stairs, then stopped, stricken at the sight of Lord Dare standing with his hand in Elaine's.

Clutching her delicate lavender wrapper and at least two of her embroidered shawls, she demanded in trembling accents to know what Elaine was about.

Quelling Elaine with a mischievous look, Lord Dare answered for her. "She's about getting herself engaged."

"To be married?" Aunt Augusta shrieked, grasping the banister to prevent an utter collapse. "No wonder the house is in such a rare set-about!"

"Do you object?"

"Of course I object! My health will never endure the strain!" she declared vehemently. "The announcement in *The Gazette*. The choosing of the trousseau. The guests. The wedding feast. Oh! I know I will have strong convulsions."

"Not during the ceremony, I hope. You will quite put the curate off his lines. And that would create an impediment of a new sort. That would never do."

His complete callousness made her wince. She held a thin hand to her palpitating heart. "I see that you are both made for each other," she declared in tragic tones. She cast a burningly reproachful look at Elaine. "Sharper than a serpent's tooth," she muttered portentously if rather obscurely, then tottered away to the comfort of her room and her vinaigrette.

Elaine, enchanted by the program Aunt Augusta had described, could only observe wryly, "It's a good thing she didn't catch sight of Mandeville. Seeing a lump the size of a hen's egg on his head might have brought on a fit of the vapours. I don't know what effect poor Elcho's wound might have had. Probably strong hysterics." She spoke more seriously than she had intended, for indeed, despite the fact that the wound was not fatal, the sight of it had almost had that effect on herself.

Seeing her distress, Lord Dare squeezed her hand sustainingly. "Forget Aunt Augusta," he recommended in a deep voice. "Also," he continued, "She'll endure our wedding ceremony with fortitude, I hope. Forget Lord Elcho. And Lord Mandeville. The Regent will deal with those two traitors summarily, I promise you."

He led her into the drawing-room, settling her on the scroll-back sofa and sliding his arm about her waist. Elaine leaned her head against his strong shoulder, raising yet another matter. "And what will happen to the Regalia?" she asked.

"I have already arranged a safe and quiet route for their return to Edinburgh with the assistance of a series of Flyers," Dare replied. "The Regalia Commission will discover them safely in their chest and never suspect for a moment their temporary disappearance."

Elaine blinked and lifted her head to look at him with new eyes. How could he have it all so well in hand? she wondered, utterly bewildered. "Already arranged..." she repeated feebly. "But how...why..."

He was watching the changing expressions on her face with amused interest. "My dear girl," he said, chuckling, "I've been striving to restore the Regalia ever since Prinny discovered the gaol guard's betrayal! The guard informed us that Mandeville had bribed him, and that both Mandeville and Elcho had stolen the treasures. We immediately set to work, hoping to return the Regalia without upheaval in order to avoid any unpleasant repercussions from the theft."

"We?"

He nodded. "Yes." He regarded her thoughtfully a moment. "Did you never suspect? Sometimes I dared to hope that you saw through my pose." His mouth tightened. "At other times, I feared you believed it all too implicitly." Seeing that she was still perfectly perplexed, he lifted his hand in a gesture of revelation. "I am, in effect, Prinny's agent. Have been from the start. I often do commissions for Prinny, you see. Trying to live down my father's memory after all, I suppose. Trying to do good to somebody so I could lift up my head with some pride." He gave a short laugh. "And I enjoy the excitement, I admit. Prinny trusts me, strangely enough. You must have observed how he relies on me."

Elaine found her voice with difficulty. "But I thought..." She caught herself up guiltily.

"That I had stolen the Regalia, on a dare?" His eyes held hers.

She nodded, feeling quite ashamed. How could she ever have suspected him?

"I'd rather steal away a greater treasure than that, my dear."

"What?"

"Your heart."

She flung herself into his welcoming arms and assured Lord Dare, between kisses, that he had already irrevocably fulfilled that ambition.

"Do you mean that you love me, despite my reprehensible character?" His eyes gleamed, and he held her to him.

She gurgled and caressed his cheek. "Why, I love you *because* of it."

He became perfectly still, then he gave a sigh that seemed drawn from the depths of his being. His whole body seemed to relax against hers. Then he smiled crookedly. "Well, my dear, I hope that you won't be unduly disappointed to learn that mine is not a truly bad character. You see, I took advantage of my father's notoriety. Indeed, the ton was more than ready to believe me to be following in my father's footsteps. And I cultivated this reputation for recklessness and daring as a blind for my real activities as Prinny's agent."

She looked at him with respect. How brave he was, and strong! Then her humour got the better of her, and her eyes began to dance. "How grossly you have been deceiving me," she chided him, a smile quivering at her lips despite her grave demeanour. "It is a blow to discover that I love a man of real integrity, after all. But I believe I will recover.''

His face became tinged with colour, and a curiously proud smile hovered about his mouth as he responded promptly, "Not from your love, I hope."

"Never from that."

He squeezed her so tightly that she could not breathe, and when he released her, she collapsed laughing against his broad chest, aglow with happiness. "But what a new light this confession sheds on all your behaviour," she commented after a moment. "I understand now why you were in the alley the day I fell into the tunnel's subsidence."

"Yes. I was following Mandeville, hoping he would lead me to the Regalia. He haunted Farrington Place so much that I knew they must be hidden here."

"A very astute conclusion," she said admiringly.

"Yes, wasn't it? I even attempted a foray in the house myself the night of my fox hunt. I returned to Farrington Place after all the others had left, hoping to search for the Regalia. But you interrupted me!"

"As did Mandeville and Elcho!"

He smiled, relishing the memory. "Yes, they had begun to suspect my activities and thus cherished no very tender feelings for me."

"No, their feelings were very obviously violent."

"As are yours?"

She blushed under his burning look, and her heart pounded violently. To alleviate the intensity of her emotions, she took to pulling at a button on his waistcoat. "I don't know why I suspected you of having stolen the Regalia . . ." she started.

"You didn't suspect anything," he interrupted her very kindly. "You knew me positively to be an incorrigible rakeshame and so leaped to a very logical conclusion."

"Well, you *are* a rakeshame, no matter what you say. A Devil's Dare."

"Call me Charles!" he commanded.

"Charles," she obeyed meekly, still pulling at his button.

He took her busy hand in his and held it in a warm clasp. "But I *have* won our dare, haven't I? You *have* succumbed to my dubious charms, have you not? I know I succumbed to your definite charms the moment I set eyes on you. My God, what spirit you have! I love you, my dear. I began falling in love with you from the very start."

She blushed with pleasure and returned the warm clasp with her hand. "How could I resist your original way of wooing me? You involved me in fox hunts, races, and duels. You insulted me repeatedly. Of course I succumbed to your charms. I love you, too."

His eyes twinkled down into hers. "How flat life will seem now that I have no more challenge to meet," he teased.

"Were you serious about wanting to marry me?"

He pulled her to him roughly so that her hands opened across his broad chest, and in her ear he whispered, "With all my heart." His mouth closed over hers, stilling any response. They both emerged breathless.

"Then," Elaine said in a voice shaken with emotion, "I dare you to make me a happy woman for the rest of my life."

This challenge the Devil's Dare accepted with alacrity.

Harlequin Regency Romance™

COMING NEXT MONTH

#11 VANESSA by Clarice Peters
Vanessa Whitmore, twenty-four, has no claim on
beauty, but she is an "original." When her fiancé
seemingly jilts her to marry Viscount Peregren's
intended, Vanessa and Perry become the talk of the
town. Overhearing the Viscount call her an
"antidote" is enough to cause a scene, and Vanessa is
banished to the country, from whence she is
summoned to France. Viscount Peregren, against his
better judgment, becomes involved, and soon finds
himself amidst fiancés found, fiancés jilted, lovers
crossed, duels designated, smuggled bodies and
schemes aplenty, until the only solution that will
answer is to marry Vanessa and keep her out
of trouble!

#12 SOPHIE'S HALLOO by Patricia Wynn
Sophia Corby was declared a changeling by her father.
She was his only offspring who didn't care a fig for
hunting. Now that she was nineteen, it was time to
marry her off. Preferably to someone of his choice.
Sophie's gentle nature was immediately attracted to
Sir Tony Farnham, for he enjoyed town life
immensely and felt no need to hunt. Displeased with
his daughter's preference, Sir Corby put forward a
Corinthian no one could resist. But the deepening ties
between Sophie and Tony could not be torn asunder
by her father's will or by a Corinthian's charm, and
Tony's patience and generous nature finally ran the
fox to the ground.

Have You Ever Wondered If You Could Write A Harlequin Novel?

Here's great news—Harlequin is offering a series of cassette tapes to help you do just that. Written by Harlequin editors, these tapes give practical advice on how to make your characters—and your story—come alive. There's a tape for each contemporary romance series Harlequin publishes.

Mail order only

All sales final

COMING SOON...

Indulge a Little
Give a Lot

An irresistible opportunity to pamper
yourself with free* gifts and help a
great cause, Big Brothers/Big Sisters
Programs and Services.
*With proofs-of-purchase plus postage and handling.

Watch for it in October!